The kick caught Halford just beneath the ribs and he doubled over, trying to protect his head. He told himself he would not cry out. He would not give the pirates the satisfaction.

"How..." Halford rasped, not lifting his face. "How did you get on board?"

"Wouldn't you like to know?" Jakis asked.

"I certainly would!" came another voice. A strange voice. Deep and dark. Not coarse like the voices of the sub-human pirates, but polished, the sort of voice a holograph opera villain would be proud of.

The lights went out.

"What's going on?" Jakis asked.

"A question I should very much like the answer to," came that dark voice again.

"Lights up, boys!" Jakis cried.

"Who's there?" Jakis asked. "Show yourself!"

"As you wish." Blue light flowered in the darkness near at hand. The voice had come from much closer, and Halford saw a spike of gleaming crystal rise and fall. It was the blade of a highmatter sword, its edge sharp enough to cut between molecules, its substance bright and cold as distant stars.

—from "The Night Captain"
by Christopher Ruocchio

BAEN BOOKS edited by HANK DAVIS

The Human Edge by Gordon R. Dickson
The Best of Gordon R. Dickson
We the Underpeople by Cordwainer Smith
When the People Fell by Cordwainer Smith

The Technic Civilization Saga
The Van Rijn Method by Poul Anderson
David Falkayn: Star Trader by Poul Anderson
Rise of the Terran Empire by Poul Anderson
Young Flandry by Poul Anderson
Captain Flandry: Defender of the Terran Empire
by Poul Anderson
Sir Dominic Flandry: The Last Knight of Terra
by Poul Anderson
Flandry's Legacy by Poul Anderson

The Best of the Bolos: Their Finest Hour
created by Keith Laumer

A Cosmic Christmas
A Cosmic Christmas 2 You
In Space No One Can Hear You Scream
The Baen Big Book of Monsters
As Time Goes By
Future Wars . . . and Other Punchlines
Worst Contact
Things from Outer Space
If This Goes Wrong . . .

BAEN BOOKS edited by CHRISTOPHER RUOCCHIO

Star Destroyers with Tony Daniel
Space Pioneers with Hank Davis
Overruled! with Hank Davis
Cosmic Corsairs with Hank Davis
World Breakers with Tony Daniel
Sword and Planet (forthcoming)
Time Troopers with Hank Davis (forthcoming)

To purchase any of these titles in e-book form,
please go to www.baen.com.

COSMIC CORSAIRS

EDITED BY
Hank Davis AND
Christopher Ruocchio

COSMIC CORSAIRS

This is a work of fiction. All the characters and events portrayed in this book are fictional, and any resemblance to real people or incidents is purely coincidental.

A Baen Books Original

Baen Publishing Enterprises
P.O. Box 1403
Riverdale, NY 10471
www.baen.com

ISBN: 978-1-9821-2569-1

Cover art by Don Maitz

First printing, August 2020
First mass market printing, October 2021

Distributed by Simon & Schuster
1230 Avenue of the Americas
New York, NY 10020

Library of Congress Control Number: 2020021149

Pages by Joy Freeman (www.pagesbyjoy.com)
Printed in the United States of America

10 9 8 7 6 5 4 3 2 1

DEDICATION

Christopher has been kind enough to let me dedicate this anthology to Jeanne Marie Caggiano, former editorial coworker, strikingly intelligent lady, and dazzlingly beautiful friend. If she ever decides to skipper a pirate ship, whether seagoing or spacegoing, I'm putting in for world's oldest cabin boy.

—Hank Davis

ACKNOWLEDGMENTS

Our thanks to those authors who permitted the use of their stories, and to the estates and their representatives who intervened for those authors unreachable without time travel (we raise a glass to absent friends). Among the very helpful agents deserving thanks are Spectrum Literary Agency, the Richard Meredith Agency, the Virginia Kidd Agency, Barry N. Malzberg, and David Drake. For help and advice, many thanks to John O'Neil and his *Black Gate* webzine, R.K. Robinson, Jason McGregor, Chris Willrich, Rich Horton, Marie Bilodeau, and others I'm unforgivably forgetting. And thanks to the Internet Speculative Fiction Database (ISFDB.org) for existing and being a handy source of raw data, and to the devoted volunteers who maintain that very useful site.

CONTENTS

INTRODUCTION

Yo-Ho-Ho and a Bottle of Oxygen

A few anthologies ago, I went into detail in the introduction to *The Baen Big Book of Monsters* about why giant monsters, from Kong to Godzilla to *The Amazing Colossal Man*, have lots of scientific problems. There are many reasons for not taking them seriously. But against this is the fun factor. Giant monsters are *fun*! The introduction was a lot longer, but this sums up its argument well enough.

And space pirates? Come *on*, now.

All sorts of arguments can be advanced about how unlikely they are. Time was that the seas thronged with cargo ships that a well-armed, but lighter, faster sailing ship could overtake and plunder, but would such be true of space commerce, if space commerce ever comes into reality?

Well, it might, in the not-so-near future, if technology keeps advancing. New energy sources and new methods of propulsion, perhaps based on scientific discoveries we cannot even foresee, might make space travel easy and not as costly as it is at present. It might become profitable to mine the Moon (will environmentalists object?), or the other planets, and in particular the asteroids, which are not at the bottom of a deep gravity well or even a shallow one, like Luna's. If space travel becomes cheap enough to make a more or less honest buck, it would be cheap enough for less honest (dare I say scurvy?) individuals to hijack it. And besides, with government being inherently scurvy, there might even be space privateers. (While pirates are private contractors, privateers do the same dirty work, but as more or less official agents of a government.)

And even if the Solar System is uninhabited by anyone but those ape spawn from the third planet out, so that there will be no trade in valuable Martian or Venusian works of art and relics, if interstellar travel becomes possible (and cheap enough), maybe wealthy collectors will pay fabulous sums for Vegan or Altairan artwork, providing a stimulus for third parties (call them "pirates" for lack of a more dignified term) to intercept it en route and offer it to yet another wealthy collector.

This is, of course, all supposition, but in the meantime, while we're waiting on somebody, possibly Elon Musk, to found a Moon or Mars colony, we can still ride paper spaceships for fun. However many objections can be raised against space piracy becoming a reality, the idea is undeniable *fun*.

I think another objection that might have been raised in the past is a dead issue now. Once upon a time, space opera, the classic adventure story of SF, akin to the shoot-em-up western known as "horse opera," was regarded as an embarrassment—something that was keeping SF from being recognized as a valid literary form, not real cultchuh, er, culture. If that was the case, then stories of space pirates (the horror, the horror) had to be a prime offender.

In 1970 I was attending a Pittsburgh SF convention, and the very famous, somewhat notorious guest of honor was chairing a panel discussion on Women's Liberation (the term "feminism" was not back in use yet). The writer was a torchbearer for the New Wave, which was being hailed as the wave of the future, sweeping aside all that trashy pulp stuff of past SF. He took a moment from denouncing a recent story collection, for not having strong women, to also berate it for having (wait for it) *space pirates*.

Well, that was five decades ago. The fiery writer chairing the panel (who, I should say, was undeniably talented, even if I rarely agreed with his polemics) is no longer with us, and we've had *Star Trek* (which the writer disliked, particularly after they bought a script from him and actually *changed* it!) come back from the dead and all but take over the world. *Star Wars* (b. 1977) is also threatening to take over the world. SF-based games are threatening to take over the world, at least virtually. SF and fantasy dominate the bestseller lists. With all these threats to the world, who needs pirates? But they are there.

And there's also *Doctor Who*, for which that writer expressed admiration in a paperback cover blurb. I wonder if he ever saw the Whovian installment that involved space pirates?

Maybe space opera isn't SF's most dignified face, but it's standing astride the public conscienceness like a colossus (I steal from the best). Why not space pirates?

And if you're reading this (unless you're looking at it online) you hold in your hands, whether or not a skull and crossbones is tattooed on either of them, a plump package of space adventures, involving space buccaneers of all sorts: from one-man operations to whole pirate fleets; from pirates fighting against tyrannical governments to the scum of space who may or may not get what they deserve.

I'm also glad to say that several stories herein by Leiber, Blish, Robertson, and others are being reprinted for the first time since they appeared in magazines and then walked the plank into pulp oblivion. A number of other stories appear for the first time anywhere. Carysa Locke's is a short adventure from the universe of her bestselling telepathic space pirates series. There's also a story from another bestselling writer, Sarah A. Hoyt, accompanied by her talented son. And one from the co-editor who deserves all the credit and none of the blame for this anthology: Christopher Ruocchio.

There are, as usual, unfortunate absences. I particularly regret that circumstances wouldn't permit including stories by the King and Queen of space adventure, Edmond Hamilton and Leigh Brackett. Maybe if there's a sequel to this book, it might still come to pass. Write your congressman!

And a very recent space pirate tale by William Ledbetter, "Broken Wings," might be here, except we were beaten to it by a colleague. You can find it in David Afsharirad's *Year's Best Military and Adventure SF #6*, also from Baen, a book I heartily recommend, and not just for that story.

Finally, we had to reluctantly pass over a trio of good novellas: "The Man from the Big Dark" by John

Brunner, "Galactic North" by Alastair Reynolds (look for it in his story collection with the same title), and a true classic, "Piracy Preferred" by the legendary John W. Campbell (1930). All good, but too long. At least we managed to include Leiber's bordering-on-novella length "They Never Come Back."

There was, alas, never any question of including Murray Leinster's terrific novel, *The Pirates of Zan*. It was originally serialized at the end of the 1950s as *The Pirates of Ersatz* in *Astounding Science Fiction*, the cover of which had a Kelly Freas painting of a pirate boarding a spaceship with a slide rule in his teeth. (If you've never heard of slide rules, consult Wikipedia).

But enough of what couldn't be included, and enough of my babbling. Adjust your scarf and eyepatch before donning the space helmet, put that robot parrot on your shoulder, make sure your trusty blaster is charged (cutlass, regular, or laser optional), and set forth on the black sea of space for adventure, mateys!

—Hank Davis,
February 2020

Boojum

Elizabeth Bear & Sarah Monette

I was glad to include "Mongoose" by Elizabeth Bear and Sarah Monette in the 2013 Baen anthology, In Space No One Can Hear You Scream (and it's not too late to get the e-book, I might mention). Here's another dazzler by these highly talented writers set in their same strikingly original space opera universe. Living space-ships, really nasty space pirates, even nastier aliens, and a lowly crew member who deserved better. And then she ... but you should read the story to find out.

The ship had no name of her own, so her human crew called her the *Lavinia Whateley*. As far as anyone could tell, she didn't mind. At least, her long grasping vanes curled—affectionately?—when the chief engineers patted her bulkheads and called her "Vinnie," and she ceremoniously tracked the footsteps of each crew member with her internal bioluminescence, giving them light to walk and work and live by.

The *Lavinia Whateley* was a Boojum, a deep-space swimmer, but her kind had evolved in the high tempestuous envelopes of gas giants, and their offspring still spent their infancies there, in cloud-nurseries over eternal storms. And so she was streamlined, something like a vast spiny lionfish to the earth-adapted eye. Her sides were lined with gasbags filled with hydrogen; her vanes and wings furled tight. Her color was a blue-green so dark it seemed a glossy black unless the light struck it; her hide was impregnated with symbiotic algae.

Where there was light, she could make oxygen. Where there was oxygen, she could make water.

She was an ecosystem unto herself, as the captain was a law unto herself. And down in the bowels of the engineering section, Black Alice Bradley, who was only human and no kind of law at all, loved her.

Black Alice had taken the oath back in '32, after the Venusian Riots. She hadn't hidden her reasons, and the captain had looked at her with cold, dark, amused eyes and said, "So long as you carry your weight, cherie, I don't care. Betray me, though, and you will be going back to Venus the cold way." But it was probably that—and the fact that Black Alice couldn't hit the broad side of a space freighter with a ray gun—that had gotten her assigned to Engineering, where ethics were less of a problem. It wasn't, after all, as if she was going anywhere.

Black Alice was on duty when the *Lavinia Whateley* spotted prey; she felt the shiver of anticipation that ran through the decks of the ship. It was an odd sensation, a tic Vinnie only exhibited in pursuit. And then they were underway, zooming down the slope of the gravity well toward Sol, and the screens all around Engineering—which Captain Song kept dark, most of the time, on the theory that swabs and deckhands and coal-shovelers didn't need to know where they were, or what they were doing—flickered bright and live.

Everybody looked up, and Demijack shouted, "There! There!" He was right: The blot that might only have been a smudge of oil on the screen moved as Vinnie banked, revealing itself to be a freighter, big and ungainly and hopelessly outclassed. Easy prey. Easy pickings.

We could use some of them, thought Black Alice. Contrary to the e-ballads and comm stories, a pirate's life was not all imported delicacies and fawning slaves. Especially not when three-quarters of any and all profits went directly back to the *Lavinia Whateley*, to keep her healthy and happy. Nobody ever argued. There were stories about the *Marie Curie*, too.

The captain's voice over fiber optic cable—strung beside the *Lavinia Whateley*'s nerve bundles—was as clear and free of static as if she stood at Black Alice's elbow. "Battle stations," Captain Song said, and the crew leapt to obey. It had been two Solar since Captain Song keelhauled James Brady, but nobody who'd been with the ship then was ever likely to forget his ruptured eyes and frozen scream.

Black Alice manned her station and stared at the screen. She saw the freighter's name—the *Josephine Baker*—gold on black across the stern, the Venusian flag for its port of registry wired stiff from a mast on its hull. It was a steelship, not a Boojum, and they had every advantage. For a moment she thought the freighter would run.

And then it turned and brought its guns to bear.

No sense of movement, of acceleration, of disorientation. No pop, no whump of displaced air. The view on the screens just flickered to a different one, as Vinnie skipped—apported—to a new position just aft and above the *Josephine Baker*, crushing the flag mast with her hull.

Black Alice felt that, a grinding shiver. And had just time to grab her console before the *Lavinia Whateley* grappled the freighter, long vanes not curling in affection now.

Out of the corner of her eye, she saw Dogcollar, the closest thing the *Lavinia Whateley* had to a chaplain, cross himself, and she heard him mutter, like he always did, *Ave, Grandaevissimi, morituri vos salutant.* It was the best he'd be able to do until it was all over, and even then he wouldn't have the chance to do much. Captain Song didn't mind other people worrying about souls, so long as they didn't do it on her time.

The captain's voice was calling orders, assigning people to boarding parties port and starboard. Down in Engineering, all they had to do was monitor the *Lavinia Whateley*'s hull and prepare to repel boarders, assuming the freighter's crew had the gumption to send any. Vinnie would take care of the rest—until the time came to persuade her not to eat her prey before they'd gotten all the valuables off it. That was a ticklish job, only entrusted to the chief engineers, but Black Alice watched and listened, and although she didn't expect she'd ever get the chance, she thought she could do it herself.

It was a small ambition, and one she never talked

about. But it would be a hell of a thing, wouldn't it? To be somebody a Boojum would listen to?

She gave her attention to the dull screens in her sectors and tried not to crane her neck to catch a glimpse of the ones with the actual fighting on them. Dogcollar was making the rounds with sidearms from the weapons locker, just in case. Once the *Josephine Baker* was subdued, it was the junior engineers and others who would board her to take inventory.

Sometimes there were crew members left in hiding on captured ships. Sometimes, unwary pirates got shot.

There was no way to judge the progress of the battle from Engineering. Wasabi put a stopwatch up on one of the secondary screens, as usual, and everybody glanced at it periodically. Fifteen minutes ongoing meant the boarding parties hadn't hit any nasty surprises. Black Alice had met a man once who'd been on the *Margaret Mead* when she grappled a freighter that turned out to be carrying a division's-worth of Marines out to the Jovian moons. Thirty minutes ongoing was normal. Forty-five minutes. Upward of an hour ongoing, and people started double-checking their weapons. The longest battle Black Alice had ever personally been part of was six hours, forty-three minutes, and fifty-two seconds. That had been the last time the *Lavinia Whateley* worked with a partner, and the double-cross by the *Henry Ford* was the only reason any of Vinnie's crew needed. Captain Song still had Captain Edwards' head in a jar on the bridge, and Vinnie had an ugly ring of scars where the *Henry Ford* had bitten her.

This time, the clock stopped at fifty minutes, thirteen seconds. The *Josephine Baker* surrendered.

❖   ❖   ❖

Dogcollar slapped Black Alice's arm. "With me," he said, and she didn't argue. He had only six weeks seniority over her, but he was as tough as he was devout, and not stupid either. She checked the Velcro on her holster and followed him up the ladder, reaching through the rungs once to scratch Vinnie's bulkhead as she passed. The ship paid her no notice. She wasn't the captain, and she wasn't one of the four chief engineers.

Quartermaster mostly respected crew's own partner choices, and as Black Alice and Dogcollar suited up—it wouldn't be the first time, if the *Josephine Baker*'s crew decided to blow her open to space rather than be taken captive—he came by and issued them both tag guns and x-ray pads, taking a retina scan in return. All sorts of valuable things got hidden inside of bulkheads, and once Vinnie was done with the steelship there wouldn't be much chance of coming back to look for what they'd missed.

Wet pirates used to scuttle their captures. The Boojums were more efficient.

Black Alice clipped everything to her belt and checked Dogcollar's seals.

And then they were swinging down lines from the *Lavinia Whateley*'s belly to the chewed-open airlock. A lot of crew didn't like to look at the ship's face, but Black Alice loved it. All those teeth, the diamond edges worn to a glitter, and a few of the ship's dozens of bright sapphire eyes blinking back at her.

She waved, unselfconsciously, and flattered herself that the ripple of closing eyes was Vinnie winking in return.

She followed Dogcollar inside the prize.

They unsealed when they had checked atmosphere—no sense in wasting your own air when you might need it later—and the first thing she noticed was the smell.

The *Lavinia Whateley* had her own smell, ozone and nutmeg, and other ships never smelled as good, but this was...this was...

"What did they kill and why didn't they space it?" Dogcollar wheezed, and Black Alice swallowed hard against her gag reflex and said, "One will get you twenty we're the lucky bastards that find it."

"No takers," Dogcollar said.

They worked together to crank open the hatches they came to. Twice they found crew members, messily dead. Once they found crew members alive.

"Gillies," said Black Alice.

"Still don't explain the smell," said Dogcollar and, to the gillies: "Look, you can join our crew, or our ship can eat you. Makes no never mind to us."

The gillies blinked their big wet eyes and made fingersigns at each other, and then nodded. Hard.

Dogcollar slapped a tag on the bulkhead. "Someone will come get you. You go wandering, we'll assume you changed your mind."

The gillies shook their heads, hard, and folded down onto the deck to wait.

Dogcollar tagged searched holds—green for clean, purple for goods, red for anything Vinnie might like to eat that couldn't be fenced for a profit—and Black Alice mapped.

The corridors in the steelship were winding, twisty, hard to track. She was glad she chalked the walls, because she didn't think her map was quite right, somehow, but she couldn't figure out where she'd gone wrong. Still, they had a beacon, and Vinnie could always chew them out if she had to.

Black Alice loved her ship.

She was thinking about that, how, okay, it wasn't so bad, the pirate game, and it sure beat working in the sunstone mines on Venus, when she found a locked cargo hold. "Hey, Dogcollar," she said to her comm, and while he was turning to cover her, she pulled her sidearm and blasted the lock.

The door peeled back, and Black Alice found herself staring at rank upon rank of silver cylinders, each less than a meter tall and perhaps half a meter wide, smooth and featureless except for what looked like an assortment of sockets and plugs on the surface of each. The smell was strongest here.

"Shit," she said.

Dogcollar, more practical, slapped the first safety orange tag of the expedition beside the door and said only, "Captain'll want to see this."

"Yeah," said Black Alice, cold chills chasing themselves up and down her spine. "C'mon, let's move."

But of course it turned out that she and Dogcollar were on the retrieval detail, too, and the captain wasn't leaving the canisters for Vinnie.

Which, okay, fair. Black Alice didn't want the *Lavinia Whateley* eating those things, either, but why did they have to bring them *back?*

She said as much to Dogcollar, under her breath, and had a horrifying thought: "She knows what they are, right?"

"She's the captain," said Dogcollar.

"Yeah, but—I ain't arguing, man, but if she doesn't know..." She lowered her voice even farther, so she could barely hear herself. "What if somebody *opens* one?"

Dogcollar gave her a pained look. "Nobody's going to go opening anything. But if you're really worried, go talk to the captain about it."

He was calling her bluff. Black Alice called his right back. "Come with me?"

He was stuck. He stared at her, and then he grunted and pulled his gloves off, the left and then the right. "Fuck," he said. "I guess we oughta."

For the crew members who had been in the boarding action, the party had already started. Dogcollar and Black Alice finally tracked the captain down in the rec room, where her marines were slurping stolen wine from broken-necked bottles. As much of it splashed on the gravity plates epoxied to the *Lavinia Whateley*'s flattest interior surface as went into the marines, but Black Alice imagined there was plenty more where that came from. And the faster the crew went through it, the less long they'd be drunk.

The captain herself was naked in a great extruded tub, up to her collarbones in steaming water dyed pink and heavily scented by the bath bombs sizzling here and there. Black Alice stared; she hadn't seen a tub bath in seven years. She still dreamed of them sometimes.

"Captain," she said, because Dogcollar wasn't going to say anything. "We think you should know we found some dangerous cargo on the prize."

Captain Song raised one eyebrow. "And you imagine I don't know already, cherie?"

Oh shit. But Black Alice stood her ground. "We thought we should be *sure*."

The captain raised one long leg out of the water to shove a pair of necking pirates off the rim of her tub. They rolled onto the floor, grappling and clawing, both fighting to be on top. But they didn't break the kiss. "You wish to be sure," said the captain. Her dark eyes had never left Black Alice's sweating face. "Very well. Tell me. And then you will know that I know, and you can be *sure*."

Dogcollar made a grumbling noise deep in his throat, easily interpreted: *I told you so.*

Just as she had when she took Captain Song's oath and slit her thumb with a razorblade and dripped her blood on the *Lavinia Whateley*'s decking so the ship might know her, Black Alice—metaphorically speaking—took a breath and jumped. "They're brains," she said. "Human brains. Stolen. Black-market. The Fungi—"

"Mi-Go," Dogcollar hissed, and the captain grinned at him, showing extraordinarily white strong teeth. He ducked, submissively, but didn't step back, for which Black Alice felt a completely ridiculous gratitude.

"Mi-Go," Black Alice said. Mi-Go, Fungi, what did it matter? They came from the outer rim of the Solar System, the black cold hurtling rocks of the Öpik-Oort Cloud. Like the Boojums, they could swim between the stars. "They collect them. There's a black market. Nobody knows what they use them for. It's illegal, of course. But they're...alive in there. They go mad, supposedly."

And that was it. That was all Black Alice could manage. She stopped and had to remind herself to shut her mouth.

"So I've heard," the captain said, dabbling at the steaming water. She stretched luxuriously in her tub. Someone thrust a glass of white wine at her, condensation dewing the outside. The captain did not drink from shattered plastic bottles. "The Mi-Go will pay for this cargo, won't they? They mine rare minerals all over the system. They're said to be very wealthy."

"Yes, Captain," Dogcollar said, when it became obvious that Black Alice couldn't.

"Good," the captain said. Under Black Alice's feet, the decking shuddered, a grinding sound as Vinnie began to dine. Her rows of teeth would make short work of the *Josephine Baker*'s steel hide. Black Alice could see two of the gillies—the same two? She never could tell them apart unless they had scars—flinch and tug at their chains. "Then they might as well pay us as someone else, wouldn't you say?"

Black Alice knew she should stop thinking about the canisters. Captain's word was law. But she couldn't help it, like scratching at a scab. They were down there, in the third subhold, the one even sniffers couldn't find, cold and sweating and with that stench that was like a living thing.

And she kept wondering. Were they empty? Or were there brains in there, people's brains, going mad?

The idea was driving her crazy, and finally, her fourth off-shift after the capture of the *Josephine Baker*, she had to go look.

"This is stupid, Black Alice," she muttered to herself as she climbed down the companionway, the beads in her hair clicking against her earrings. "Stupid, stupid, stupid." Vinnie bioluminesced, a traveling spotlight, placidly unconcerned whether Black Alice was being an idiot or not.

Half-Hand Sally had pulled duty in the main hold. She nodded at Black Alice and Black Alice nodded back. Black Alice ran errands a lot, for Engineering and sometimes for other departments, because she didn't smoke hash and she didn't cheat at cards. She was reliable.

Down through the subholds, and she really didn't want to be doing this, but she was here and the smell of the third subhold was already making her sick, and maybe if she just knew one way or the other, she'd be able to quit thinking about it.

She opened the third subhold, and the stench rushed out.

The canisters were just metal, sealed, seemingly airtight. There shouldn't be any way for the aroma of the contents to escape. But it permeated the air nonetheless, bad enough that Black Alice wished she had brought a rebreather.

No, that would have been suspicious. So it was really best for everyone concerned that she hadn't, but oh, gods and little fishes, the stench. Even breathing through her mouth was no help; she could taste it, like oil from a fryer, saturating the air, oozing up her sinuses, coating the interior spaces of her body.

As silently as possible, she stepped across the threshold and into the space beyond. The *Lavinia Whateley* obligingly lit the space as she entered, dazzling her at first as the overhead lights—not just bioluminescent, here, but LEDs chosen to approximate natural daylight, for when they shipped plants and animals—reflected off rank upon rank of canisters. When Black Alice went among them, they did not reach her waist.

She was just going to walk through, she told herself. Hesitantly, she touched the closest cylinder. The air in this hold was so dry there was no condensation—the whole ship ran to lip-cracking, nosebleed dryness in the long weeks between prizes—but the cylinder was cold. It felt somehow grimy to the touch, gritty and oily like machine grease. She pulled her hand back.

It wouldn't do to open the closest one to the door—and she realized with that thought that she was planning on opening one. There must be a way to do it, a concealed catch or a code pad. She was an engineer, after all.

She stopped three ranks in, lightheaded with the smell, to examine the problem.

It was remarkably simple, once you looked for it. There were three depressions on either side of the rim, a little smaller than human fingertips but spaced appropriately. She laid the pads of her fingers over them and pressed hard, making the flesh deform into the catches.

The lid sprang up with a pressurized hiss. Black Alice was grateful that even open, it couldn't smell much worse. She leaned forward to peer within. There was a clear membrane over the surface, and gelatin or thick fluid underneath. Vinnie's lights illuminated it well.

It was not empty. And as the light struck the grayish surface of the lump of tissue floating within, Black Alice would have sworn she saw the pathetic unbodied thing flinch.

She scrambled to close the canister again, nearly pinching her fingertips when it clanked shut. "Sorry," she whispered, although dear sweet Jesus, surely the thing couldn't hear her. "Sorry, sorry." And then she turned and ran, catching her hip a bruising blow against the doorway, slapping the controls to make it fucking *close* already. And then she staggered sideways, lurching to her knees, and vomited until blackness was spinning in front of her eyes and she couldn't smell or taste anything but bile.

Vinnie would absorb the former contents of Black Alice's stomach, just as she absorbed, filtered, recycled, and excreted all her crew's wastes. Shaking, Black Alice braced herself back upright and began the long climb out of the holds.

In the first subhold, she had to stop, her shoulder against the smooth, velvet slickness of Vinnie's skin, her mouth hanging open while her lungs worked. And she knew Vinnie wasn't going to hear her, because she wasn't the captain or a chief engineer or anyone important, but she had to try anyway, croaking, "Vinnie, water, please."

And no one could have been more surprised than Black Alice Bradley when Vinnie extruded a basin and a thin cool trickle of water began to flow into it.

Well, now she knew. And there was still nothing she could do about it. She wasn't the captain, and if she said anything more than she already had, people were going to start looking at her funny. Mutiny kind of funny. And what Black Alice did *not* need was any more of Captain Song's attention and especially not for rumors like that. She kept her head down and did her job and didn't discuss her nightmares with anyone.

And she had nightmares, all right. Hot and cold running, enough, she fancied, that she could have filled up the captain's huge tub with them.

She could live with that. But over the next double dozen of shifts, she became aware of something else wrong, and this was worse, because it was something wrong with the *Lavinia Whateley*.

The first sign was the chief engineers frowning and going into huddles at odd moments. And then Black Alice began to feel it herself, the way Vinnie was... she didn't have a word for it because she'd never felt anything like it before. She would have said *balky*, but that couldn't be right. It couldn't. But she was more and more sure that Vinnie was less responsive somehow, that when she obeyed the captain's orders, it was with a delay. If she were human, Vinnie would have been dragging her feet.

You couldn't keelhaul a ship for not obeying fast enough.

And then, because she was paying attention so hard she was making her own head hurt, Black Alice noticed something else. Captain Song had them cruising the gas giants' orbits—Jupiter, Saturn, Neptune—not going in as far as the asteroid belt, not going out as far as Uranus. Nobody Black Alice talked to knew why, exactly, but she and Dogcollar figured it was because the captain wanted to talk to the Mi-Go without actually getting near the nasty cold rock of their planet. And what Black Alice noticed was that Vinnie was less balky, less *unhappy*, when she was headed out, and more and more resistant the closer they got to the asteroid belt.

Vinnie, she remembered, had been born over Uranus.

"Do you want to go home, Vinnie?" Black Alice asked her one late-night shift when there was nobody around to care that she was talking to the ship. "Is that what's wrong?"

She put her hand flat on the wall, and although she was probably imagining it, she thought she felt a shiver ripple across Vinnie's vast side.

Black Alice knew how little she knew, and didn't even contemplate sharing her theory with the chief engineers. They probably knew exactly what was wrong and exactly what to do to keep the *Lavinia Whateley* from going core meltdown like the *Marie Curie* had. That was a whispered story, not the sort of thing anybody talked about except in their hammocks after lights out.

The *Marie Curie* had eaten her own crew.

So when Wasabi said, four shifts later, "Black Alice, I've got a job for you," Black Alice said, "Yessir," and hoped it would be something that would help the *Lavinia Whateley* be happy again.

It was a suit job, he said, replace and repair. Black Alice was going because she was reliable and smart and stayed quiet, and it was time she took on more responsibilities. The way he said it made her first fret because that meant the captain might be reminded of her existence, and then fret because she realized the captain already had been.

But she took the equipment he issued, and she listened to the instructions and read schematics and committed them both to memory and her implants. It was a ticklish job, a neural override repair. She'd done some fiber optic bundle splicing, but this was going to be a doozy. And she was going to have to do it in stiff, pressurized gloves.

Her heart hammered as she sealed her helmet, and not because she was worried about the EVA. This was a chance. An opportunity. A step closer to chief engineer.

Maybe she had impressed the captain with her discretion, after all.

She cycled the airlock, snapped her safety harness, and stepped out onto the *Lavinia Whateley*'s hide.

That deep blue-green, like azurite, like the teeming seas of Venus under their swampy eternal clouds, was invisible. They were too far from Sol—it was a yellow stylus-dot, and you had to know where to look for it. Vinnie's hide was just black under Black Alice's suit floods. As the airlock cycled shut, though, the Boojum's own bioluminescence shimmered up her vanes and along the ridges of her sides—crimson and electric green and acid blue. Vinnie must have noticed Black Alice picking her way carefully up her spine with barbed boots. They wouldn't *hurt* Vinnie—nothing short of a space rock could manage that—but they certainly stuck in there good.

The thing Black Alice was supposed to repair was at the principal nexus of Vinnie's central nervous system. The ship didn't have anything like what a human or a gilly would consider a brain; there were nodules spread all through her vast body. Too slow, otherwise. And Black Alice had heard Boojums weren't supposed to be all that smart—trainable, sure, maybe like an Earth monkey.

Which is what made it creepy as hell that, as she picked her way up Vinnie's flank—though *up* was a courtesy, under these circumstances—talking to her all the way, she would have sworn Vinnie was talking back. Not just tracking her with the lights, as she would always do, but bending some of her barbels and vanes around as if craning her neck to get a look at Black Alice.

Black Alice carefully circumnavigated an eye—she didn't think her boots would hurt it, but it seemed discourteous to stomp across somebody's field of vision—and wondered, only half-idly, if she had been sent out on this task not because she was being considered for promotion, but because she was expendable.

She was just rolling her eyes and dismissing that as borrowing trouble when she came over a bump on Vinnie's back, spotted her goal—and all the ship's lights went out.

She tongued on the comm. "Wasabi?"

"I got you, Blackie. You just keep doing what you're doing."

"Yessir."

But it seemed like her feet stayed stuck in Vinnie's hide a little longer than was good. At least fifteen seconds before she managed a couple of deep breaths—too deep for her limited oxygen supply, so she went briefly dizzy—and continued up Vinnie's side.

Black Alice had no idea what inflammation looked like in a Boojum, but she would guess this was it. All around the interface she was meant to repair, Vinnie's flesh looked scraped and puffy. Black Alice walked tenderly, wincing, muttering apologies under her breath. And with every step, the tendrils coiled a little closer.

Black Alice crouched beside the box and began examining connections. The console was about three meters by four, half a meter tall, and fixed firmly to Vinnie's hide. It looked like the thing was still functional, but something—a bit of space debris, maybe—had dented it pretty good.

Cautiously, Black Alice dropped a hand on it. She

found the access panel and flipped it open: more red lights than green. A tongue-click, and she began withdrawing her tethered tools from their holding pouches and arranging them so that they would float conveniently around.

She didn't hear a thing, of course, but the hide under her boots vibrated suddenly, sharply. She jerked her head around, just in time to see one of Vinnie's feelers slap her own side, five or ten meters away. And then the whole Boojum shuddered, contracting, curved into a hard crescent of pain the same way she had when the *Henry Ford* had taken that chunk out of her hide. And the lights in the access panel lit up all at once—red, red, yellow, red.

Black Alice tongued off the *send* function on her headset microphone, so Wasabi wouldn't hear her. She touched the bruised hull, and she touched the dented edge of the console. "Vinnie," she said, "does this *hurt*?"

Not that Vinnie could answer her. But it was obvious. She was in pain. And maybe that dent didn't have anything to do with space debris. Maybe—Black Alice straightened, looked around, and couldn't convince herself that it was an accident that this box was planted right where Vinnie couldn't...quite...reach it.

"So what does it *do*?" she muttered. "Why am I out here repairing something that fucking hurts?" She crouched down again and took another long look at the interface.

As an engineer, Black Alice was mostly self-taught; her implants were second-hand, black market, scavenged, the wet work done by a gilly on Providence Station. She'd learned the technical vocabulary from

Gogglehead Kim before he bought it in a stupid little fight with a ship named the *V. I. Ulyanov*, but what she relied on were her instincts, the things she knew without being able to say. So she *looked* at that box wired into Vinnie's spine and all its red and yellow lights, and then she tongued the comm back on and said, "Wasabi, this thing don't look so good."

"Whaddya mean, don't look so good?" Wasabi sounded distracted, and that was just fine.

Black Alice made a noise, the auditory equivalent of a shrug. "I think the node's inflamed. Can we pull it and lock it in somewhere else?"

"No!" said Wasabi.

"It's looking pretty ugly out here."

"Look, Blackie, unless you want us to all go sailing out into the Big Empty, we are *not* pulling that governor. Just fix the fucking thing, would you?"

"Yessir," said Black Alice, thinking hard. The first thing was that Wasabi knew what was going on—knew what the box did and knew that the *Lavinia Whateley* didn't like it. That wasn't comforting. The second thing was that whatever was going on, it involved the Big Empty, the cold vastness between the stars. So it wasn't that Vinnie wanted to go home. She wanted to go *out*.

It made sense, from what Black Alice knew about Boojums. Their infants lived in the tumult of the gas giants' atmosphere, but as they aged, they pushed higher and higher, until they reached the edge of the envelope. And then—following instinct or maybe the calls of their fellows, nobody knew for sure—they learned to skip, throwing themselves out into the vacuum like Earth birds leaving the nest. And what if, for a Boojum, the solar system was just another nest?

Black Alice knew the *Lavinia Whateley* was old, for a Boojum. Captain Song was not her first captain, although you never mentioned Captain Smith if you knew what was good for you. So if there *was* another stage to her life cycle, she might be ready for it. And her crew wasn't letting her go.

Jesus and the cold fishy gods, Black Alice thought. Is this why the *Marie Curie* ate her crew? Because they wouldn't let her go?

She fumbled for her tools, tugging the cords to float them closer, and wound up walloping herself in the bicep with a splicer. And as she was wrestling with it, her headset spoke again. "Blackie, can you hurry it up out there? Captain says we're going to have company."

Company? She never got to say it. Because when she looked up, she saw the shapes, faintly limned in starlight, and a chill as cold as a suit leak crept up her neck.

There were dozens of them. Hundreds. They made her skin crawl and her nerves judder the way gillies and Boojums never had. They were man-sized, roughly, but they looked like the pseudoroaches of Venus, the ones Black Alice still had nightmares about, with too many legs, and horrible stiff wings. They had ovate, corrugated heads, but no faces, and where their mouths ought to be sprouted writhing tentacles.

And some of them carried silver shining cylinders, like the canisters in Vinnie's subhold.

Black Alice wasn't certain if they saw her, crouched on the Boojum's hide with only a thin laminate between her and the breathsucker, but she was certain of something else. If they did, they did not care.

They disappeared below the curve of the ship, toward the airlock Black Alice had exited before clawing her way along the ship's side. They could be a trade delegation, come to bargain for the salvaged cargo.

Black Alice didn't think even the Mi-Go came in the battalions to talk trade.

She meant to wait until the last of them had passed, but they just kept coming. Wasabi wasn't answering her hails; she was on her own and unarmed. She fumbled with her tools, stowing things in any handy pocket whether it was where the tool went or not. She couldn't see much; everything was misty. It took her several seconds to realize that her visor was fogged because she was crying.

Patch cables. Where were the fucking patch cables? She found a two-meter length of fiber optic with the right plugs on the end. One end went into the monitor panel. The other snapped into her suit comm.

"Vinnie?" she whispered, when she thought she had a connection. "Vinnie, can you hear me?"

The bioluminescence under Black Alice's boots pulsed once.

Gods and little fishes, she thought. And then she drew out her laser cutting torch and started slicing open the case on the console that Wasabi had called the *governor*. Wasabi was probably dead by now, or dying. Wasabi, and Dogcollar, and . . . well, not dead. If they were lucky, they were dead.

Because the opposite of lucky was those canisters the Mi-Go were carrying.

She hoped Dogcollar was lucky.

"You wanna go *out*, right?" she whispered to the *Lavinia Whateley*. "Out into the Big Empty."

She'd never been sure how much Vinnie understood of what people said, but the light pulsed again.

"And this thing won't let you." It wasn't a question. She had it open now, and she could see that was what it did. Ugly fucking thing. Vinnie shivered underneath her, and there was a sudden pulse of noise in her helmet speakers: screaming. People screaming.

"I know," Black Alice said. "They'll come get me in a minute, I guess." She swallowed hard against the sudden lurch of her stomach. "I'm gonna get this thing off you, though. And when they go, you can go, okay? And I'm sorry. I didn't know we were keeping you from..." She had to quit talking, or she really was going to puke. Grimly, she fumbled for the tools she needed to disentangle the abomination from Vinnie's nervous system.

Another pulse of sound, a voice, not a person: flat and buzzing and horrible. "We do not bargain with thieves." And the scream that time—she'd never heard Captain Song scream before. Black Alice flinched and started counting to slow her breathing. Puking in a suit was the number one badness, but hyperventilating in a suit was a really close second.

Her heads-up display was low-res, and slightly miscalibrated, so that everything had a faint shadow-double. But the thing that flashed up against her own view of her hands was unmistakable: a question mark.

<?>

"Vinnie?"

Another pulse of screaming, and the question mark again.

<?>

"Holy shit, Vinnie!... Never mind, never mind.

They, um, they collect people's brains. In canisters. Like the canisters in the third subhold."

The bioluminescence pulsed once. Black Alice kept working.

Her heads-up pinged again: <ALICE> A pause. <?>

"Um, yeah. I figure that's what they'll do with me, too. It looked like they had plenty of canisters to go around."

Vinnie pulsed, and there was a longer pause while Black Alice doggedly severed connections and loosened bolts.

<WANT> said the *Lavinia Whateley*. <?>

"Want? Do I *want* . . . ?" Her laughter sounded bad. "Um, no. No, I don't want to be a brain in a jar. But I'm not seeing a lot of choices here. Even if I went cometary, they could catch me. And it kind of sounds like they're mad enough to do it, too."

She'd cleared out all the moorings around the edge of the governor; the case lifted off with a shove and went sailing into the dark. Black Alice winced. But then the processor under the cover drifted away from Vinnie's hide, and there was just the monofilament tethers and the fat cluster of fiber optic and superconductors to go.

<HELP>

"I'm doing my best here, Vinnie," Black Alice said through her teeth.

That got her a fast double-pulse, and the *Lavinia Whateley* said, <HELP>

And then, <ALICE>

"You want to help *me*?" Black Alice squeaked.

A strong pulse, and the heads-up said, <HELP ALICE>

"That's really sweet of you, but I'm honestly not

sure there's anything you can do. I mean, it doesn't look like the Mi-Go are mad at *you*, and I really want to keep it that way."

<EAT ALICE> said the *Lavinia Whateley*.

Black Alice came within a millimeter of taking her own fingers off with the cutting laser. "Um, Vinnie, that's um...well, I guess it's better than being a brain in a jar." Or suffocating to death in her suit if she went cometary and the Mi-Go *didn't* come after her.

The double-pulse again, but Black Alice didn't see what she could have missed. As communications went, *EAT ALICE* was pretty fucking unambiguous.

<HELP ALICE> the *Lavinia Whateley* insisted. Black Alice leaned in close, unsplicing the last of the governor's circuits from the Boojum's nervous system. <SAVE ALICE>

"By eating me? Look, I know what happens to things you eat, and it's not..." She bit her tongue. Because she *did* know what happened to things the *Lavinia Whateley* ate. Absorbed. Filtered. Recycled. "Vinnie... are you saying you can save me from the Mi-Go?"

A pulse of agreement.

"By eating me?" Black Alice pursued, needing to be sure she understood.

Another pulse of agreement.

Black Alice thought about the *Lavinia Whateley*'s teeth. "How much *me* are we talking about here?"

<ALICE> said the *Lavinia Whateley*, and then the last fiber optic cable parted, and Black Alice, her hands shaking, detached her patch cable and flung the whole mess of it as hard as she could straight up. Maybe it would find a planet with atmosphere and be some little alien kid's shooting star.

And now she had to decide what to do.

She figured she had two choices, really. One, walk back down the *Lavinia Whateley* and find out if the Mi-Go believed in surrender. Two, walk around the *Lavinia Whateley* and into her toothy mouth.

Black Alice didn't think the Mi-Go believed in surrender.

She tilted her head back for one last clear look at the shining black infinity of space. Really, there wasn't any choice at all. Because even if she'd misunderstood what Vinnie seemed to be trying to tell her, the worst she'd end up was dead, and that was light-years better than what the Mi-Go had on offer.

Black Alice Bradley loved her ship.

She turned to her left and started walking, and the *Lavinia Whateley*'s bioluminescence followed her courteously all the way, vanes swaying out of her path. Black Alice skirted each of Vinnie's eyes as she came to them, and each of them blinked at her. And then she reached Vinnie's mouth and that magnificent panoply of teeth.

"Make it quick, Vinnie, okay?" said Black Alice, and walked into her leviathan's maw.

Picking her way delicately between razor-sharp teeth, Black Alice had plenty of time to consider the ridiculousness of worrying about a hole in her suit. Vinnie's mouth was more like a crystal cave, once you were inside it; there was no tongue, no palate. Just polished, macerating stones. Which did not close on Black Alice, to her surprise. If anything, she got the feeling Vinnie was holding her ... breath. Or what passed for it.

The Boojum was lit inside, as well—or was making herself lit, for Black Alice's benefit. And as Black Alice clambered inward, the teeth got smaller, and fewer, and the tunnel narrowed. Her throat, Alice thought. I'm inside her.

And the walls closed down, and she was swallowed.

Like a pill, enclosed in the tight sarcophagus of her space suit, she felt rippling pressure as peristalsis pushed her along. And then greater pressure, suffocating, savage. One sharp pain. The pop of her ribs as her lungs crushed.

Screaming inside a space suit was contraindicated, too. And with collapsed lungs, she couldn't even do it properly.

alice.

She floated. In warm darkness. A womb, a bath. She was comfortable. An itchy soreness between her shoulder blades felt like a very mild radiation burn.

alice.

A voice she thought she should know. She tried to speak; her mouth gnashed, her teeth ground.

alice. talk here.

She tried again. Not with her mouth, this time.

Talk . . . here?

The buoyant warmth flickered past her. She was . . . drifting. No, swimming. She could feel currents on her skin. Her vision was confused. She blinked and blinked, and things were shattered.

There was nothing to see anyway, but stars.

alice talk here.

Where am I?

eat alice.

Vinnie. Vinnie's voice, but not in the flatness of the heads-up display anymore. Vinnie's voice alive with emotion and nuance and the vastness of her self.

You ate me, she said, and understood abruptly that the numbness she felt was not shock. It was the boundaries of her body erased and redrawn.

!

Agreement. Relief.

I'm . . . in you, Vinnie?

=/=

Not a "no." More like, this thing is not the same, does not compare, to this other thing. Black Alice felt the warmth of space so near a generous star slipping by her. She felt the swift currents of its gravity, and the gravity of its satellites, and bent them, and tasted them, and surfed them faster and faster away.

I am you.

!

Ecstatic comprehension, which Black Alice echoed with passionate relief. Not dead. Not dead after all. Just, transformed. Accepted. Embraced by her ship, whom she embraced in return.

Vinnie. Where are we going?

out, Vinnie answered. And in her, Black Alice read the whole great naked wonder of space, approaching faster and faster as Vinnie accelerated, reaching for the first great skip that would hurl them into the interstellar darkness of the Big Empty. They were going somewhere.

Out, Black Alice agreed and told herself not to grieve. Not to go mad. This sure beat swampy Hell out of being a brain in a jar.

And it occurred to her, as Vinnie jumped, the

brainless bodies of her crew already digesting inside her, that it wouldn't be long before the loss of the *Lavinia Whateley* was a tale told to frighten spacers, too.

Elizabeth Bear was a winner of the 2005 John W. Campbell Award for Best New Writer, then went on to win a Hugo Award for her story, "Tideline," and another Hugo for her novelette, "Shoggoths in Bloom." She has won several British Science Fiction Awards, and her first novel, *Hammered*, won the Locus Award. A prolific writer, her most recent novels include *Chill*, *The White City*, and *Ad Eternum*. She has also collaborated with Sarah Monette on the novel *Companion to Wolves*. She has had the unusual distinction of having a line from her *Seven for a Secret* quoted on an episode of the TV show *Criminal Minds*. She lives in New England. Her website is www.elizabethbear.com.

Sarah Monette was born and raised in Oak Ridge, Tennessee, began writing at the age of twelve, and hasn't stopped yet. Appropriately, her PhD in English Literature was earned with a dissertation on ghosts in English Renaissance revenge tragedy. Her novels include *Melusine*, *The Virtu*, *The Mirador*, and *Corambis*. She has written under the pseudonym of Kathryn Addison. She won the Spectrum award in 2003 for her short story "Three Letters from the Queen of Elfland," and many of her short stories have been cited on Best of the Year lists and included in anthologies of the year's best SF and/or fantasy.

Currently teaching a course in seventeenth-century literature, she lives in Wisconsin with four cats, a husband, and an albino bristlenose plecostomus. Her website is www.sarahmonette.com. I (Hank) included another collaboration by the authors, their Lovecraftian space opera "Mongoose," in my Baen anthology, *In Space No One Can Hear You Scream*. In my intro to that chilling tale, I mentioned that "Boojum" was set in the same universe, and recommended it. And now, you can see how right I was.

A Relic of the Empire

Larry Niven

Here's an early entry in Larry Niven's famed and now-classic "Known Space" series. The space pirates swooped down on the planet and the apparently ineffectual explorer on it, figuring they had nothing to fear from him. Too bad they didn't understand that knowledge is power, and he was the one with the knowledge...

When the ship arrived, Dr. Richard Schultz-Mann was out among the plants, flying over and around them on a lift belt. He hovered over one, inspecting with proprietary interest an anomalous patch in its yellow foliage. This one would soon be ripe.

The nature-lover was a breadstick of a man, very tall and very thin, with an aristocratic head sporting a close-cropped growth of coppery hair and an asymmetric beard. A white streak ran above his right ear, and there was a patch of white on each side of the chin, one coinciding with the waxed spike. As his head moved in the double sunlight, the patches changed color instantly.

He took a tissue sample from the grayish patch, stored it, and started to move on...

The ship came down like a daylight meteor, streaking blue-white across the vague red glare of Big Mira. It slowed and circled high overhead, weaving drunkenly across the sky, then settled toward the plain near Mann's *Explorer*. Mann watched it land, then gave up his bumblebee activities and went to welcome the newcomers. He was amazed at the coincidence. As far as he knew, his had been the first ship ever to land here. The company would be good... but what could anyone possibly want here?

Little Mira set while he was skimming back. A flash of white at the far edge of the sea, and the tiny blue-white dwarf was gone. The shadows changed abruptly, turning the world red. Mann took off his pink-tinged goggles. Big Mira was still high, sixty degrees above the horizon and two hours from second sunset.

The newcomer was huge, a thick blunt-nosed cylinder twenty times the size of the *Explorer*. It looked old: not damaged, not even weathered, but indefinably old. Its nose was still closed tight, the living bubble retracted, if indeed it had a living bubble. Nothing moved nearby. They must be waiting for his welcome before they debarked.

Mann dropped toward the newcomer.

The stunner took him a few hundred feet up. Without pain and without sound, suddenly all Mann's muscles turned to loose jelly. Fully conscious and completely helpless, he continued to dive toward the ground.

Three figures swarmed up at him from the new-comer's oversized airlock. They caught him before he hit. Tossing humorous remarks at each other in a language Mann did not know, they towed him down to the plain.

The man behind the desk wore a captain's hat and a cheerful smile. "Our supply of Verinol is limited," he said in the trade language. "If I have to use it, I will, but I'd rather save it. You may have heard that it has unpleasant side effects."

"I understand perfectly," said Mann. "You'll use it the moment you think you've caught me in a lie." Since he had not yet been injected with the stuff, he decided it was a bluff. The man had no Verinol, if indeed there was such an animal as Verinol.

But he was still in a bad hole. The ancient, ren-ovated ship held more than a dozen men, whereas Mann seriously doubted if he could have stood up. The sonic had not entirely worn off.

His captor nodded approvingly. He was huge and square, almost a cartoon of a heavy-planet man, with muscularity as smooth and solid as an elephant's. A Jinxian, for anyone's money. His size made the tiny shipboard office seem little more than a coffin. Among the crew his captain's hat would not be needed to enforce orders. He looked like he could kick holes in hullmetal, or teach tact to an armed Kzin.

"You're quick," he said. "That's good. I'll be asking questions about you and about this planet. You'll give truthful, complete answers. If some of my questions get too personal, say so; but remember, I'll use the Verinol if I'm not satisfied. How old are you?"

"One hundred and fifty-four."

"You look much older."

"I was off boosterspice for a couple of decades."

"Tough luck. Planet of origin?"

"Wunderland."

"Thought so, with that stick-figure build. Name?"

"Doctor Richard Harvey Schultz-Mann."

"Rich Mann, hah? Are you?"

Trust a Jinxian to spot a pun. "No. After I make my reputation, I'll write a book on the Slaver Empire. Then I'll be rich."

"If you say so. Married?"

"Several times. Not at the moment."

"Rich Mann, I can't give you my real name, but you can call me Captain Kidd. What kind of beard is that?"

"You've never seen an asymmetric beard?"

"No, thank the Mist Demons. It looks like you've shaved off all your hair below the part, and everything on your face left of what looks like a one-tuft goatee. Is that the way it's supposed to go?"

"Exactly so."

"You did it on purpose then."

"Don't mock me, Captain Kidd."

"Point taken. Are they popular on Wunderland?"

Dr. Mann unconsciously sat a little straighter. "Only among those willing to take the time and trouble to keep it neat." He twisted the single waxed spike of beard at the right of his chin with unconscious complacence. This was the only straight hair on his face—the rest of the beard being close-cropped and curly—and it sprouted from one of the white patches. Mann was proud of his beard.

"Hardly seems worth it," said the Jinxian. "I assume

it's to show you're one of the leisure classes. What are you doing on Mira Ceti-T?"

"I'm investigating one aspect of the Slaver Empire."

"You're a geologist, then?"

"No, a xenobiologist."

"I don't understand."

"What do you know about the Slavers?"

"A little. They used to live all through this part of the galaxy. One day the slave races decided they'd had enough, and there was a war. When it was over, everyone was dead."

"You know quite a bit. Well, Captain, a billion and a half years is a long time. The Slavers left only two kinds of evidence of their existence. There are the stasis boxes and their contents, mostly weaponry, but records have been found too. And there are the plants and animals developed for the Slavers' convenience by their tnuctip slaves, who were biological engineers."

"I know about those. We have bandersnatchi on Jinx, on both sides of the ocean."

"The bandersnatchi food animals are a special case. They can't mutate; their chromosomes are as thick as your finger, too large to be influenced by radiation. All other relics of tnuctipun engineering have mutated almost beyond recognition. Almost. For the past twelve years I've been searching out and identifying the surviving species."

"It doesn't sound like a fun way to spend a life, Rich Mann. Are there Slaver animals on this planet?"

"Not animals, but plants. Have you been outside yet?"

"Not yet."

"Then come out. I'll show you."

❖　　　❖　　　❖

The ship was very large. It did not seem to be
furnished with a living bubble, hence the entire lifesys-
tem must be enclosed within the metal walls. Mann
walked ahead of the Jinxian down a long unpainted
corridor to the airlock, waited inside while the pressure dropped slightly, then rode the escalator to the
ground. He would not try to escape yet, though the
sonic had worn off. The Jinxian was affable but alert;
he carried a flashlight-laser dangling from his belt,
his men were all around them, and Mann's lift belt
had been removed. Richard Mann was not quixotic.

It was a red, red world. They stood on a dusty plain
sparsely scattered with strange yellow-headed bushes. A
breeze blew things like tumbleweeds across the plain,
things which on second glance were the dried heads
of former bushes. No other life-forms were visible. Big
Mira sat on the horizon, a vague, fiery semicircular
cloud, just dim enough to look at without squinting.
Outlined in sharp black silhouette against the red
giant's bloody disk were three slender, improbably tall
spires, unnaturally straight and regular, each with a
vivid patch of yellow vegetation surrounding its base.
Members of the Jinxian's crew ran, walked, or floated
outside, some playing an improvised variant of baseball,
others at work, still others merely enjoying themselves.
None were Jinxian, and none had Mann's light-planet
build. Mann noticed that a few were using the thin
wire blades of variable-knives to cut down some of
the straight bushes.

"Those," he said.

"The bushes?"

"Yes. They used to be tnuctip stage trees. We
don't know what they looked like originally, but the

old records say the Slavers stopped using them some decades before the rebellion. May I ask what those men are doing in my ship?"

Expanded from its clamshell nose, the *Explorer*'s living bubble was bigger than the *Explorer*. Held taut by air pressure, isolated from the surrounding environment, proof against any atmospheric chemistry found in nature, the clear fabric hemisphere was a standard feature of all campermodel spacecraft. Mann could see biped shadows moving purposefully about inside and going between the clamshell doors into the ship proper.

"They're not stealing anything, Rich Mann. I sent them in to remove a few components from the drives and the comm systems."

"One hopes they won't damage what they remove."

"They won't. They have their orders."

"I assume you don't want me to call someone," said Mann. He noticed that the men were preparing a bonfire, using stage bushes. The bushes were like miniature trees, four to six feet tall, slender and straight, and the brilliant yellow foliage at the top was flattened like the head of a dandelion. From the low, rounded eastern mountains to the western sea, the red land was sprinkled with the yellow dots of their heads. Men were cutting off the heads and roots, then dragging the logs away to pile them in conical formation over a stack of death-dry tumbleweed heads.

"We don't want you to call the Wunderland police, who happen to be somewhere out there looking for us."

"I hate to pry—"

"No, no, you're entitled to your curiosity. We're pirates."

"Surely you jest. Captain Kidd, if you've figured out a way to make piracy pay off, you must be bright enough to make ten times the money on the stock market."

"Why?"

By the tone of his voice, by his gleeful smile, the Jinxian was baiting him. Fine; it would keep his mind off stage trees. Mann said, "Because you can't *catch* a ship in hyperspace. The only way you can match courses with a ship is to wait until it's in an inhabited system. Then the police come calling."

"I know an inhabited system where there aren't any police."

"The hell you do."

They had walked more or less aimlessly to the *Explorer's* airlock. Now the Jinxian turned and gazed out over the red plain, toward the dwindling crescent of Big Mira, which now looked like a bad forest fire. "I'm curious about those spires."

"Fine, keep your little secret. I've wondered about them myself, but I haven't had a chance to look at them yet."

"I'd think they'd interest you. They look definitely artificial to me."

"But they're a billion years too young to be Slaver artifacts."

"Rich Mann, are those bushes the only life on this planet?"

"I haven't seen anything else," Mann lied.

"Then it couldn't have been a native race that put those spires up. I never heard of a space-traveling race that builds such big things for mere monuments."

"Neither did I. Shall we look at them tomorrow?"

"Yes." Captain Kidd stepped into the *Explorer*'s airlock, wrapped a vast hand gently around Mann's thin wrist and pulled his captive in beside him. The airlock cycled and Mann followed the Jinxian into the living bubble with an impression that the Jinxian did not quite trust him.

Fine.

It was dark inside the bubble. Mann hesitated before turning on the light. Outside he could see the last red sliver of Big Mira shrinking with visible haste. He saw more. A man was kneeling before the conical bonfire, and a flickering light was growing in the dried bush-head kindling.

Mann turned on the lights, obliterating the outside view. "Go on about piracy," he said.

"Oh, yes." The Jinxian dropped into a chair, frowning. "Piracy was only the end product. It started a year ago, when I found the puppeteer system."

"The—"

"Yes. The puppeteers' home system."

Richard Mann's ears went straight up. He was from Wunderland, remember?

Puppeteers are highly intelligent, herbivorous, and very old as a species. Their corner on interstellar business is as old as the human Bronze Age. And they are cowards.

A courageous puppeteer is not regarded as insane only by other puppeteers. It *is* insane, and usually shows disastrous secondary symptoms: depression, homicidal tendencies, and the like. These poor, warped minds are easy to spot. No sane puppeteer will cross a vehicular roadway or travel in any but the safest available fashion or resist a thief, even an unarmed thief. No sane puppeteer will leave his home system, wherever that may be, without his painless method of suicide, nor will it walk an alien world without guards—nonpuppeteer guards.

The location of the puppeteer system is one of the puppeteer's most closely guarded secrets. Another is the painless suicide gimmick. It may be a mere trick of preconditioning. Whatever it is, it works. Puppeteers cannot be tortured into revealing anything about their home world, though they hate pain. It must be a world with reasonably earthlike atmosphere and temperature, but beyond that nothing is known...or was known.

Suddenly Mann wished that they hadn't lit the bonfire so soon. He didn't know how long it would burn before the logs caught, and he wanted to hear more about this.

"I found it just a year ago," the Jinxian repeated. "It's best I don't tell you what I was doing up to then. The less you know about who I am, the better. But when I'd got safely out of the system, I came straight home. I wanted time to think."

"And you picked piracy? Why not blackmail?"

"I thought of that—"

"I should hope so! Can you imagine what the puppeteers would pay to keep that secret?"

"Yes. That's what stopped me. Rich Mann, how much would you have asked for in one lump sum?"

"A round billion stars and immunity from prosecution."

"Okay. Now look at it from the puppeteer point of view. That billion wouldn't buy them complete safety, because you might still talk. But if they spent a tenth of that on detectives, weapons, hit men, et cetera, they could shut your mouth for keeps and also find and hit anyone you might have talked to. I couldn't figure any way to make myself safe and still collect, not with that much potential power against me.

"So I thought of piracy.

"Eight of us had gone in, but I was the only one who'd guessed just what we'd tumbled into. I let the others in on it. Some had friends they could trust, and that raised our number to fourteen. We bought a ship, a very old one, and renovated it. She's an old slowboat's ground-to-orbit auxiliary fitted out with a new hyperdrive; maybe you noticed?"

"No. I saw how old she was."

"We figured even if the puppeteers recognized her, they'd never trace her. We took her back to the puppeteer system and waited."

A flickering light glimmered outside the bubble wall. Any second now the logs would catch . . . Mann tried to relax.

"Pretty soon a ship came in. We waited till it was too deep in the system's gravity well to jump back into hyperspace. Then we matched courses. Naturally they surrendered right away. We went in in suits so they couldn't describe us even if they could tell humans apart. Would you believe they had six hundred million stars in currency?"

"That's pretty good pay. What went wrong?"

"My idiot crew wouldn't leave. We'd figured most of the ships coming into the puppeteer system would be carrying money. They're misers, you know. Part of being a coward is wanting security. And they'd most of their mining and manufacturing on other worlds, where they can get labor. So we waited for two more ships, because we had room for lots more money. The puppeteers wouldn't dare attack us inside their own system." Captain Kidd made a sound of disgust. "I can't really blame the men. In a sense they were right. One ship with a fusion drive can do a hell of a lot of damage just by hovering over a city. So we stayed.

"Meanwhile the puppeteers registered a formal complaint with Earth.

"Earth hates people who foul up interstellar trade. We'd offered physical harm to a puppeteer. A thing like that could cause a stock-market crash. So Earth offered the services of every police force in human space. Hardly seems fair, does it?"

"They ganged up on you. But they still couldn't come after you, could they? The puppeteers would have to tell the police how to find their system. They'd hardly do that; not when some human descendant might attack them a thousand years from now."

The Jinxian dialed himself a frozen daiquiri. "They had to wait till we left. I still don't know how they tracked us. Maybe they've got something that can track a gravity warp moving faster than light. I wouldn't put it past them to build it just for us. Anyway, when we angled toward Jinx, we heard them telling the police of We Made It just where we were."

"Ouch."

"We headed for the nearest double star. Not my idea; Hermie Preston's. He thought we could hide in the dust clouds in the trojan points. Whatever the puppeteers were using probably couldn't find us in normal space." Two thirsty gulps had finished his daiquiri. He crumpled the cup, watched it evaporate, dialed another. "The nearest double star was Mira Ceti. We hardly expected to find a planet in the trailing trojan point, but as long as it was there, we decided to use it."

"And here you are."

"Yeah."

"You'll be better off when you've found a way to hide that ship."

"We had to find out about you first, Rich Mann. Tomorrow we'll sink the *Puppet Master* in the ocean. Already we've shut off the fusion drive. The lifters work by battery, and the cops can't detect that."

"Fine. Now for the billion-dollar—"

"No, no, Rich Mann. I will not tell you where to find the puppeteer planet. Give up the whole idea. Shall we join the campfire group?"

Mann came joltingly alert. *How* had the stage trees lasted this long? Thinking fast, he said, "Is your autokitchen as good as mine?"

"Probably not. Why?"

"Let me treat your group to dinner, Captain Kidd."

Captain Kidd shook his head, smiling. "No offense, Rich Mann, but I can't read your kitchen controls, and there's no point in tempting you. You might rashly put someth—"

WHAM!

The living bubble bulged inward, snapped back. Captain Kidd swore and ran for the airlock. Mann stayed seated, motionless, hoping against hope that the Jinxian had forgotten him.

WHAM! WHAM! Flares of light from the region of the campfire. Captain Kidd frantically punched the cycle button, and the opaque inner door closed on him. Mann came to his feet, running.

WHAM! The concussion hurt his ears and set the bubble rippling. Burning logs must be flying in all directions. The airlock recycled, empty. No telling where the Jinxian was; the outer door was opaque too. Well, that worked both ways.

WHAM!

Mann searched through the airlock locker, pushing sections of spacesuit aside to find the lift belt. It wasn't there. He'd been wearing it; they'd taken it off him after they shot him down.

He moaned: a tormented, uncouth sound to come from a cultured Wunderlander. He *had* to have a lift belt.

WHAMWHAMWHAM. Someone was screaming far away.

Mann snatched up the suit's chest-and-shoulder section and locked it around him. It was rigid vacuum armor, with a lift motor built into the back. He took an extra moment to screw down the helmet, then hit the cycle button.

No use searching for weapons. They'd have taken even a variableknife.

The Jinxian could be just outside waiting. He might have realized the truth by now.

The door opened. . . . Captain Kidd was easy to find, a running misshapen shadow and a frantic booming voice. "Flatten out, you yeastheads! It's an attack!" He hadn't guessed. But he must know that the We Made It police would use stunners.

Mann twisted his lift control to full power.

The surge of pressure took him under the armpits. Two standard gees sent blood rushing to his feet, pushed him upward with four times Wunderland's gravity. A last stage log exploded under him, rocked him back and forth, and then all was dark and quiet.

He adjusted the altitude setting to slant him almost straight forward. The dark ground sped beneath him. He moved northeast. Nobody was following him—yet.

Captain Kidd's men would have been killed, hurt, or at least stunned when the campfire exploded in their faces. He'd expected Captain Kidd to chase him, but the Jinxian couldn't have caught him. Lift motors are all alike, and Mann wasn't as heavy as the Jinxian.

He flew northeast, flying very low, knowing that the only landmarks big enough to smash him were the spires to the west. When he could no longer see the ships' lights, he turned south, still very low. Still nobody followed him. He was glad he'd taken the helmet; it protected his eyes from the wind.

In the blue dawn he came awake. The sky was darker than navy blue, and the light around him was dim, like blue moonlight. Little Mira was a hurtingly bright pinpoint between two mountain peaks, bright enough to sear holes in a man's retinae. Mann unscrewed his helmet, adjusted the pink goggles over his eyes. Now it was even darker.

He poked his nose above the yellow moss. The plain and sky were empty of men. The pirates must be out looking for him, but they hadn't gotten here yet. So far so good.

Far out across the plain there was fire. A stage tree rose rapidly into the black sky, minus its roots and flowers, the wooden flanges at its base holding it in precarious aerodynamic stability. A white rope of smoke followed it up. When the smoke cut off, the tree became invisible . . . until, much higher, there was a puff of white cloud like a flak burst. Now the seeds would be spreading across the sky.

Richard Mann smiled. Wonderful, how the stage trees had adapted to the loss of their masters. The Slavers had raised them on wide plantations, using the solid-fuel rocket cores inside the living bark to lift their ships from places where a fusion drive would have done damage. But the trees used the rockets for reproduction, to scatter their seeds farther than any plant before them.

Ah, well . . . Richard Mann snuggled deeper into the yellow woolly stuff around him and began to consider his next move. He was a hero now in the eyes of humanity-at-large. He had badly damaged the pirate crew. When the police landed, he could count on a reward from the puppeteers. Should he settle for that or go on to bigger stakes?

The *Puppet Master*'s cargo was bigger stakes, certainly. But even if he could take it, which seemed unlikely, how could he fit it into his ship? How would he escape the police of We Made It?

No. Mann had another stake in mind, one just as valuable and infinitely easier to hide.

What Captain Kidd apparently hadn't realized was that blackmail is not immoral to a puppeteer. There are well-established rules of conduct that make blackmail perfectly safe both for blackmailer and victim. Two are that the blackmailer must submit to having certain portions of his memory erased, and must turn over all evidence against the victim. Mann was prepared to do this if he could force Captain Kidd to tell him where to find the puppeteer system.

But how?

Well, he knew one thing the Jinxian didn't....

Little Mira rose fast, arc blue, a hole into hell. Mann remained where he was, an insignificant mote in the yellow vegetation below one of the spires Captain Kidd had remarked on last night. The spire was a good half mile high. An artifact that size would seem impossibly huge to any but an Earthman. The way it loomed over him made Mann uncomfortable. In shape it was a slender cone with a base three hundred feet across. The surface near the base was gray and smooth to touch, like polished granite.

The yellow vegetation was a thick, rolling carpet. It spread out around the spire in an uneven circle half a mile in diameter and dozens of feet deep. It rose about the base in a thick turtleneck collar. Close up, the stuff wasn't even discrete plants. It looked like a cross between moss and wool, dyed flagrant yellow.

It made a good hiding place. Not perfect, of course; a heat sensor would pick him out in a flash. He hadn't thought of that last night, and now it worried him. Should he get out, try to reach the sea?

The ship would certainly carry a heat sensor, but not a portable one. A portable heat sensor would be a weapon, a nighttime gunsight, and weapons of war had been illegal for some time in human space.

But the *Puppet Master* could have stopped elsewhere to get such implements. Kzinti, for example.

Nonsense. Why would Captain Kidd have needed portable weapons with night gunsights? He certainly hadn't expected puppeteers to fight hand-to-hand! The stunners were mercy weapons; even a pirate would not dare kill a puppeteer, and Captain Kidd was no ordinary pirate.

All right. Radar? He need only burrow into the moss/wool. Sight search? Same answer. Radio? Mental note: Do not transmit anything.

Mental note? There was a dictaphone in his helmet. He used it after pulling the helmet out of the moss/wool around him.

Flying figures. Mann watched them for a long moment, trying to spot the Jinxian. There were only four, and he wasn't among them. The four were flying northwest of him, moving south. Mann ducked into the moss.

"Hello, Rich Mann."

The voice was low, contorted with fury. Mann felt the shock race through him, contracting every muscle with the fear of death. It came from behind him!

From his helmet.

"Hello, Rich Mann. Guess where I am?"

He couldn't turn it off. Spacesuit helmet radios weren't built to be turned off: a standard safety factor. If one were fool enough to ignore safety, one could insert an "off" switch, but Mann had never felt the need.

"I'm in your ship, using your ship-to-suit radio circuit. That was a good trick you played last night. I didn't even know what a stage tree was till I looked it up in your library."

He'd just have to endure it. A pity he couldn't answer back.

"You killed four of my men and put five more in the autodoc tanks. Why'd you do it, Rich Mann? You must have known we weren't going to kill you. Why should we? There's no blood on *our* hands."

You lie, Mann thought at the radio. *People die in a market crash. And the ones who live are the ones who suffer. Do you know what it's like to be suddenly poor and not know how to live poor?*

"I'll assume you want something, Rich Mann. All right. What? The money in my hold? That's ridiculous. You'd never get in. You want to turn us in for a reward? Fat chance. You've got no weapons. If we find you now, we'll kill you."

The four searchers passed far to the west, their headlamps spreading yellow light across the blue dusk. They were no danger to him now. A pity they and their fellows should have been involved in what amounted to a vendetta.

"The puppeteer planet, of course. The modern El Dorado. But you don't know where it is, do you? I wonder if I ought to give you a hint. Of course you'd never know whether I was telling the truth."

Did the Jinxian know how to live poor? Mann shuddered. The old memories came back only rarely, but when they came, they hurt.

You have to learn not to buy luxuries before you've bought necessities. You can starve learning which is which. Necessities are food and a place to sleep, shoes and pants. Luxuries are tobacco, restaurants, fine shirts, throwing away a ruined meal while you're learning to cook, quitting a job you don't like. A union is a necessity. Boosterspice is a luxury.

The Jinxian wouldn't know about that. He'd had the money to buy his own ship.

"Ask me politely, Rich Mann. Would you like to know where I found the puppeteer system?"

Mann had leased the *Explorer* on a college grant. It had been the latest step in a long climb upward. Before that . . .

He was half his lifetime old when the crash came. Until then boosterspice had kept him as young as the ageless idle ones who were his friends and relatives. Overnight he was one of the hungry. A number of his partners in disaster had ridden their lift belts straight up into eternity; Richard Schultz-Mann had sold his for his final dose of boosterspice. Before he could afford boosterspice again, there were wrinkles in his forehead, the texture of his skin had changed, his sex urge had decreased, strange white patches had appeared in his hair, and there were twinges in his back. He still got them.

Yet always he had maintained his beard. With the white spike and the white streak it looked better than ever. After the boosterspice restored color to his hair, he dyed the patches back in again.

"Answer me, Rich Mann!"

Go ride a bandersnatch.

It was a draw. Captain Kidd couldn't entice him into answering, and Mann would never know the pirate's secret. If Kidd dropped his ship in the sea, Mann could show it to the police. At least that would be something.

Luckily, Kidd couldn't move the *Explorer.* Otherwise he could take both ships half around the planet, leaving Mann stranded.

The four pirates were far to the south. Captain Kidd had apparently given up on the radio. There were water and food syrup in his helmet; Mann would not starve.

Where in blazes were the police? On the other side of the planet?

Stalemate.

❖   ❖   ❖

Big Mira came as a timorous peeping Tom, poking its rim over the mountains like red smoke. The land brightened, taking on tinges of lavender against long, long navy blue shadows. The shadows shortened and became vague.

The morality of his position was beginning to bother Dr. Richard Mann.

In attacking the pirates, he had done his duty as a citizen. The pirates had sullied humanity's hard-won reputation for honesty. Mann had struck back.

But his motive? Fear had been two parts of that motive. First, the fear that Captain Kidd might decide to shut his mouth. Second, the fear of being poor.

That fear had been with him for some time.

Write a book and make a fortune! It looked good on paper. The thirty-light-year sphere of human space contained nearly fifty billion readers. Persuade one percent of them to shell out half a star each for a disposable tape, and your four-percent royalties became twenty million stars. But most books nowadays were flops. You had to scream very loud to get the attention of even ten billion readers. Others were trying to drown you out.

Before Captain Kidd, that had been Richard Schultz-Mann's sole hope of success.

He'd behaved within the law. Captain Kidd couldn't make that claim, but Captain Kidd hadn't killed anybody.

Mann sighed. He'd had no choice. His major motive was honor, and that motive still held.

He moved restlessly in his nest of damp moss/wool. The day was heating up, and his suit's temperature control would not work with half a suit.

What was that?

It was the *Puppet Master*, moving effortlessly toward him on its lifters. The Jinxian must have decided to get it under water before the human law arrived.

. . . Or had he?

Mann adjusted his lift motor until he was just short of weightless, then moved cautiously around the spire. He saw the four pirates moving to intersect the *Puppet Master*. They'd see him if he left the spire. But if he stayed, those infrared detectors . . .

He'd have to chance it.

The suit's padded shoulders gouged his armpits as he streaked toward the second spire. He stopped in midair over the moss and dropped, burrowed in it. The pirates didn't swerve.

Now he'd see.

The ship slowed to a stop over the spire he'd just left.

"Can you hear me, Rich Mann?"

Mann nodded gloomily to himself.

Definitely, that was it.

"I should have tried this before. Since you're nowhere in sight, you've either left the vicinity altogether or you're hiding in the thick bushes around those towers."

Should he try to keep dodging from spire to spire? Or could he outfly them?

At least one was bound to be faster. The armor increased his weight.

"I hope you took the opportunity to examine this tower. It's fascinating. Very smooth, stony surface, except at the top. A perfect cone, also except at the top. You listening? The tip of this thing swells from an eight-foot neck into an egg-shaped knob fifteen feet across. The knob isn't polished as smooth as the rest of it. Vaguely reminiscent of an asparagus spear, wouldn't you say?"

Richard Schultz-Mann cocked his head, tasting an idea.

He unscrewed his helmet, ripped out and pocketed the radio. In frantic haste he began ripping out double handfuls of the yellow moss/wool, stuffed them into a wad in the helmet, and turned his lighter on it. At first the vegetation merely smoldered, while Mann muttered through clenched teeth. Then it caught with a weak blue smokeless flame. Mann placed his helmet in a mossy nest, setting it so it would not tip over and spill its burning contents.

"I'd have said a phallic symbol, myself. What do you think, Rich Mann? If these are phallic symbols, they're pretty well distorted. Humanoid but not human, you might say."

The pirates had joined their ship. They hovered around its floating silver bulk, ready to drop on him when the *Puppet Master*'s infrared detectors found him.

Mann streaked away to the west on full acceleration, staying as low as he dared. The spire would shield him for a minute or so, and then...

"This vegetation isn't stage trees, Rich Mann. It looks like some sort of grass from here. Must need something in the rock they made these erections out of. Mph. No hot spots. You're not down there after all. Well, we try the next one."

Behind him, in the moments when he dared look back, Mann saw the *Puppet Master* move to cover the second spire, the one he'd left a moment ago, the one with a gray streak in the moss at its base. Four humanoid dots clustered loosely above the ship.

"Peekaboo," came the Jinxian's voice. "And goodbye, killer."

The *Puppet Master*'s fusion drive went on. Fusion flame lashed out in a blue-white spear, played down the side of the pillar and into the moss/wool below. Mann faced forward and concentrated on flying. He felt neither elation nor pity but only disgust. The Jinxian was a fool after all. He'd seen no life on Mira Ceti-T but for the stage trees. He had Mann's word that there was none. Couldn't he reach the obvious conclusion? Perhaps the moss/wool had fooled him. It certainly did look like yellow moss, clustering around the spires as if it needed some chemical element in the stone.

A glance back told him that the pirate ship was still spraying white flame over the spire and the foliage below. He'd have been a cinder by now. The Jinxian must want him extremely dead. Well—

The spire went all at once. It sat on the lavender plain in a hemisphere of multicolored fire, engulfing the other spires and the Jinxian ship; and then it began to expand and rise. Mann adjusted his attitude to vertical to get away from the ground. A moment later the shock wave slammed into him and blew him tumbling over the desert.

Two white ropes of smoke rose straight up through the dimming explosion cloud. The other spires were taking off while still green! Fire must have reached the foliage at their bases.

Mann watched them go with his head thrown back and his body curiously loose in the vacuum armor. His expression was strangely contented. At these times he could forget himself and his ambitions in the contemplation of immortality.

Two knots formed simultaneously in the rising smoke trails. Second stage on. They rose very fast now.

"Rich Mann."

Mann flicked his transmitter on. "You'd live through anything."

"Not I. I can't feel anything below my shoulders. Listen, Rich Mann, I'll trade secrets with you. What happened?"

"The big towers are stage trees."

"Uh?" Half question, half an expression of agony.

"A stage tree has two life cycles. One is the bush, the other is the big multistage form." Mann talked faster, fearful of losing his audience. "The forms alternate. A stage tree seed lands on a planet and grows into a bush. Later there are lots of bushes. When a seed hits a particularly fertile spot, it grows into a multistage form. You still there?"

"Yuh."

"In the big form the living part is the tap root and the photosynthetic organs around the base. That way the rocket section doesn't have to carry so much weight. It grows straight up out of the living part, but it's as dead as the center of an oak except for the seed at the top. When it's ripe, the rocket takes off. Usually it'll reach terminal velocity for the system it's in. Kidd, I can't see your ship; I'll have to wait till the smoke—"

"Just keep talking."

"I'd like to help."

"Too late. Keep talking."

"I've tracked the stage trees across twenty light-years of space. God knows where they started. They're all through the systems around here. The seed pods spend hundreds of thousands of years in space; and when they enter a system, they explode. If there's a habitable world, one seed is bound to hit it. If there isn't, there're lots more pods where that one came from. It's immortality, Captain Kidd. This one plant has traveled farther than mankind, and it's much older. A billion and a—"

"Mann."

"Yah."

"Twenty-three point six, seventy point one, six point nil. I don't know its name on the star charts. Shall I repeat that?"

Mann forgot the stage trees. "Better repeat it."

"Twenty-three point six, seventy point one, six point nothing. Hunt in that area till you find it. It's a red giant, undersized. Planet is small, dense, no moon."

"Got it."

"You're stupid if you use it. You'll have the same luck I did. That's why I told you."

"I'll use blackmail."

"They'll kill you. Otherwise I wouldn't have said. Why'd you kill me, Rich Mann?"

"I didn't like your remarks about my beard. Never insult a Wunderlander's asymmetric beard, Captain Kidd."

"I won't do it again."

"I'd like to help." Mann peered into the billowing smoke. Now it was a black pillar tinged at the edges by the twin sunlight. "Still can't see your ship."

"You will in a moment," the pirate moaned . . . and Mann saw the ship. He managed to turn his head in time to save his eyes.

Larry Niven is renowned for his ingenious science fiction stories solidly based on authentic science, often of the cutting-edge variety. His Known Space series is one of the most popular "future history" sagas in SF and includes the epic novel *Ringworld*, one of the few novels to have won both the Hugo and Nebula awards, as well as the *Locus* and Ditmar awards, and which is recognized as a milestone in modern science fiction. Four of his shorter works have also won Hugos. Most recently, the Science Fiction and Fantasy Writers of America have presented him with the Damon Knight Memorial Grand Master Award, given for Lifetime Achievement in the field. Lest this all sound too serious, it should be remembered that one of his most memorable short works is "Man of Steel, Woman of Kleenex," a not-quite-serious essay on Superman and the problems of his having a sex life. Niven has also demonstrated a talent for creating memorable aliens, beginning with his first novel, *World of Ptaavs*, in 1966. A reason for this, Niven writes, is that, "I grew up with dogs. I live with a cat and borrow dogs to hike with. I have a passing acquaintance with raccoons and ferrets. Associating with nonhumans has certainly gained me insight into alien intelligences." This ingenious creativity with aliens is not just limited to the intelligent sort, and here, alien vegetation provides a launching pad to drive the story.

The Night Captain

Christopher Ruocchio

It doesn't take much—or many hands—to hijack a ship while the crew's in cold sleep, but then it doesn't take many people to save it. With the ship's ordinary crew on ice for a long voyage between the stars, the security of the vessel is down to her night captain, a junior officer with relatively little experience. But when a routine refueling stop opens the ship up to attack, it's down to the night captain and his skeleton crew to save their human cargo from piracy...only the night captain may not be alone...

CHAPTER 1
BLADES IN THE NIGHT

Five years of darkness already. Five years since they set sail from Forum and the primary crew went to their icy beds. Five years of night.

Five years...and another twenty to go before they

reached Nessus. Once upon a time, a single twenty-five-year night cruise would have been enough for an officer to live out his commission. There were times—none of them in living memory—when Roderick Halford might have expected to retire on landfall at Nessus and settle into a life of desk work or a posting with one of the civil services. He might have settled down, started a family, kept a modest estate in the countryside of some backwater world in the Expanse and lived out his days in peace.

That was before the war. Before the Cielcin. Before he'd been assigned to ferry Lord Hadrian Marlowe's Red Company from the core to the frontlines and back. He supposed he shouldn't complain. He had the easy job: mind the ship at warp between the stars, keep the lights on and the ship fueled—on schedule and on course. The Imperial Legions survived off the back of officers like himself, ferrymen whose job was to run the ship while the more senior officers and combat personnel slept in cryonic fugue, awaiting deployment when they arrived at their destination. It was not a glamorous posting, but it was honest work . . . if lonely and quiet.

This was to be Halford's third voyage as night captain aboard the venerable battleship. By its end, he would count forty-seven years of service on this commission. Nearly twice the minimum of what a night officer might have served in peacetime. He was grateful his palatine genetics ensured that he still had centuries to look forward to. There was always the chance the war would end before he was too old to enjoy it.

Maybe.

It was quiet. The *Tamerlane* was always quiet during these long nights. More than ninety thousand souls called the old *Eriel*-class vessel home—Mad Marlowe's Red Company—but fewer than a hundred of those still drew breath. The rest slumbered in icy coffins, awaiting the trumpet blast.

Halford's footfalls rang in the metallic silence, mingling with the pulsing of the music through the conduction patches behind his ears as he went about his morning jog. The ship was quieter than usual, without the distant hum of the warp drives undergirding everything, and through the windows he beheld not the violet fractals of space-at-warp, but the seeming static stars, distant and cold.

They'd put into port at the fuel depot 0.1 light-years out of Nagapur system three days ago to refuel the ship's antimatter reservoirs. A short layover, but one that allowed the novelty of fresh faces and an opportunity for the night crew to explore the ring-station's scant offerings.

He could see the station through the slit windows of the *Tamerlane*'s equator, a promenade that circled the arrowhead-shaped battleship beneath the armored dorsal hull. Each morning, Halford liked to jog two or three miles of the ship's length before attending to his duties. The *Tamerlane* was vast, a dozen miles end-to-end, with dozens of decks and hundreds of chambers, so much of it disused and sealed off while the main crew slept. It was good for a captain to make his rounds, however slowly, to be apprised of problems and things in need of repair during the long and silent crossing between the stars.

"How long until we're ready to depart again?" he asked, slowing his jog. He leaned against the rail, looking down from the promenade to where the ranks of

Sparrowhawk lighters slumbered in their berths, wings folded for deployment above their mag-tubes. One of the lighter craft had its cockpit open, and a repair kit lay abandoned by some workman on the strand above the little black starship. Halford frowned; he wasn't aware that one of the mechanics was working on the lighters.

"Another five hours, captain," came the lieutenant's reply. "Port authority's finished refueling, but we need to pass safety clearance."

Five hours . . . that was enough time to shower and have a quick meal before it was time to be off. His lieutenants had said there was a restaurant not far from the gangway that served curries in the Nagapuran style. It would be nice to have something not synthesized or grown on board. Nagapur was to be their last and only stop on this voyage, and this would be Halford's last opportunity for a meal prior to departure. "Very good, Kessan. I'm nearly done here."

"I'll keep you apprised if anything changes, sir," said Lieutenant Kessan. "But all's quiet and smooth."

Halford hissed and made the sign of the sun disc. It would not do to so tempt fate.

"Tell the port authority we'll have all the paperwork cleared in five hours time. I want us leaving on schedule." A couple hours would not make much difference in a journey of twenty years, but Roderick Halford was not going to be the man who made Lord Hadrian Marlowe late. The Devil of Meidua was His Radiance the Emperor's newest Knight Victorian, and this mission in the Expanse was of crucial importance to the war effort, everyone said. Thinking better of his thoughts of a final expedition off-ship, he said,

"Send Yuri to the station; have him pick up food for the bridge crew. On me."

Kessan's voice brightened, "Aye, sir."

It was a trifle, but morale was built on trifles.

Halford resumed his run. It was early in his day for such food, but five hours was enough time. At any rate, Kessan and Yuri and many of the others were just coming to the end of their shifts, and they'd had the thankless task of watching the fuel gauges rise all through the night. One of the section bulkheads cycled as he approached, permitting him to pass beneath the sloping arch into the next length of bay. His music played on, rough sounds urging him forward.

Nothing quite like a run to shake the blood loose in the early morning.

The bulkhead hissed shut behind him, and ahead the promenade stretched for nearly half a mile to the next one. Through the high, narrow windows, he could see Nagapur Station's white limbs turning in outer space's limitless day, like a fleet of pale-masted ships swaying at anchor in time to his music. Halford was a man of schedules, of databases and time charts. He could appreciate the orderly beauty of the station's mechanics, and of the mechanisms that triggered lights and doors as he progressed. It was what had attracted him to the role of a night captain in the first place: the maintenance of order. The quiet, careful hours. The clear goals.

The next bulkhead opened, beeped, closed behind him.

Feet drummed the metal floor, rattling where the promenade ran over another bank of Sparrowhawks waiting in their mag tubes. He passed doors on his right that opened onto halls that led inward, past offices and armories toward the tram line that ran along the *Tamerlane's* spine from bow to stern clusters. Above his head, pipes gleamed and mechanisms clicked with clockwork precision, controlling the shutters that controlled the narrow windows. Even his footsteps were a part of that gearwork symphony. A part of the ship, as was he.

The next bulkhead did not open. Halford drew up, waved a hand at the overhead sensor. He frowned. That shouldn't happen. He checked the lights on the door panel. All systems were blue. A glitch? Still frowning, he punched the door controls, keyed the door to open.

It didn't move.

The only reason the bulkhead would be non-responsive was if the environment beyond were compromised, but if there were a hull breach or radiation leak, there would be alarms.

"Kessan, check the E-12 bulkhead on the equator. I think there's a fault," Halford said, and watched disquiet grow on his face reflected in the black alloy of the door.

Kessan didn't answer.

"Lieutenant?" he asked. Still nothing. "Lieutenant Kessan, this is Commander Halford. I said check the E-12 bulkhead on the equator. Do you copy?"

Silence.

Real silence.

Halford turned. None of the shutter controls in the ceiling above were moving.

Something was very wrong. Cycling channels on his wrist-terminal, he checked behind his ears to make sure he'd not sweated off the conduction patches. They were still there. Broadcasting on all ship channels, he said, "Commander Halford to *Tamerlane*, do you read? I'm having trouble raising the bridge. Can anyone confirm?" Even the port authority should have been able to hear him. "What in Earth's name is going on?"

Had there been a systems error? He didn't like to think what sort of error could have stopped all shipboard communications and jammed up the doors. He turned back and returned down the length of the promenade to the last bulkhead he'd passed through. There was no sense panicking yet. There were surely a dozen explanations for the broken door, and any number of things might have happened to the comm system.

The other door would not open, nor the round portal of the first side door.

"Halford to bridge, do you copy?"

Silence.

"Damn it." He let the terminal fall, muttering to himself. There was a manual override on one of the interior doors not far down. He found the yellow lever and pulled, forcing the maintenance hatch open just wide enough to shoulder his way through. The old mechanisms clearly had not been used in decades. He'd make a note to have them oiled. The access way paralleled one of the common corridors, all gunmetal and low, red lighting. Halford hurried along it toward the center of the ship. Though he was quite sure he'd never traveled along this particular access tunnel before, he knew it should terminate near hydroponics and the tramway that ran along the center of the vessel.

Halford pressed on, twice pausing to try his terminal

again with no success. He might have been alone on the mighty vessel—alone in all the world. He wondered if the port authority had noticed the fault on their end. Surely they would send a team to the airlocks as soon as they noticed the trouble with the comms. Nagapur Station was small by the standards of Legion fuel depots, so there was no excuse for ignorance.

"They'll have it sorted before you get to the door at this rate, Halford," he muttered to himself. He couldn't imagine what had gone wrong. There was no excuse for a systems failure on this scale. His people were inspecting the ship constantly.

Could it be foul play? Unlikely. Piracy at refueling stations was not unheard of, but at a Legion depot? It just didn't seem possible.

The doors opened on another manual lever, but this hatch did not grind like the first and opened smoothly. The corridor beyond was dark, and emergency lighting had taken hold, red as the lighting in the maintenance passage.

The night captain swore.

For power to be out in this section, they were looking at something far worse than a mere technical fault. His hands went to his belt, but he remembered—too late—that he was wearing his exercise gear. He had no belt. No glowsphere, no torch, no plasma burner. He was unarmed and unequipped, unprepared for whatever was going on.

"Halford to bridge," he tried his terminal again, but the line was dead as ancient kings. "Do you copy? Damn it."

Hydroponics was just ahead. Aquaculture provided produce sufficient to supplement the crew's diet of bromos hyper-oats, even when the *Tamerlane* was fully staffed. The section comprised several long, half-cylinder chambers that paralleled the central tram line. If the tram was down—and Halford was sure it was—the greenhouses would be one way for him to work his way along the *Tamerlane's* long axis and reach the bridge.

That was when he heard it.

"Ryude said it weren't far, right?"

"Should be right ahead."

"You hear something?"

"No. You?"

"I thought..."

"Move it, Jakis! Captain said there ain't much time!"

Captain? Halford stopped in the mouth of the access way. They weren't talking about him. Stowaways? On the *Tamerlane?* It shouldn't be possible. But he didn't know any man named Ryude, and there was certainly no man called Jakis amongst the skeletal night crew. Halford cursed silently. He should have had his sidearm, should at least have been wearing a stunner. He looked back and forth, trying to catch sight of the owners of those two voices. Even in the dark, he should be able to see the men. They'd sounded so close.

"Told you!" said the first voice, the man called Jakis.

A hand seized Halford by the collar and spun him about. The night captain slammed against the bulkhead with enough force to knock the wind out of him. Gasping, Halford got his hands up to guard.

"What's this then?" said the owner of the second voice, a short, powerfully built man with a face like weathered stone. "One of the crew?"

There was something *off* about the two men. They were too short, too broad in the shoulder. Were they mutants? Tank grown homunculi bred for rough labor? Their arms were thicker than their necks, and both men wore gray environment suits with badly scarred ceramic armor painted a burnt red color. One thing was certain: they were no members of his crew.

"Who the hell are you?" Halford asked, and he was pleased to find his voice was steady.

"Who are we?" asked the man called Jakis. "Ain't it fucking obvious?"

The other man raised his voice and shouted. "Doran! Gann! Got us a live one here!"

Two more of the strange homunculi emerged from an open side passage and slouched closer. "Looks high-born, this one," said one.

Jakis nodded. "That he does." The craggy man leaned forward. He stank to high heaven. "What's your name, man?"

"Commander Roderick Halford. This is my ship." He realized his mistake the moment after he stopped talking.

"Your ship, is it?" the fellow asked. "This is just our lucky day. Caught the captain, lads!" The men around slapped one another on the shoulders. "Has to be a record, that."

Four of them . . .

The door to the maintenance shaft was still open, and he knew the way was clear back the way he'd come. If he could make it to the hatch, he could close it, buy a little time, find another way forward and sound the alarm.

Invaders. Pirates . . . on his ship? How? How could pirates get aboard an Imperial battleship? Why would they dare?

"I see you looking, *captain*," said Jakis. "Don't try anything, or my lads here'll beat you bloody."

Halford clenched his jaw. He'd never been in a proper fight, and he wasn't looking to start now. Discretion was the better part of valor, was it not? Better to run and fight another day. There was nothing he could do unarmed and alone.

He saw his window and dove.

One huge ham fist rose and socked him in the belly, nearly lifting him from his feet. His teeth rattled, and he gasped, staggering back. How he managed to keep his feet was anyone's guess. The brute hit like a sledgehammer, and it took all Halford's concentration just to remember to breathe.

"Thought I told you not to try anything, little man!" Jakis said, massaging his knuckles. "Ryude will want you alive." He made a sign, and another blow took Halford in the side of the head. He folded like a house of cards, face cracking against the floor panels. The night captain had a dim impression of legs crowding around him like a forest of angry red trees.

The first kick caught him just beneath the ribs and he doubled over, trying to protect his head. The next took him in the back, and he clenched his jaw to stop from accidentally biting his tongue. Halford told himself he would not cry out. He would not give the pirates the satisfaction.

"Woo lads!" said one of the others. Gann maybe. "Don't want him broke. Captain's after ransom, remember. He's no good dead!"

"How..." Halford rasped, not lifting his face. "How did you get on board?"

"Wouldn't you like to know?" Jakis asked, and though

Halford did not raise his eyes, he could imagine the ogre's leer clear enough.

"I certainly would!" came another voice. A strange voice. Deep and dark. Not coarse like the voices of the sub-human pirates, but polished, the sort of voice a holograph opera villain would be proud of.

The lights went out.

All the lights went out. Only the pale indicators on the pirates' suits still gleamed red and white.

"The hell?"

"What's that?" Jakis asked. "What's going on?"

"A question I should very much like the answer to," came that dark voice again. "Identify yourselves!"

"Lights up, boys!" Jakis cried. A moment later, four suit lamps blazed, white cones illuminating the way down the hall to either side.

"There!" one of the pirates shouted.

A stunner flashed, and Halford thought he saw the whirl of a black cloak at the edge of the lamplight.

"Missed me," the voice said.

Halford righted himself, scuttled away from the pirates like an upset crab. The voice was familiar to him, but he couldn't quite place it. It was one of the officers, but it couldn't be. They were all on ice. In fugue. Or should have been.

"Who's there?" Jakis asked. "Show yourself!"

"As you wish."

Blue light flowered in the darkness near at hand. The voice had come from much closer, and Halford saw a spike of gleaming crystal rise and fall. It was the blade of a highmatter sword, its edge sharp enough to cut between molecules, its substance bright and cold as distant stars. By its pale radiance the commander saw a tall, thin man dressed in armorial black, an officer's greatcoat fluttering about his shoulders. The blade sheared through one of the pirates effortlessly, slicing the man in half from shoulder to the opposing hip bone. The night captain saw blood and heard a wet slap as the two parts of the man hit the deck. The blade cut effortlessly, without resistance . . . and vanished.

One of the pirates yelled and fired his stunner wildly in the direction of the newcomer, but the muzzle flash revealed only empty hallway. The man in black was gone, twisting away faster than the homunculi and their suit lamps could track. Halford sat frozen against the corridor wall, paralyzed. He'd never been in any sort of combat situation before, never seen a man—even an enemy—die, much less die so awfully. In the quasi-dark, he kept seeing the split shape of the dead pirate falling.

"Where'd he go?" Jakis asked. "Doran?"

"He got Doran!" said one of the others.

"Captain won't like this . . ."

"Quiet!" Jakis hissed. "You hear that?"

In the darkness, Halford saw the shimmer and flash of knives. The three men held blades at the ready, supporting their stunners as they looked up and down the hall, casting their pale lamps to and fro. That was common practice for fighters aboard starships. There was no telling what system or environment seal an errant shot or arc of plasma might damage.

"Still got the captain, though . . ." one said, his beam glaring in Halford's face. "Didn't run when he had the chance."

"Rot the captain," Jakis said. "Where's the other one? He can't have gone far."

Combat had moved the three men down the hall to one side, and Halford looked back. From his vantage point he could see down the hall and across to the far side where the hatch to the maintenance tunnel still stood open. Just inside he could make out a black shape standing, barely lit by backscatter from the three pirates' lamps.

The fellow raised a long, white finger to his lips.

Halford swallowed.

The lamps all shifted, all turned the wrong way a moment after.

Because he was listening for it, Halford heard the dry snap of a bootheel on the metal floor. A moment after, the blue light blossomed once again as the exotic nuclei of the highmatter sword changed energy states and coagulated on the air. Its radiance was a thing utterly without warmth. Like moonlight, it cast pale highlights on the hall, on the pirates, and on the man who held the weapon and pointed it at his quarry.

Tall he was and thin, broad-shouldered and clad from head to toe in black: black tunic over black trousers with a double stripe of darkest red to hide the outer seams. Polished black boots cuffed below the knee. The coat he wore was blacker still, high-collared and long-tailed. Of silver were its buttons, and silver too were the buckles on boots and waist and sleeve. And his face! Pale, pointed, and unsmiling it was beneath a wild mane of hair blacker than his clothing.

And Halford knew him.

The pirates whirled and fired, but their stunner bolts all pinged off the newcomer's shield curtain, pale fractals shimmering in the gloom.

"Get him!" Jakis yelled, and rushed forward.

Abandoned by his men, the big homunculus charged alone. He tried to catch the arm of the man in black as he raised his sword and held it long enough to stab his foe, and though he caught the wrist it was no good. The man in black turned and sliced clean through Jakis's arm. The pirate did not so much as scream, but staggered back, staring at the stump in numb disbelief. He must never have faced highmatter before. In an ordinary ceramic sword, there would not have been enough force behind so small a movement to so much as scratch his armor...

Highmatter needed no force.

The man in black thrust his sword out, skewering Jakis beneath the lungs. He stepped forward, dragging the blade up and out through the bigger man's shoulder, leaving a smooth, horrible gash through every rib he had. Halford shut his eyes, and so didn't see how the third pirate met his end. He opened them on a crash and saw the fourth man had fallen, scrabbling backwards, his knife and stunner abandoned in his horror.

"I yield!" the man said. "I yield!" It was the one called Gann, flat eyes wide in the glow of his own lamp.

The man in black stood over him, sword clean and shining in his hand. "Who are you? And what are you doing on my ship?"

"Your ship?" Gann echoed, stupidly. His eyes found Halford, sitting on the floor himself. "I thought *he* was the captain?" The other raised his sword, threatening. Gann's voice jumped an octave as he answered, "What's it look like? You're being robbed."

The tip of the highmatter blade flicked up, hovered mere fractions of an inch from Gann's chin. "That isn't what it looks like to *me*," the man in black said.

"Captain will be on his way out by now," Gann said. "We were just having a look round."

"What are you after? Weapons?" That made sense. Attacking a Legion vessel like the *Tamerlane* at a fuel depot mid-warp—when it was at its most vulnerable, its least manned—there was an elegance to it that Halford could respect.

The pirate pushed himself away from the blade and back against the edge of the corridor. "Ransoms. Legion ships got officers. Nobile houses will pay rich for their boys and girls back. Or the Empire will."

Halford frowned. "Ransoms?" he spoke barely above a whisper. The pirates were after ransoms, which meant they'd be raiding the cubiculum, the sleeper cells many floors above, beneath the *Tamerlane's* dorsal hull.

The man in black laughed. "You picked the wrong ship for that," he said, and even with his back turned Halford could hear the grin in his voice. "Do you know what ship this is?"

"*Tamerlane*," Gann said.

"Very good, you can read," the man in black glanced back at Halford, and for the first time Halford realized he was wearing a pair of red glass spectacles over his eyes. Had they allowed him to see in the dark? "Do you know who I am?"

The pieces seemed to come together in Gann's slow, subhuman mind. "You're not . . . Lord Marlowe?"

"Got it in one."

Gann's eyes went wide, and without warning he lurched to one side, rolling to try and get his knees under him on his way to his feet. The blue blade flashed and took one of Gann's legs out from under him. He toppled to the ground with a cry and a yelp of pain as his stump collided with the deck plates. "You were supposed to be in fugue!"

"Sorry to disappoint you," said Hadrian Marlowe, planting his foot squarely on the squat homunculi's chest. "You're going to bleed out from that leg of yours, and quickly. So answer my questions, if you want to live: Where is your captain now?"

"Gone above!" Gann said, not even hesitating. "Went to take your sleepers himself."

"And how many men has he got with him?"

"Fifty!" Gann almost shouted, voice cracking.

Marlowe's blade flicked down, notching the man's armored shoulder. "No," he said. "How many?"

"About twenty," Gann said, wincing. "Rest of us split up. Teams of four like us."

"Why?"

"Diversion," he groaned as Marlowe pressed his heel into his chest. "We were going to set hydroponics on fire. Burn your crops."

"Villains!" Halford managed to say. He'd found his feet at last, and his voice with them.

"Good of you to join us, Commander," Lord Marlowe said.

The night captain had the good grace to look down at his feet. He knew he ought not to have locked up like that. It was no way for an officer of His Radiance's Legions to act under pressure. He'd dishonored himself, his ship, and his crew.

But this was not the time to reflect on it.

"Where is your ship?" Lord Marlowe had turned back to Gann bleeding beneath him.

The homunculus shook his dull-featured head.

"How did you get on board?" Halford came forward,

careful not to step in any of the blood that puddled on the deck. He did not envy whoever would have to clear the bodies away when this was all over. Clearing his throat, the night captain asked, "Did the port authority help you?"

Rather than answer, Gann raised a hand. Marlowe saw something there a moment before Halford did and leaped away, blade flashing, severing the last pirate's hand at the wrist. A thin stream of violently orange fluid fountained from a hose woven into the fabric of the pirate's suit, filling the air with the faintly sweet stench of a chemical accelerant.

Gann had tried to torch Marlowe.

Lord Hadrian didn't hesitate. A single bounding step closed the distance between him and Gann. The blue sword flashed, and its point drew a red line across Gann's exposed neck and gouged the wall behind him. Stepping neatly back, Marlowe unkindled his sword. The blade and gleaming quillions vanished in a faint mist.

"We have to move quickly, commander," Marlowe said, shaking the blood from his hydrophobic clothes. "Arm yourself."

CHAPTER 2
DIVIDE AND CONQUER

"Where are we going, lord?" Halford asked, keeping pace beside the black-clad palatine.

"To the cubiculum," Lord Marlowe said, not breaking stride. "If they're after ransoms, that's where they'll be." He almost laughed. "They picked the wrong ship to rob, I tell you. They won't get much for our people."

Halford did not interrupt. "Aristedes is nobile, and Koskinen...a few of the junior officers."

Unable to help himself, the night captain added, "And me."

"And you..." Marlowe answered. "But the rest of them? The Empire wouldn't spend a spare bit on Corvo and the others..." Marlowe had turned the emergency lighting back on in the hallway from an override console half-concealed behind a panel in the wall, and red light shone on his pale face as he looked back. "We have to get up to C-Deck."

Halford frowned. "The lifts won't be operable."

"Our friends got down somehow."

"May I ask a question, lord?"

Hadrian Marlowe pre-empted his commander, saying, "Why am I not in fugue?"

Halford blinked. They said Mad Marlowe could see the future—could he read minds as well? "Well...yes."

"A man in my position, Commander Halford, does not get much time to himself. I often wait years before going into the freeze on these long journeys, besides..." Lord Marlowe's voice trailed off, and he paused a moment, one hand on an arch that supported the canted walls of the corridor. "I have bad dreams."

The commander had no idea what to say to that. You couldn't dream in fugue. It wasn't possible. Men in fugue did not so much as breathe: heart function and metabolism were all but halted, and brain activity hovered microns above nil. Men in fugue were as good as corpses. They could not dream. But Halford was not about to brand the Lord Commandant a liar, especially not to his face. He'd met Hadrian Marlowe only twice before: once on Forum at an officers' meeting and again on the occasion of his transfer to the *Tamerlane*. As night crew, Halford had expected to have virtually no contact with the *Tamerlane's* master.

His counterpart, the primary ship's captain Otavia Corvo, was a barbarian. A Norman homunculus nearly seven feet tall that Marlowe had brought in from the wild space beyond Imperial borders. Much of Marlowe's crew was composed of such misfits. They said his lover was a witch, a clanswoman of the vile Tavrosi who made congress with machine daimons and mingled her flesh with technologies unholy in the eyes of Mother Earth. Halford had seen her only briefly: a darksome, unpleasant-looking creature with reddish-black hair and a dreadfully pale complexion, her left arm covered in those unsightly tattoos the clansmen wore. Pretty enough in her own way, he supposed. For a woman, and a low-born foreigner to boot.

"Commander?" Lord Marlowe had asked a question, and Halford had to shake himself out of his reflection.

"Sorry, my lord."

"Are you all right?"

The junior man inhaled sharply and stood a little straighter. "Quite, sir. It's only...I've not seen action before."

Marlowe's face darkened, brows pulling down. "A highmatter sword's an ugly way to start." He brandished the unkindled hilt in his fist. "I'm sorry. But I need you here, commander. Are you with me?"

Halford shook himself. "Aye, sir."

"Top man." Marlowe turned away and resumed his progress down the hall. "They must have climbed down the maintenance shaft parallel to the lifts. It'll be a long climb." He groaned. "Why did they have to take out the power?"

The night captain grimaced. They'd have to climb more than twenty decks to reach C-Deck where the sleepers lay in their icy beds, and in the heavy false gravity of the suppression field, no less.

The suppression field . . . the suppression field was still active.

"They didn't," Halford said, clearing his throat. "The suppression field's still on."

Marlowe didn't break stride. "And?" Halford stopped in his tracks. Marlowe's voice had gone so cold that Halford felt almost flash-frozen to the spot. He hadn't meant to give offense, and said as much. "Get to your point." Lord Marlowe stopped, realizing his subordinate had stopped following him. He turned back, eyes hidden behind his red lenses.

"Artificial gravity should have failed when we went to emergency power, but it didn't." Halford adjusted the awkward drape of the shield-belt he had taken from one of the slaughtered pirates. "That suggests we didn't go to emergency power at all. My lord, I think they've hacked the ship's datasphere." If he expected Lord Marlowe to interrupt him, the night captain was surprised. The dark lord only looked at him. He continued. "If we can get to the racks, I might be able to restart the system, get us control of the comms and the locks."

"And we'll be able to contact the bridge?" Marlowe asked.

Halford blinked. "And security." He frowned, thinking of his officers spread throughout the ship, each of them unaware of what was going on. "The racks are down and aft, in engineering. If we hurry...we can be there in...fifteen minutes?"

Marlowe was shaking his head. "We can't abandon the sleepers to our friends, Commander Halford." He turned away in a whirling of black coat. "Head for the racks; I'll handle the cubiculum."

"Alone?" Halford hurried after his lord. "But we don't know how many of them there are!"

"And they don't know we're coming," Marlowe said. "I'll try and head them off, buy some time for you to get the comms working and alert security." The palatine knight clapped Halford on the shoulder in what was meant to be a comradely way. "Move fast. I don't know how much time we've got." He drew back, and gesturing at his ear, he said, "Call me when you're done."

And with that he turned and hurried off down the hall, a darker shadow moving against the blackness. Halford watched him go, standing gormless in the hall. The man had just run off into the bowels of their crippled starship to face Emperor only knew what with little more than a sword in hand.

"Mad Marlowe, indeed," he muttered.

Halford had never visited the racks alone before, let alone when the lights were out. His breath frosted the air, rose and vanished in the red gloom. He held the pirate's plasma burner in unsteady hands, advancing between the rows of ytterbium crystal storage.

The racks were situated to the rear of the old battleship, on the highest of the engineering decks, above the manifold turbines and reactors and the antimatter reservoir that powered the vessel's faster-than-light drives. The banks of crystal storage and processors had to be kept cold, and so relied on the same liquid helium coolant that maintained the antimatter's magnetic containment systems.

But he was right.

The air around him was so dry he felt the moisture being leeched from him. His cold sweat cracked on his skin.

It was full of droning. Had power really been cut, all but the core systems would have dropped dead and left the room silent. All about Halford resounded the faint groan of fans and magnetic drives. Here and there a microfilm deck whirred. Indicator lights winked at him from the banks to either side: red and blue and yellow.

The machines were active. They were still drawing power.

Trying not to think of Lord Marlowe and the way the pirates had fallen in bloody pieces all around him, Halford pressed forward one careful step at a time. His own breath came louder than that of the machines, ragged and uneven.

His mind concocted shapes in the waiting shadows ahead, but each step revealed only empty darkness. He was alone. And yet the pirates must have sent a man down here. Someone had tampered with the ship's computer—unless they had a mole aboard. But that was surely impossible!

Or they might have hacked the system portside, said a more optimistic voice in his ear. It was possible that these lowlifes had a man on the station's work crews. It was also possible these lowlifes *were* the station's work crews. He shook his head, dismissing these considerations. They didn't matter. All that mattered was restoring the comms and alerting Kessan and Yuri on the bridge.

He didn't have much time. Marlowe was surely making the long climb to the cubiculum at that very moment. When he got there, his lordship would need support, would need Halford manning the doors, the lifts, the lighting grid. The cameras.

These thoughts consumed him as he reached the end of the row and turned a corner. He didn't even see the cables until it was too late. He tripped and had to hop comically on one foot until he regained his balance, swearing under his breath all the while. He caught the next rack with one hand to steady himself, twisting to look back.

"What the...?" He pointed the plasma burner's torch beam at the offending bit of machinery.

A collection of braided cables, red and silver, looped from the back of the machines and puddled near the floor where some hurried workman had improperly replaced them in the slot between black-to-back rows of sleek, black towers. Halford crouched, tugged the tangle free. Someone had cut the ties that secured the cables in neat bundles. Why?

He had his answer a moment later. A thin glass wire—ephemeral almost as spider's silk—hung amidst that chaos. Halford followed it, traced one end to the back of the nearest computer tower and the other... like a fisherman pulling his quarry from the depths, Halford tugged on the line until he fished out a little black box.

In spite of the danger of the situation, Halford laughed. It was an antenna. At least that answered the question of how the pirates had gotten control of the ship's systems—though how they'd gotten the antenna installed was a question for another time. With a savage grin, he tugged the device free. He dropped it at his feet and crushed it with his heel.

The lights did not come back on, but then he'd not expected them to. Finding the antenna had been a stroke of good fortune. He swept the rows with his torch beam. On reflection, maybe fortune had had little to with it. The sabotage was obvious. They must not have counted on any of Halford's skeleton crew making it down to this level with the comms disabled and the doors mostly locked.

If memory served, the command terminal was dead ahead, in the far corner against the rack room's outer wall. Memory did serve, and a few simple keystrokes were enough to conjure the holograph display, tiled panels blossoming ghostlike in the darkened chamber.

Halford laughed again. He may be have been worse than useless up against those pirates, but he'd guessed their problem in one. The ship's computer was still operable; it was only that the network was down. Each terminal, each console, each system on the *Tamerlane* was a point that formed the datasphere web, but most were only appendages. The machines in the rack room were the spine, and the interlopers with their antenna had severed it. But it was a surprisingly simple error to correct.

"Kessan!" Halford spoke into his terminal. "Kessan, this is Halford, do you read?"

"Sir?" the familiar voice came in a moment later. "Sir, there's been some sort of systems fault. We're sealed on the bridge. Comms were down until—"

The night captain overrode his lieutenant. "We're under attack. Lord Marlowe and I found four pirates on the mezzanine near hydroponics."

"Pirates?" Kessan said, then, "Marlowe? He's awake?"

"Yes and yes," Halford snapped, "and how it is none of us knew his lordship was still out of the ice is a question for another time. I'm in engineering. Our guests backdoored their way into our datasphere, attached an antenna direct to the mainframe. I've taken care of it. Marlowe's on his way to the cubiculum on C. Pirates are after highborn ransoms."

"We don't have many of those," Kessan replied, repeating what Marlowe himself had said.

"No, we don't." As he spoke, Halford brought up security feed after security feed, trying to get eyes on Marlowe. How had the pirates gotten past security in the first place to install their antenna? Surely *something* would have flagged on their sensors. "But alert the security teams. I want all hands to converge on the cubiculum as fast as possible. Lord Marlowe needs backup."

"Where is he now?"

"Climbing one of the maintenance shafts." Halford's eyes swept over the display again, searching.

There he was! One of the holograph panels displayed the black shape of a man climbing the maintenance shaft parallel to the lift's vacuum tube. Halford wasn't too late! More holograph panels opened about him, flowering in the air until Halford stood in the center of an arc of little ghostly screens. He tabbed through them, camera after camera displaying rank after rank of icy creches like the cells of a beehive: the frigid beds of nearly ninety thousand undead. For a moment, he felt as if all the *Tamerlane* were unrolled before his eyes. Every corridor, every bay and cabin, every spire and airlock and hold. He saw the back of Kessan's head at the central holography well on the bridge, and the equatorial promenade where he'd been about his morning run. He saw Marlowe still climbing level after level to reach their enemy—and he saw the enemy themselves, dark shapes moving in the aisles beneath the frosty faces of the fugue creches.

"Lord Marlowe," he said, changing channels on his wrist-terminal. "Halford to Marlowe."

The nobile's voice came strained. "I take it you've solved our computer problem?" For a moment, the black shape climbing the ladder faltered.

"Yes, my lord," he said, and relayed what he had explained to Kessan.

"But how did they get hardware *into* engineering without our knowledge?" Marlowe asked and resumed climbing.

"I'm not sure," Halford answered. "My lord, there must be thirty of them where you're heading."

To the night captain's astonishment, Hadrian Marlowe did not stop climbing for an instant. He only asked, "I trust you've alerted security."

"On their way."

"How many?"

"Twenty."

"*Noyn jitat!*" his lordship swore. Halford did not recognize the language. Was it Jaddian? "It'll be an all-out firefight if we attack them in the sleepers' hold," Marlowe said. "Security will have to stand down."

Halford swallowed. "But . . . my lord."

"Any stray shot in that hold could damage one of

the sleeper pods. We'll *lose* people." Marlowe paused, and Halford saw the way his shoulders hunched on the holograph. "We have to let them pull the pods they want. We'll hit them on the run back—do you know how they got in?"

"No, lord." He'd been looking, but all the airlocks were clear. "They must have cut through the hull somewhere. No sign on the airlocks. They can't have cut through the dorsal hull. It's two meters of adamant at its thickest . . ."

"You think they came in through the bottom?"

"I think they came in near engineering. Think about it: they had to get at the datasphere core here."

Marlowe was silent a moment. "Lock yourself in, Commander Halford. If you're right, you'll have company."

Halford hurried to find the controls that sealed engineering. His reset had temporarily unlocked the doors again, and he heard the distant squeal and clank of pneumatics slamming bolts into place. There was nothing to be done for the manual lock on the hatch he'd used to get in, unless . . .

His eyes drifted to the plasma burner on the console to his right. Grimacing, Halford snatched it up. "What are you going to do, lord?"

"Sound the general alarm," Lord Marlowe replied. "We need to flush them out."

Midway down the aisle toward the hatch, Halford stopped. "If I do that, they'll know we're onto them."

"Good," Marlowe answered. "It's time they were on the defensive."

Something clanged in the rows off to Halford's left, and he flinched, jerking his plasma burner up, spare hand thumbing his pilfered shield-belt. The barrier's energy curtain snapped into place with a static crackling and the bitter smell of ozone—but it was only another of the doors cycling shut.

The rest was silence.

Shaking himself, Halford hurried back along the aisle, breath rising in white clouds made pink by the low light. The hatch was dead ahead: a pill-shaped aperture secured with the familiar yellow lever. He leaned on it, felt the gears grind closed. Fumbling with the weapon's dials, Halford set the burner to steady state and aimed at the base of the lever. A stream of violet plasma fountained forth, fusing the lever in place. Heat wafted off the weapon in waves, alien in the sterile cold of the rack room. The fused metal gleamed white hot in the darkness. Halford took aim at each of the bulky hinges in turn. They could repair the hatch in flight if they had to. One ruined door was a small price to pay.

Something rattled in the walls—or was it in the room behind him? Halford whirled.

There was nothing there.

"Jumping at shadows, Roderick..." he muttered to himself, and jogged back to the console. "I'm sealed in," he said, tamping one finger to the conduction patch behind his ear to make sure the thing was seated properly.

Marlowe's answer came through loud and clear. "Very good, Commander. I'm in position."

"What exactly are you going to do?"

"Just...drive our friends toward the lifts and have security in position," came the reply.

Halford relayed all this to Kessan and Yuri on the

bridge. Toggling through panel after panel, the night captain called up the controls for the general alarm.

"On your mark, lordship," he said, hand hovering over the ghostly button projected on the console.

"Just do it, Roderick!" Marlowe barked.

Halford slapped the holograph. The button dissolved, and three things happened at once.

First, the lights flared on: white and blinding after so much time in the soft, red darkness.

Second, alarms blared: rough and raucous where before the sleeping ship had seemed so silent.

And last—almost unnoticed in the instant before all that light and sound—a trigger clicked right behind him.

Halford froze.

CHAPTER 3
AS ABOVE, SO BELOW

"Step away from the console with your hands above your head, sirrah," came a smooth voice from the space behind Halford. "And drop the plasma burner. You'll not be needing it."

Halford did not move. He stayed hunched over the command console. Turned out his paranoia was not misplaced. Those noises he'd thought he'd heard inside the rack room *had* come from inside the rack room.

Vwaa-vwaa! The alarms wailed. Lights red and white flickered and flashed. He could pretend not to have heard his attacker, though what good that would have done was a mystery to him.

"I said turn around with your hands on your head!" the other man shouted.

There was nothing for it. Halford turned, plasma

burner still in his hand, and faced the strangest creature he had ever seen. If it was a homunculus, it was of a different stock and race than those Lord Marlowe had dispatched outside hydroponics. Where those creatures were bulky, this man—if man it was—was thin as a rail, his torso cadaverous beneath shoulders too wide and arms too long and gangling. What was worse, the creature's torso was too short by a third, the legs too long like the arms, giving the impression of a man stretched as if on one of the Chantry's torture racks.

It wore no helmet, and the only feature that hinted that it was a man and no woman was the voice. That had been deep and commanding. The face was androgyn, bleach-white and hairless, reminding Halford of nothing so much as the alien Cielcin he had seen in war holographs.

But this was no Cielcin. Cielcin did not speak the tongues of men—and at any rate, this Cielcin had horns and eyes large as a man's fist. They had no nose, no ears, and wore black armor of organic style, evoking the shape of muscle and bone. This creature wore a tattered green coat over what looked like a scratched suit of combat armor that might once have been mirror-polished and smooth.

"Are you Ryude?" Halford asked, recalling the name of the captain Gann and his lot had mentioned.

The creature brandished its weapon, a high-powered phase disruptor. "I said hands up, sirrah!"

Halford raised his hands, forgetting that he was shielded and so relatively safe.

"Drop the weapon!" the stranger said.

Panic gripped him, and he said, "I am Commander Roderick Halford, captain of this ship." Perhaps that information would give the creature pause. Halford's eyes flickered from the monster's face to the blue slit gleaming at the muzzle of its phase disruptor.

"Captain is it, *commander*?" the fellow sneered. "Then surrender! Step away from the console, and you'll not be harmed."

"Who are you?" Halford asked, hands still in the air. "What are you?" He had to do something. Without him, Marlowe and the security team would be at the mercy of the pirates. He had no way of knowing if Kessan and Yuri on the bridge had access to the security cameras given the ship's current state. He had no idea what the pirates had done to his ship, what worked and didn't, and if he stood down and stepped aside, this creature would have control of all of it. He glanced back at the arc of security feeds shining in the air above the console. He thought he saw the crystal spike of Marlowe's sword flash on two of the screens. Had he engaged the bulk of the pirates? Were those shots ringing out on other feeds? Was the security team with him?

Halford felt powerless before his enemy, just as he had been useless in the hall. He was an officer of the Imperial Legions, but he did not feel like one. He felt like an idiot child, as if his life as an officer had only ever been a presumptuous form of play. He was no soldier. He wasn't even a night watchman. He was a glorified baggage porter, unworthy of title and rank. He was nothing more than the remaindered scion of a lesser house, a spare son who'd chosen an easy posting for the promise of promotion to a desk job.

Well, serving Mad Marlowe had put an end to those dreams.

"Put the gun down, commander!" the stranger said again, brandishing its phase disruptor. "It's ransoms we're after."

Halford didn't reply, nor was he sure what madness moved his hand. But move he did, jerking his borrowed plasma burner down to fire wildly at his assailant. Violet plasma arced free, rushing forth in a continuous stream that lanced toward his foe in a tight arc that looped like a solar flare. It was still set to continuous stream.

The stranger fired. Blue lightning cracked against Halford's shield, and he flinched. His assailant dove to the right, long limbs skittering spiderlike across the metal floor, fingers leaving fine scratches on the enameled steel, its tattered coat smoldering.

To Halford's astonishment, the creature ignored its burning coat and neither removed it nor extinguished its flames. Halford guessed how the pirates had cheated security and come aboard.

"You're an Extra!" Halford said. The creature was more machine than human. Halford was willing to bet his body was steel from the neck down. A full prosthetic. There was no telling what other hardware the creature concealed in its body, but it must have had the means to bypass ship's security and make it to the very heart of the *Tamerlane*. That thought gave Halford pause. He'd never seen a demoniac before, one of the barbarian witches who traded their humanity for metal. He clenched his fist about the grip of his burner to keep his hand from shaking. Machine or man, his opponent wore no shield. He still had a chance.

"You missed me!" the Extra said.

Halford glanced back at the monitors. Mad Marlowe

stood alone, his back against the wall as he dogged the pirates' steps. On several of the panels, Halford saw the floating coffin-shapes of fugue creches pushed or dragged through the air by a motley crew of men and homunculi. Word must not have gotten through to Kessan and Yuri, after all. They must not have had access to the security feeds, either. They were blind, with no idea where to send the security team.

Another shot crackled off his shield's curtain, and Halford snapped his attention back to his opponent. The machine-man lumbered forward, shoulder first. Halford bit his tongue as the impact took him, and he felt his feet leave the ground. Then the ground was above him. It took the commander a moment to realize his enemy had flipped him ass-over-tea-kettle and slapped him against the floor. Still, he had the presence of mind to roll away. Some piston in the other man's leg wheezed as he turned, stumbling about to loom over his fallen prey.

The night captain scrabbled to his knees and opened fire. An arc of plasma shot forth, bathing the monster's knee. The Extra did not slow its advance, for metal feels no pain. Fingers hard as iron seized Halford by the scruff of his shirt and half-lifted him from his knees. The other hand—the hand that held the phase disruptor—cracked down across his face. Halford felt a tooth crunch. At least one. His vision blurred as he hit the deck again and spat blood on the deck.

"You should have come quietly, commander," the man said. "It would have been easier on you."

Lying on his belly, Halford looked up. The machine-man stood over him, tattered coat still smoldering like a demon out of the oldest, foulest fables. The metal of its left leg glowed cherry red, but it didn't seem to mind.

"Don't be afraid," it said. "You'll be with the rest of your people soon. Once the Empire pays up, you'll be right back here." The stranger leveled his weapon at Halford—more for effect than anything. Halford was still shielded, still proof against disruptor fire. "You're a naval officer. Naval officers don't die unless their ship does. It's your men who'll get it if you don't tell them to stand down." Was that bitterness in the creature's voice? Had he been a soldier, once? When he was a man?

Over the monster's shoulder, Halford saw Hadrian Marlowe's image again. The palatine knight had gotten round the retreating pirates. Wherever they were going, wherever their escape shuttle was, Marlowe had put himself between them and it. They were running right into him.

But he was alone, and so in a sense he was running into them. Sharp as his sword was, and deadly, he could not fight twenty men. He was mad. His vision still blurred, Halford cocked his head.

No. Marlowe wasn't mad. He meant not to fight twenty men, but to engage them. To engage them because the only alternative he had was to let his people go, and the only way he would allow that to happen was over his dead body.

They said Hadrian Marlowe could not be killed. Halford had heard the stories. Pallino, who was troop commander of the first thousand, said he'd seen Marlowe cut down in single combat with a prince of the inhuman Cielcin. He wasn't the only one. Perhaps it was true. Perhaps Marlowe did not fear death because it could not touch him. Or perhaps... perhaps he feared it and stood anyway.

Stood.

Spitting blood and bits of broken tooth, Roderick Halford turned and surged to his feet. He would run clean down the aisle and lose himself in the racks. He would get away long enough to call in the order on his terminal. The Extra might get him, but its people would not get away. He expected iron fingers on his arms at any moment; expected to tumble down again; expected the cold muzzle of the phase disruptor rammed against his chin, his back; expected the cold snap of lightning burning down nerve channels.

Expected unconsciousness.

Expected death.

He heard a clatter, but did not turn back. Racks of black computer towers flashed past him as sirens wailed. Red lights and blue winked at him like distant stars. And nothing happened.

Nothing *happened*.

No lightning. No disruptor fire. No grasp of iron fingers.

He turned back.

The machine-man had fallen, half-veiled in smoke from its burning jacket. It dropped its gun, both hands gone to its glowing knee. Unshielded as it was, the plasma had scorched the exposed metal . . . and fused it to the bone. The creature's one leg had stuck in position, its complex and delicate mechanics reduced to a bar of honest steel. The Extra had tried to chase him and fallen.

Heart hammering, vision blurred, face bruised and dripping blood, Halford raised his burner and was surprised to find his hand was steady.

He fired.

The pale, androgynous face vanished in a nimbus of purple fire. Headless, the metal hulk keeled over. Dead.

Halford staggered against the rack of computers at his left. Dropping his smoking gun, his fingers fumbled the controls on his wrist-terminal. "This is Halford," he said, and his mouth ached. "All security forces converge on C-Level near lift carousel 13. Repeat. All security forces converge on C-Level near lift carousel 13." It hurt to speak, but he tried not to think about it. Broken teeth and a fractured orbital could be repaired easily enough. He would sleep it off in fugue while the surgeons plied their trade.

Lift carousel 13 would put the security team behind the pirates, would split their attention with Marlowe. His lordship would have a chance. Stepping round the ruined hulk of his enemy, Halford sank into the seat before the security monitors.

"Can you see what's happening?" he asked his men on the bridge.

"No, sir," Yuri replied. "Feeds are still down on our end."

Halford nodded and did not answer.

Hadrian Marlowe stood alone. The alarm rang all about, lights flashing red and white. Any minute now, the doors ahead would open and his quarry would come rushing through. His shield was holding steady, but he didn't like his chances against twenty armed men, even shielded. He tested the weight of his sword unkindled in one hand, pressed the palm of the other against the door.

Any second now . . .

Surprise would win him a brief advantage. He might cut down a few before those in the rear noticed. They'd rush him, hoping to overwhelm him and take away his sword. They'd succeed in time. Twenty-to-one. Fifteen-to-one. Ten. It was all the same. But he would not let them take his people away.

Gunfire sounded on the far side of the door, and the sounds of distant shouting issued through the steel.

"Halford?" he asked. The night captain had gone quiet minutes before. He was certain the fellow was dead. "Halford, do you copy?"

The door opened an instant later, and he saw the whites of his enemies' eyes. The blue blade shone constant against the red-white flash of the alarms. He saw those whites go wider and pressed forward, pivoting to one side as the lead pirates shoved the first floating creche forward. The blue sword drew down, slicing through suit and sailor alike. Disruptor fire flashed from behind, filling the air. A stray shot coruscated against his shield curtain, and he surged forward, dragging his blade through a flat arc that severed the arm from another man.

That first fugue creche bumped against the wall behind like an old crate tossed on the sea. Hadrian kicked it clear of the fighting and slashed through the long knife of a third pirate. The man threw the busted weapon and retreated, fumbling with his sidearm.

"Security's coming," came the night captain's words on the line. "Was attacked. Sorry."

Roderick Halford's voice sounded broken.

"Good!" Marlowe replied, seizing the second floating coffin in the line. He shoved it forward, catching one of the pirates in the gut. The man grunted and fell, the coffin floating over him. Marlowe let it slide, striding past the downed man with a casual sweep of his sword. At the other end of the hall, the figures of men in the black suits and white armor of security personnel appeared, guns blazing. Rather than be caught in the crossfire, Hadrian doubled back behind the last of the floating fugue crèches, dragging it to one side of the broad hall. Frost rimed the surface of the chamber, and through violet suspension fluid he beheld the darkly chiseled face of Captain Otavia Corvo, fast asleep.

This reminder of what it was these pirates meant to take from him lit a fire in the young lord, and with a cry he vaulted over Corvo's sleeper pod, lashing out with his sword.

Left. Right.

Two men fell dead, and a moment after, two more closed in. Before he could turn and face them, huge arms wrapped about his waist. Big fat-fingered hands seized his sword hand, trying to immobilize him. A shot rang out, and the arms about his waist slackened. Twisting, Hadrian forced his blade down toward the man's opaque black visor. Closer. Closer. The pirate resisted, but Hadrian Marlowe threw both hands behind the weapon. The pirate was strong, made stronger by the gene tailoring that made the homunculus what he was. But Hadrian was a child of the breeding looms of the Imperial High College.

He was stronger.

The blade met no resistance as it passed through black glass and the flesh beneath it. Slowly, the homunculus's grip slackened. He crumpled slowly.

Breathing hard, Hadrian looked around, holding his sword at the ready.

But the battle was over.

Soldiers in the black-and-white hurried forward, their disruptors raised. The last of the pirates threw down their weapons. Blade still in hand, Hadrian advanced toward the nearest of these: a tall, thin man in faceless matte gray.

The pirate said nothing.

"Where is your ship?"

Quiet at last.

Halford hadn't moved from the terminal chair. His head swam. About and above him, the monitors flickered with movement. He saw little, remembered less. The remaining pirates were escorted to the brig pending release to the port authority. Marlowe led the team onto the pirate's shuttle where it had cut through the hull in one of the lower sections, in deep among the engine clusters.

It was over.

Cool hands on his face. A woman's voice. Another's—a man's.

"Got smashed up real bad," one of them said.

"Can you patch him up?"

"Can, lordship," the medtech answered. That other voice . . . the dark, sardonic one. That was Marlowe. Halford could just barely see Hadrian Marlowe: a white patch atop a dark blur to one side. How long had he been sitting in that chair? Hours? Days? "Be a few months growing the new teeth in. Don't think there's damage. Pupil response is good."

"Punched me in the mouth . . ." Halford tried to say. He wasn't sure if the words came out.

The dark blur moved to stand before him, and

Halford felt a hand on his shoulder. Marlowe's hand. Marlowe's face was still a blur.

"You saved our people, commander," he said, and squeezed the hand of Halford's shoulder. "You saved me, come to think of it." He drew back, and for an instant his face floated into focus. He'd removed those ridiculous dark spectacles. Without them, Halford thought he looked a hundred years older. It was the same sharp face, the same pointed nose and chin, the same gaunt cheekbones—but the eyes were far away. They were not the eyes of a young man—and Hadrian Marlowe was a young man, not much older than Halford himself.

But those eyes...they were like distant stars.

The men all said Marlowe was mad, but was it madness if all the stories about him were true?

Halford didn't know the answer.

Christopher Ruocchio is the author of *The Sun Eater*, a space opera fantasy series, as well as the Assistant Editor at Baen Books, where he has co-edited four anthologies. He is a graduate of North Carolina State University, where he studied English Rhetoric and the Classics. Christopher has been writing since he was eight and sold his first novel, *Empire of Silence*, at twenty-two. To date, his books have been published in five languages.

Christopher lives in Raleigh, North Carolina, with his wife, Jenna. He may be found on both Facebook and Twitter with the handle "TheRuocchio."

Pirate Chance

Carysa Locke

Piracy is outlawed in the Commonwealth, and so is being a telepath. Unfortunately for Pallas, she is both. Worse, she's a fugitive on the run from her own mother: the most dangerous pirate of all, their Queen. Pallas will do whatever it takes to keep her young daughter safe, and keep them both from being discovered. But when an imminent pirate attack threatens her new job and new life, she'll have to choose between staying hidden and fighting for what she holds most dear. This story is part of the larger fabric of Carysa Locke's bestselling Telepathic Space Pirates series, available on Amazon, Kobo, and all retailers where books are sold.

CHAPTER 1

The space skipper at table six was cheating.

There was one every rotation. Most pilots who made their living ferrying people and goods across the endless black had biotech enhancements. Sometimes legal, sometimes not. Usually, it wasn't a problem. Scanners caught the tech and logged it when they came through the doors. Top of the line holorecorders monitored the gambling floor every moment, and plainclothes surveillance drones mingled among the guests. But someone always thought they could get clever and win a little extra hard coin.

This guy was good, subtle even. It was clearly not his first time. The implants in his hands quickened his reflexes. Old tech, and legal. The nanobots in his eyes were newer, and decidedly illegal, with a high-end scrambler to keep them from being detected. Among other things, they monitored and recorded the other guests and his dealer without their permission. They also calculated the chits dealt, an unfair advantage over the house.

The scanners didn't log it. The drones missed it. But Pallas caught the flow of his thoughts as they brushed against her mental shields. She signaled the nearest drone and kept moving, sweeping her gaze past the pilot and on to another table as security closed in, so no one would associate her with the tag.

Her aptitude for detecting cheaters had won her this job, and as long as she could keep doing it, there would be food on the table and airtight walls around her young daughter. Those were her priorities, right after staying unnoticed and unremarkable. Unfortunately, she was skirting the line of that last bit, but survival sometimes demanded she take risks.

Behind her, a brief scuffle erupted.

"You can't touch me, I got rights!" The pilot loudly declared his innocence as he was marched off the floor.

Pallas highly doubted that on multiple levels. No standard skipper made enough credit or hard coin to afford that level of scrambler. He had to moonlight as something else. She'd only used her Talent to read his surface thoughts, so she didn't know what it was, and she didn't care. It had nothing to do with her.

In most ways, the position of compliance officer for the Helix Waystation was the perfect job. She spent her days walking the gambling floor and keeping an eye on anyone entering the waystation doors. She had company-provided room and board, so no record of a rental property or housing bill existed. And she was a short transit tube away from any number of ships and a clear jump path out of here. If she needed to grab Mercy and run, she could do so in minutes.

That was worth the risk of occasionally using her telepathic Talent to do her job.

The datalink on her wrist pinged, and she lifted it to eye level. A tiny hologram of her daughter's face popped up. As always, Pallas's heart did a little flip. The older her daughter got, the more she looked like her grandmother.

Not only was it a dangerous connection to the very woman hunting them relentlessly, but it hurt. It hurt that she saw almost nothing of Aidan in their daughter's face. Pallas always looked for him, but Mercy just didn't look like her father. Instead, she was growing more and more to look like Lilith, Pallas's mother and the woman responsible for Aidan's death.

Her hair was long and dark, her skin the same bronze as Pallas's own. Her eyes were the same startling green. The almond shape of her eyes, her pert nose, the slant of her cheekbones and jaw, all of them promised to develop into the striking looks that drew people to Lilith so effortlessly and, to a lesser degree, to Pallas, who had never managed to duplicate her mother's charismatic presence.

"Mom, can I go over to Kylie's place to work on a project for school?"

Pallas frowned. At almost thirteen, Mercy was at an age where friends were of vital importance, and as often as they moved around the galaxy, they'd been few and far between. Like them, Kylie lived on-station with her family. They'd been here fourteen months now, and Pallas had met Kylie. She seemed like a nice, normal girl. But her family worked the fuel station side of Helix, and as a consequence, their living quarters were extremely close to the space dock. Anyone who wanted to take Mercy could snatch her and be gone before Pallas could get to her.

Seeing her hesitation, Mercy rushed to fill the silence. "I'll take my splicer. I promise I'll be careful."

The splicer could hack into station security with the press of a button, setting off alarms and locking down the dock. It had cost Pallas nearly every piece of hard coin they had, but it was worth it to make sure her daughter couldn't be taken from her. Helix might be a good place to disappear, but it was also one of the central waystations along the most traveled shipping quadrant in the Commonwealth. It was high traffic, and the very features that made it a safe place to disappear would also make it very difficult to track someone once they left.

Mercy's eyes widened in a guileless look Pallas knew well. "Please? It's for astrogation, and I always mess up the calculations. Kylie's *really* good at them."

She couldn't keep Mercy isolated. It was only going

to get more difficult from now on. Once she was a teenager, boys would become an issue. The standard rebellious phase, as her daughter struggled to find her own identity, was something that their lifestyle would only make more challenging.

The harder she tried to cage her, the more risks Mercy might take to escape those bonds.

"I want you home for dinner," Pallas said finally. She kept talking over Mercy's squeal of excitement. "And you'll send me regular check-ins."

"I know, I know. I promise. Thanks, Mom!"

"Mercy—"

But the holo blipped out as her daughter cut the connection. Pallas let it go. Mercy already knew everything she was going to say. At some point, as a parent you had to stop and trust that the lessons you'd tried to teach had sunk in.

Sighing, she resumed her rounds. They were busy today. A passenger liner and three merchant vessels were docked, as well as the usual collection of smaller ships passing through. Most waystations offered little more than refueling and resupply, with expensive, small entertainment kiosks that might or might not be functional. But Helix was one of the larger hubs, and it featured a full-service space dock for repairs, a gambling floor, a shopping center, a spa, a dozen restaurants, and various other shops and entertainment offerings. Over two thousand families lived here full time, with a transient population of about ten thousand more on any given day.

The gambling house was nearly always busy. People who made their living traveling space tended heavily toward drinking and gambling. Spending coin on material goods made little sense for someone who lived in a berth of less than a hundred square feet. Entertainment was the vice of choice.

"Rayla." Hudson Parish, the gaming floor's head of security fell into step beside her. There was always something bland in his tone when he said the name she'd assumed. Hudson was good at his job, and he had annoyingly good instincts for a man with no mental Talent at all. He could feel something was off about the perfectly acceptable background she'd handed him when she'd applied for this job. He could feel something off about her, as well.

They wouldn't be staying here long enough for him to take his suspicions any further. She never stayed long in any one place. In the meantime, she monitored his surface thoughts whenever he was around her, and gently nudged him in other directions when he focused on her or Mercy too much.

"Mr. Parish," she said, her voice crisp and neutral.

This afternoon, his attention wasn't on her at all. He didn't even flick a glance her way as they paced along together.

Hmm. Unusual. She opened her shields just a bit and let his surface thoughts skim past. She got impressions more than specifics. A worry to increase station security, and something about temporarily lowering the house betting cap to limit the hard coin on the floor.

"Your presence is needed downstairs," he said.

Surprised, she hesitated for a moment before recovering her stride. He turned toward her then, his dark eyes a little cool and far more analytical than she liked. She always felt somehow that she was under a microscope with him, though he had no biotech enhancements to catalog or record her.

In his fifties, he was a fit man, single, and reasonably good looking, with one of the top positions on the station. More than a few female employees had tried to get his attention in a more personal way.

Pallas would do anything she could to deflect it.

He kept his fair hair cut short, and there was something in the way he held himself that said he had a military background, though she'd never caught a hint of it in his thoughts. He wore a navy colored suit with a lighter blue shirt, and a silver link flashed at his collar, engraved with intricate scrollwork. Real silver, and not cheap. The suit was tailored and made of a cotton-silk blend. Again, the real stuff, though likely enhanced with self-cleaning features.

In contrast, Pallas wore the most serviceable off-the-rack clothes she could get, synth-cloth and usually second-hand. Today, she was in black pants and a green synth-silk blouse that matched her eyes. It was more striking than she liked, but Helix wanted the employees walking the floor to blend in and look better than merely functional.

"Problem?" Hudson asked.

"No." They never called her downstairs. Why would he ask for her now? "My shift has another hour and twenty minutes."

"Nathan will take the rest of your shift. This is more important." Smoothly, he turned and gestured off the floor, in the direction of one of the service lifts for staff. Although from the outside the gesture probably looked deferential, Pallas knew it wasn't.

All right then. Obediently, she followed his directive and began making her way to the lift.

Pallas controlled her breathing and her physical

responses, but her mind raced. Did they really need her downstairs for some reason, or had Hudson finally penetrated the false identity she'd handed him when he hired her? Or worse, had she slipped up with her Talent and been noticed?

Talent was outlawed and widely feared in the Commonwealth. People were whisked away by the government and never seen again when they weren't being bought and sold on the black market for their skills.

It took effort for Pallas to remain relaxed as they entered the lift together and started down. She folded her hands casually in front of her, debating the wisdom of prodding him for information. Hudson was the sort who divulged exactly what he wanted, when he wanted, and not the kind to be easily manipulated, by Talent or otherwise.

"What's going on?" she asked finally, figuring the question was generic enough to be safe.

"You'll find out soon enough," he said cryptically.

Damn the man. Pallas frowned. "Will this take longer than my shift? I'm supposed to pick up Mercy this afternoon from school." She lied smoothly, with the ease of long practice and familiarity.

His penetrating gaze flicked to her face, his expression unreadable. "No. You should be done in plenty of time." His thoughts told her nothing, his natural shields unusually strong for a null. She could get past them, but she didn't want to risk it.

The lift stopped, and she followed him out. Down here was the working underbelly of the casino. The offices, meeting rooms, employee lockers, and three levels below this, the vault. Hudson led her down the hall past two conference rooms, and into a small office. Two security drones stood to either side of the door. Inside was seated the skipper she'd flagged for cheating just a short time ago.

Some of her unease slid away. Perhaps this was merely a follow up to the earlier incident.

Curious, she waited as Hudson crossed the room and took a seat behind the desk. They were in his office, she realized, noting the old fashioned book-shelves filled with actual paper books, a rarity beyond measure in many corners of the galaxy. There was a decided lack of holopics and vids anywhere in the room, and a masculine stamp to the desk and decor.

The pilot fixated on her.

"Is she in charge?" He cast an anxious glance back and forth between Pallas and Hudson. "Did you tell her?"

Hudson deliberately didn't answer his questions. "Mr. Scarsdale here has information to trade," he said instead. He didn't look at Pallas, yet was clearly speaking to her. She kept her face expressionless; she had no power to make any trades on behalf of Helix. If anyone in this room did, it was Hudson. So why bring her into this?

"That's right, that's right," the pilot, Scarsdale, said. "No security report, and I give you guys my info. It's good, I swear."

A security report would get his license flagged. He might even lose it altogether.

Hudson sat back in his chair, his hands folded. "Why don't you tell Ms. Porter what you have to trade."

Eager to do so, Scarsdale practically bounced in his seat. "They're coming here," he said, "planning to hit Helix."

Pallas frowned. Was he talking about a gang of thieves? Despite popular vids showcasing otherwise, thieves rarely targeted casinos. Their security was too tight. Even the street level pickpockets that filled the spaceport avoided the gambling floor. Too many holorecorders and surveillance officers for their liking.

"Who?" she asked, prompting the pilot when he didn't continue.

He stared up at her, his eyes wide and a little jittery with either fear or something he was on. He wiped a nervous hand on his thigh. "Pirates."

CHAPTER 2

The word jolted through Pallas like an electric current. The moment seemed frozen, the world around her slowing as her heartbeat accelerated and adrenaline flooded her body. Her vision washed white and all she could think was that Mercy was half the station away and she had to get to her.

It took her a few seconds to realize Scarsdale had continued speaking.

"... I'm not saying anything else without an agreement."

"Ms. Porter?" Hudson's voice seemed to come from far away. Pallas realized she had to respond or risk rousing his suspicions about her further.

Swallowing a ball of anxiety, she forced her mouth to shape words. "Why would pirates target Helix?" Everything shifted back into focus and she was suddenly desperate to know the answer.

One of the reasons she'd chosen this station was its position in the middle of the Commonwealth.

Pirates kept to the fringes. They'd been chased out of civilized space for the Talent they wielded, and they rarely ventured too far back in.

"Don't know." A stubborn look settled over Scarsdale's features. "But they are, and I got good info for you."

His surface thoughts gave her no clues. His focus was solely on his determination to keep his license and get out of this situation. For a second, Pallas imagined prying open his mind and pulling out the information she wanted. It would be easy. He was only human, a null, with no shields to speak of.

But if she did that, there was a strong chance Hudson would realize what was happening. He was perceptive, and he was watching both of them very closely. She forced herself to wait. She folded her hands in front of her and focused on breathing in slowly, then breathing out again. She had to remain calm and get answers.

None of this addressed the question of why she was here. Pallas sent Hudson a pointed look, one eyebrow raised. Right now, she wished him out of this room, but since that wasn't going to happen she'd have to figure out what he wanted with her.

Getting her unspoken message, he reached into an inner pocket on his suit jacket and pulled out a chit. He set it on the desk. Scarsdale followed the movement like a dog watching its next meal, his gaze glued to that chit.

Pallas had only seen them a handful of times before, and always in the hands of a whale, one of their regulars with deep pockets and a habit of betting large and often.

"I see you know what this is," Hudson said.

"A house chit," Scarsdale said.

"Yes. Access to one of our best rooms, as much food and drink as you want . . . and even a ten thousand credit gift you can take with you, or spend at any game you want in the casino." Hudson leaned forward. "Your nano-implants will remain deactivated, of course."

The pilot's head bobbed up and down.

"But first, you're going to tell us about these pirates."

Scarsdale's hand drifted toward the chit.

Hudson's fingers closed over it. "The pirates."

"And you won't report me to the authorities?"

"Why should we care what tech you put into your body? So long as you aren't using it here."

"All right, all right." He swiped a nervous hand across his mouth. "They hired me. Paid for these." He pointed to his eyes. "So I could, like, look for things. Not just video, but scanning for security, like that. It's all copied to a data packet that gets uploaded automatically back to them, and I get to keep the tech."

"The pirates hired you, put nanotech in your eyes, and sent you here to scout our security?"

The pilot nodded.

Hudson frowned. "What else?"

"What do you mean what else? That's good info."

"Did you send the data?"

"Three packets worth, before you tagged me."

Before he decided his new eyes had other uses and started cheating, Pallas thought.

"When are they planning to hit us?"

"How should I know? It's not like I'm part of their crew."

Hudson drummed his fingers on the desk, still caging the chit beneath them. "Current circumstances would indicate otherwise."

"I'm not a fucking mind leech." Scarsdale's scowled, his face growing red with anger.

Hudson ignored him, looking at Pallas. "What do you think?"

She hesitated. What was he looking for? "He's telling the truth," she said. "As far as I can tell."

"Course I am."

"My thought as well." Abruptly, Hudson stood up. He lifted the chit with deft fingers and tucked it back inside his suit.

"Hey, that's mine!"

Hudson signaled the security drones by the door. They moved forward, each taking one of the pilot's arms.

"What the hell? You said I could go. You said I could have the chit. We had an agreement!"

"I don't make agreements with thieves," Hudson said coldly. "You'll enjoy our hospitality in a private room until I can verify what you've said. Once I have, you'll be free to go." Hudson leaned closer to the other man. "However, if you've lied to me, I'll turn you over to the port authority and let them deal with you."

As Scarsdale sputtered and protested, the drones led him from the room.

"Oh," Hudson called after him. "And either way, you're blacklisted from the Helix."

The door slid shut, cutting off the man's increasingly loud protests. Silence reigned, so complete that it made Pallas uncomfortably aware of the room's soundproofing capabilities. Hudson could do anything he wanted inside these walls, and no one standing outside the door would be aware.

Of course, those limits didn't apply to Pallas. She

eyed him, considering her options. Her instincts warned her to grab Mercy and run. Get off Helix, get out of here before the pirates arrived. But she couldn't just run without tipping Hudson off, and he wouldn't just let her go. He'd want answers, want to know why, and he'd use his drones and everything else at his command to get them. Pallas would have no choice but to use her Talent. Every square inch of this place had holorecorders.

She did not need holos of herself circulating the Commonwealth with the words "dangerous fugitive" attached.

"You're the best spotter I've ever hired," Hudson said into the silence.

It was not what Pallas had expected him to say. "Thank you," she said, still cautious.

"His story seems too incredible to believe. Why would pirates target us?"

It was a good question. Pallas had been thinking about the answer for some time. "Casinos hold as much hard coin on the premises as some banks," she offered. "And some might think a waystation casino is an easier mark than, say, a place like Windfall." Windfall was the newest, largest gaming establishment in the Commonwealth.

"Perhaps, but our security is tighter. A bank would be easier."

That was arrogance. Banks were located, for the most part, on planets. A space station made a much better target than a planet. However, coming this deep into the Commonwealth just for a haul of hard coin, however large, didn't seem like a compelling enough reason.

Pirates were not average thieves. While they did have a use for the Commonwealth's economy, they much preferred a more direct target: a new ship to add to the fleet would always be more valuable than money.

A thought occurred to Pallas. It sent a shiver through her body that she struggled to keep hidden. Her fingers tightened together.

What if they knew? What if the pirates weren't coming here to steal anything at all? What if they planned to recover something they'd lost? She had to resist the urge to ping Mercy's datalink and check on her daughter.

She had to get out of this room.

"It seems like an unnecessary risk, when they can easily target a ship more valuable than what we keep in our vault," Hudson mused.

"Yes, I agree," Pallas said.

"Perhaps Scarsdale is wrong. Maybe whoever he's working for is a common thief with delusions of grandeur."

"Perhaps." But Pallas didn't think so.

Hudson glanced at her sharply. "You disagree?"

She hesitated. It might behoove her to guide him in a direction away from pirates and all they entailed. But it didn't really matter, did it? Whatever happened to this place after she left, there was nothing she could say or do right now to prevent it.

"I just think there is a general fear associated with pirates." She chose her words carefully. "They were exiled because their abilities are so dangerous. They're the monsters in the dark. What they are carries a death sentence in the Commonwealth. Who would be foolish enough to pretend to be them?"

Hudson snorted. "You would be surprised. But I take your point." Abruptly, he moved back behind his desk. "Thank you for your insights. You may return to your shift, but please do not speak of any of this to anyone."

"Of course." That was it? Pallas was surprised, but if it got her out of here faster, she was good with it.

As she moved to the door, Hudson spoke again. "Rayla, you have excellent instincts. Please make use of them and keep an eye out for anyone else out of place. Scarsdale might not be their only scout, or . . ."

As his sentence trailed off, alarm coursed through Pallas, reviving the adrenaline of before. Hudson was right, and she'd been blind not to think of it sooner. People came and went from the casino all day long. It wouldn't take a great deal of skill for someone Talented to blend in with the crowd. Pallas herself was proof of that.

The pirates could already be here.

CHAPTER 3

As soon as she was back on the gaming floor, Pallas pinged Mercy's datalink. No answer. She pulled up the station directory and found Kylie's parents. Her father was working but her mother was home. She pinged her datalink.

A woman in her mid-thirties with fair hair and an easy smile answered, her holo appearing above Pallas's wrist unit. They'd met twice before. She worked in hospitality and her name was Beth. She lived a normal life with her family, where the most dangerous thing in her background was the fine she'd paid three years ago for importing unregistered produce without the proper paperwork.

Pallas knew, because she'd run a thorough check into the whole family when Mercy and Kylie became friends. Technically illegal, but also not the most illegal thing Pallas did on a daily basis.

"Rayla, hi! Were you looking for Mercy? The girls are deep into building a three-dimensional astrogation diorama of the quadrant." Beth laughed. "I don't know if our synthesizer will ever be the same, and I'm not sure how we're going to fit it out the front door to take to school in the morning."

Pallas forced a smile. "Sounds like they're having fun."

"Oh, they are . . ."

Pallas half-listened as Beth described the school project. Her attention was caught by the profile of a man standing near the bar. He looked familiar. He wasn't playing any of the myriad games on the floor. Their bells, music, and loud promises of riches meant to catch his attention washed over and around him as though he didn't hear them. There was something off in the way he stood, not drinking or talking to anyone, just watching the floor. Hunting for something, or someone.

Cold iced the blood in her veins.

Pallas reached for her Talent, a hair's breadth from dropping her shields and slamming him into the bar. The dozen clean glasses lined up on the counter would break, and the shards of glass would stab through his throat, bleeding him out in seconds. Everyone would think it was a terrible accident, and by the time they realized something more sinister had happened, she'd be halfway to the spaceport with her daughter.

The man turned. His face lit up with a smile as one of the servers bounced across the floor and threw herself into his arms with a squeal of delight. They embraced, and Pallas blinked and let her grasp on her Talent go. Her body shook with the release of tension.

Beth chattered on about the girls' school project. "...I'm not sure Mr. Escobar meant the diorama to fill half the dining room." Beth paused. "Rayla, are you all right?"

"Fine." She wasn't.

"Did you...did you need to speak with Mercy?"

Clearly, her acting skills were failing her. Calculations ran through her mind. Beth's place was close to the spaceport.

"I'm going to need to work late," she said. "I was hoping Mercy could stay at your place for dinner tonight."

"Oh! Oh yes, we would love to have her." Clearly relieved and back on familiar ground, Beth made small talk while Pallas went through the motions of responding.

She signed off as quickly as she could and escaped into one of the back hallways marked for staff only. It took her another minute to find an open break room and lock herself inside.

Only then did she allow herself to feel the panic flooding her system.

She'd almost killed a man. An innocent man visiting his girlfriend at work.

She'd never killed before. Taken memories, yes. Mentally incapacitated, when absolutely necessary. But she'd never taken a life. That was something her mother did, casually, and often cruelly. Pallas had promised herself she would never be like Lilith. She would raise Mercy to be better, and to do that, she had to model different choices. Harder choices.

Memories crowded close, nearly swallowing her whole. Aidan's face swam into focus, blurred and softened by the passage of time. Familiar grief stabbed through her. She remembered his laugh, the kindness in his brown eyes and the way they'd crinkled at the corners when he smiled. He'd been a gentle soul, not hard enough or dangerous enough to please Lilith as a suitable match for her daughter.

The Talented had started life as soldiers and assassins. They were an army that won a war, and after it was done, their masters turned against them. In answer, they fled the Commonwealth and took on the mantle of pirates, fighting a new war for survival. Gifted with strong mental powers that made regular men into living weapons, the pirates were the most lethal military force in the galaxy.

Lilith was their Queen. No daughter of hers was going to pair with a man not of her choosing. Pallas thought she could stand up to her mother and make her own choices. When Aidan died, she thought it was an accident. A terrible tragedy that left her grief-stricken and alone with an infant daughter.

She should have known better. It was three years before she knew the truth. Three years before Mercy's own Talent began to show itself, and Lilith's true motivations came to light.

Like her grandmother, Mercy was special. Lilith had killed Aidan to prevent Pallas from having a child. She hadn't known that Pallas was already pregnant. If they'd stayed, she'd have killed Mercy, too.

In her experience, once someone started killing as a solution to problems, it became an answer that was all too easy. Pallas was never going to go down that road.

She took a deep breath, feeling the cool air fill her lungs, letting it out slowly as she let the memories wash through her.

She'd allowed herself to grow complacent. For ten years, she'd moved from place to place quickly, never staying long, never building relationships or allowing herself the luxury of long term goals. When she came to Helix fourteen months ago, she'd let herself believe that maybe this was far enough, deep enough into the Commonwealth to be safe. She'd allowed herself to think that after all of this time, they'd finally stopped hunting. A decade of running was long enough, wasn't it?

But the cold truth was that it would never be enough. The pirates were loyal to Lilith. They would never stop. The people in the Commonwealth hated and feared what she was, what Mercy was. They could never be safe, never have a real home here. She'd been stupid to forget that, even for a moment.

Today was a wakeup call. They'd been in one place too long. It was time to pack up and move on. She'd burn this identity, collect Mercy, and disappear. It didn't matter when the pirates were coming, or why. It was time to go.

Calm once again, she took a moment to double-check her appearance. Her dark hair was still perfectly coiffed, her clothes neat, and her green eyes reflected a resolve as comfortable as an old friend. No one looking at her could guess at the secrets that lurked beneath the surface.

Standing alone and unobserved, Pallas took a risk. She reached out with her telepathy on a tight mental thread narrowed to just one person. Just in case they weren't the only telepaths on this station.

Mercy.

There was a long hesitation before her daughter answered.

Mom? The single word question was so soft and cautious Pallas had to strain to hear it. She'd drilled into Mercy the importance of never using her gifts unless she had to. They couldn't risk detection.

My shift is almost done. When it's over, I'm coming to get you, and we're leaving.

Leaving? Although she was no empath, Pallas could practically feel the vibrations of her daughter's disappointment and sense of loss. It filled her with regret. Mercy deserved better. She'd finally begun to put down roots, to build friendships, and now all of that was being ripped away.

Are we ever coming back?

The plaintive note in Mercy's mental voice broke Pallas's heart. *No, probably not.*

But the astrogation project is due tomorrow. We're almost done, and we—

Mercy.

The lights flickered. The floor vibrated beneath Pallas's feet, the station rumbling as though an earthquake moved through it. An alarm began to sound, and the station's AI spoke over the comm system. *"Please remain calm. Helix Waystation is on lockdown. For your safety, please remain where you are until further notice. Security protocols are in effect."*

Mom? What's happening?

The rumbling stopped, but Pallas wasn't foolish enough to think that meant the danger was over.

Stay at Kylie's. I'll come for you.

She cut the connection before Mercy could respond. If pirates had boarded the station, the last thing she needed was someone else picking up the conversation.

Her wrist unit pinged. "All operators and officers, please report to the gaming floor. All wait staff, keep guests calm, distribute free drinks and complimentary chits. Members of station security, report to your commanding officers."

Pallas ignored the directive. She left the break room and hurried down the hall to the nearest stairwell. Lifts would be locked down without using a station ID, and she didn't want anyone noticing her movements.

She took the steps two at a time. In the fourteen months she'd been on Helix, there had never been a lockdown. Now they had one less than an hour after receiving a warning about an impending pirate attack.

She had to assume the worst.

CHAPTER 4

Pallas entered her quarters ten minutes after the first alert sounded. Everything had gone quiet for now. They didn't want to alarm the guests, of course. Security had their own channel for communications. She'd listened in for the first few minutes but ultimately found the chatter distracting.

Pirates, collision, whatever had happened or was happening, her goal remained the same: get Mercy and get clear.

She changed clothing quickly. If she needed to

run, she wasn't wearing heels. Two bags waited in the closet, already packed and ready. One for her, and one for Mercy. She took them both down to the bare essentials, shoving everything into one bag.

She was in and out in under two minutes.

A few fellow employees passed her in the back hallways. None of them stopped her or questioned what she was doing. A mild sense of panic seemed to have infected everyone. She heard two wait staff talking as she squeezed by them.

"...explosion at the space dock. Have you heard anything about casualties?"

"No one is telling us anything! My sister works at the dock..."

The buzz of thoughts against her shields was so loud a headache began to beat behind her eyes. The more agitated nulls became, the more they projected. Right now, everyone was agitated. She strengthened her shields and hoped Mercy remembered her lessons.

Turning, she jogged down the last flight of stairs. She had to cross the gaming floor to hit the transit tube, and that's when things would get hard. Right now, the tube would be locked down. She'd have to override the system.

She didn't have the clearance for that. But Hudson did.

Taking a deep breath, she cracked open her shields. An onslaught of jumbled thoughts hit her, and she flinched. It took her longer than she liked to sort through them and narrow in on one particular mind. It helped that she'd spent a decent amount of time tracking his thoughts over the past few months.

He was at least a level below her. She'd have no

business down there, where only casino executives and security forces roamed.

Time to dust off her Talent and put it to use. She'd just have to hope that doing so wasn't painting a target on her back.

There was a knack to directing people's thoughts. It took a subtle skill to keep someone's mind from acknowledging what they were seeing, and that's what Pallas had to do to move invisibly through the casino. She took her time, moving methodically and reminding herself that steady progress was better than being stopped and questioned.

She was so focused on her task that she didn't notice the danger until it was too late. She should have realized that the station AI had been silent for too long. She should have remembered that emergency protocols during a lockdown had security at every major entrance in and out of a level.

But it wasn't until she was nearly to Hudson that it occurred to her something was very wrong. This was just one floor above the vault; it should have been crawling with security. It was *the* access point to everything the casino held most dear.

So, where was everyone?

She'd located Hudson's mind before, but now she homed in on his thoughts.

Some people didn't think in words, so much as images. Hudson was like that. Reading him was a bit like interpreting a series of artistic holos. In an emergency situation, she'd have expected him to be a company man, worried about the house's bottom line. Instead, his thoughts were focused on the safety of the guests.

Underneath that was a primal fear, a focus on personal survival. Hudson was in the executive office, and he was not alone.

Pallas stopped dead in the corridor. She was at both a crossroads and an impasse. She needed Hudson to get to the spaceport. Hudson was in a room being held against his will. To get to him, she'd have to confront the very threat she needed to avoid.

She wrestled with herself for all of fifty seconds.

When she walked into the executive office, it was to see Florian Carter dead on the floor. The Helix Station Director had never been her favorite person, but he didn't deserve to be murdered. She couldn't dwell on him when there were others still alive in the room. Hudson, of course, and Quinla Terantine, Carter's executive assistant. She was huddled behind his desk, trying to make herself as small as possible.

A man stood over her armed with a plasma rifle. It was standard military issue, common across the galaxy. He could have been a mercenary, a soldier, or even station security. But he wasn't. Pallas looked at the gun and the sloppy, disheveled appearance of his armored clothing. Her gaze lingered on the greasy strands of his hair and the unshaven scruff across his jaw. Her mouth thinned.

Whatever flaws her mother had, she'd always demanded a certain excellence from her crews. Whoever this was, he wasn't like the pirates Pallas remembered.

There were two other men in the room, both of them pirates. She felt the buzz of their minds behind their shields, power contained by walls much stronger than those of nulls like Hudson and Quinla.

The man looming over the executive assistant leaned

down to her, jabbing the barrel of his gun into her ribs. Small and delicate looking, Quinla let out a whimper and closed her eyes. He chuckled, drawing the barrel up her side.

Pallas had no idea what his Talent was. What any of them might be capable of. Telepathy and telekinesis were a given, but there were other, far more dangerous mental abilities. The smart move would be to pull the codes she needed from Hudson's head, hope she could do it while still directing everyone's attention away from herself, and get the hell away while she could.

She had Mercy to think about. She shouldn't risk herself for a couple of nulls.

Pallas sighed. She walked out of the room, dropped the barriers and redirects she was using to hide, and then walked back in.

"Rayla," Hudson said, clearly shocked to see her. "You shouldn't be down here. Go, run!"

Her hands were already raised to show she was unarmed, but the pirates swung their guns on her anyway.

"Who the hell is this?" One of the strangers stepped forward. He seemed a bit more together than the other two. His armored clothing was at least on straight and looked clean. His hair, though long, was neatly tied back. There was an air of authority about him that the other two lacked.

"You must be the Captain," she said. Every crew had one. "My name is Rayla." The lie flowed so smoothly off her tongue after ten years of hiding and lying, she almost believed it herself. "I'm not sure why you're here, but you should go."

Hudson closed his eyes. She caught the image of her death from him. He expected them to kill her.

"Aren't you a fiery one." The pirate exchanged a look with his compatriot. They both smiled. They didn't see a threat. Pallas was small in stature, and right now she was keeping a tight hold on her Talent, locking it down.

Deliberately, she smiled at them. This guy wasn't highly ranked. At best, he captained a corvette. Maybe even a skiff. What the hell were they doing targeting a waystation in the heart of the Commonwealth?

The leader stepped closer to her. She took a better look at his shields. Solid, but flawed. Lazy. After all, they only had a few nulls to worry about, right?

"I think we've found a pressure point we can use," he said, smiling down at her. "Sounds to me like you two know each other." He gestured to Hudson. "Let's have a bit of fun."

He grabbed Pallas by the arm and shoved her, hard. She landed on the thick rug Mr. Carter had imported from Nessius at great personal expense. She dug her fingers into the red and gold whorls patterned into the wool.

It had been a long, long time since she'd used her Talent. *Really* used it. She might be too rusty. Their shields might be stronger than she thought.

"Rayla, I'm so sorry."

She had to tune Hudson's voice out. She couldn't spare him her attention right now. Her focus had to be on the three pirates.

There were more, of course. There was no way a crew of three had decided to raid this station alone. But for now, these were the only ones who mattered.

"Now," the leader said to Hudson, "I think it's time you give us those codes." He gestured to Rayla. "Or we kill this one in front of you. Slowly."

They already had the codes. Taking them from Hudson's mind would have been child's play for a telepath of any skill. Now they were just tormenting him for fun.

"I can't do that," Hudson said. "I am responsible for the lives on this station. With those codes, you could kill every single person aboard. They would give you complete control."

"That's true." The leader nodded, then gestured toward Pallas.

The man who had so enjoyed tormenting Quinla stepped forward. Pallas caught the dark flash of his thoughts as he reached down. He enjoyed inflicting pain. His hand closed over her hair, and Pallas's breath hissed through her teeth as he hauled her up, tears pricking her eyes.

She shut out the pain, centering herself.

The pirate holding her by the hair leaned so close she could smell the onion on his breath. She felt him prod at her mental shields.

Time's up, she thought.

She saw the moment he realized she wasn't a null. A slow frown spread across his face, his eyes narrowing. He opened his mouth.

All at once, she dropped her shields.

Her Talent, chained for so long, roared forward with more strength than she'd planned. It crashed through him, tearing his shields apart like old cloth ripping at a seam. She slammed into his mind and he reeled back, dropping her.

Pallas's Talent filled the crevices of his mind. She read him, every thought, every fear, every embarrassing moment and secret thrill. Her hooks sank deep and held tight.

"Durkin, what—" Before he could finish his sentence, Pallas moved on to the leader, her Talent cresting over his shields even as Durkin fell to the floor and curled up in a fetal position, whimpering like a child. His mind lay bare to her, and she saw his intention. How he fled just ahead of a larger crew. How he'd overheard talk of a huge score and meant to claim it for himself.

The third man swung his plasma rifle, aiming it at her. A twist of her hand spun it out of his grasp and sent it crashing across the room. Telekinesis wasn't her most powerful Talent, but it was strong enough.

While he gaped at her, she swept aside his shields as though they were made of paper. In the next moment, she had all three pirates in her grip.

It was too easy. Pallas was a skilled telepath, and after all this time she had a finely honed specialization with memory. The very fabric that made someone who they were. It hung before her like a tapestry, woven of millions of threads. Impossibly intricate and completely individual. If she cut one, several more unraveled. If she cut them all, they wouldn't remember their own names.

Killing them might have been kinder.

"Who—who are you?" the leader asked. Terror widened his eyes; he could feel what she was poised to do.

Pallas could have told him. In that moment, it would no longer matter if he knew who she was. She could have said *my mother is Lilith, your Queen*. But some secrets were too dear. She didn't dare whisper the truth, even now.

She couldn't take the chance.

"No one important," she said wearily. A different kind of truth.

While he gaped at her in disbelief, she took his memory.

CHAPTER 5

Pallas left them alive. She was not cruel, as her mother would be. She left them most of their childhoods. Swathes of memory and their sense of self she allowed to remain untouched. But anything dangerous, anything that had built in them the viciousness and sadism she sensed, that she took.

And of course, anything to do with Helix Waystation and her.

When she was done, weariness weighed her down. She lifted a hand to her head, tucking her hair back into place. Her arm felt impossibly heavy.

Across the room, Quinla still huddled behind the desk. Only now, she watched Pallas with terror. Well, wasn't that just perfect? Save a null and suddenly in their eyes, she was a monster.

No matter. Quinla wouldn't remember her. None of them would.

She turned to Hudson. He, too, watched her with newfound knowledge in his dark eyes. She could see him making the connections. For him, it was like everything he hadn't realized he'd known was suddenly coming together.

"I don't suppose there's any point in asking for my last payday?" she asked.

He blinked slowly. His brows had drawn into a

scowl, and she could see the suspicion and anger forming, the fear.

"No," she murmured. "I didn't think so."

"You—" he said. "You're one of them."

She sighed. "Yes, I'm Talented." There was no point in denying it.

"All this time—all these months you've worked beside us—"

Impatient, she waved a hand. "Yes, yes. The monstrous telepath worked with you day in and day out, reading your thoughts and invading your privacy. You're fortunate to be alive."

"It's not funny," he said.

"I didn't say it was." She looked at him seriously. "You do understand that the thoughts of the average person are actually quite boring, and that being Talented is just as much a curse in this galaxy as it is anything?"

He just stared at her.

"Never mind." She rose to her feet, each movement clumsy and slow. "I'll take those codes now."

His mouth tightened, mutinous and determined. And then, of course, he thought of them.

Pallas was too tired to smile. "Thank you." She had to remove herself from his memory. His, Quinla's, anyone else she'd spent a great deal of time with. "Not that you'll remember."

Hudson staggered to his feet, regaining some of his authority and getting angrier by the second. "Rayla—"

"It's Pallas," she said. Mostly because she was so incredibly weary of hearing names that weren't her own.

He stopped, regrouped. "If you think you can just walk out of here—"

"Yes, that is exactly what I am going to do."

She crossed the room, stepping right into his personal space. He lurched back. When she raised her hand to his lapel, he flinched.

"For what it's worth, you were a good boss," she said. "Fair. Strict. I appreciated both about you." She reached inside his jacket with two fingers and lifted out the house chit.

His face turned thunderous at this blatant theft. Tucking it away, she decided enough was enough, and she pulled on all of the threads in his mind connected to her or Mercy.

A moment later he blinked at her, clearly dazed.

"Who are you?" he asked, swaying. His gaze moved beyond her to rest on the three pirates, all of them lying sprawled and unconscious on the floor. "What's going on?"

"Quinla," Pallas said as she tugged on those same threads in the executive assistant's mind. "I think Mr. Parish could use some water." A deft push had the woman rising to her feet and crossing to a small side table with a pitcher of water and several empty glasses. It was usually best to keep people at familiar tasks while they recovered.

"I'm afraid I must be going now," Pallas said. She retrieved her bag from where she'd dropped it just inside the door. "Thank you for the hospitality. Helix has truly been a wonderful stay." Right up until it wasn't.

Pallas slipped out the door. No one stopped her.

Fatigue made it feel as though she walked in sand, each step heavy and plodding. But she couldn't afford to rest. These were just the screw-ups, the rejects in a stolen skiff trying to get the jump on a big score. The real pirates were coming, and the score they were after was her.

Pallas didn't intend to be here when they arrived.

It took her longer than she would have liked to find the room with Scarsdale in it. To be fair, she was moving a lot slower than usual. Hudson's code opened the door, and she found it little more than a cell inside. More barren than a hotel room, with barely the necessities.

The pilot, Scarsdale, popped up off the narrow bed. His hair stood up on one side, a crease marring his face where it had pressed against the bed in sleep. He stared at her, mouth slightly agape. She was clearly not who he'd been expecting.

Pallas held up the house chit. "I hear you have a ship," she said. "Still interested in a deal?" He wasn't her first choice, but she needed off this station.

Besides, his mind held information she needed. Like, who specifically had hired him. With his nano-implants deactivated, he was no threat to her, and she would simply remove any memory of her once they got to . . . wherever she was going next. A fringe world, maybe. It didn't seem as though the core worlds were as safe as she'd hoped.

Slowly, Scarsdale smiled. His eyes never left the chit.

Mercy. Pallas contacted her daughter as she pulled the pilot from his cell.

Mama! Most days, Mercy considered *mama* too immature to use anymore. It was a measure of how frightened she'd been that she used it now.

I'm on my way.

Everyone's afraid, Mercy said, her voice small. *They say pirates boarded the station.*

There was a thread of tension to the words that Pallas interpreted as terror. Mercy had every reason for her fear. To her, pirates were not thieves roaming the cosmos. They were the family that wanted her dead. The grandmother that would kill her if she ever got her hands on her.

Mercy was a threat to Lilith's rule. Pallas would do anything, sacrifice everything, to keep her daughter safe.

I took care of it, baby, she said to reassure her. And then, because she believed in being truthful with her child, she didn't stop there. *But more are coming.*

We're leaving? There was none of Mercy's earlier reluctance now. She understood all too clearly what was at stake.

As soon as I can reach you.

I'm ready.

Pride swelled in Pallas. Of course she was ready. Mercy had learned her lessons well. No matter what happened, no matter what the future held, she would survive.

All she'd ever needed was a chance.

Carysa Locke has been writing stories since she started with horrible *Star Wars* fanfic in the sixth grade. (Trust me, it was bad!) Her love of Science Fiction and Fantasy began in childhood with her parents, who were both fans of the genre and avid readers. She lives in the Pacific Northwest, with her husband and two rescue dogs. Her Telepathic Space Pirates series is based on a roleplay game her best friend created and ran for their gaming group from 2004 to 2006. Although much has changed and evolved as the books have been written, many of the characters began life on sheets with dice rolls.

They Never Come Back

Fritz Leiber

Here's that rarity that warms an editor's frozen lump of a heart: a never before reprinted story by a Grand Master of SF and Fantasy. The science may be a bit odd, though I think it was a more legit speculation in 1941, and a couple of things may upset the overly PC reader, but it's a fast-moving extravaganza of space pirates, survival in space, and true love. Fasten your seatbelts and enjoy the space-warping ride.

"Hey you! What's your business?"

Bart Harlan, standing on the catwalk that circled the upper rim of the docking-cradle, did not immediately answer the shouted question. He clung to the thin handrail, bracing himself against the sheets of rain which drove across the almost deserted landing and stared wearily down into the shadowy interior of the cradle.

It was about the grubbiest looking space-tramp he'd ever seen. Its weblike outer skin of molybdo-barium meteor cushionings was tarnished black, except where recent gouges revealed shining metal. One boarding grapple was badly bent; it would not quite fold back into the housing, and stuck out like a broken finger.

The isoquartz space ports showed no lights; they peered like dead eyes from behind the molybdobarium interweave.

A trip to the repair cradles was certainly in order; no spaceship inspector would ever OK a tramp like that, unless the bribe was pretty steep.

Suddenly Bart Harlan lifted his head to the driving rain and laughed grimly. To think that it was only twenty-four hours since the *Sphinx* should have landed in this very docking cradle! Should have landed. That terrible radio announcement was burned into his memory: "Friends, it is with deepest grief we announce that the spaceship *Sphinx*, earthward from Mars, lost contact with its warp about a half an hour ago. The cause is unknown. Aboard were Professor Wilkerson, who captained his own ship, his daughters Ann and Lucy, Navigator Williams, and three crew members. Professor Wilkerson, as you all know, is a distinguished member of the Scientists' Central Committee, and..."

Bart shook his head despairingly. Those announcements were always the same. Death knells. Because no spaceship ever came back once it lost contact with the warp along which it had been traveling. This was due to the nature of extraterrestrial navigation, which was entirely different from what a scientist of the early twentieth century would have imagined.

Ships did not move freely through space. They clung to space warps—invisible lines along which the gravitational pull between the various planets of the solar system was concentrated. The discovery of the existence of these warps toward the end of the twentieth century—and the possibility of intensifying them by special projectors—had revolutionized the science of physics and made space travel possible.

However, once a ship lost its warp, because of an explosion or some other serious accident, it was doomed. It could not navigate. It was too small an object to be seen by telescope. It could not even be reached by radio, since the long radio waves had been found to travel chiefly along warps, except for short distances. Therefore "They never come back" was the grimmest proverb in the dangerous Extraterrestrial Traffic—four words a spaceman seldom said but was always thinking.

Bart gripped the guard rail until his knuckles showed white. His thoughts had turned, for the thousandth time, to Ann Wilkerson. Laughing, madcap Ann. The girl who, in spite of the trouble between them, meant all the world to him. What was there left for him now?

His chief aim in life had been lost when they'd expelled him from I.I.E.N. (International Institute of Extraterrestrial Navigation). His expulsion had begun the trouble between him and Ann; her father had forbidden her to see him. And now Ann was gone.

Why, he asked himself furiously, was he hanging around this docking cradle? It couldn't bring her back. Nothing could bring her back, except possibly his theory...and now he would never be given a chance to prove that theory.

A gust of wind buffeted him, and he almost slipped from the catwalk. "An easy death," he thought, without feeling any especial emotion except a chilling misery. "Why not?"

"Hey, you up there! Are you deaf? What's your business?"

Bart stared down incuriously into the cradle. He could just about make out the speaker, and no more. A little man standing outside an open entry port. He seemed to be staring upward and using one hand to shield his face from the rain. There was an urgent ring to his voice.

When he saw that Bart was looking at him, he called again, but this time in a more confidential tone. "Did Vanetti send you?"

Still Bart did not answer. Why should he bother to? He felt completely out of touch with the concerns of the people around him, now that Ann was gone.

The little man seemed to interpret his silence as a kind of qualified agreement, for he went on, "Well, you're a navigator, aren't you?"

Bart was about to tell him he'd made a mistake, when a daring thought leapt into his mind. After all, why shouldn't he? He had nothing to lose. He was a navigator in everything but name. He'd completed his seven-year course at I.I.E.N. before he'd been kicked out and disqualified. He'd seen more than a billion miles of student service. He knew more than most of the men who were graduated with honors.

This tramp looked as if it needed a navigator badly enough to take a chance and—most important of all—it would be traveling along the same warp from which Wilkerson's ship had vanished; otherwise it wouldn't be in this particular cradle.

A growing excitement sent the blood whipping up into his face. Bart had a theory about what might happen to ships that lost contact with their space warp...and the captain of a tramp might be just the man to listen to a wild rescue plan.

Of course, if he were caught navigating without credentials, it would mean ten years in the Mars Penal Colony. But it was worth it. It was worth it!

"Hey, you, looking at the rain! Can't you talk?"

Bart leaned over and waved him a vague salute. "Be right down."

As he descended the narrow spiral stairs, he let his gaze rove over the landing field. To a man of an earlier age, it would have looked like nothing so much as a collection of silvery gas tanks, but to a man of the twenty-first century it meant cradles, warp intensifiers—the highway to the Martian and Venusian frontiers.

There were few signs of activity. A couple of repairmen clad in synthetic rubber were working on the nearest cradle. A tiny, beetlelike runabout scuttled past and vanished into the curtain of rain which blotted out the further cradles. Somewhere a loudspeaker was monotonously shouting a name.

Bart entered the short passageway that led to the interior of the cradle. At closer view the tramp presented an even more disreputable appearance. There didn't seem to be a single exterior fitting that had been serviced for months. And the general stench was nostril-wrinkling; Mars dirt and Venus dirt, as well as Earth dirt, were in evidence.

Yet he liked the lines of the ship; they promised speed. It was a 2067 Willis-Lang Archangel, he decided; not a bad model at all. He noted the name above the entry port. The *Molly R.*

"Well, you took your time, all right. What was

the idea of going up on the catwalk? Giving us the once-over?" said the little man, who turned out to be a thin-faced, beak-nosed Londoner. Bart nodded noncommittally.

"Well, come on. Captain's going space-crazy waiting for you." But before the Londoner went through the port of the *Molly R*, he reached up mechanically and touched the name plate of the ship—a spaceman's typical "good luck" gesture. Spacemen were notoriously superstitious, more so even than the early aviators had been.

Bart duplicated the gesture and then followed, feeling his way along the unlit center passage. His mind was an excited confusion of vague hopes and vaguer plans, yet somehow he felt that he had a hunch.

He decided against asking why the lights weren't on. The less he said, the better.

He stumbled into the large bunk room and then pulled up short, realizing his guide had stopped and that he was in the presence of half a dozen men. At first he could hardly discern the outlines of their figures. It was damnably dark, with the only light coming from a grimy iso-quartz side port. He heard an intermittent metallic tapping that somehow set his teeth on edge. Then, as his eyes became accustomed to the darkness, forms and faces began to appear, as if emerging from a fog.

"Here's your navigator, Captain Driscoll."

It was his guide who spoke. Bart turned to the one who had been addressed. He made out small, watery eyes peering at him from a reddish complexioned face. Captain Driscoll's hunched, wiry body gave the impression of restless energy. He was snuffing nervously and brushing his nose with his thumb.

"So you're a navigator, eh...eh?"

"I can navigate," answered Bart. The first flame of his excitement had burned out. He was cautious and alert.

The captain chuckled shortly. "Oh, so that's how it is. You can navigate but you're not a navigator, eh? There's a difference, isn't there, boys?"

A chorus of affirmative grunts answered him. Bart found a certain ironic amusement in the abnormally lax discipline, in the way the captain fraternized with his crew. The textbooks never mentioned spaceships like this one.

Most of the men were sprawled in the bunks. There was a tall, leather-skinned Mongolian, whom Bart later discovered was always simply referred to as "Chinaman." Sitting next to the captain, as close as to dwarf him, was a great fat hulk with hands like paws and a face disfigured by space-frostbite; he was addressed as "Morgan."

Again Bart heard the measured metallic tapping, but could not locate it.

"Well, at least the guy Vanetti sent us isn't talkative." The malicious voice came from an upper bunk, from which a youthful, pasty face peered down—a white blur in the semidarkness.

"Shut up, Kid," said Morgan thickly, without turning his head.

Bart decided it would be wisest to lay his cards on the table. "Vanetti didn't send me. I just happened along."

Immediately the atmosphere became taut, hostile. Captain Driscoll snuffed twice and then questioned sharply, "But why did you say you could navigate?"

"Because I can."

"What's your name?"

"Bart Harlan."

Silence. Then a husky, commanding voice from the darkest corner of the bunkroom. "Wait a minute, Driscoll. I think I've heard of this guy."

Bart made out a pair of legs dangling from an upper bunk.

"Who is he, Lesher?" questioned Driscoll.

The legs slipped down and Lesher advanced, limping slightly. He was a stocky, stoop shouldered man, whose face was covered with a network of premature wrinkles and whose black eyes had the cold, hawk-like stare of the veteran spaceman. Locks of greasy black hair straggled down his forehead from under his pilot's cap, which was pushed back on his head. His right hand was missing. In its place was a steel claw with three prongs which could open and shut. He was rapping it thoughtfully against a tobacco tin. This was the sound Bart had been unable to place.

"Yeah, I know him all right. Saw his picture in the Spaceman's Gazette three months back. Same guy. Got kicked out of I.I.E.N. for getting smart with your professors, didn't you?"

Bart nodded. There was a perceptible lessening of the hostile tension. The men looked at Bart with a new interest.

Just then his guide, who had left the bunkroom, returned. "Vanetti phoned."

"What did he say, Wilson?" questioned Driscoll.

"Can't get a navigator for us—at least today. Says they all tell him that the job is..."

Bart didn't quite catch the last word. It was cut short

by a villainous glare from Lesher. But he thought it was "risky." His suspicions of the unkempt crew of the *Molly R* were increased. But he felt no desire to back out. The thought of Ann Wilkerson held him like a magnet, even though he realized his theory of what might have happened to the *Sphinx* was wild and improbable.

And, after all, no legitimate spaceship would think of taking an uncertified navigator. Just what was Driscoll planning, Bart wondered?

Navigators were not easy to obtain in any case. They were the aristocrats of the Extraterrestrial Traffic. It took a highly intelligent man with a peculiarly intuitive mathematical ability to get through the seven year course at I.I.E.N., to master the lore of the space warps, the theory of fourth-dimensional torques, the calculus of hyperspace. In an emergency only the highly specialized knowledge of a navigator could suggest the right maneuver to save a ship.

An unspoken conference seemed to be going on inside the darkened bunkroom of the *Molly R*. Captain Driscoll turned to each of his crew in turn, and received a nod or a noncommittal shrug of the shoulders. Bart knew they were "passing" on him.

"Well, Harlan," said Driscoll finally, "I can offer you the pay of a certified navigator. Our destination is ... well, Mars. What do you say, eh?"

"I'll take it."

"Very good. We slide into the warp at 7:15 tonight."

"That'll hardly give me time to get my tables and calculators, or my clothes."

"You won't need 'em. Will he, boys, eh?" Driscoll replied. "Last navigator we had ran out on us and left all his things behind. He was certified, eh, boys?"

Bart felt the hair on the back of his neck bristling in a reaction of mingled excitement and apprehension.

"Well, Harlan, this is our complete crew. Lesher's our senior pilot. Morgan's our engineer."

Bart acknowledged the informal introductions with a nod. Perhaps it was the name Morgan that made him think of an ancient-day pirate crew. The leather-skinned Chinaman; the beak-nosed Wilson; the pasty-faced Kid; the hulking engineer with his disfiguring spaceburns (in another age they would have been cutlass-slashes); the illusively pale-eyed Captain Driscoll; and especially the brooding Lesher with a three pronged hook instead of a hand—all made an unpleasant and sinister picture in the eerie halflight.

The picture stuck in his mind long after Wilson had taken him to the navigator's tiny private cabin, with an injunction to "lie low until the inspector's come and gone." Just what sort of a mess had he gotten himself into?

Thoughts of Ann came between him and this speculation. Yet he felt his earlier mood of enthusiasm evaporating and despair beginning to return. How could he ever interest Driscoll in his rescue plans?

He realized that his wild hope was built on a very flimsy foundation. Just his unverified theory that spaceships which lost contact with their warp sometimes spiralled around that warp until repeated meteor impacts broke up the circular movement and they contacted a "sun warp" and started on the slowly accelerating plunge toward the sun.

If true, the theory meant that "they sometimes came back"—that there was a faint chance of rescue, if one was on the lookout. But it was only a wild speculation, Bart told himself bitterly. He began to think he was a fool, and acting like a fool. Getting mixed up with Heaven knew what deviltry, just because of a wild inspiration born of despair.

He found his lips forming the words "They never come back" and, mainly to find mental escape, he began to check over the charts and calculating machines of his predecessor—the navigator who had run out and left his things behind him.

Bart found them complete and in good order, and the longer he contemplated them the more he found himself wondering just why they had been left behind. A case of desertion? He studied the signature his predecessor had inscribed on the fly leaves of his books. A firm, neat "John Richards, Navigator."

There was a metallic tapping at the door. Lesher entered, touching his steel claws to his lips to enjoin silence.

Bart noticed that the passage lights had been turned on. Before the door closed he heard the captain saying in a hearty voice, "Well, inspector, I guess you've seen about all there is aboard, eh...?"

And the oily reply, "Yes, it's OK, Driscoll. I won't need to bother to interview your navigator, since you say his papers are all in order."

The words could mean only one thing. Bribery.

"Mister Harlan," said Lesher, leaning against the bunk and running his hand through his straggling hair, "I got a little question that's bothering me. Do you know enough about space-torques to be able to slip a ship from one warp to another, when the warps happen to intersect?"

"Certainly, though it's a ticklish job. Requires considerable calculation. Only to be adopted as an emergency measure. Why's it bothering you, Lesher?"

"Just a theoretical interest, Mister Harlan. Just theoretical. Well, you better get up to the control room soon. About an hour and we'll be sliding into the warp." And he slouched off.

A queer question, thought Bart. Warp slipping was a maneuver that was almost never used. Since the gravitational warps changed their positions with the movements of the planets, they occasionally passed through each other and momentarily intersected. But why should Lesher be interested in such a matter? Hadn't Captain Driscoll said their destination was Mars?

Bart decided Lesher must have been trying to test his knowledge. He shook his head dubiously and prepared to go up to the control room.

As he was gathering up the books of tables a thin ledger fell out of one. He hastily inspected it and found it to be Richards' diary. He wondered why a deserter would happen to leave such a thing behind. Moved by curiosity, he rapidly scanned the last pages. They proved to be a record of the *Molly R's* trip in from Mars.

The final entry sent a spasm of emotion through him. It read, "The Chinaman's just talked with the ship ahead of us on the warp. It's the *Sphinx*, owned by Professor Wilkerson of the Scientists' Central Committee. I told Lesher he was running too close behind it for safety, but he won't pay any attention to me. I was a fool ever to have signed up on this damned ship. Never again. Of course, I made a complaint to Driscoll. As usual he told me he'd talk to Lesher about it. But he never will, the shifty-eyed little incompetent. I'll make it hot for him when I talk to the Navigators' Bureau. And I'll do that as soon as we reach Earth. But what can I do now? Nothing, except take some caffeine tablets and wait up in the control room so as to be ready for emergencies. Of course, Lesher won't like it. Damn him. The man gives me the creeps, always fiddling around with that steel claw."

There the entry ended. Bart's first thought was that this explained why Richards had left the ship so suddenly. He had gone to register a complaint; and, of course, Driscoll was probably anxious to get away from Earth before an injunction could be brought against the *Molly R.*

Bart's second reaction was a reawakening of his earlier excitement. So the *Molly R* had talked to the *Sphinx.* That might give him additional information as to the exact point of disappearance.

There came another knock at the door. He hastily pocketed the diary.

"Lesher wants you up in the control room pretty quick." It was the scar-faced engineer who spoke.

"Say," blurted out Bart, "How long were you talking to the *Sphinx* before it was lost?"

Morgan stared at him dumbly. His face seemed to turn a trifle pale. Bart realized he had touched a tender point in spaceman's superstition—the fear of mentioning lost ships by name.

"What, that ship? Yeah, we maybe talked to her. Can't say when. You better get up forward."

The next hour Bart spent mostly with Lesher, making routine calculations and checkups. Meanwhile the crew stowed the scanty cargo. Wilson came up and made a cursory inspection of the control room fittings and of the forward valve chamber, through which a man in a space suit could reach the outer hull if vital repairs were needed in transit.

Bart noticed that the crew were able workers, but weak on cooperation. There were several exchanges of hot language. Once Morgan and the Kid almost came to blows trying to decide whose job it was to service the starboard propulser. With every delay the nervousness of the men seemed to increase.

Finally, the checkup was completed and the fuel tanks filled with hydrocarbon-synthetic. Warning signals were exchanged with the engineers in charge of the spacewarp intensifiers under the cradle.

Lesher slid into the pilot's seat and switched on the electromagnetic artificial gravity. A double force bound each member of the crew to the metal floor of the ship; for the first moment it felt like walking on flypaper.

In two minutes the *Molly R* would hit the warp. "Hope you won't mind my asking," said Bart to Lesher, "but I heard you talked to the *Sphinx* on your last trip. I happen to be interested in her." He felt he must convince someone of the feasibility of his rescue plans. Otherwise the risk he was running as an uncertified navigator would be in vain.

The black-eyed pilot did not take his hand or claw off the controls, but his head swung around quickly. "Why do you ask that?"

"Because I happened to know some of the people aboard and..."

The warning light gleamed yellow. Lesher picked up the mike of the ship's individual sound system and barked a warning. "We're elevating!" Then he threw in a switch and slowly drew back a lever. The nose of the *Molly R* began to rise.

Now the two gravity systems, the artificial and the natural, began to oppose one another, until it was hard to keep footing. Bart settled back into his all-rubber seat behind the navigator's keyboard.

Gray, rainswept sky became visible through the observation port. When the hull was vertical to the Earth, the movement ceased.

"Why the devil," said Lesher in a curiously low voice, "do you have to talk about the *Sphinx*? Listen to me, Harlan; forget that ship. Are you trying to jinx our start?"

Bart was taken aback by this display of superstition from a competent man, even though he knew he should have expected it. "But, you see, I've a special interest in the *Sphinx*," he ventured.

Now Lesher's eyes were fixed on the chronometer, watching the fractional seconds. Bart pressed three buttons on the navigator's keyboard. The yellow light began to blink rapidly.

"Harlan, why are you on board?" Lesher's question was abrupt and knifelike.

"You know at least one good reason. I need the money," Bart temporized, realizing it was not a good time to press his point.

The light gleamed green. Lesher began to draw back the propulser and centralizer levers, notch after notch. A purring sound became audible, rising to a vibrant hum. The *Molly R* quivered as if it were a live thing feeling for the lines of force of the warp. Finally it seemed to settle itself, like a cat about to spring.

Bart braced himself, his eyes concentrating on the keyboard.

"OK, Harlan. I'll just tell you one thing more. Merely good advice. Don't ever try to back down on us."

The vibrant hum rose to a crescendo. The *Molly R* whipped up into space.

CHAPTER II
CASTAWAYS

Cold, implacably chilling. The silence of interplanetary space. The unpleasant feeling of giddiness that comes with the absence of gravitation or its equivalent. The trembling nervousness that is supposed to be partly due to the unimpeded action of cosmic and subcosmic rays. Above all, the terrible loneliness of a lost and battered ship, a ship that could never come back.

Ann Wilkerson put down the can of tungsten-plastic. That is, she placed it in the air about a foot from one of the side walls, and it wavered and hung. Then she blew on her knuckles and drew on her fur-lined mittens. How long, she thought, would her horrible, futile vigil last?

It was thirty-one hours since the catastrophe, and still the mangled hulk of the *Sphinx* was not perceptibly nearer the sun. Just how far it had moved from the warp she could not tell, for the control room was destroyed.

Indeed, the whole ship was destroyed, torn open, air sucked out, save for the aft cabin in which she and Lucy had been locked by her father when he realized that the boarders were pirates.

Her father . . . Ann tried not to think of him, and of Navigator Williams and the rest of the crew. All, all dead. Smashed by explosive bullets. Blown to pieces in the final explosion.

"Ann," called a faint voice, "Ann, come close to me. Don't stay away." Lucy was huddled against the ceiling, which was a little warmer than the rest of the cabin, since the sunlight was now striking on that side. Her face was drawn, eyes pale, lips trembling.

When Ann put her arms around her, she buried her face in her sister's thick fur collar and began to sob.

"Ann," she said, "I know we've got to die. I can face that. It's being so far away from earth, and all alone. And waiting, waiting, waiting! I'm afraid of the emptiness outside. Stay close to me, Ann."

For a few minutes the girls clung silently to one another. The cabin was illuminated by a beam of sunlight which came through the tiny ceiling port. Not the warm, diffracted sunlight of Earth, but the strange, harsh sunlight of interplanetary space.

The front cabin wall had been buckled inward by the final explosion, and was here and there daubed with tungsten-plastic, the universal quick repair agent. It was still airtight.

In one corner was the small radio sending set which Ann had almost succeeded in repairing and hooking up to the auxiliary generator, miraculously intact; the spare parts and tools hung about it as if by magic in the gravitationless space. Tied to a wall were two space suits, semi-rigid affairs resembling those of a diver.

It was all so hopeless, thought Ann, with a shudder. But she must go on trying. She must! Otherwise she wouldn't have the power to comfort Lucy, to give Lucy something to cling to.

No, she had to keep working; trying to fix up a radio transmitter, although she knew radio was almost useless except when sending along a warp. She had to keep daubing suspicious looking cracks with tungsten-plastic, listening for meteor impacts. She had to keep working for fourteen hours more. By that time the aft oxygen tank and the oxygen canisters of the space suits would be empty.

But, as she held her frightened younger sister, one finger hooked around a ceiling fixture so they wouldn't drift away, she couldn't keep her thoughts from circling back to the catastrophe.

It had all come so unexpectedly. Of course, she had known of the priceless supply of isotrium-concentrate her father was bringing back to the vaults of the S.C.C. (the Scientists' Central Committee).

Discovered on Mars and only recently isolated in workable quantities, isotrium was yet unplaced in the table of elements—indeed, it bid fair to upset the whole theory of subatomic physics. Sensational stories about the "Martian metal" or "Super-radium" had already appeared in the popular press—stories which detailed its destructive action on human flesh, its inertness toward carbon, and its weird cold glow.

But the S.C.C. had not yet revealed that isotrium-concentrate acted as a catalyst to release atomic energy without generating heat, to dissipate all elements with the exception of carbon. The S.C.C. had a monopoly of the dangerous stuff, which was priceless if for no other reason than that it was never offered for sale.

But whoever could have dreamed of piracy on the space warps? Ann had always thought that nothing could happen to her father; he was too high in the councils of the S.C.C., which wielded as much influence as the government itself. Nevertheless, disaster had struck him down.

It had begun when the tramp traveling the warp behind them had called for help. The *Molly R.* Only Williams had been at all suspicious, and her father brusquely overrode his objections.

"They tell us their fuel tanks are burning, Williams,"

he had said, "and we can't leave them to roast like mice in an oven."

Ann remembered his stern expression, his dignified air of command. The two ships were quickly slowed down and brought together, side by side. "Tandem warping" the maneuver was called.

Then the boarding grapples were interlocked, the telescopic boarding port pushed out and fitted into the entry port of the *Molly R.* Ann recalled Williams standing at the end of the boarding port and saying, "I can't smell the fire, Professor Wilkerson."

Those were his last words. There was the characteristic whine of an explosive bullet, and his suit mushroomed out and splattered.

After that...nightmare! Her father hurrying Lucy and herself into the aft cabin, locking the door against her bewildered, terrified objections; then striding back, gun in hand—she watched him through the intercabin port. Then further explosions, shoutings, screams of men in deathly pain. Her father rushing back again toward the locked door, his shirt all bloody, and collapsing just outside. And she unable even to get to him!

Then those men—the great fat one and the one who had a hook instead of a hand. One of them was carrying the small chest of solid carbon which contained the isotrium. Ann had fainted.

The final blast had awakened her. It rocked the whole ship. It destroyed the artificial gravity system, for Ann found herself floating in the air. When she managed to get to the intercabin port, she saw what had happened. The forward part of the ship was a twisted ruin. Had she not been quick with the tungsten-plastic, the aft cabin would have lost its air too.

The space pirates had evidently left a charge behind them to complete their work of destruction and blow the *Sphinx* off the warp. She and Lucy had survived—but they were doomed.

Lucy's sobbings ceased. When she lifted her head there was a strange little smile on her face. "Ann, I want to go and look at the earth again."

Ann released her, and she pushed off diagonally across the cabin to a dark space port and hung there, hungrily staring.

Ann went back to finish up her work on the radio transmitter. She became so absorbed in it that part of the weight of her misery lifted. Mechanical work became peculiarly simplified in a gravitationless system; you could leave a couple of parts hanging poised in the air while you hunted for the right tool; you never had to waste time grubbing around on the floor after fallen screws and bolts.

There was a dull crack and the cabin shook slightly. A meteor. Immediately Ann pushed off in the direction of the can of tungsten-plastic. Then she waited until she located a faint hiss of escaping air. It was in the extreme stern.

She pushed off again, found the danger spot—a bolt which had been previously loosened—and squeezed out a blob of plastic. Air pushed the viscous metalloid partly into the crevice before it hardened into a neat patch. The hissing stopped. Ann went back to her work.

Lucy clung to the dark space port, as if she would never tire of gazing at the earth. "It's so beautiful, Ann," she said in a wistful voice. "It's not nearly so big as the Moon is when you see it from Earth, a hazy green crescent, dappled with white. Those are the clouds. The rest of it's black, outlined against the stars. Just think, it's sunrise there along that line between the dark part and the hazy green. And off to one side is the crescent Moon. The Moon looks ever so small, Ann."

"You'd better come away now, Lucy," said Ann, dreading another outburst. "It's cold there, and you must be freezing. Besides, I think I've got the radio in shape, and I'm going to try to send off a message."

Lucy turned her head. "Why do you go on bothering about that radio. It just makes it so much worse. You know no one can hear us. You know there's no chance."

"But there may be. We don't seem to have drifted far from the warp. We may still be within radio range."

"What difference can that make? We can't be saved. You know what they say..." her lips faltered on the words, "They never come...back. Now that means us, Ann."

Ann fought against her own rising sense of doom. "We've got to keep trying," she managed to say. But Lucy's words kept sounding in her ears. "They never come back...never come back...never."

Suddenly she found herself thinking of Bart Harlan. He was the one person she ever remembered finding fault with that grim proverb. "Loony Bart" the other fellows at I.I.E.N. used to call him.

His square-jawed face and smiling eyes swam up into her memory. She wondered if she still loved him. Dear, crazy Bart. It was almost a year since he'd been expelled in disgrace because of his wild pranks and disregard of authority; almost a year since her father had forbidden her to speak to him. She had obeyed, because her father's word was law. She had even thought she was beginning to forget him. And now his face seemed to smile at her, and to hold out hope.

Desperately she sought to remember his theory about lost ships. What was it? Something about the possibility of them circling the warp they had lost, caught in the space field that surrounded each warp... and even getting back near their warp for a time, if the conditions were right...

"Ann, dear," called Lucy in a voice that was dangerously near to breaking, "the Earth looks so tiny and far away. It makes me frightened."

Ann's momentary mood of hopefulness vanished at the words, and she found herself plunged into a reaction of black despair. After all, she thought, Bart was only a student with wild ideas. How could there be anything to his theory? Her father had told him it was nonsense. And he'd been expelled from I.I.E.N. That proved he was a person you couldn't take seriously, didn't it?

So it was with a feeling of futility that Ann pushed the levers and buttons that controlled the auxiliary generator. A faint humming filled the cabin. With listless fingers she adjusted the transmitter, picked up the microphone, and began.

"Spaceship *Sphinx* sending. Spaceship *Sphinx* sending. Can you aid us? We are completely disabled. We lost contact with Mars-Earth warp 17 at about 4:15 Tuesday, Universal Time. We were about 3,400,000 miles from Earth when we lost contact. This is Ann Wilkerson sending. We do not seem to have drifted very far. You may be able to sight us. Can you aid us? Spaceship *Sphinx* calling..."

She repeated the message three times, her voice

becoming more and more mechanical with each utterance. Then, thinking of the missing isotrium, she added an explanation.

"We were boarded by pirates from the freighter *Molly R*. They murdered all the crew, including Professor Wilkerson. They wrecked the *Sphinx*. They have in their possession the box of isotrium-concentrate which Professor Wilkerson was bringing from Mars. It is of the utmost importance that the isotrium be returned to the Scientists' Central Committee. The safety of mankind may depend upon it. One of the pirates had lost his hand and wore a steel hook in its place. Spaceship *Sphinx* calling…"

She felt Lucy tugging at her wrist. "Your voice sounds like a ghost's. There's no hope for us, is there? Let me stay close to you, Ann. We'll die soon, won't we?"

Again Ann took Lucy into her arms and comforted her. She was not angry. Stronger nerves than Lucy's had been broken by the overpowering loneliness of interplanetary space, even in ships that were not doomed. Isolation from the environment of Earth was a thing to which the nervous system of mankind was not yet adjusted. Hospitals were full of cases of "space neurosis" and "cosmic shock." Victims of "space phobia," "gravitational dementia," and similar mental disorders crowded the insane asylums. How could she blame Lucy for giving way to despair?

Thinking these thoughts, Ann became aware of her own tiredness and misery. Her imagination set diabolically to work, picturing the vast, airless abyss around her—in every direction millions of miles of frigid emptiness. The absence of gravitational pull made everything seem like an evil nightmare; an irrational fear of falling took possession of her. She wanted to scream, to beat against the metal walls, to hide her eyes, to huddle into one of the lockers and pull the door tight behind her.

It was only by the greatest effort that she prevented herself from crying out. *If Lucy sees my face now,* she thought, *we'll both go mad.*

There was a deafening impact. The wall of the cabin against which they had been poised, rushed away from them, leaving them momentarily isolated in the air. The opposite wall struck them and sent them grotesquely sprawling.

Lucy shrieked. Ann clutched at a wall fixture, missed it, managed to catch hold of the leg of an anchored table. Various loose objects were bounding and sailing about erratically, as if in a gigantic dice-box. She dodged a flying screwdriver. Dazed, she could only think, "a hundred pound meteor, or heavier." Then on her horrified ears there burst the loud hiss of escaping air. She made out three separate hissings, which meant at least three leaks.

The sound banished her fear. She did not search for the tungsten-plastic; she knew the metalloid would be useless in this emergency; the leaks sounded too big—they would take too long to patch.

A glance at the falling gauge of the oxygen tank showed that it too had been cracked open. Before she realized it, she had hold of Lucy and was propelling her toward the wall where the spacesuits were tied.

Speed was everything now. Working with all the energy and efficiency she could command, she forced Lucy's legs into the heavy, semi-rigid fabric of one suit.

"My wrist, Ann," said Lucy. "My wrist hurts."

Already her voice sounded unnaturally faint and muffled. That meant the air pressure was falling rapidly.

"Put your arms in here," Ann commanded, as if her sister were a child. "You've just got to." Her words, or the tone of them, had their effect. Lucy compliantly wriggled into the suit, helped to fasten the hermetic seams, and to adjust the cold-resistant helmet of glass-synthetic.

Ann manipulated the valve that controlled the oxygen canister, then reached for the second suit. She experienced a sudden attack of faintness. She could nearly hear the hissing of the escaping air. If she wasn't quick now, she'd get the "space bends" from the rapidly diminishing pressure, she realized; bubbles of nitrogen would form in her blood system, agonizing, paralyzing.

It seemed to take ages to slide her legs into the clumsy trousers. The cabin swam around her. There was a ringing in her ears, to which she knew no real sound corresponded. Fighting dizziness, she pulled on the arms of the suit. As she reached for the helmet she realized that her consciousness was going fast. Her fingers felt thick and numb; she couldn't seem to move them. The ringing in her ears was deafening. Everything was spinning and turning red...

Lucy made the convulsive movement of a person just recovering from a shock. Her bewildered eyes encountered her sister. She saw Ann's nerveless hands, swathed in the heavy gloves of the spacesuit, fumbling futilely with the hermetic seams.

If Lucy had been fully conscious of what was happening, she might have acted differently and given way to terror. As it was, she responded with a kind of dreamlike decisiveness to her sister's plight. Her hands automatically sought out and fastened the hermetic seams, tightened the helmet, flooded the suit with life-giving oxygen.

"How long have we left?" questioned Lucy.

"About two hours of oxygen in each canister. How long was I unconscious?"

"It seemed forever. I thought you were dead. Maybe half an hour. I don't know."

For a while they clung together in their clumsy suits, trying to shut out the thought of the terrible emptiness that had invaded the very cabin. It occurred to Ann that she might as well open the emergency entry port—it made no difference now. What did anything matter now?

Slowly the spasm of terror passed. The feeling that she must do something, no matter how hopeless it was, came back to her. She disengaged herself from Lucy's embrace and made her way to the radio.

She could not tell if it was still all in order. No matter. She adjusted the controls as best she could in the darkness. She worked the microphone into her suit through the special pocket that had hermetic slits both inside and out.

"Spaceship *Sphinx* calling... Spaceship *Sphinx* calling..."

CHAPTER III
UNMASKED

The *Molly R*, a million miles out, drove swiftly along warp 17. The metal hull was filled with the faint, deep hum of the great centralizing rotor, which held the ship in warp, and the more strident humming of the two propulsers.

Lesher still sat at the controls. Bart Harlan, pacing nervously back and forth, marveled at the facility with which the senior pilot manipulated his metal claw. He seemed to prefer it to his good hand.

An automatic bell began to jangle, indicating that a large meteor had entered the electric field around the ship. Lesher consulted the indicators. "We'll have to bend warp around her, Harlan," he said, and then barked a warning into the mike.

The jangling increased in volume. The ship gave a sudden, sickening lurch, then straightened out. The jangling died away. Bart released his grip and stared out of the wide observation port into the harsh darkness, which glittered with incredibly brilliant stars. The sun lay astern, but its light was invisible except when momentarily reflected by a stray fragment of meteoric material.

Bart was on edge. Getting away from Earth had been a trying business—his first solo navigation job, and an illegal one at that. But he was oblivious of nervous fatigue. Now that he was actually out in space, thoughts of Ann Wilkerson and the vanished *Sphinx* dominated his mind. Hopes and fears, wild plans for rescue—all worked together to produce a condition of almost painful mental excitement.

Although he knew the *Sphinx* had been at least three million miles out when it lost contact with its warp, he found his eyes peering anxiously forward, searching. Smiling grimly, he remembered what the psychologists had to say about the ease with which fixed ideas and monomanias are generated in interplanetary space.

What, he asked himself, would be his best course? Lesher had refused even to talk about the *Sphinx*, on the grounds that it would bring bad luck. Should he try Captain Driscoll? That seemed the only way. Broach the subject cautiously; point out how profitable would be the rescue of such a distinguished world figure as Professor Wilkerson; the money side ought to appeal strongly to Driscoll.

Lesher interrupted these cogitations. "What's eating you, Harlan? Looking for a new asteroid? Watch out for your nerves; you don't know this game like I do. Better go and have some grub. Chinaman'll be coming up to relieve me soon. Get a rest. I'll be needing you later."

The veteran pilot's hawklike face seemed to Bart to be the very incarnation of the spirit of the old-fashioned, superstitious spaceman. There was something inhuman about it, something that partook of the cold, untempered emptiness of space itself.

Bart walked back and pushed open the door leading aft. It was a heavy, all-metal affair which, when closed and bolted, sealed off the control room hermetically from the rest of the ship—a precaution in case of serious accident to the after part of the hull.

On his way to the bunkroom he passed the leather-faced Chinaman, who recognized his presence with an expressionless nod. But Bart hardly noticed him. His thoughts were occupied with plans as to how the search was to be conducted once he had persuaded Captain Driscoll to attempt the rescue of the *Sphinx*.

He pictured the *Molly R* cruising along at a relatively slow rate, one man stationed at the meteor finder (for it ought to register a derelict ship as well

as a meteor), another at the all-way peritelescope,
another at the radio . . . himself busy with calculations
according to his theory.

He tried not to think that Driscoll might refuse. He
tried to forget the fixedness with which most spacemen
held to the proverb "They never come back."

Back in the bunkroom the Kid was opening a tin
of beefsteak. The tin had a double cover; the opening
of the outside one started a chemical process which
heated the contents.

He greeted Bart. "Well, if it isn't our Uncertified
Navigator. Morgan tells me you're no fake. Says you
really can navigate. I admit I had my doubts."

Bart only half heard him. He was absorbed in
mentally reviewing a theorem in dimensional torques.

The Kid opened the second cover of the tin, swearing because he burned his hand in the process, and
attacked his beefsteak. Then, talking with his mouth
full and waving a fork, he proceeded to try to impress
Bart with the fact that he was generally a tough guy.
He related several wild and semi-criminal escapades
in which he figured as the main character. Vanity
seemed to be the Kid's most distinguishing feature.

Bart, still pondering the knotty theorem, only made
a pretense of listening and gave noncommittal answers
to the frequent demands for praise. Gradually the
Kid's tone became more confidential. He liked hearing
himself talk uninterrupted.

"Say, Harlan, I don't envy you your job. Lesher
told you what happened to Richards, that guy we had
before you, didn't he?"

Bart nodded. He hadn't heard the beginning of
the question.

"Still, Harlan, you're lucky to get in with a bunch of boys like us. How much extra cash is the skipper giving you? Hasn't told you yet, eh? Take my advice, Harlan old man, don't let him gyp you. Of course, the rest of us deserve the most, because we did the job. Still, you ought to get a fair share. Boy, we sure needed you. It was a ticklish business, waiting there in the docking cradle while Vanetti was trying to get us a navigator. We didn't dare stay long on Earth. We were expecting an official visit any minute, not from the regular inspectors, but from the S.C.C. men—and they can't be bribed. I was sure nervous."

Bart had finally begun to listen to him. "What the devil are you talking about?" he asked.

The Kid stared at him, then burst into a high, giggly laugh. "Do you mean to tell me Driscoll hasn't given you the dope yet? Or Lesher?"

Bart shook his head impatiently.

"Well, stew me, if that ain't funny! Why, I don't see why I shouldn't tell..." The Kid checked himself suddenly. His mouth hung open. He was staring over Bart's shoulder.

"Talking again, are you?" Lesher's voice carried an overtone of menace. The pilot limped forward to the table. "This youngster just loves to hear himself spiel, Mister Harlan." He tapped the Kid on the chest with his claw hand, and the Kid shrank back from the contact. Lesher's voice took on an ingratiating quality. "Don't pay any attention to what he says, Mister Harlan. He's just a young punk trying to make out he's tough. Aren't you?"

The Kid's answer was an unintelligible mumble. His eyes were fixed fascinatedly on the claw.

Bart rose to his feet. "I'd go and get myself a good rest now, Mister Harlan, if I was you." Lesher used his claw to puncture a fresh can. "Hold on, though, that ain't the right way to your cabin."

"I know it isn't," said Bart. "I want to see the captain first."

Captain Driscoll seemed to be startled at Bart's entrance. At least, he fumbled nervously with a black box of peculiar appearance which lay on his desk. But Bart took no notice of these actions.

"Sir," he said, "I have a proposition to lay before you. If successful, it would result in a large profit for you."

A look of complete bewilderment came into Driscoll's watery eyes, as if Bart's statement was the last thing in the world he'd expected to hear. He snuffed twice and brushed his nose with his thumb. "Go ahead," he said.

Bart was in his element. Now that he could talk of his real reason for signing on the *Molly R*, his voice became confident and compelling. He spoke briefly and to the point. He began by showing the large reward that would fall to the man who rescued the *Sphinx*. He outlined his theory about ships which lost contact with their warps. He minimized the old superstitions. He pointed out that the rescue attempt would involve no danger whatsoever, only a temporary reduction in speed. He explained how a slight readjustment of the meteor finding apparatus would greatly increase its range.

But he was so absorbed in his own argument that he did not notice how Driscoll's eyes went wide at the first mention of the *Sphinx*, how Driscoll stopped his nervous fidgeting at the talk of rescue plans, and went rigid. Finally, he did not notice the small shuffling noises behind him.

"With a corresponding stepping up of the frequency of the finder," he was saying, "the range might even be increased to twenty or thirty thousand miles, and that should enable us to..."

He was jerked backward, off his feet. He felt a cruel choking pain in his neck. Taken by surprise, he struggled wildly, futilely.

"And now," he heard Lesher's harsh voice, "it's about time we put our proposition to Mister Harlan."

And Morgan's nervous squeak, "Throw him out, I say. Throw him out like Richards, to freeze in space."

Bart began to take in the situation. He realized that Lesher had slipped the claw into the neckband of his shirt and was twisting it tight. Seeing that resistance was futile, one man against three, he lay still.

Lesher released the pressure slightly. The feeling of dreamlike abstraction that had haunted Bart since he boarded the *Molly R* dropped away from him. He began dimly to sense the astounding truth about the *Molly R* and its crew. Chance words and expressions, the Kid's boasting, Driscoll's nervousness—things he had not consciously noted at the time—began to hook up rapidly in his mind.

Then his eyes chanced to light on the black box on Driscoll's desk. He noted the initials on it—A.A.W.S.C.C. That could only mean "Andrew A. Wilkerson, Scientists' Central Committee."

The truth burst on him like a thunderclap. And with the truth came the realization that, if he made a false move, it might mean death by cold and suffocation in outer space.

"Throw him out," Morgan was repeating. "He'll try to wreck our plans, like Richards did. These navigators are all alike. Let's throw him out and take our chances when we get to Mars."

"And try to sell that stuff on Mars?" asked Lesher contemptuously, pointing with his free hand to the black box. "Oh, no, Morgan, we wouldn't have a chance. We left Earth for the same reason, didn't we? Our fortune's in that box, a fortune for each man jack of us. And the only place we can sell it is on asteroid 87, where there's a rich maniac who doesn't ask questions. He's the man who's hiring us to do this job, isn't he? And the only way we can get to asteroid 87 is to slip from this warp into the Venus-87 warp. They're due to intersect. But I can't turn the trick. It takes a navigator, so help me. We could have done it easily last trip if Richards hadn't balked. Do you get me?"

It was obvious to Bart that, out here in space, Lesher was the real boss of the *Molly R.* "I don't care," said Morgan. "He'll try to wreck us. He's crazy. Talking about rescuing ships! Only a crazy man talks that way. Throw him out to freeze. I tell you, he's a jinx."

Lesher snarled an imprecation. "You fool, can't you understand anything but motors? If it hadn't been for your hurrying, we might have persuaded Richards to help us. And if you want to talk about jinxes, I'll tell you something. There's only one jinx on this ship, and I won't breathe easy until we get rid of it. It's that!" And he pointed again at the square black box.

Morgan, taken aback, squinted his eyes in puzzlement. "I don't get you," he said slowly. "It's our fortune in that box, just like you said before. And I still don't see why we can't open it up a mite and have a look at it. We can't even be sure the right stuff's there. One look couldn't hurt."

A spasm of mingled exasperation and anger twisted Lesher's face, and Bart winced as the pressure on his neck was momentarily increased.

"Listen, Morgan," continued Lesher, and his words were drops of corrosive, "if you so much as touch that box, so help me, I'll claw you to strips. You fat pig, that isotrium is powerful enough to burn you to death before you could get the box shut."

Morgan's face set in resentful, angry lines, but Captain Driscoll, who had thus far taken no part in the swift exchange of words, began to rap nervously on the desk. "Quit it, boys," he interjected. "Lesher's right—both about Harlan and this box." Then he opened a drawer in his desk and brought out an ugly snubnosed explosive-bullet revolver. He set it to explode on contact, rather than at a specified range, and laid it down near his hand. "Let him go, Lesher," he said, "and you put our proposition to him."

Bart found himself jerked to his feet and deposited in a chair. The pressure on his collar relaxed completely, but his throat still pained him severely. He rubbed it and coughed to get his speech back.

"It's this way, Mister Harlan," began Lesher, taking the center of the stage and using a mockingly ingratiating tone of voice. "It's this way. We need your help, Mister Harlan, but if I may say so, you need ours too, as you can well understand if you've been listening closely to Mister Morgan's recent remarks. He's full of cute ideas, our Mister Morgan is, and he sometimes persuades me to put them into practice. I guess you understand that part of it, all right. Is your neck still bothering you? Too bad. Well, here's the proposition. We've got a commodity for which we can only find a buyer on asteroid 87.

And, being in a hurry, we want to get there as fast as we can. With your technical knowledge, Mister Harlan, you can do the warp-shifting trick for us. If you pull it off—and you ought to—everything will be fine and dandy, and Captain Driscoll will be pleased to give you a five thousand dollar bonus. If you make a slip—well, Mister Harlan, you've heard about what happened to poor Mister Richards. I don't like to talk about such things. Still, I must say I can think up cuter ideas than Morgan here when I get going. When you come to think about it, getting shoved out into space is a mighty quick and painless death. Morgan—I hope he won't mind my saying it—sort of lacks imagination. Suppose, just as a matter of scientific research, we was to lock you in your cabin with the box of isotrium—open. They say it's nasty what happens to you, but of course some men have got to be martyrs to science. Well, Mister Harlan, what's your answer?"

Bart was thinking quickly now. He knew he had to be convincing. "I want ten thousand," he demanded.

"That's quite all right, Harlan. Ten thousand it is," said Driscoll swiftly—too swiftly.

"Second point. How am I to know you won't pitch me out as soon as I've shifted warps for you?"

Lesher smiled like a satisfied cat. "Why, Mister Harlan, don't go putting ideas into our heads. I'm afraid the only thing you can do is trust us. I'd be glad to put it in writing, but that wouldn't be any help to you on the *Molly R*, would it now? So we'll have to consider it as a gentlemen's agreement. Does that satisfy you?"

"Third point," said Bart, deciding the risk was worth taking, "I'd like to know how the *Sphinx* is mixed up in all of this."

Their reaction to the question surprised him. He had expected blustering anger. Instead he saw faces grow pale. Morgan stepped back involuntarily. Spaceman's superstition! They'd pirated a ship, and now they were afraid to mention its name.

For the first time in his life Bart fully realized how being out in space exaggerated the human mind's weakness for fears and taboos.

Lesher was the first to recover. "Any more talk like that, Harlan, and we'll let Morgan do what he wants with you."

The fat engineer was repeating, "He's crazy, I tell you. Talks about rescuing ships. Crazy. They never come back, you fool! Do you hear me, they never come back!" His voice rose to a hoarse yell, then abruptly broke off as he got control of himself.

"Come on," said Driscoll. "Let's get Harlan up front and start calculating the shift. Morgan, don't let yourself go like that. Call Wilson and have him keep a gun on Harlan every second."

"Shall we go forward, Mister Harlan?" murmured Lesher, picking up the automatic.

CHAPTER IV
RESCUE IN SPACE

"I tell you, there's a jinx on the *Molly R.*"

Morgan was holding forth in the control room. The passage of three hours had not improved the condition of his nerves. On the surface the fat man seemed only obstinately argumentative, but Bart sensed that underneath lay fear. Morgan was talking to hide that fear.

All the crew members but the Kid and Captain Driscoll were in the control room. The Chinaman was in the pilot's seat, his immobile face fixed on the onrushing void. Wilson was dividing his attention between Bart and the radio. He kept the automatic close at hand. His double job made him irritable and he shifted about uneasily.

Lesher was keeping tabs on Bart's calculations, as far as he was able, and discussing the mechanical aspect of the warp-changing maneuver.

"We're jinxed," the engineer repeated, "and we're fools to be putting our lives in the hands of a crazy, double-crossing navigator."

"Forget it, can't you?" whined Wilson petulantly. Lesher raised his eyes from the table which Bart had littered with penciled theorems, and slips and graphs from the calculating machines.

"Yes, shut up, Morgan! Everything's OK. And everything will be OK if you don't mess up the engines when we change warps. Which you're apt to do the way you're feeling. Go back to your bunk and try to pull yourself together."

"It is not good to talk of jinxes," muttered the Chinaman, making a quick, ritualistic gesture with his left hand. Bart had already learned that the Oriental was a dimensionalist—a member of a pseudo-religious cult which professed to have established psychic communication with creatures and spirits in other dimensions of reality. The gesture was intended to ward off evil influences.

"I'm all right," said Morgan belligerently. "My nerves are like iron."

But Bart noticed that his hands were trembling

slightly. For a time there was an uncomfortable silence in the control room.

It was broken when Wilson announced that he was getting a message from the ship behind them on the warp. Lesher lifted his head. "I didn't know there was any ship due to leave so soon," he said. "Who is she, Wilson?"

"The University of Minnesota."

Lesher spun round in his chair. "An S.C.C. boat, so help me!" he rasped. "What do they want with us?"

"Oh, nothing . . . nothing," replied Wilson jerkily. "Just wanted to say 'hello' and check our position."

"Just wanted to check our position? That's all they would say? I don't like it," said Lesher. Then he stopped himself, seeming to realize the bad effect his words were having on the others' nerves, and changed his tone. "Though it's nothing to worry about, boys. We'll be off this warp in less than two hours, and then we can thumb our noses at all the S.C.C. boats in creation. I guess we must be going through a powerful thick belt of subcosmic rays right now. We've no other cause to feel jittery."

But Bart, pushing buttons on a calculator, could tell that these reassuring remarks did not have the effect on the others that Lesher desired. They seemed to strike a sour chord. The jumpiness of the crew gave Bart a feeling of hope. It meant they would be easier to deal with if a crisis came up.

It occurred to him that he might be able to increase their nervousness. He directed a seemingly casual question at the Chinaman. "Why did you say just now that it isn't good to talk of jinxes?"

"Because there are others who may hear—spirits

from other dimensions of reality—creatures my fore-fathers knew dimly as demons," replied the leather-faced Oriental, repeating the ritualistic gesture. "If they hear us talk of unlucky things that may happen, they seek to make them happen. They know the way to our world, though we do not know the way to theirs—except for the Master Dimensionalist."

"Now he's started," whined Wilson. "It's a lot of rot. Blooming rot."

"You mean," continued Bart innocently, "that even the empty space around us is filled with what you call spirits? That out there"—he pointed to the star sprinkled observation port—"there are things who are watching us?"

As Bart hoped, it was Morgan rather than the Chinaman who answered him. "Don't start that!" yelled the engineer in a sudden spasm of trembling, which he tried to pass off as anger. "Don't start that or I'll kill you! Don't start talking about . . . about the ships that never come back."

Bart shrugged his shoulders, as if he hadn't any such matter in mind.

Morgan subsided impotently, clenching his fists to hide the outward signs of his fear. Again silence descended on the control room, but it was a silence that ate at the nerves like an acid, a silence that fostered panic. Superstitions that could be laughed away on Earth took on a monstrous and compulsive reality in the isolation of interplanetary space. Even Lesher had trouble concentrating on the results of Bart's calculations.

After about ten minutes Wilson began to mutter, and to adjust and readjust the dials of the radio. "I don't know what it is," he said in answer to Lesher's question. "It's very faint. No, it's not the S.C.C. ship. There, it's coming a little louder now. No, curse it, I've lost it again."

"Maybe the ship ahead of us on the warp?"

Wilson, fumbling with the dials, shook his head. "No, I don't think so. Somehow the sound doesn't have warp quality. It's . . . queer."

"What do you mean, it hasn't warp quality?" Lesher interrogated jerkily. "It's got to have warp quality. We're a sight too far from Earth to be reached by radio except along the warp, so help me. You're imagining things. Turn up the amplifier and let's all hear it."

An eerie murmuring filled the control room. There was a varying cadence about it that suggested speech, though it was too low and confused with static for individual words to be intelligible. But something about the tone and pitch of it sent Bart's heart pounding. He looked at the other men, and saw fear on the faces of the Chinaman and Morgan.

The latter was squeaking, "What's that word it's saying? What's that word it's saying?"

Suddenly the static lifted and the voice came through, loud and clear. It filled the control room. "Spaceship *Sphinx* calling. Spaceship *Sphinx* calling."

Morgan's fat body quaked convulsively in panic. There was a gurgling sound in his throat. Then he ran aft, stumbling. Wilson, moved by irrational fear, grabbed up the automatic.

A wild exaltation filled Bart, for he recognized Ann's voice; yet at the same time he felt curiously calm, as if he were playing at a game of skill with the crew of the *Molly R* and waiting his chance to make a decisive move.

He watched the drawn faces of Lesher and Wilson. He heard the Chinaman mumbling wildly about "voices from another dimension." The meteor finder began to jangle raucously. Wilson almost dropped the automatic. Captain Driscoll's voice came faintly from aft, barking questions. The jangling increased swiftly in volume.

Bart guessing its meaning, strained his eyes at the observation port. Lesher shouted at the Chinaman, "Bend warp, you fool! Bend warp!" The Chinaman lost his head. In stead of bending warp, he decreased speed, yanking levers violently. He decreased speed much too quickly. Inertia pulled at them with sickening force. Wilson pitched forward across the floor. Lesher, halfway to the pilot's seat, was forced to cling to an anchored table for support. Bart did likewise. For three full minutes inertia gripped them tight, dragged at their flesh, made their veins stand out.

The Chinaman was pressed against the control board. The jangling of the meteor finder had become an earsplitting din. Finally the torment lessened. Then things happened with a startling rapidity, though to Bart it seemed almost slow, he saw each action so clearly. Captain Driscoll came staggering up the corridor, a gun in one hand, blood dripping from a gash in his cheek. Wilson half rose to his feet, holding his head and whimpering. Lesher struggled to pull the Chinaman off the controls.

Then Bart saw it. The thing loomed up like an illusion—so close to the *Molly R* that it half obscured the observation port. Parts of the battered hull reflected blinding glitters of sunlight; others were in so deep shadow as to be invisible. It was a picture impossible on earth—all highlights, weird, frightening.

"Look," cried Bart, seizing his chance, "Look! It's the *Sphinx!*"

The others turned to the port. The sight of the hulk, hanging there magnified and unreal, changed confusion into panic. The Chinaman threw Lesher to one side and fled. Wilson followed him. Together they bowled over Driscoll and carried him along with them. The control room was empty save for Bart and Lesher.

A few steps brought Bart to the door through which the others had fled. He slammed it shut and shoved the bolts into place. Then he turned to deal with Lesher. The veteran pilot had meanwhile managed to escape the grip of terror and drag his eyes away from the monstrous hulk of the *Sphinx*. He came at Bart with a rush, swinging his hook up at Bart's jaw, like a fisherman trying to catch a game fish through the gills. The hook gouged Bart's chin, but failed to catch the jawbone. He stepped to one side, tripped Lesher with his foot, at the same time swinging a blow at his back. Lesher's head hit the floor with a sickening thump and his body went limp. Bart knew that for the time being he was master of the *Molly R.*

He noted that the derelict *Sphinx* was slowly floating past them, and set the controls so that the *Molly R* backed warp at the same rate of speed. In that way he kept the two ships approximately abreast, though about fifty yards apart. Then he went to the radio and attempted to talk with Ann.

He could get no reply, although he continued to hear her voice at short intervals monotonously repeating the words "Spaceship *Sphinx* calling." His eyes narrowed. Evidently she could send, but not receive.

Just then Ann began a coherent message. "The

Sphinx was boarded by pirates from the *Molly R.* They murdered the entire crew, including Professor Wilkerson. They..." Then her voice broke. "I can't send much longer," came the faint words. "Oxygen running low... soon exhausted... intense cold... for the present, this is Ann Wilkerson... signing off."

Bart beat his palm with his fist. He knew he could not grapple the *Sphinx*, since the grapples were located and operated from amidships. Yet he could not delay. Ann, he thought, might be near death... horribly frightened... alone.

There was only one way. He must cross over in a space suit. Having reached this decision, his movements became precise and efficient. He silenced the bell of the meteor finder. He taped the unconscious Lesher's arms and feet. He locked the ship's controls.

He calculated it would take Driscoll and his crew at least fifteen minutes to cut through the bolted door, once they had recovered from their panic. Scooping up the automatic Wilson had dropped, he returned to the radio and attempted to contact the S.C.C. ship travelling behind them on the warp. He couldn't raise their operator.

Not wasting an instant, he put a fresh metal tape in the attached phonographic device and cut the following message: "Spaceship *Molly R* stalled on warp 17, about 3,257,300 miles from Earth. Aboard are the wreckers of Wilkerson's *Sphinx*. I temporarily have them locked up aft. They are desperate. Take all precautions in boarding us. Meanwhile I am attempting to rescue a survivor from the *Sphinx* which is floating derelict near our warp. Navigator Harlan sending. This is a phonographic message."

He set the radio to broadcast his call at half minute intervals, hoping against hope that it would be believed; he knew that the detail about the derelict *Sphinx* would raise doubts in the mind of the average spaceman. Perhaps he shouldn't have mentioned it. But there was no time now to make a change.

He glanced at the clock. Five minutes gone, and still no sounds to indicate Driscoll and the others were cutting at the bolted door. Jerking a space suit from a locker, he made his way to the emergency port, which consisted of two hermetic doors with a valve chamber between them in which the pressure could be decreased slowly. Getting into the suit, he shifted the automatic to an outer pocket.

Then a thought occurred to him. He went to the locker where tools and spare parts were kept and selected a dozen heavy rods and wrenches. With these he filled the other pockets. As he was adjusting his glass-synthetic helmet he spared another glance for the clock. Three more minutes gone.

From behind the bolted door there began to well up the characteristic muffled roar of an oxyacetylene torch. Fifteen minutes to go. He hurried into the valve chamber and adjusted the air-control to decrease pressure at the highest possible rate of speed. His head swam. He fought to retain consciousness. The gauge went down, down, finally hit bottom.

He was in a comparative vacuum. His blood, confined only by the relatively weak air-pressure his suit could generate, pounded in his arteries. Then, suddenly, the red spots stopped dancing in front of his eyes, and his head cleared.

He opened the outer door. Before and beneath him

was black, starry emptiness. Poised about fifty yards off was the torn hull of the *Sphinx*, transfigured by the sun, which Bart could not yet see, into a mass of grotesque highlights. He noted that stern showed a smooth, unbroken surface. That was where he could expect to find Ann, and so that was where he would have to direct his jump.

Bart knew that at this distance from the sun and from any planet, gravitational attraction was negligible. Nevertheless, the fact that he was still in the artificial gravitation system of the *Molly R* gave him the eerie feeling that he would fall straight down as soon as he sprang from the outer port. With an effort he conquered the inhibition, poised himself, and gave a vigorous push, as if he were making a standing broad jump.

Space received him. The sudden loss of gravity and weight made it seem like diving into water. Then he was out of the shadow of the *Molly R*. The sudden blast of harsh, unrefracted sunlight was almost like a physical blow. He saw the *Sphinx* rushing at him.

He clutched the meteor cushioning before the rebound had a chance to drive him away. Edging his way along, he reached the stern without finding any entry. It was agonizingly slow work, especially when he thought of Driscoll and his desperate crew at work on the connecting door. Pausing, he took a large wrench out of his pocket and began to pound on the hull; the sound, transmitted by the metal, might reach Ann.

Then he started back on the other side. He had gotten no more than a few feet when he noticed an open emergency port ahead of him. The helmet of a space suit was projecting from it. Sunlight revealed the face in the helmet. It was Ann's.

In a few moments Bart was beside her. But there was no time for him to try to read the words her lips were forming, nor to drink in the wild, startled beauty of her white face and reddish golden hair, which made an incredibly exotic picture against the background of stabbingly brilliant stars. Now that the first part of his mission was accomplished, his mind was dominated by the thought of an oxyacetylene flame hungrily eating its way through a metal door. How long had he been gone? Eight minutes? Ten? Twelve? He quickly put his arm around Ann and started to worm his way over the hull. It never once occurred to him there might be another survivor aboard.

When she tried to hold back, he remorselessly broke her grip and pulled her after him. He attributed her actions to panic, and he knew there was no time to reason with her, even if he were able to make himself heard. As he pushed off toward the *Molly R*, holding Ann tight to his side, his foot slipped against the meteor cushioning. This changed the direction of his push and he saw that they were going to miss the *Molly R* and careen beyond it into the void.

Using his free hand, he took a heavy connecting rod out of his pocket and hurled it with all his might in a direction exactly opposite that of the *Molly R*. He did the same with another rod and a large wrench. It worked. The force of the reaction changed the direction of their course. They swung around in a broken curve, and he managed to clutch the open door of the valve chamber.

It was the work of a moment to get inside. Then his feverish fingers sought the air control, and the pressure began to mount. He did not wait for it to equalize completely with the pressure inside the control room, so when he got the inner door open it swung outward with a bang and narrowly missed hitting him. Then they were inside.

All this while he had hardly spared a glance for Ann. Fingering the explosive-bullet automatic with his clumsy gloves, Bart looked around quickly and could see no change, save for a dull glow around the lock of the door leading aft, which showed where the oxyacetylene torch was at work. Lesher still seemed to be in the same position on the floor. Bart looked at the clock and saw he had scarcely been gone eight minutes.

He smiled grimly as he started to unloose his helmet. Then he heard Ann's voice. Now that they were in atmosphere again, it would carry through her space suit.

"Oh, Bart," she was saying. "I've been trying to tell you. Lucy's in the *Sphinx*. Our air supply was almost exhausted when I heard your tapping and went to investigate. I couldn't get her to come to the port with me. She may be suffocating by now. I tried and tried to tell you."

CHAPTER V
VICTORY

It was a moment before the meaning of her words filtered through to Bart's intelligence, before he realized how completely he had misinterpreted her words about the death of her father and the entire crew. He felt like an athlete who, at the end of a gruelling mile run, is told he must begin another race in two minutes.

Ann noticed Lesher's motionless form. Her eyes went wide in horror and surprise. "That man," she managed to say. "That man...the same one..."

Bart understood. He slipped off his helmet and went close to her. He started to undo the fastenings of her suit, then changed his mind.

"Ann," he said, "you've got to understand. As you see, this is the *Molly R*, the ship that pirated the *Sphinx*. Before I learned that, I'd signed on as navigator. I had a wild notion of persuading them to attempt to rescue the *Sphinx*. Then I found out the truth. Ann, that man with the hook is helpless. The rest of the crew are locked aft. Take this gun, and shoot to kill if they burn their way through the door. Keep your space suit on. It might be necessary to abandon ship quickly. I'll put in a fresh canister of oxygen; here it is. I've got to go back and get Lucy. And you...you have to trust me."

Ann stared at him, trying to piece together what he was saying. It all seemed so incredible to her, like a queer mixture of dream and reality. Bart's appearance...her rescue...Lucy's plight...and then this ship and that man with the hook. But after a moment she saw what she must do, and nodded her head in sudden determination and gripped the automatic firmly.

Before replacing his own helmet, Bart hurried over to the control panel and switched on the ship's individual sound system. "Driscoll!" he shouted. "Driscoll! If you manage to burn a hole in that door I'll spray a dozen explosive bullets through it. I don't care what happens to the *Molly R*. I'm giving you fair warning."

To his relief he heard the roar of the torch die away. He didn't hope to stop them, but he figured they might delay a few minutes making preparations for a gun fight before they went back to work on the door. And he desperately needed those minutes.

Then he was back in the valve chamber. In a pocket of his space suit was an extra oxygen canister and a flashlight. Again he lowered pressure rapidly, and this time he had to fight harder to keep from going under. With a sickening fear, he realized that the nervous strain was beginning to tell on him.

After the air gauge hit bottom it took him longer to recover than it had on his first trip. Everything seemed to take longer, to require a greater exertion of will power. On the first trip he had been thinking chiefly of Ann. Now he lacked that incentive and found himself weighing dangers.

Moreover, he was leaving Ann behind, in deadly peril. He found that it took a distinct effort to open the outer door. And when he stared into the black abyss, his knees shook and the cold seemed to cut through him like a frosty knife. "Can't waste a second. Can't waste a second," he kept mumbling to himself.

He noted that the derelict had drifted fifteen or twenty yards further away. The distance looked enormous. As he bent his legs and pushed off he felt that it was the action of a terrible nightmare—not of sane reality.

Then he found his hands clutching meteor cushionings, and his fear left him. He climbed directly over the hull this time, making straight for the open port. He waited for a moment to switch on his flashlight, and then pushed in.

It was like a diver entering a ship on the deep ocean bottom. His flashlight made a spot of brightness on the opposite wall...nothing more. Lucy's eyes were closed when he found her. Unconscious or dead, he thought mechanically, as he replaced her used-up oxygen canister with the fresh one. He cursed because his fingers fumbled and slipped as he screwed it tight and adjusted the valve. Half his thoughts were on another girl...Lucy's face began to blur under his anxious eyes, and Bart had to fight down another spasm of nervous weakness.

Getting out the port and up over the hull was a maddeningly slow business. It was difficult towing Lucy, because she could not adjust herself to his movements.

Halfway over the hull he sensed an independent movement from her. The next moment he was involved in a grotesque struggle with a panic-stricken girl who kicked and squirmed convulsively. Her eyes were the white-rimmed orbs of stark terror. He caught a glimpse of blood about her mouth, where she had bitten her lip.

He managed to hold her away from the hull so she could find nothing to grip but his arm. When Bart finally saw the *Molly R*, his heart sank. The off-warp drift of the *Sphinx* was increasing rapidly and now fully one hundred yards separated the two ships.

Lucy managed to touch the hull at the last moment, and her struggles greatly altered the direction of his push, so that they were headed for a point forty feet from the *Molly R*. One after another he threw away his remaining wrenches and heavy rods, using all the force at his command. Reaction gradually rectified their course, but he could see they were going to miss contact by a few scant inches.

He knew that struggling wouldn't shift their direction one iota. At the last second he remembered his flashlight. It plummeted off, and his free hand closed on a fixture of the grapple housing.

This time he had struck the *Molly R* amidships and he had to work his way forward, avoiding the ports for fear they might be noticed.

But when he reached the control room section he spared a glance on a small side porthole. His horror stricken eyes remained glued to what he saw. Lesher was free and struggling with Ann. "Fool, fool," thought Bart, "to forget his claw could cut through any tape that confined his arms!"

Evidently Lesher had managed to surprise Ann, for she had dropped her gun and was clinging with both hands to the arm which bore the claw. Her space suit protected her somewhat from his blows and kicks, but it was an unequal struggle. Soon he would free his claw to tear and rip.

No time to operate the valve chamber. No time to struggle with Lucy. It meant danger to Ann and them all, but it was the only way.

He swung Lucy against the interweave, saw her clutch and hold. Then he was yanking himself forward into the valve chamber at a reckless pace. He did not quite close the outer door, but kept tight hold of its handle with his left hand. With his right he worked speedily at the lock of the inner door, keeping as far away from it as he could.

It slammed open with a great crash. The sudden rush of escaping air drove the outer door wide open and Bart with it. The force of the blast whipped his body out so that it was at right angles to the hull. If it hadn't been for his grip on the outer door he would have been blown away from the ship altogether.

A flurry of papers—the ones bearing the calculations for the warpshifting maneuver—swept out through the port. Then came Lesher, powerless in the grip of the momentary hurricane, his eyes already beginning to bulge in a ghastly way from the sudden decrease in air pressure. He was clutching at his throat.

Bart's eyes, drawn by a morbid fascination, followed him. The pilot's body shot rapidly off into space, surrounded by the flurry of papers. Now that they were in an almost perfect vacuum, papers and man both moved at the same rate of speed—diminishingly black shapes against the stars, save where the sun made fantastic highlights.

That sight had the same effect on Bart as if he were plunged from a frightening dream into an even deeper nightmare—so deep that he did not remember his actions for the next few minutes. His last thought was that Ann, protected by her space suit, must have been able to hold on to something and keep from being blown out of the control room. But he was also aware that a space suit could not have shielded her completely from the physiological effects of the sudden change in pressure.

When consciousness began to come back to Bart, he was inside the control room and fumbling with the fastenings of his space suit. He only vaguely knew where he was. The first thing he saw was the clock. He noted that the minute hand had moved a quarter of the way around the dial since he'd last looked at it. What had happened? Wasn't there something important connected with the clock?

He tried to remember. His mind was dazed. The vision of Lesher's body rocketing out into space came back to him, and he winced. He felt a twinge of pain where Lesher's hook had gouged his jaw. He raised his hand to his cheek and was dully surprised when it encountered the smooth glass-synthetic of his helmet. His slow, struggling thoughts shifted from Lesher to the rest of the crew.

He turned around and looked stupidly at the door leading aft. A circular section of the metal glowed cherry red. In the center of this section was a small hole in which another metal was bubbling and fuming like very thick liquid rubber. That must be tungsten-plastic, he thought. Its presence puzzled him. What was tungsten-plastic doing here? Why had they closed the hole they had made with the torch?

Then he remembered. He had emptied the control room of air to save Ann. At about the same time Driscoll and the others must have cut through—and immediately been forced to close the hole to keep air in the aft part of the ship. In his mind's eye he pictured the sort of patch they'd made: a small metal plate sealed down over the hole with a great blob of tungsten-plastic.

But Ann. What had happened to Ann?

It was as if some obstruction snapped in his mind, and memory came back with a rush. He looked rapidly around him. Ann was lying on the floor near the control board. Lucy was kneeling beside her and shaking her. Both girls still wore their space suits. And, even as Bart watched, he saw Ann's lips part and quiver, saw her eyelids flutter open. She had come through!

As he moved to help Lucy, he figured out what he had done during the blank in his memory. He noted that the door of the valve chamber was locked shut. The quality of the light told him the control room was once more filled with air; a glance at the pressure gauge confirmed this.

He could hardly believe it, yet he realized that while he was unconscious or "space mad," he must have rescued Lucy from where he had left her clinging to the outer hull; further, he must have brought her into the control room, locked the valve chamber, and reopened the ventilators which had automatically shut when the pressure fell.

He helped Lucy undo the fastenings of Ann's helmet and her own. Ann's eyes sought his. She gripped his hand feebly and managed a smile. He soon convinced himself that she had not been seriously injured, and that with a little rest she ought soon to recover.

Then, ignoring Lucy's questions, he made for the radio. His phonographic message was still sending. He switched it off and spoke into the mike. "Navigator Harlan speaking. Can you hear me, *University of Minnesota*?"

"Thank God, sir," came the immediate reply. "I was beginning to think you were done for. You still have the crew locked aft?"

"Yes, but I can't tell for how long."

"We're coming at top speed. Is your position the same?"

"Yes. 3,257,300 miles out, approximately."

"Then we're still about 500,000 miles short. Can you back-warp to meet us?"

"I don't dare to. It would give the crew a chance to gum up the motors and wreck us."

"Of course. In any case we ought to be up with you in about half an hour. How did you know they had wrecked the *Sphinx*?"

"They partly revealed it to me themselves, thinking I would aid in their escape. And I've seen a square black box with Professor Wilkerson's initials on it."

He heard a flurry of excited conversation at the other end, and a man's voice—not the operator's—saying, "That may be the isotrium." Then the operator questioning, "Do you mean a box, or just a black valise?"

"I mean a square black box," said Bart. "I'd never seen anything just like it before. The material it was made of puzzled me. Looked like solid carbon."

"That's it!" came the second voice, and then something sounding like "But I can't believe it because of the other thing he said."

There followed a pause. Apparently they were conferring. When Bart heard the operator again, the man sounded hesitant.

"One other thing, Harlan. I believe we got part of your phonographic message wrong. The way it sounded to us, you spoke of sighting the *Sphinx*."

"I did. You didn't get it wrong."

"But man, that's impossible."

"It's true nevertheless. And I can prove..."

"But I tell you it's impossible. No lost ship can be found. The *Sphinx* was utterly destroyed."

Bart struggled to keep his temper. He knew he was fighting against accepted scientific theory. "Listen," he said, "I can prove it. I not only found the *Sphinx*, but I also rescued the two survivors—Wilkerson's daughters, Ann and Lucy. Do you want to talk with them?"

Another pause. Bart called to Lucy to come to the radio if she could leave Ann. In a moment she was beside him. Just then the second voice spoke to Bart directly. It was dry and matter-of-fact.

"Listen, Harlan, I am Carlstrom of the Scientists' Central Committee. I think I know you. You're the Harlan who was expelled from I.I.E.N. aren't you? Frankly, I can't believe your story. What you say about the ill-fated *Sphinx* prevents me from taking you seriously. I presume from what you last said that you have a female accomplice who will attempt to imitate the voice of one or both of Professor Wilkerson's daughters. Harlan, I don't know what motives you have for this deception, but let me tell you that you can't get away with it. Frankly, I have serious doubts of..."

Lucy cut in excitedly. "Professor Carlstrom, you've got to believe us. We were rescued from the *Sphinx*. It's true what he says, all true."

At this Carlstrom seemed to be taken aback. His voice was uncertain when he spoke again. "I can't believe you are Lucy Wilkerson."

"But I am. Why, Professor Carlstrom, do you remember how you visited us just about six weeks ago, and you and father spent the evening discussing the properties of isotrium, and I asked you questions about your work in the antarctic?"

Bart saw that Ann was standing beside him and Lucy. He put out his hand to support her, but she didn't need it. "Professor Carlstrom," she said in an eager voice, "you must try to satisfy your doubts. Any further proof you demand, we can give. Only no time must be lost in getting us out of this terrible ship. Every minute increases our danger."

Carlstrom's voice was strident with excitement. "Listen, Ann—if you are Ann Wilkerson—answer me one question. It's something no stranger could know. What was the real cause of your mother's death?"

"She died while collaborating with my father in his attempts to isolate isotrium," replied Ann in a hollow whisper. "It was completely hushed up. Her death coincided with the successful isolation of isotrium-beta. It was later diagnosed as isotrium poisoning, type three."

Carlstrom's "By Heaven, it checks!" seemed more an involuntary exclamation than a statement. "Listen, Ann and Lucy, we're coming at top speed. I still can't believe what Harlan says, but I trust you. In less than half an hour we'll lay alongside the *Molly R* and ..."

Bart was no longer listening. He had just received a disquieting shock. Through the opposite space port, dim because of the double refraction of iso-quartz and glass-synthetic, he had seen the malignant face of the Kid.

His mind set rapidly to work reconstructing the activities of Driscoll and the others. Probably they had never guessed that he had left the control room. Therefore, when air began to suck through the hole they had cut, it had very likely convinced them that both Bart and Lesher were dead. Rather than take any chances, they had hustled the Kid into a space suit and sent him out through the aft valve chamber to find out what sort of leak the control room had sprung and if it could be repaired.

Now that they knew the truth, they would undoubtedly recommence their cutting at the door.

"Ann," said Bart, "You and Lucy stick to the radio. Keep in contact with Carlstrom, so we can let him know of any unforeseen developments. Don't bother to take off the rest of your space suits; it's possible we may need them in a hurry." Then a frightening thought occurred to him, and he hurried to the valve chamber and double bolted the door securely from the inside. That would prevent the Kid from playing the same trick on him that he had played on Lesher.

Bart's mind had become a hotbed of fears. Wasn't it just barely possible, he thought, that Driscoll might try to flood the control room with some kind of poison gas? The chemicals available on a spaceship would make it easy to manufacture cyanogen or odorless phosgene.

Rather than take a chance, he jammed the ventilators shut. He and Ann and Lucy could easily get along for half an hour on stale air. If the worst came to the worst, they could always resume their helmets. Mightn't it be better to do that right away, and empty the control room of air as a protection? He decided against it. It would be too great a strain on Ann, and it would make cooperation with *The University of Minnesota* very difficult. Moreover, he had used the trick once; the others were undoubtedly prepared for it.

Within five minutes after he had sighted the Kid's face, he heard the sound of the oxyacetylene torch. He repeated his warnings to Driscoll over the ship's sound system. But the answer was a bloodcurdling laugh which he recognized as Morgan's, followed by an almost unintelligible jumble of curses and threats. He thought he could make out the words, ". . . burn you, like Lesher said."

Bart secured the explosive-bullet automatic he had given to Ann, and directed the girls to take a crouching position near the radio and out of the line of fire. He sensed that both were near the breaking point.

The minutes dragged slowly on. The metal door glowed more and more brightly. *The University of Minnesota* kept announcing its rapid changes in position as it approached. It was a race between the S.C.C. ship and the torch, but the torch was winning. Soon a tiny hole appeared in the door, and through it the bluish, incandescent flame hissed like a serpent's tongue.

Bart's nervously exhausted mind kept picturing the five faces on the other side—so vividly that it seemed almost like a kind of clairvoyance. The hate-laden, swinish eyes of Morgan; the baleful glare of the superstitious Chinaman; the chalk-white face of the Kid, its mouth twisted into a nasty grimace; the set features and thin, fear-pursed lips of Wilson; the malefic, pale eyes of Driscoll, light blue like the flame of the torch—Bart felt that he saw them all, that waves of murderous hate were emanating from them and beating against his brain. Five desperate men, driven almost insane with rage, uncertainty, and panic.

He almost wished that Lesher were still with them. Lesher at least would have had the force of character to control them, to fight down their hysteria.

The hole grew in size, became a horizontal cut; then another cut at right angles, and then another. The flame moved implacably. When *The University of Minnesota* was still one hundred thousand miles away, an incandescent square of metal fell with a dull clang to the floor. Simultaneously a bullet sang past Bart's head and spattered against the wall.

Bart replied, sending three bullets through the opening, one on top of the other. He heard a shriek of pain and saw a metal plate lifted into place to bar the opening. Stalemate!

But that was not long the case. He had estimated only too well the mad desperation of the men he was up against. For he heard Driscoll's voice shouting faintly.

"Harlan, don't think we haven't guessed by now that you're an agent of the S.C.C. Listen, we've got a box of isotrium in here. Harlan, that stuff is a thousand times more powerful than radium. It kills any man who's near it and not protected by metal. If you won't surrender, you and those women with you, we're going to dump it through the opening. Think fast, Harlan. It's not a nice death."

"Don't let him do it, Bart," cried Ann wildly. "He only knows the minor properties of isotrium—things that have been published in magazines. If he takes it out of its container, it will destroy the whole ship. Melt it down to cold electrons. Stop him!"

But it was Driscoll's voice that answered her. "Don't think you can fool us with a lot of fairy tales. We'll see to it that we're protected. You're going to get it. Right away."

"Quick!" hissed Bart. "We've got to abandon ship. Tell Carlstrom. Put on your helmets. It's the only hope. Driscoll's crazy enough to do what he says."

"Think fast, Harlan," came the voice through the door. "We're about to give it to you."

As they entered the valve chamber, they saw the plate that covered the hole lifted slightly aside. Within fifteen seconds they were pushing off from the ship. This time the *Sphinx* was a good two hundred yards away, but Ann and Lucy pushed with him and they crossed the gap.

Then they turned to watch the *Molly R.* What they saw etched itself indelibly on their minds. At first they noted no change. Then gradually the forward part of the ship began to glow pale green, as if it had been lightly brushed with radium. The glow grew in intensity and spread to the aft part of the ship, until the entire hull gleamed coldly, like some monstrous, phosphorescent fish from the lightless ocean deeps.

There was no sparkle, no shimmering, no pulsation— only an implacably intensifying glow. But the awesome change did not end there. Slowly the *Molly R* became semi-transparent. It looked like a ship of luminous glass. Bart could vaguely discern the outlines of the compartment walls and of the motors and the various fixtures. For a moment he thought he saw movement. Tiny forms of men rushing frantically about like trapped insects. Dissolving men of glass seeking escape from a dissolving ship.

Then there came an acceleration in the incredible process. Stars became visible through the hull. Swiftly the glow decreased in intensity. The outlines of the *Molly R* became vague and mistlike. Soon what had been a spaceship was no more than a vague luminescence—a nebulosity that might have been as distant as the Milky Way. Then it was gone.

They were alone in the cosmic blackness, which the brilliance of the stars and the harsh light of the sun, with its fantastically flaming corona, served only to emphasize and intensify. Bart realized that his breath was coming in heavy and measured gasps—such was the spell of evil fascination the vanishing of the *Molly R* had cast on him.

He clasped Ann closer and felt her shivering through the clumsy thickness of the space suits. By what a narrow margin, he thought, had they escaped the fate of Morgan and the Chinaman, of Wilson, the Kid, and Captain Driscoll; save for the high vacuum between the two ships, the cataclysmic action of the isotrium might readily have passed from the *Molly R* to the *Sphinx.*

His gaze idly roamed the empty cosmos. Near the sun he noted two tiny crescents, the larger greenish, the smaller silver. Those were the Earth and the Moon.

Then full realization of their predicament came to them. Only the S.C.C. ship *University of Minnesota* stood between them and certain death from suffocation or cold. Would they sight the derelict? It was more likely that, not finding the *Molly R,* they would continue on their way, suspecting a plot or an elaborate hoax.

He felt despair take root in him. He felt the cold sucking hungrily at him.

Ann and Lucy were both pulling at him, trying to attract his attention, pointing toward the Earth. At first, he did not understand what they were trying to convey. Then he saw it too—a dull star that lay in the same direction as Earth but inside the blackness of the unillumined part of Earth's disk! It wavered—it moved—it grew momently brighter. It could only be *The University of Minnesota,* traveling along the warp at a reduced rate of speed now it had reached the zone in which it expected to find the *Molly R.*

Bart fumbled in his pocket for the explosive-bullet automatic, set the control for the bullets to explode at a range of two hundred yards. *The University of Minnesota* had almost reached them. He aimed carefully at a spot about one hundred yards ahead of its prow and fired once, twice, three times. The bullets flashed like rockets as they burst.

The University of Minnesota drove past, then began to decrease speed, stopped, and slowly back-warped.

They saw heads outlined against the portholes. Slim telescopic grapples reached out for them.

An hour later, Ann, Lucy, and Bart were sitting in Carlstrom's cabin, and the S.C.C. ship was headed back for Earth. "We know so little of space," the distinguished scientist was saying. "We are like children blundering around in the dark. To think that today I have witnessed the first rescue of a lost ship. It is a milestone in the history of extraterrestrial navigation. And you, Harlan, were expelled from I.I.E.N.?"

"That's right, I'm afraid."

Carlstrom rubbed his wrinkled cheek reflectively, and smiled. "Well, Harlan, that just goes to show what mistakes we old fellows make sometimes. Of course, it was as much your faith in your theory as the theory itself that found the *Sphinx*. The S.C.C. were interested in the *Molly R* and had ordered the authorities to hold it pending an investigation. When we learned it had nevertheless left Earth, I was detailed to follow it to Mars. Well, it is gone now, and the isotrium with it. But we can talk of those matters later. Now you all need rest and further medical attention."

"I still feel it's all a dream," said Lucy, shivering and smiling all at once. "I keep thinking I'll wake up aboard the wreck of the *Sphinx*."

Carlstrom shook his head sadly. "Science lost a great man when your father perished. I know how it must grieve you. Now, Miss Lucy and Miss Ann, you'll be alone in the world, won't you?"

The sisters nodded their heads, but Ann's eyes sought Bart's, and found them.

Fritz Leiber (1910–1992) began his writing career in a 1939 issue of the now-legendary fantasy magazine, *Unknown*, with "Two Sought Adventure," which introduced his popular and enduring characters, Fafhrd and the Gray Mouser. The pair of itinerant swordsmen and thieves would return in a host of short stories, novellas, and novels, marking a high point in the fantasy subgenre of sword and sorcery, a term which Leiber coined. He may be best remembered for the Mouser and Fafhrd yarns, but he was equally adept at horror fiction, and often appeared in another classic fantasy magazine, *Weird Tales*. And of course, he was a master of science fiction. In 1981, the Science Fiction Writers of America made it official, naming him a SFWA Grand Master. His many other honors include being the Guest of Honor at the 1951 and 1979 World SF Conventions and a total of six Hugo Awards, two Nebula Awards, and three World Fantasy Awards—one of them for lifetime Achievement. The Horror Writers Association also recognized his importance to their field, presenting him in 1988 with their Bram Stoker award for lifetime achievement. In 2001, he was inducted into the Science Fiction Hall of Fame. More could be cited, but space is limited, unlike Leiber's talent. It's a genuine pleasure to bring back into print for the first time since its 1941 publication a rousing space adventure from early in this young titan's career.

Redeemer

Gregory Benford

While the seagoing pirates of old prowled the waves in ships with crew numerous enough to overwhelm a ship laden with valuable cargo, that was a consequence of the available technology—setting out to sea by oneself would likely be a suicide mission. But technology advances and one man in a starship might be able to pirate another ship. Particularly with most of the crew in cold sleep, and only three crewmembers awake and not expecting his arrival. Besides, he had virtue, or at least a virtuous argument on his side. Not that he wasn't expecting a big payday...

He had trouble finding it. The blue-white exhaust plume was a long trail of ionized hydrogen scratching a line across the black. It had been a lot harder to locate out here than Central said it would be.

Nagara came up on the *Redeemer* from behind, their blind side. They wouldn't have any sensors pointed aft. No point in it when you're on a one-way trip, not expecting visitors and haven't seen anybody for seventy-three years.

He boosted in with the fusion plant, cutting off the translight to avoid overshoot. The translight rig was delicate and still experimental and it had already pushed him over seven light-years out from Earth. When he got back to Earth there would be an accounting, and he would have to pay off from his profit anything he spent for over-expenditure of the translight hardware.

The ramscoop vessel ahead was running hot. It was a long steel-gray cylinder, fluted fore and aft. The blue-white fusion fire came boiling out of the aft throat, pushing *Redeemer* along at a little below a tenth of light velocity. Nagara's board buzzed. He cut in the mill-mag system. The ship's skin, visible outside through his small porthole, fluxed into its superconducting state, gleaming like chrome. The readout winked and Nagara could see on the situation board his ship slipping like a silver fish through the webbing of magnetic field lines that protected *Redeemer*.

The field was mostly magnetic dipole. He cut through it and glided in parallel to the hot exhaust streamer. The stuff was spitting out a lot of UV and he had to change filters to see what he was doing. He eased up along the aft section of the ship and matched velocities. The magnetic throat yawning up ahead sucked in the interstellar hydrogen for the fusion motors. *Redeemer*'s forward mag fields pulsed to shock-ionize the hydrogen molecules ahead, then ate them eagerly. He stayed away from that. There was enough radiation up there to fry you for good.

Redeemer's midsection was rotating but the big clumsy-looking lock aft was stationary. Fine. No trouble clamping on.

The couplers seized *clang* and he used a waldo to manually open the lock. He would have to be fast now, fast and careful.

He pressed a code into the keyin plate on his chest to check it. It worked. The slick aura enveloped him, cutting out the ship's hum. Nagara nodded to himself.

He went quickly through the *Redeemer*'s lock. The pumps were still laboring when he spun the manual override to open the big inner hatch. He pulled himself through in the zero-g with one power motion, through the hatch and into a cramped suitup room. He cut in his magnetos and settled to the grid deck.

As Nagara crossed the desk a young man came in from a side hatchway. Nagara stopped and thumped off his protective shield. The man didn't see Nagara at first because he was looking the other way as he came through the hatchway, moving with easy agility. He was studying the subsystem monitoring panels on the far bulkhead. The status phosphors were red but they winked green as Nagara took three steps forward and grabbed the man's shoulder and spun him around. Nagara was grounded and the man was not. Nagara hit him once in the stomach and then shoved him against a bulkhead. The man gasped for breath. Nagara stepped back and put his hand into his coverall pocket and when it came out there was a dart pistol in it. The man's eyes didn't register anything at first and when they did he just watched the pistol, getting his breath back, staring as though he couldn't believe either Nagara or the pistol was there.

"What's your name?" Nagara demanded in a clipped, efficient voice.

"What? I—"

"Your name. Quick."

"I . . . Zak."

"All right, Zak, now listen to me. I'm inside now and I'm not staying long. I don't care what you've been told. You do just what I say and nobody will blame you for it."

"Nobody . . . ?" Zak was still trying to unscramble his thoughts and he looked at the pistol again as though that would explain things.

"Zak, how many of you are manning this ship?"

"Manning? You mean crewing?" Confronted with a clear question, he forgot his confusion and frowned. "Three. We're doing our five-year stint. The Revealer and Jacob and me."

"Fine. Now where's Jacob?"

"Asleep. This isn't his shift."

"Good." Nagara jerked a thumb over his shoulder. "Personnel quarters that way?"

"Uh, yes."

"Did an alarm go off through the whole ship, Zak?"

"No, just on the bridge."

"So it didn't wake up Jacob?"

"I . . . I suppose not."

"Fine, good. Now, where's the Revealer?"

So far it was working well. The best way to handle people who might give you trouble right away was to keep them busy telling you things before they had time to decide what they should be doing. And Zak plainly was used to taking orders.

"She's in the forest."

"Good. I have to see her. You lead the way, Zak."

Zak automatically half turned to kick down the hatchway he'd come in through and then the questions came out. "What—who *are* you? How—"

"I'm just visiting. We've got faster ways of moving now, Zak. I caught up with you."

"A faster ramscoop? But we—"

"Let's go, Zak." Nagara waved the dart gun and Zak looked at it a moment and then, still visibly struggling with his confusion, he kicked off and glided down the drift tube.

The forest was one half of a one hundred meter long cylinder, located near the middle of the ship and rotating to give one g. The forest was dense with pines and oak and tall bushes. A fine mist hung over the tree tops, obscuring the other half of the cylinder, a gardening zone that hung over their heads. Nagara hadn't been in a small cylinder like this for decades. He was used to seeing a distant green carpet overhead, so far away you couldn't make out individual trees, and shrouded by the cottonball clouds that accumulated at the zero-g along the cylinder axis. This whole place felt cramped to him.

Zak led him along footpaths and into a bamboo-walled clearing. The Revealer was sitting in lotus position in the middle of it. She was wearing a Flat-lander robe and cowl just like Zak. He recognized it from a historical fax readout.

She was a plain-faced woman, wrinkled and wiry, her hands thick and calloused, the fingers stubby, the nails clipped off square. She didn't go rigid with surprise when Nagara came into view and this bothered him a little. She didn't look at the dart pistol more than once, to see what it was, and that surprised him, too.

"What's your name?" Nagara said as he walked into the bamboo-encased silence.

"I am the Revealer." A steady voice.

"No, I meant your name."

"That is my name."

"I mean—"

"I am the Revealer for this stage of our exodus."

Nagara watched as Zak stepped halfway between them and then stood uncertainly, looking back and forth.

"All right. When they freeze you back down, what'll they call you then?"

She smiled at this. "Michele Astanza."

Nagara didn't show anything in his face. He waved the pistol at her and said, "Get up."

"I prefer to sit."

"And I prefer you to stand."

"Oh."

He watched both of them carefully.

"Zak, I'm going to have to ask you to do a favor for me."

Zak glanced at the Revealer and she moved her head a few millimeters in a nod. He said, "Sure."

"This way." Nagara gestured with the pistol to the woman. "You lead."

The woman nodded to herself as if this confirmed something and got up and started down a footpath to her right, her steps so soft on the leafy path that Nagara could not hear them over the tinkling of a stream on the overhead side of the cylinder. Nagara followed her. The trees trapped the sound in here and made him jumpy.

He knew he was taking a calculated risk by not taking Jacob, too. But the odds against Jacob waking up in time were good and the whole point of doing it this way was to get in and out fast, exploit surprise. And he wasn't sure he could handle the three of them together. That was just it—he was doing this alone so he could collect the whole fee, and for that you had to take some extra risk. That was the way this thing worked.

The forest gave onto some corn fields and then some wheat, all with UV phosphors netted above. The three of them skirted around the nets and through a hatchway in the big aft wall. Whenever Zak started to say anything Nagara cut him off with a wave of the pistol. Then Nagara saw that with time to think, Zak was adding things up and the lines around his mouth were tightening, so Nagara asked him some questions about the ship's design. That worked. Zak rattled on about quintuple-redundant failsafe subsystems he'd been repairing until they were at the entrance to the freezing compartment.

It was bigger than Nagara had thought. He had done all the research he could, going through old faxes of *Redeemer*'s prelim designs, but plainly the Flatlanders had changed things in some later design phase.

One whole axial section of *Redeemer* was given over to the freeze-down vaults. It was at zero-g because otherwise the slow compression of tissues in the corpses would do permanent damage. They floated in their translucent compartments, like strange fish in endless rows of pale, blue-white aquariums.

The vaults were stored in a huge array, each layer a cylinder slightly larger than the one it enclosed, all

aligned along the ship's axis. Each cylinder was two
compartments thick, a corpse in every one, and the
long cylinders extended into the distance until the
chilly fog steaming off them blurred the perspective
and the eye could not judge the size of the things.
Despite himself Nagara was impressed. There were
thousands and thousands of Flatlanders in here, all
dead and waiting for the promised land ahead, circling
Tau Ceti. And with seventy-five more years of data
to judge by, Nagara knew something this Revealer
couldn't reveal: the failure rate when they thawed
them out would be thirty percent.

They had come out on the center face of the bulwark
separating the vault section from the farming part.
Nagara stopped them and studied the front face of the
vault array, which spread away from them radially like
an immense spider web. He reviewed the old plans in
his head. The axis of the whole thing was a tube a
meter wide, the same translucent organiform. Liquid
nitrogen flowed in the hollow walls of the array and
the phosphor light was pale and watery.

"That's the DNA storage," Nagara said, pointing at
the axial tube.

"What?" Zak said. "Yes, it is."

"Take them out."

"What?"

"They're in failsafe self-refrigerated canisters, aren't
they?"

"Yes."

"That's fine." Nagara turned to the Revealer. "You've
got the working combinations, don't you?"

She had been silent for some time. She looked at
him steadily and said, "I do."

"Let's have them."

"Why should I give them?"

"I think you know what's going on."

"Not really."

He knew she was playing some game but he couldn't see why. "You're carrying DNA material for over ten thousand people. Old genotypes, undamaged. It wasn't so rare when you collected it seventy-five years ago, but it is now. I want it."

"It is for our colony."

"You've got enough corpses here."

"We need genetic diversity."

"The System needs it more than you. There's been a war. A lot of radiation damage."

"Who won?"

"Us. The outskirters."

"That means nothing to me."

"We're the environments in orbit around the sun, not sucking up to Earth. We knew what was going on. We're mostly in Bernal spheres. We got the jump on—"

"You've wrecked each other genetically, haven't you? That was always the trouble with your damned cities. No place to dig a hole and hide."

Nagara shrugged. He was watching Zak. From the man's face Nagara could tell he was getting to be more insulted than angry—outraged at somebody walking in and stealing their future. And from the way his leg muscles were tensing against a foothold Nagara guessed Zak was also getting more insulted than scared, which was trouble for sure. It was a lot better if you dealt with a man who cared more about the long odds against a dart gun at this range, than about the principle. Nagara knew he couldn't count on

Zak ignoring all the Flatlander nonsense the Revealer and others had pumped into him.

They hung in zero-g, nobody moving in the wan light, the only sound a gurgling of liquid nitrogen. The Revealer was saying something and there was another thing bothering Nagara, some sound, but he ignored it. "How did the planetary enclaves hold out?" the woman was asking. "I had many friends—"

"They're gone."

Something came into the woman's face. "You've lost man's *birthright*?"

"They sided with the—"

"Abandoned the planets altogether? Made them unfit to *live* on? All for your awful *cities*—" and she made a funny jerky motion with her right hand.

That was it. When she started moving that way Nagara saw it had to be a signal and he jumped to the left. He didn't take time to place his boots right and so he picked up some spin but the important thing was to get away from that spot fast. He heard a *chuung* off to the right and a dart smacking into the bulkhead and when he turned his head to the right and up behind him a burly man with black hair and the same Flatlander robes and a dart gun was coming at him on a glide.

Nagara had started twisting his shoulder when he leaped and now the differential angular momentum was bringing his shooting arm around. Jacob was already aiming again. Nagara took the extra second to make his shot and allow for the relative motions. His dart gun puffed and Nagara saw it take Jacob in the chest, just right. The man's face went white and he reached down to pull the dart out but by that time the nerve inhibitor had reached the heart and abruptly Jacob stopped plucking at the dart and his fingers went slack and the body drifted on in the chilly air, smacking into a vault door and coming to rest.

Nagara wrenched around to cover the other two. Zak was coming at him. Nagara leaped away, braked. He turned and Zak had come to rest against the translucent organiform, waiting.

"That's a lesson," Nagara said evenly. "Here's another."

He touched the keyin on his chest and his force screen flickered on around him, making him look metallic. He turned it off in time to hear the hollow boom that came rolling through the ship like a giant's shout.

"That's a sample. A shaped charge. My ship set it off two hundred meters from *Redeemer*. The next one's keyed to go on impact with your skin. You'll lose pressure too fast to do anything about it. My force field comes on when the charge goes, so it won't hurt me."

"We've never seen such a field," the woman said unsteadily. "Outskirter invention. That's why we won."

He didn't bother watching Zak. He looked at the woman as she clasped her thick worker's hands together and began to realize what choices were left. When she was done with that she murmured, "Zak, take out the canisters."

The woman sagged against a strut. Her robes clung to her and made her look gaunt and old.

"You're not giving us a chance, are you?" she said.

"You've got a lot of corpses here. You'll have a big colony out at Tau Ceti." Nagara was watching Zak maneuver the canisters onto a mobile carrier. The young man was going to be all right now, he could tell that. There was the look of weary defeat about him.

"We need the genotypes for insurance. In a strange ecology there will be genetic drift."

"The System has worse problems right now."

"With Earth dead you people in the artificial worlds are *finished*," she said savagely, a spark returning. "That's why we left. We could see it coming."

Nagara wondered if they'd have left at all if they'd known a faster than light drive would come along. But no, it wouldn't have made any difference. The translight transition cost too much and only worked on small ships. He narrowed his eyes and made a smile without humor.

"I know quite well why you left. A bunch of scum-lovers. Purists. Said Earth was just as bad as the cylinder cities, all artificial, all controlled. Yeah, I know. You flatties sold off everything you had and built *this*—" His voice became bitter. "Ransacked a fortune—*my* fortune."

For once she looked genuinely curious, uncalculating. "Yours?"

He flicked a glance at her and then back at Zak. "Yeah. I would've inherited some of your billions you made out of those smelting patents."

"You—"

"I'm one of your great-grandsons." Her face changed. "No."

"It's true. Stuffing the money into this clunker made all your descendants have to bust ass for a living. And it's not so easy these days."

"I ... didn't ..."

He waved her into silence. "I knew you were one of

the mainstays, one of the rich Flatlanders. The family talked about it a lot. We're not doing so well now. Not as well as you did, not by a thousandth. I thought that would mean you'd get to sleep right through, wake up at Tau Ceti. Instead—" he laughed—"they've got you standing watch."

"Someone has to be the Revealer of the word, grandson."

"Great-grandson. Revealer? If you'd 'revealed' a little common sense to that kid over there he would've been alert and I wouldn't be in here."

She frowned and watched Zak, who was awkwardly shifting the squat modular canisters stenciled GENETIC BANK. MAX SECURITY. "We are not military types."

Nagara grinned. "Right. I was looking through the family records and I thought up this job. I figured you for an easy setup. A max of three or four on duty, considering the size of the life-support systems and redundancies. So I got the venture capital together for time in a translight and here I am."

"We're not your kind. Why can't you give us a chance, grandson?"

"I'm a businessman."

She had a dry, rasping laugh. "A few centuries ago everybody thought space colonies would be the final answer. Get off the stinking old Earth and everything's solved. Athens in the sky. But look at you—a paid assassin. A 'businessman.' You're no grandson of mine."

"Old ideas." He watched Zak.

"Don't you see it? The colony environments aren't a social advance. You need discipline to keep life-support systems from springing a leak or poisoning you. Communication and travel have to be regulated for simple safety. So you don't get democracies, you get strong men. And then they turned on us—on Earth."

"You were out of date," he said casually, not paying much attention. "Do you ever read any history?"

"No." He knew this was part of her spiel—he'd seen it on a fax from a century ago—but he let her go on to keep her occupied. Talkers never acted when they could talk.

"They turned Earth into a handy preserve. The Berbers and Normans had it the same way a thousand years ago. They were seafarers. They depopulated Europe's coastline by raids, taking what or who they wanted. You did the same to us, from orbit, using solar lasers. But to—"

"Enough," Nagara said. He checked the long bore of the axial tube. It was empty. Zak had the stuff secured on the carrier. There wasn't any point in staying here any longer than necessary.

"Let's go," he said.

"One more thing," the woman said.

"What?"

"We went peacefully, I want you to remember that. We have no defenses."

"Yeah," Nagara said impatiently.

"But we have huge energies at our disposal. The scoop fields funnel an enormous flux of relativistic particles. We could've temporarily altered the magnetic multipolar fields and burned your sort to death."

"But you didn't."

"No, we didn't. But remember that."

Nagara shrugged. Zak was floating by the carrier ready to take orders, looking tired. The kid had been easy to take, to easy for him to take any pride in doing it. Nagara liked an even match. He didn't even mind losing if it was to somebody he could respect. Zak wasn't in that league, though.

"Let's go," he said.

The loading took time but he covered Zak on every step and there were no problems. When he cast off from *Redeemer* he looked around by reflex for a planet to sight on, relaxing now, and it struck him that he was more alone than he had ever been, the stars scattered like oily jewels on velvet were the nearest destination he could have. That woman in *Redeemer* had lived with this for years. He looked at the endless long night out here, felt it as a shadow that passed through his mind, and then he punched in instructions and *Redeemer* dropped away, its blue-white arc a fuzzy blade that cut the darkness, and he slipped with a hollow clapping sound into translight.

He was three hours from his dropout point when one of the canisters strapped down behind the pilot's couch gave a warning buzz from thermal overload. It popped open.

Nagara twisted around and fumbled with the latches. He could pull the top two access drawers a little way out and when he did he saw that inside there was a store of medical supplies. Boxes and tubes and fluid cubes. Cheap stuff. No DNA manifolds.

Nagara sat and stared at the complete blankness outside. *We could've temporarily altered the magnetic multipolar fields and burned your sort to death*, she had said. *Remember that.*

If he went back she would be ready. They could

rig some kind of aft sensor and focus the ramscoop fields on him when he came tunneling in through them. Fry him good.

They must have planned it all from the first. Something about it, something about the way she'd looked, told him it had been the old woman's idea.

The risky part of it had been the business with Jacob. That didn't make sense. But maybe she'd known Jacob would try something and since she couldn't do anything about it she used it. Used it to relax him, make him think the touchy part of the job was done so that he didn't think to check inside the stenciled canisters.

He looked at the medical supplies. Seventy-three years ago the woman had known they couldn't protect themselves from what they didn't know, ships that hadn't been invented yet. So on her five-year watch she had arranged a dodge that would work even if some System ship caught up to them. Now the Flatlanders knew what to defend against.

He sat and looked out at the blankness and thought about that.

Only later did he look carefully through the canisters. In the lowest access drawer was a simple scrap of paper. On it someone—he knew instantly it must have been the old woman, or somebody damned like her—had hand-printed a message.

> If you're from the System and you're reading this on the way back home, you've just found out you're holding the sack. Great. But after you've cooled off, remember that if you leave us alone, we'll be another human settlement

someday. We'll have things you'll find useful. If you've caught up with *Redeemer* you certainly have something we want—a faster drive. So we can trade. Remember that. Show this message to your bosses. In a few centuries we can be an asset to you. But until then, keep off our backs. We'll have more tricks waiting for you.

When he popped out into System space the A47 sphere was hanging up to the left at precisely the relative coordinates and distance he'd left it. A47 was big and inside there were three men waiting to divide up and classify and market the genotypes and when he told them what was in the canisters it would all be over, his money gone and theirs and no hope of his getting a stake again. And maybe worse than that. Maybe a lot worse. He squinted at A47 as he came in for rendezvous. It looked different.

Some of the third quadrant damage from the war wasn't repaired yet. The skin that had gleamed once was smudged now and twisted gray girders stuck out of the ports. It looked pretty beat up. It was the best high-tech fortress they had and A47 had made the whole difference in the war. It broke the African shield by itself. But now it didn't look like so much. All the dots of light orbiting in the distance were pretty nearly the same or worse and now they were all that was left in the system.

Nagara turned his ship about to vector on the landing bay, listening to the rumble as the engines cut in. The console phosphors rippled, blue, green, yellow as Central reffed him.

This next part was going to be pretty bad. Damned bad. And out there his great-grandmother was on the way still, somebody he could respect now, and for the first time he thought the Flatlanders probably were going to make it. In the darkness of the cabin something about the thought made him smile.

Gregory Benford is a physicist, educator, and author. He received a BS from the University of Oklahoma and a PhD from the University of California, San Diego. Benford is a professor of physics at the University of California, Irvine, where he has been a faculty member since 1971. He is a Woodrow Wilson Fellow and a Visiting Fellow at Cambridge University. He has served as an advisor to the Department of Energy, NASA, and the White House Council on Space Policy. He is the author of over twenty novels, including *In the Ocean of the Night, The Heart of the Comet* (with David Brin), *Foundation's Fear, Bowl of Heaven* (with Larry Niven), *Timescape,* and *The Berlin Project.* A two-time winner of the Nebula Award, Benford has also won the John W. Campbell Award, the British Science Fiction Award, the Australian Ditmar Award, and the 1990 United Nations Medal in Literature. In 1995 he received the Lord Foundation Award for contributions to science and the public comprehension of it. He has served as scientific consultant to the NHK Network and for *Star Trek: The Next Generation.*

Trading Up

Sarah A. Hoyt & Robert A. Hoyt

When one space pirate pirates another space pirate's ship, which one is the good guy? Or is it none of the above? And when there's serious sibling rivalry involved, it underlines that there's no feud like a family feud...

The air was thick with the kind of fog you only got when hundreds of people traveling with limited access to hygienic facilities frequented a station that didn't invest much in its air filters. Faraway Bay, like many black market transit points, didn't go in for excessive convenience, let alone comfort, since they knew you didn't have much choice.

"I'm getting out of the business," said Harding, pulling himself a little more upright.

"You? Why? And how? What's your old man think of this?" said Midluk, his forehead creasing.

Harding took a swig of Supernova. Technically, he could have drunk alcohol, instead of a fizzer—nobody on the Bay cared, and his liver could handle far more toxic things than that without it affecting his growth. But he'd never understood why someone would voluntarily disadvantage themselves with a pleasant sedative—you never knew when you might need to fight.

"Why is my business. How is where you come in. As for my father, I haven't cared what he thought for quite some time, thanks."

A Volboque waitress wandered by with a tray of drinks. Presumably—given the hiring practices for the humans—she was what her species considered buxom. There was perhaps a certain plumpness about the vestigial tentacles on her flank. She gurgled.

"Another beer, honey?" the tongue twister on her belt translated robotically.

"Yeah, that's fine." said Midluk, distractedly. He stared at Harding for a beat longer than was comfortable. He seemed to be thinking about something fairly hard.

"Frankly, you're a damned good black market trader. You know that?" he said, after a while.

Harding nodded. He'd been raised to it, so there was no point in false modesty.

"And I bet you could make real money if you turned pirate. That old Dad of yours trained you boys well."

Harding just shrugged. "Doubtlessly. Kill a man, take his ship, that's piracy in a nutshell. Not much to it."

"Yeah, well, so far, people haven't had much luck killing you or taking yours, and from what I hear, plenty have tried. That's what we old-timers call career potential. No telling what you could go on to do, with experience," Midluk continued.

"All in all, I'm certainly leaving behind a bright future in the shadows," Harding agreed.

"Well," Midluk said at last, "then I guess I ain't got no choice but to help you, because damned if I need that kind of competition. What is it you need, exactly?"

"Leverage, or some kind of in at a legitimate trade academy. Some place willing to stamp a diploma on me, so that I have something to show stations and docks where I'm trying to get listed."

"That's it? Why not just approach them directly? You're more than qualified to sign up at an academy. You could probably pass any entrance exam cold."

"Yes, but I've previously run up bounties working out to millions in GalBlue credits in various systems. I suspect I need to go the extra parsec for an academy to take me on."

Midluk paused.

"A fair point." He scratched his chin. "So happens I might know a way to help you. But it's not going to come free."

"I suspected that would be the case. What's your price?"

"It's not money. I've got a job needs doing, and you might be just the person to do it."

There is a phrase: "Who guards the guards?" It was a variant of this that was currently pre-occupying Harding: "Who pirates the pirates?"

People like Midluk, who had been working in piracy, privateering, or the black market for a while, eventually did something not dissimilar to what freetraders did. Once they had enough money, they'd buy a cushy office on a station and start managing a fleet, rather than personally captaining a ship between various places.

This increased your security and comfort, and it meant that you weren't personally in the thick of it if something went pear-shaped en route. Unfortunately, it also meant you weren't in the thick of it if something went pear-shaped en route—some less experienced captain still on his way up was.

Midluk had had two shipments of black market weapons mysteriously disappear: ship, crew, and all. It was especially sensitive because the weapons in question had been pirated from The Counsel of Six Worlds, needed in a regional uprising C6W was hoping to suppress. If arms dealers ever used the word "synergy," they would have used it here. C6W ended up more poorly armed, and the rebels ended up as well armed as the people doing suppression work, and thus were more likely to stick around to be future customers.

The shipments disappearing made things more complicated, especially since Midluk could hardly ask C6W to investigate. For all he knew, they were actually the cause, though he suspected not. The Counsel wasn't known for being modest. They also had some rather sharp opinions on pirates, largely of the kind delivered by judges and preceding executions. That left him without much of anyone to turn to.

That was where Harding had the opportunity to be useful. He could captain a ship on the route and find out what was going on.

And so it was that Harding found himself at the helm of *Fool's Paradise*, a twenty-kiloton freighter with—apparently—nothing more than a high-efficiency slow-boat engine and minimal armament, on a renegade stringline past the Achilles mini-belt on the way from Sensora, in Counsel space, to Lapis, which was held by the Thratian Compact. It was to pirates what a nice juicy steak is to a wolf, and Harding was the hunter with the hotshot, crouching nearby. With some work he'd talked Midluk out of sending the usual cargo—it had been tricky, but if the hijacking was this reliable, all he stood to do was lose stock. Midluk, for his part, had found a way to ensure that the cargo was still *somewhat* valuable if by a minor miracle it arrived safely. Since Midluk didn't want to risk his men, Harding was the only crew—*Fool's Paradise* might have a couple dozen souls at full capacity, but it didn't need them, certainly not to be bait.

Harding didn't wait long for the wolves to come out. As the ship rode the makeshift stringline nodes out past the belt, suddenly alarms started ringing, and the Threader abruptly lost the string. The ship shuddered violently, as all the physical space that was being pulled out of the stringline's core and pushed into the area around it came flooding back.

Space has a density of around one lone hydrogen atom per cubic centimeter, and stringlines usually "pulled" several cubic light-years out of their stable low-density center and into the much higher-density annulus around their edges. The technology that achieved it was complicated, involving a form of paramatter nicknamed "transferium", capable of buffering almost infinite loads of energy. This was helpful because the stringline's stabilizing energy relied partially on the fact that somewhat less than one and a half yottatons of hydrogen ions per cubic light-year got compressed into a much, much smaller space at the annulus edge, generating theoretical energy up to a hundred petajoules as the hydrogen ions dimerized. In effect, the rim was one, long, tubular star. When broken, stringlines could—in fact engineers said that if properly designed they would automatically—handle withdrawing the area of active reaction to the respective portions up- and down-stream until continuity was re-established. This had the happy side effect of ensuring that if the stringline "snapped," provided the Threader was able to ease the ship off the string properly and weather the massive gravity shockwave, the pilot wasn't immediately immolated by the equivalent of the biggest man-made hydrogen explosion in history, because much of that energy had already been spent. Instead, he was merely stuck in the middle of deep space.

In Harding's case, he was also facing down what was clearly a mid-sized yacht turned into an after-market battle cruiser. Whoever was piloting it was well-funded. As he pulled it up on his viewscreen, he appraised it with a professional eye—very dark strategically placed hull plating, probably paramatter with a layer of prismatic shielding designed to diffuse lasers; wall-to-wall magnetic nodes, which made the ship look a bit like it had a fine layer of metallic hair, but which could capture and dissipate most plasma or ion-based weapons; a variety of heavy armaments from conventional railguns to ship-scale hotshots, and if Harding was the one betting, a whole other set of less legal armaments currently concealing itself.

Harding didn't bother firing up the comms. A smaller raiding ship with a boarding party was already dispatched and inbound. He merely noted its estimated impact site, and then he stood up and moved quickly to the bod-pod near the captain's chair, which he'd pre-configured to equip his suit and helmet. The suit snapped smartly into place around him, and he lifted his arm to look at an uplink to the ship's computer he'd prepared in advance. They weren't standard on Midluk's ships, but Harding had insisted.

Making his way down toward the airlock, he brought up the ship's engineering systems on his screen. There was a distant crash and a much gentler shuddering than the one when they dropped out of Stringspace, as the pirate vessel bored into the starboard side of the mess, somewhat aft of the bridge.

Harding touched the screen and shut down the lights in the room. He crawled into a maintenance access tunnel that led into the mess. As the ship doors opened, he heard muted swearing.

"Musta hit the damned electrical line on the way in. Say, where is everybody?"

"Cap'n says he couldn't find much crew. Guess old Midluk's having trouble hiring these days. Always some interference from popping the stringline, though, so stay alert."

"Aye, sir!"

The men walked into the mess hall. One by one, the electric doors around them closed, counter-clockwise.

"Oh, how cute. The captain is trying to barricade us in. Phillips, blow that door over there, would you?"

A brute of a man pulled a set of breaching charges and made his way toward the door. From his concealed position in a maintenance tunnel under the mess, Harding watched him and counted under his breath. He overrode the forward airlock, and with judicious use of closing air-seals, made a direct line to the room adjacent to the mess. Then, just as the man reached the door, he pushed a button.

The door whooshed open a moment before the breaching charge was placed.

"What the—"

The air flooded out of the mess, pulling the men off balance. The one with the explosives went flying headlong as the air from the mess evacuated through the narrow tunnel created by the now-open door. He barely managed to catch himself, two rooms down. The others grabbed onto tables and chairs long enough for the initial evacuation of the air to pass.

Harding flipped on the lights and burst from the maintenance tunnel. The men didn't have time to dim their visors and were blinded by the time Harding was upon them.

He killed the officer with a fully powered hotshot within a second. The next two men, barely starting to react, had their hearts cauterized before they got much further. A fourth man managed to actually get his own hotshot in hand, but he never got the chance to fire it before a wave of concentrated heat hit him in the brain. A flicker caught Harding's eye, and almost instinctively he tapped his screen to close the door right as the explosives expert threw a grenade. The door snapped shut in front of it, and the door behind the unlucky man snapped shut a moment later. There was a bang, and Harding opened the door with his hotshot raised, in case the man had somehow taken cover. Instead, he was laying against the far door, peppered in shrapnel.

The man raised his head, weakly.

"Who—are—?" he said, and those were his last words.

Harding inspected the bodies. The suits weren't nearly as nice as the ship, which probably meant the owner had hired contractors. They'd be mercs, probably—experienced but not exceptional, and used to fighting other mercs or disorganized pirates that mostly preyed on free traders.

Question was, where to go from here? *Fool's Paradise* was in fact more than it seemed—it was an old blockade runner, and although it didn't look like it, its engines could actually get it up to quite a clip at full burn. The light armament was original—it kept the weight down, as did a number of other design features of the ship. Initially Harding had planned to figure out what they were up against, find a ship beacon and some other parameters that could be locked onto, and get away. C6W wasn't about to come to his aid at the moment—but an anonymous tip of a pirate in the area and a tracking key for finding them could initiate a much better-armed and equipped search than almost any trader could afford to start. Midluk had channels for getting that info out.

That had been the theory, anyway. Harding hadn't counted on a ship quite that intimidating. First, he would never get out of range of the full complement of weapons aboard it, no matter how quickly he spun up the engines. Second, even if by some miracle he did, he actually misdoubted the ability of first-line C6W ships to go toe-to-toe with that ship. They would be sufficient for normal pirates, but this was not a normal pirate. And by the time they mobilized the cavalry, the captain would know he'd been made and be on his way to greener pastures.

That left just one choice.

Harding grabbed a couple of things off of the explosive expert's body and climbed into the ship that the men had used to bore into the side of the *Fool's Paradise*. With a couple of deft taps, he interfaced with the raiding ship. After all, it had to have a way of returning back to its home ship once it was finished.

As the airlock at the front closed and the borer disengaged, Harding smiled to himself. Time to play against the pirates at their own game—kill a man, steal his ship.

The raiding vessel navigated itself methodically back to the mothership and landed in a vac-bay on the side. It lowered into place and, using large electromagnets, aligned and docked. Harding didn't waste any time, arming one of the mines he had stolen and erupting through the door as it opened, a conventional pistol he'd brought with him raised.

He had tempo. The welcoming party was emerging onto the deck from a crew airlock as he burst forth. He tossed the armed grenade and got in cover behind the raiding vessel. He waited until he felt the floor rattle from the shrapnel and hot gas hitting the deck with force, then rolled his body smartly out of cover and began picking off targets. Hotshots lost lethality with distance, just like lasers, but a metal slug, unimpeded by air resistance and unswerved by gravity, could be quite deadly in space.

There were just twelve men out of probably twice that many still standing when Harding emerged from cover. With deadly accuracy, he picked off the six most alert ones as he closed the distance. He ducked behind a set of cargo containers, holstered the pistol, armed another grenade, and waited for a breath while pulling out a fresh hotshot. Then he tossed the grenade from the left side of the container. Quickly, he rolled to the right and got another man in the head as he watched the grenade. He ducked back behind cover, and the grenade exploded. The same instant, Harding blind fired—accurately, as it turned out— over the top of the cargo container into a man who had run toward his cover position to get away from the grenade, slid behind the thin end of the cargo container, and shot a man flanking him from what had been his left, then dived prone and shot a third survivor as he made a break for the doors. He looked at the sprawled figures on the deck, picked out two and shot them both in the head. One of them started to rise as Harding aimed, only to find out the hard way that the opossum gambit had not worked out.

Harding pulled out a knife. The edge came to life, glowing brilliant purple-white. He cut easily through the suit and into the arm of one of the men on the deck, exposing a small device implanted in his flesh. Walking to the doors, he pulled open a small compartment on his arm computer. He placed the chip inside and flipped a small lever with his finger. A coverplate closed on the chip, and metal pins were driven into it at key positions in the process, allowing the device to interact with it.

Harding closed the device with the chip inside and ran his arm by the airlock's reader. The door opened.

As the inner airlock door opened, he was presented with an empty hallway. Hotshot drawn, he shot the wall in a very specific location near the closed airlock. Then, he opened his helmet. The faceplate flipped down flush with his chest, and the upper portion retracted behind his head in one smooth motion. Suddenly, over the speakers, there came a voice.

"Well, well, brother. I thought I recognized the fighting style. What brings you to my humble abode?"

Harding looked up at a nearby camera and shrugged.

"Strictly business. I guess I shouldn't be surprised. What series are you?"

"Emperors. Augustus Vaxel. You?"

"Harding Vaxel. I don't believe I've had the pleasure."

"No, but I may dimly recall you killing off Napoleon in one of Daddy's little games a few years back."

Harding shrugged. "Could be. I don't keep track anymore."

"Nor do I, to be honest. Back to business?"

"By all means."

Doors opened all the way down the hallway, and armed men began pouring out.

Five minutes and thirty-one seconds later, Harding was in a side-room, ankle-deep in corpses, and the remaining guards were hiding around various corners, taking potshots into the hallway in the hopes he'd stick his head out. Both his original burners were discarded, his pistol was empty, the remainder of his stolen grenades were expended along with all but one of his the door-breaching charges, and he was breathing heavily.

"That was impressive, I'll grant you. But this isn't going to do you any good, Harding," said the speakers.

"Mm?" said Harding. There was a distant whooshing sound. Harding flipped his helmet closed and grabbed onto a locker. There were a few moments of high wind, and then the hallway was empty.

Harding patched into comms via his own ship outside, and from there, communicated with the bridge.

"Looks like you were trying for some poetic justice, hm?"

He stepped out of cover. Guards who had been caught without suits were floundering in the airless hall. He shook his head.

"You know—I didn't want to be trapped, so my door was blasted to stay open. But theirs weren't. You could have saved them." There was a trace of emotion in his voice for the first time. He started back up for the bridge.

"Given the underperformance in certain areas of my workforce I decided to do a little headcount reduction. Anyway, what do you care? You killed dozens of my men."

Harding mounted a ladder and swarmed up it with ease.

"True, but I didn't kill dozens of *my* men. That's bad practice."

He emerged at the top.

"Heaven forefend. But maybe worry less about them than yourself. Wanna know a little secret?"

Harding came to a huge set of bulkhead doors faced in material so black it looked like a hole. The plating extended several feet into the surrounding hallway.

"Well, well, you've got paramatter riot doors."

"Yes I do. Even I probably couldn't breach these. Not even if I could turn the *Cutthroat*'s guns on itself. And the life support is still providing oxygen to my portion of the ship. Now, yours, that's another story. And incidentally—"

There was a thirty-second series of dull thumps as

the ship's cannons fired. There was a burst of static and crackling over the speaker relay.

"How unfortunate—looks like you're stuck here. Mysteriously, your ship seems to have been cut in half. Don't worry, though, I spared your comm uplink so we could share this very special moment. How's that oxygen supply looking?"

"Honestly, I'm surprised you only just got around to doing that."

"Now, I know what you're thinking. A lingering death by suffocation sounds boring. The good news is, I have reinforcements back at base. They'll be here in a few minutes, and then you'll have something to keep you busy while you wait to suffocate. Who knows, one might get lucky and kill you. Although then again—"

A turret dropped down from the ceiling and began strafing the area with hotshot bolts. Harding dived for the ladder.

"—a more personalized mercy killing isn't off the table. If at any time it's all a bit much for you, feel free to get near the automated defense turrets."

"Not likely," said Harding, as he slid down the ladder.

"Hey, a boy can dream."

It wasn't, Harding reflected, the best situation he'd been in. His ship's weapons, if he could access them and power them, still probably couldn't dent the *Cutthroat*. He had access to comms, but even if he could report exactly what the C6W needed to know in a way that would convince them to send the kind of firepower necessary, they'd be likely to kill both of them. Augustus knew that. He had reason to be confident. His position seemed unassailable.

Although—an idea began to form in Harding's

mind—perhaps the key wasn't to attack his position successfully, but to turn it from an untouchable defensive position into an indefinite siege.

He had a plan.

He hit the bottom of the ladder and rolled, ducking into a room off the side of the hallway and getting behind cover there as another automatic turret took a potshot from inside the room. He tapped his arm computer. *Fool's Paradise* still had functional scanners—he could use that. He brought up the schematics and tapped to bring up a 3D projection in his visor.

The bridge was, sure enough, impenetrable. The sensors couldn't even get through the paramatter shielding it so that was all he could ascertain. But density scans revealed another interesting fact—the decking between engineering and the crew quarters was standard thickness, and while the rooms themselves were well-guarded with turrets, the maintenance tubes were not.

Harding took a pair of hotshots off of guards that had asphyxiated near the door, and slung one over his back. These were military-grade hotshots, Thermalyte G-14s, differentiated from the commonly sold G-12 civilian models mostly by the fact that you could run them over with a tank and still probably fire effectively. This was useful but quadrupled the cost, which the average being in most systems—not encountering many tanks on a daily basis—usually didn't go for.

One interesting, we-swear-it-wasn't-intentional-honest aspect of the design by Thermalyte was that, where the civilian models spread the wiring out across the weapon's body, the military models had one particularly well-armored "node" on the side and ran multiple redundant wires out to key parts that needed coordinating. This meant that if you had the right tool—and people like Harding kept one handy—you could open the compartment, at which point you could do things like override the pulse limiter. It took only a few simple snips of key wires and twisting together one particular pair, which Harding now did to the second gun. He looked at the schematic of the room on his arm, worked out the angle to fire at the turret, and poked his head up long enough to take one lightning quick shot. The gun fired a massively powerful bolt, ionizing the air in front of Harding such that the explosion knocked him back into the wall with force. This would probably have been okay, if the energy wasn't channeled through the much smaller surface area of the gun on his back. He felt his shoulder pop and grimaced. But the turret, which normally would laugh off a hotshot blast no problem, had it much worse. The beam of thermal energy was so intense as to reduce it to molten slag. Harding crawled across the now-exposed gap to the maintenance chute and pulled himself inside, favoring his injured arm.

"Heading into the maintenance tunnels, eh? That'll be a bit annoying for my men," said Augustus.

"Wanted a change of scenery," Harding said, gritting his teeth against the pain as he crawled toward the crew quarters.

"Remind me to install some cameras in those on my next ship."

"Your engineers probably won't like that. You'd be amazed what they can get up to in here."

"Well, in the meantime, how about we make this more interesting?"

There was a click at the nearest maintenance hatch. Harding pushed on it experimentally. It wouldn't budge.

"You installed locks?"

"Well, these'd be a bit of a security risk otherwise. No telling who might use them to sneak around. You'll also find that the access panels are locked shut, in case you had some brilliant plan involving them."

Harding cursed, very convincingly, he thought. Augustus seemed to only half buy it, but lapsed into silence while he waited for Harding's next move.

At last, Harding reached the appropriate maintenance hatch. He looked at his modified burner. He needed something a little more violent and a little less hot if he was going to get through this. He didn't fancy crawling through molten metal. But still, it would be best if it was directed, or else it would be no better than setting off the mine in here, and he'd probably end up cooked. So, let's see—if you were field-stripping this, you might remove the focusing tube, and it should still fire, Harding thought to himself. Now if you tweaked the length of the pulse down, you'd probably melt all the internal wiring as it handled the energy load, but then again, if the pulse was short enough, it only needed to sustain it for a fraction of a second. And now—

He arranged himself carefully relative to the maintenance hatch, lined up the gun, and after a second of hesitation, fired. The gun truly walloped him, driving him straight back into the wall and knocking his shoulder again. He let out a long, soundless stream of air. The burst of undirected, high temperature, high pressure air didn't quite ionize the air this time, but the pressure wave knocked the hatch off its hinges. He dropped the oven-hot gun full of fused wiring, limply worked the remaining breaching grenade out, and armed it.

"You're just full of surprises, aren't you?"

"Oh, the best is yet to come," said Harding, jaw tensed.

He tossed the breaching charge, and rolled behind the corner in the maintenance tunnel. The charge exploded, leaving a person-sized hole in the floor.

Harding leapt out of the maintenance tunnel and into the hole in the floor just outside. And promptly dropped about fifteen feet onto the bulkhead below. On the up side, he was able to roll. On the downside, what he rolled on was his injured arm, which finally managed to pop it all the way out of its socket.

The engineering deck looked grim. There had only been a couple of engineers aboard—not unusual on smaller ships—but they weren't essential unless something went wrong, and Augustus either knew that or was uncharacteristically reckless. They'd suffered the same fate as the guards.

"Oh, here's some interesting news, Harding. I see that my reinforcements have arrived. I'll just let them know you're in the engine room, shall I?"

Good, he's distracted, Harding thought.

He only had a few seconds. He limped to a computer terminal and interfaced with it. The navigation screen came up. He selected his target on his arm computer, which translated it directly into engine maneuvers to be performed based on the ship's location and position sensors. He programmed the sublight engines for full burn and engaged. The chip from a recently deceased engineer who had collapsed at his terminal authorized the maneuvers. Then, he wheeled around—rocking sideways

as the ship's engines turned to face their destination—
and pulled open a panel behind him with his good arm.
Sooner or later, everything came down to connections.
A captain might nominally have total control over his
ship, but if the wires between the bridge and the engine
room were cut, then all the software overrides in the
world wouldn't save them. Harding pulled out his knife
and made quick work of these. Then, for good measure,
he went to the console and cut the wires inside that.

The ship finished turning into position, and then
engaged sublight thrusters. Harding went tumbling
across the floor until he wound up rolling against the
wall. He struggled upright, took one deep breath, and
broke into a run. He couldn't slow down. He had an
idea how the next two minutes were going to play out.
He needed to get into the security office.

"Okay, damn it, you've got me, Harding. I can't
shut it off. Where are you taking us?"

The radio was crackling. The *Fool's Paradise* was
quickly receding behind them.

"Oh, just a little place called Hastings, in the Thratian Compact's space. I seem to recall that they have
some pretty stiff fines for piracy, dealing contraband—
pretty rough, and that's if you *can* pay them."

"Oh, I'm quaking. Only not very much, because my
men and I can simply walk down there and override
the engines in person, and you—"

All the doors snapped shut. Harding was locked
in the office.

"—are going to get to sit by and watch. And don't
bother trying to open that door. The late Jack Landall,
whose chip you stole, no longer has permission to do
so. Now, you do give me an idea, though. After all

the damage you've caused to my ship, maybe we'll send *your* body to the Compact for the bounty. I bet you've done a bit of black market trading yourself."

Harding started to shrug, barely stopping in time to avoid agony.

"You can certainly try. I'll be ready."

"Oh, I see. That's why you're in the security office instead of heading directly back to the escape pods. Not up to a fight, all of a sudden? Shoulder bother you, perhaps? You look like you're favoring it."

Harding lifted the hotshot in his off-hand and shot the camera in the security office.

"Temper, temper. I bet you think you can control the active defenses from there. Very sorry to break the news, Harding, but I had those controls re-wired so that that is the Captain's privilege alone. Like so many things on this ship, it's a small precaution against the lack of honor among thieves. See you soon!" He laughed through the static.

At the last moment, Harding sent one last signal to *Fool's Paradise*, activating the distress beacon, and switched off his comms. They'd be useless in a moment anyway.

As it happened, the turrets had not been his objective at all. He guessed that Augustus's first move was going to be to override the doors, and that permissions would be pulled off his stolen chip, rendering it useless. But what the security office almost certainly could do was print a new chip for someone, provided they could prove they were who they said.

By coincidence, Harding could "prove" that he was Augustus.

There were probably only a few base-pairs different

between the two of them, and security offices used DNA validation methods. Ironically, the methods were so good that they had to have built-in tolerance for minor mutations caused by random UV rays and oxidative damage. On most commercial units, the tolerances allowed for the minor changes between the clones in the President and Emperor Series.

A small device extruded into which he placed his finger. It took a tiny skin biopsy and paused for a moment to process. A moment later, it made a small bell tone and authorized printing of a new copy of Augustus's chip. Harding quickly exchanged it for the chip in his arm computer.

He had access to doors again. And Augustus and his men weren't here yet.

The escape pods were actually slightly fore of the engine room, with a short hall in between them that anyone not blowing a hole in the ceiling would have to traverse.

Harding quickly slipped into the escape pod room.

He didn't dare open the escape pod itself just yet. On most ships, in the interest of ensuring complete evacuation, all the alarms would go off the moment it was opened. Instead, he queried for remote signals. And sure enough, he struck gold. The escape pod had a small independent guidance computer that had remote-access capabilities for the purpose of allowing larger stations or ships to help it navigate in, which wasn't unusual on small vessels. The ship would allow him to warm up the engines and engage various systems without actually opening the doors. He was just finishing doing this, and prepping to open the doors, run inside, finalize undocking, and escape, when the door burst open.

The boy who attacked him was his spitting image—about fourteen, jet black hair, black eyes, mildly tanned from having engineered radio-protective proteins in the skin in addition to melanin.

Augustus smiled cruelly.

"One of my scouts reported back that the security office was empty. Tricky."

Harding dived to the side and shot some of the supporting men behind Augustus, who were already leveling their hotshots. Harding took up residence behind a control console.

He heard a click. An object went flying overhead. Something much more ingrained than mere thought caused him to swing his hotshot vertically upward like a racket, and bounce the incoming grenade right back in the direction it had come from. There was a sudden scuffle and a babble of panicked voices. A wave of nausea hit him as the sudden, violent movement of his shoulder on instinct caught up with him.

There was an explosion behind him.

Harding rounded the corner, hotshot at the ready. The tight scrum of men had been thinned out significantly. Those that hadn't been killed had dived in all directions, some in, some out of the pod. He was suddenly wrenched to the side. Augustus had grabbed Harding's hotshot, and with one movement pulled it out of his weakened grip. Harding swept his legs out from under him. Augustus caught himself on his free hand while falling and made to roll upright, but Harding kicked him in the head as he flipped over, then knocked the stolen hotshot out of his hands while he was recovering from the blow. But before Augustus could draw another weapon, Harding ducked instinctively sideways as a bolt of energy shot from behind him, right through where his head had been. One of Augustus's men was still feeling lucid enough to fight, evidently. He rounded and kicked the stunned merc so hard in the jaw that he toppled over backward, then dived for the hotshot, avoiding a shot that Augustus had just taken at him. He grabbed the hotshot, and he and Augustus were suddenly both aiming at each other, Augustus half crouching, Harding laying prone with the hotshot raised.

Harding stood upright, shakily.

"Terran stand-off. I suppose it was always going to come to this."

"Your men need to learn a little discipline with explosives in enclosed spaces. Those of them still in a state to learn anything, that is."

Augustus quirked an eyebrow and grinned, the same roguish grin as Harding when he was up to something.

"To be fair, I kept my best men on my ship *with me*," he sighed heavily, "but what they lack in discipline, they make up for in disposability."

The two were just a couple of feet apart. Harding had well above human reaction speed, but nothing was fast enough for this. And sure enough, Augustus rushed him and held him up against the wall, hotshot against hotshot, barrels both pointed at the ceiling. Augustus gritted his teeth and pressed to the side slightly, and Harding's shoulder gave way.

Augustus held Harding at hotshot-point while Harding nursed his injured arm.

"You're getting soft, Harding. You don't have what it takes for this business anymore. Now sit quietly. You're probably worth more alive than dead, but only if you don't make too much work for me."

Augustus stepped back and scanned his chip to open the doors to the escape pod. Sure enough, alarms started going off.

The "pod" was actually a small independent vessel, capable of packing about a hundred people in space suits into tubes. There was a low ceiling that you could walk under while ducking, and then a ten by ten array of tubes on the floor you could open and drop into. Once inside, the tube would interface with the suits, and predesigned ports would allow the suits themselves to start an IV by taking over their auto-med capabilities. Occupants would be heavily sedated to reduce metabolic and oxygen use, and from then on it was the job of the pilot and copilot alone to navigate to help.

Harding subtly rotated the arm he was nursing so the computer on it was down toward his fingers.

"Get moving. We'll pack you into one of the sleep tubes until we figure out how to disengage the engines. With any luck, the local authorities haven't noticed us yet."

Harding smiled.

His finger pressed the button. The door closed, suddenly. There was a dull thump as the last engaged lock let loose. The escape pod fired itself off into space.

Augustus looked momentarily stunned.

"The thing about escape pods," said Harding, calmly, "is that they're designed around being found. Unless you did something ill-advised to the emergency transponder, I would guess that it's equipped with a distress signal that's making quite a radio-frequency ruckus. Which, of course, you would want, if you were stranded in deep space alone with dwindling air and a hundred sleeping crew."

"You—appreciate, I hope, that the only reason I haven't killed you yet is I'm trying to work out if there's a way to use you to improve my position," said Augustus.

He looked at Harding thoughtfully.

"You know—I still have a small vessel that my backup arrived on. I can take that. You—you can take the fall. Yes. Heck, maybe I'll pin both our records on you. Nobody can tell us apart physically, and they would have a hard time doing so genetically."

"How did you plan to get me to cooperate for that? Because, you know, if you kill me that's going to put a rather substantial question mark over the proceedings, and if you don't, first I can disagree with your story, and second, you'd need to figure out how to get me to stay still."

"Nobody is going to believe you. You're obviously trying to get out of responsibility for your crimes, Harding, or at least that's what my contacts will ensure the authorities think. As for how to get you to stay still—"

Augustus lunged with the butt of the hotshot, but Harding was still agile enough to dodge that. The two scuffled on the floor, hand to hand, each pressing for advantage. Augustus managed to get on top of his chest and knocked Harding's head against the deck, hard. Harding struggled through the blurring in his vision and ringing in his ears to punch Augustus in the throat. Augustus coughed and, sneering, grabbed Harding's shoulder and squeezed. Harding turned sideways and suppressed the urge to vomit.

And then suddenly, there was a bump.

✧   ✧   ✧

The purpose of a ship-net is to stop ships. How you stop something going at an appreciable fraction of the speed of light in a hurry, from outside, without killing all the occupants, took a great deal of engineering to work out. The solution turned out to be something like a stringline, or a time-space distortion drive, but in reverse. You dilated the space in front of the ship, and you compressed the space behind it. Put in less technical terms, you put more road in front of the ship than behind it. The downside of this approach is that it requires a massive expenditure of energy, a great deal of paramatter, and very advanced technology. All of which, as any ship engineer will tell you, boils down to one common element—obscene amounts of money.

Well, the Thratian Compact had money. It didn't collect taxes, per se, but in the space it operated in, it agreed to provide infrastructure support, protection from piracy, emergency recovery services, and many other things, at a pre-arranged, contractually established price. As the Compact worlds were a popular place to trade these days, the price of these services had gotten fairly expensive, and hence all the many wonderful things the galaxy could sell, it could buy. It also meant that, to ensure people continued ponying up these prices instead of finding outside solutions, their response time had to be very good.

The subjective experience of suddenly being caught in a ship-net was distinctive. The "net" itself was a small ship launched and designed to keep pace with your ship, attach to it, and then to essentially override your drive with its own reverse-oriented drive. So the first thing you experienced when it attached was a substantial bump as it latched onto your cargo bay. If you were currently straddling someone and threatening to knock them unconscious, it might be such a substantial bump as to toss you into the ceiling.

The next thing you experienced, as soon as your ship was safely caught, was the sound of people flooding through any available bays, because the Compact didn't like to let pirates sit around and think of ways to get out of their current predicament.

When Augustus came to, he was being restrained by armed guards. Puzzlement crossed his face as he realized that Harding was still there, talking quietly with the captain.

"Arrest—arrest that boy," he said weakly, trying to shake off the restraints.

Harding turned and gave the characteristic devilish grin that ran in the family.

The captain turned to Augustus.

"I think you'll find that Mr. Vaxel is a citizen in good standing, as of thirty-one terra-rotes ago when he contacted one of our brokers to pay his—rather substantial—debts in full."

"Wha—what?"

"Whereas *you* appear to have been engaging in stringline disruption and piracy. And a number of other potential charges pending a full investigation. I don't know what the final bounty will be, but I'd place it at eleven million, seven hundred and sixty thousand GalBlue, probably about ten times that if your credits are in GalGreen."

"Oh, no, he's not—he was piloting a ship named *Fool's Paradise*. It was full of—"

"Essential and legal medical supplies needed in

Lapis for the epidemic this year. We responded to its distress signal."

Augustus blinked.

"In what—he was riding a third party stringline. Nobody does that to carry medicine!"

"What, just because I'm turning my life around means I can't take a shortcut? The stringline itself isn't actually illegal—well, the portion of it in Compact space isn't, and that's where *Fool's Paradise* was found."

"You rotten—I bet you don't have a trading license! Nobody will buy from you."

"I'm partnered with another person who does have a trading license. It's just a simple point-to-point pick-up and drop-off, since his own fleet is terribly busy." Harding was lying, but he and Midluk had ensured the lie would hold up if investigated.

"I feel we're straying from the point—sir, can you pay your bounty at this time? We accept all major currencies. I'm happy to take down an account number." The captain brandished a small tablet.

"I—" Augustus stared at Harding, in mute disbelief.

"Well, in that case, we'll be happy to accommodate you until you can speak to a banker and line up some loans."

The constable stepped smartly forward, injected something into Augustus's neck, and he promptly passed out again.

Augustus did not, as it happened, have the credits, or the credit, to pay his debt. Unfortunately for him, the Counsel of Six Worlds, once they were notified by a certain party that he was in custody, were all too happy to pay it themselves. They had an ongoing business relationship with the Compact to help reduce piracy, especially if traders in their own territory complained about the pirate in question. The Counsel's sentence for piracy was eventual death; the exact parameters of same depended on how bored the local councilor was feeling.

Harding, as it turned out, was due a substantial portion of that bounty for actions that had helped lead to the capture of the notorious pirate. Augustus had apparently been less than discriminate, and had targeted free-traders as well as smugglers. The Compact and Counsel had differing opinions on the latter, but could agree firmly on the former. That was before the various other men aboard the ship were tallied.

Harding certainly wasn't going to complain. He'd spent nearly his last penny clearing his name in every system where his name could be cleared with money. Just like that, he was a newly minted honest trader. Unfortunately he was also a poor one. Until free-trading started paying the bills, he was going to need something to live on. Also, he was going to need a ship. As it happened, the ship of a local, notorious pirate had been impounded and put up for auction—a ship named *The Cutthroat*. Since it went up for sale in the Compact, the black-market gear wasn't stripped out of it, though a substantial disclaimer was put on it warning that about half the ship would have to be removed to fly it legally almost anywhere outside the Compact. Harding got it for a song.

As he sat for the first time at the console, there was a brief feeling that finally things were going right. He was bigger than his father's legacy, maybe for the first time in his life. This wasn't the first of his brothers he'd had a hand in killing, but it was the first time he'd done it legally.

And Midluk had come through on his promise. There was a station called *Mercurial Artifice*, whose exact location was a secret, but it housed an old trading school named Shipstone's—and Midluk knew a faculty member who owed him a favor.

Now the screen, like the future, lay before him—full of potential, but ultimately blank. He was completing applications to re-register the ship under a new name. It was required by law in order to captain an ex-pirate vessel, in a large enough subset of regions not to be worth arguing with. Mostly, to minimize the risk of shooting a free-trader.

A piece of ancient history occurred to him. In a way, both ship and station were part of a new beginning. It only made sense to tie them together. The perfect name occurred to him. He typed it and submitted it.

"Kill a man, take his ship, that's the—businessman's way."

Said the now-captain helming *The Da Vinci*, perhaps the most heavily armed future free-trader in all of the Thratian Compact.

⚔

Sarah A. Hoyt won the Prometheus Award for her novel *Darkship Thieves*, published by Baen, and has also authored *Darkship Renegades* (nominated for the following year's Prometheus Award) and *A Few Good Men*, as well as *Through Fire* and *Darkship Revenge*, novels set in the same universe. She has written numerous short stories and novels in science fiction, fantasy, mystery, historical novels and genre-straddling historical mysteries, many under a number of pseudonyms, and has been published in *Analog*, *Asimov's* and *Amazing Stories*. For Baen, she has also written three books in her popular shape-shifter fantasy series, *Draw One in the Dark*, *Gentleman Takes a Chance*, and *Noah's Boy*. Her *According to Hoyt* is one of the most outspoken and fascinating blogs on the internet, as is her Facebook group, *Sarah's Diner*. Originally from Portugal, she lives in Colorado with her husband, two sons and "the surfeit of cats necessary to a die-hard Heinlein fan."

Robert A. Hoyt was professionally published at fourteen, with a short story in a DAW anthology. Since then he's published several short stories and a novel, *Cat's Paw*. While slightly hampered by college and graduate school, he's back to writing and hard at work on a fantasy series, as well as a collaboration with Sarah A. Hoyt on a series of pulp novels in the same universe (Orphan Stars) as *Trading Up*. So look for good things from him in the future.

Breaking News
Regarding Space Pirates

Brian Trent

A space pirate "just doesn't get no respect," even after she's retired and gone straight, and when a very wealthy art collector has treasures missing from his vault full of priceless (and not always legally acquired) art objects, the cops say "yessir," and drag her to the scene of the crime. Where she ends up solving a locked room mystery, and also gives a double meaning to the story's sneaky title.

~~~

An hour ago, *Sagacious Bay Police Depart-ment* officials confirmed that AztecSky CFO Bradley Winterfig's private vault—long-championed to be the most secure in the solar system—has indeed been cracked by persons unknown. According to the state-ment viewable here, several items from Winterfig's personal collection were vandal-ized or stolen outright, making this the first known high-profile heist in Osirian history.

*The investigation appears to be proceeding
swiftly, as Sagacious Bay police are at this
very moment bringing a person of interest
to the scene of the crime.*

The colony soldiers were also the colony police, an
arrangement Jolene Fort had never cared for on other
worlds. She especially didn't like it now, as she was
forcibly escorted from *Olena's Oyster Bar* and into
the SBPD hovercar, then flown up to a docking ring
on the local S-E. Already pining for the oysters she
hadn't had a chance to sample, Fort endured the
low-g climb as a newscopter drone continually buzzed
them, shining its bright lights onto the windows to try
catching a glimpse of the mysterious passenger. The
hovercar crawled up the ladder, changed tracks, and
continued ascending to the private vault of Bradley
Winterfig.

The man himself was already there, sitting on the
ceiling.

"Jolene Fort!" Winterfig boomed as she crossed the
threshold of the airlock.

"I am," she said awkwardly, staring in astonishment at the man above her. Winterfig was the largest
specimen of humanity she had ever seen, and that
included Martian trogs and deepworld pit-fighters.
He was a massive golem of flesh clad in a flexmetal
suit-jacket and ruby-studded tie. By contrast, Jolene
was tall, slender, ebony-skinned, and wearing simple
cargo pants and a pale, sleeveless top.

An SBPD officer escorted her up along the wall to
where the massive man awaited her. A skylight interrupted the otherwise unmarred ceiling; presumably, it

was constructed of reinforced glasstic, because Jolene could see the blackness of space and Osiris's single, ringed moon.

"Sit down, please," the officer said, the holobadge displaying from her crisp black uniform as PRVT CIPRIANO. Jolene complied, adopting a Lotus-style posture across from the vault's famous owner. The skylight formed a glassy pyramid between them.

"How did you do it?" Winterfig demanded, glowering out at her from bushy black eyebrows and a staggering beard. "How did you rob my vault?"

Jolene raised an eyebrow. "I didn't rob your vault."

"You, ma'am, are a space pirate!"

"Was a pirate," Fort said with a sigh. "That was a long time ago. I gave up on all that before I left Sol system." She gazed around the vault, craning her neck to take it all in. "This is nice, Bradley."

It was, she had to admit, *very* nice.

The walls were plastered with paintings, garlanded with holocubes, and hung with rare artifacts ranging from scraps of Ashokan rockships to Martian war glass. The suits of armor ran from feudal Japanese samurai to modern IPC praetorian. There were bone masks and diamond visors. Arrowheads and buckeyballs. There were suspension discs containing vellum scrolls and ancient video game cartridges. It represented a mind-bending variety, though Jolene began to wonder if this wasn't so much a diverse historical museum as a mad hoarder's closet.

The mad hoarder addressed the cop. "Where did you find her?"

"At *Olena's Oyster Bar*."

"Did she come quietly?"

"No," replied Officer Cipriano. "She kept complaining that she hadn't sampled the oysters yet."

Fort shrugged. "They take thirty years to reach peak maturity. I'd rather not wait until the next time they're in season."

Winterfig leaned forward, rubbing his huge hands. "Jolene Fort, I'm going to ask you plain: How did you break into my vault? Where are the companions who helped you? And what have you done with the stolen treasures?"

Fort blinked her surprise. "Stolen treasures? How would you even know in all this mess?"

"Inventory!" the man shouted, and a classical podium grew out of the pewter-colored ceiling. The microfab arranged itself into a scroll that flowered open. A lengthy list of items appeared in black text on the surface, but several displayed in alarmingly scarlet font.

"Your companions stole the following items," the man said, and began to read.

> *Winterfig's collection is considered to be the largest private art collection in IPCnet, rivaling museums outside of Sol. While the full extent of his collection is not known, those pieces he has revealed in holo-tours cover approximately six thousand years of recorded history, from as far back as the Assyrian Empire to as recent as the Partisan War. Winterfig has declined to reveal precisely what items were stolen or damaged in the heist, except that they were "rare artworks"* . . .

Jolene Fort patiently listened to the astounding list of missing artifacts. "You know," she said in the pause that followed, "you could have just emailed that list to me planetside, Bradley, and asked if I knew anything."

"I shall pay handsomely for the return of these items," Winterfig said, ignoring this.

"Not that I couldn't use the money, but I haven't the foggiest idea where they are."

"You're a space pirate!"

Jolene shook her head, realizing that even across decades and light-years and new identities, she was apparently destined to have the same conversation, a Möbius strip of karmic causality with only the merest of provincial variations. "I *was* a pirate, sure. People change, Bradley. I'm now a respectable member of society."

Winterfig blasted out a sound that might have been a laugh in the more brutish periods of human history. "Respectable! Ha! I spit on your 'respectable' reputation!"

Fort shrugged and said, somewhat defensively, "Well, *some* people like me."

"How did your cohorts break in?"

"I don't have 'cohorts' anymore." She looked thoughtfully at some of the debris that floated in the air around them, and at the chunks of terracotta littering the floor and walls. It looked like the aftermath of an explosion, as opposed to the disheveled detritus from a heist. "Were there any breaches?" she asked.

Winterfig jabbed a finger at the skylight pyramid between them. "*This* skylight was shattered, before the blister membrane healed over the damage. But my vault AI confirmed that the skylight was shattered *outward.* Meaning that your thieving band *escaped* this way, but they didn't *enter* this way!"

"Is that a Martian mummy?" Fort asked, squinting at a desiccated body in a tattered spacesuit. "I know someone who would be very interested in learning you have illegal redworld artifacts here."

For a large fellow, Winterfig moved with impressive speed. One of his hands thrust out to seize her by the shirt. "Are you threatening me, you out-system scum?"

Officer Cipriano separated them. "Let's keep our hands off the suspect, okay?"

"Suspect! Ha! I spit on that! She's a *known space pirate.*"

Fort asked, "Don't you have cameras in here, Bradley? Maybe they could shed some light on what happened."

Winterfig touched the microfab podium again. Its surface lit and displayed a time-stamped video of the vault interior. The video began to play.

In the video, a large terracotta statue of an ancient warlord stood below them, where none existed now.

Fort watched the unchanging video for about a minute, and then asked, "Is anything going to happen?"

"It already happened!" Winterfig rewound the recording, and then slowed its progression to a frame-by-frame advancement. In one frame, something like a ghostly insect crawled over the camera-lens; at regular speed, it hadn't been visible.

Winterfig pulled something from his shirt pocket. There, on his palm, was a glassy insect.

"An airhound," the man boomed. "Fitted with camera and display-jack. Somehow it got inside my vault, made a visual sweep of the environment, and then positioned itself over my cameras with a static image, fooling the

AI into thinking nothing was happening while the burglars were able to go about their business undetected."

"Clever." Fort stood and began to pace around the ceiling, passing through a cloud of hovering debris that clinked against her clothing. "I think it's pretty obvious how the burglars got in. They smuggled themselves inside the terracotta warlord statue."

"Impossible!" Winterfig screamed, waving his arms around in fury, scattering floating rocks in every direction. "That statue was brought here a month ago."

Fort held out her hands as if trying to reason with a thick-headed child. "So? Did you never hear of suspended animation?"

Officer Cipriano interrupted, "Are you suggesting that the thieves smuggled themselves into a statue, then waited a month to dispatch the airhound and break out? Why would they do that?"

Fort rubbed her chin. "Last month was Mr. Winterfig's birthday, and it was heavily publicized that he celebrated right here, in his vault, entertaining various glitterati for several days. You received a lot of gifts from various sycophants, and I'm guessing one of those gifts was that statue." When he said nothing, she nodded. "That's what I thought. Your parties are known to last for weeks, so the thieves would have had to wait it out. Their suspension capsules waited inside the statue, likely with a simple monitoring array that would awaken them once a certain period of inactivity suggested the coast was clear. Only then would they have dispatched the airhound, cracked open the statue from the inside, and gone to work."

The officer frowned. "You seem to know an awful lot about this."

Jolene smiled bleakly. "*When* I was a pirate, I used that technique myself. *Allegedly*, it would have worked to get aboard the Prometheus Industries Jovian Spin Tower on Olympus Mons. Hey, Bradley—"

"It's Mister Winterfig!"

"You said that *some* things were stolen...and *some* things were vandalized. I've just explained how your statue was destroyed. Was that all?"

"No, that wasn't all." He pointed to an immense, violet-hued painting glowing faintly on the wall directly across from them. It depicted some kind of exotic landscape, rendered in extremely thick, bulging layers of radiant purples, indigos, and dusky violets. Jolene imagined it might have been beautiful at one time, but someone had indeed ruined it: the center of the painting had been gouged out, leaving an empty crater and a messy splatter-effect around the absence.

"The thieves ruined this painting!" Winterfig protested. "It was priceless! It was beautiful! It was—"

"Illegal," Jolene said, nodding.

Officer Cipriano blinked in confusion. "Illegal? Why?"

The former space pirate swallowed uncomfortably. "Because it's a Grelk painting," she said softly.

> Winterfig himself has come under criticism over the years, with several museums and historians charging that "historical artifacts are not for furnishing one man's private den." Several watchdog organizations have accused him of shady dealings, including the illegal procurement of artifacts through smuggler channels. There have even been

> persistent rumors that Winterfig is a key
> figure in the bio-art black market, trading
> in works made from rare and alien species
> such as those found on the DeGuzman
> comet cluster native to Ra System.

"Do you have any water?" Jolene Fort asked, rubbing her throat. "Damn me, it's dry in here."

Winterfig gave a withering glare. "Of course it's dry. Moisture is the enemy of art."

"I thought *you* were the enemy of art."

"*What was that?!*"

Jolene Fort turned to the police officer. "Some water, please? Seriously, it's the least you can do after denying me those oysters."

"Don't give her anything to drink until she's cooperated," Winterfig decreed.

Officer Cipriano flushed angrily. "Mr. Winterfig, I don't take orders from you. Besides, she does seem to be cooperating. And she's right; it *is* very dry in here." The cop removed a small canteen from a utility pocket on her uniform and handed it to Fort.

Fort unscrewed the cap and took a deep swig of the bottle. Then, to everyone's surprise, she opened her mouth and a warbling tentacle of water emerged. In the low gravity, it formed a shivering glob in the air that slowly crept toward the far wall.

Winterfig screamed. He tore off his flex-metal suit jacket and captured the small globule, stuffing it like a magic ball into an expensive sleeve.

Fort gave a sheepish smile. "Okay, I think I know what happened, Bradley. But first, can you tell me *exactly* when the skylight shattered?"

"11:16 p.m. last night. Blister containment snapped shut over it within ten seconds."

Fort turned to Officer Cipriano. "Can you cross-reference that time with local spaceflight-traffic coming down the space elevator?"

The cop frowned. "I can, but if you're suggesting the thieves leapt through the skylight to land on a descending ship, that's ridiculous. Breaking that skylight resulted in explosive decompression. It wouldn't be like making a skydive—they would have been flung out into the atmosphere."

"I'm willing to bet that the skylight was broken outward the *very instant* a ship with very bright lights was coming down for a landing."

"I spit on what you think, Jolene Fort!" Winterfig stomped.

Officer Cipriano touched her ear. After a moment, she said with some astonishment, "Confirmed! A cargo shuttle came within sight of the vault around 11:16 p.m. last night. And that shuttle is in a repairbay right now, because according to the flight crew they collided with some unverified debris. Apparently, something smashed into their landing lights and blew apart one of the wingrotors."

Fort allowed herself a small smile. "I'd say the 'unverified debris' hitting the ship were the very thieves you're looking for. I think when the skylight shattered, they were blown out into the sky by the decompression and got sliced and diced on impact with the rotors."

Winterfig shook his bushy head. "You're saying they committed suicide? Why would they do that?"

"I don't think it was their choice. *They* didn't shatter

the skylight, but they were blown outside when it did shatter."

"Then who the hell shattered the skylight?"

Fort pointed. "See that Grelk painting? You can always tell a Grelk painting, because of its uniquely scintillating shade of purple."

"I know more about Grelk paintings than a pirate like you would ever—"

"Do you know what they're made of?"

Winterfig closed his massive mouth. "No."

Fort's eyes grew wide. "You have artwork but don't know its history?"

The police officer interrupted, obviously warming to the discussion. "Perhaps you could tell us, Jolene?"

The former space pirate nodded and began walking along the ceiling, then down the wall to where the immense painting stood. "I'm from Earth originally," she said, "And on Earth, there once was a shade of paint known as 'mummy brown.' This was a dark pigment derived from a very particular organic component. Specifically, it was achieved by grinding up old Egyptian mummies—ancient dead people—and used by artists." Fort squinted at the glowing canvas. "Well, Grelk paintings are also made with a unique color, known as 'Grelk purple,' and that's because they're derived from Grelk larvae, illegally obtained from comets."

Officer Cipriano glowered at the CFO. "Indeed?"

His face turned bright red. "I don't know what she's talking about."

Fort continued. "Pregnant Grelk deposit their eggs just below the surface of comets. When the eggs hatch into larvae, the little newborns go into a kind of torpor and remain buried in the ice until the comet makes its sunward approach. Then, the heat melts the ice, reactivating the larva. They immediately squirm into one big mass, and scan the skies for signs of their parents' bioluminescence. When they see a cluster of lights—as distinguished from the sun—it's typically the glowing bellies of Mommy and Daddy returning to the nesting place, so the larva erupt out of the ice, hurling toward their parents." She smiled at the thought. "It's actually kind of sweet, if you think about it. The little critters latch onto their parents' bellies, and the whole family flies back out to the DeGuzman Cluster, driven by the solar wind, to begin the cycle all over again."

Winterfig began an agitated pace around the vault. "Even if what you're saying is true—which I seriously doubt—I've had this painting for years! No Grelk larvae were squirming around in the paint! These canvases were as dry as everything else in here!"

"Sure. But remember that the crooks were in cryostorage. There's a lot of water in those things. When the statue broke apart to release the thieves, a lot of that water would have released with them. You saw how water behaves in low-gravity. If *any* of that water hit the Grelk painting, it would reactivate the larvae from torpor and..."

"Are you saying that these crooks were killed by *paint*?" the CFO cried.

Fort stuffed her hands into her pockets. "Yep."

For a moment everyone seemed to stare at everyone else, gauging the reaction. The beams of the orbiting newscopter drone made the skylight pyramid flare for a moment before it passed out of sight.

Slowly, everyone's eyes slid to the glowing purple painting, with the central gobs of paint curiously—even ominously—absent, as if it had gathered itself into a central mass and then erupted off the canvas. The dusky hues still looked wet, and bubbling, and suggestive of shadowy movement within the deep layers. In fact, Jolene thought, the ruined picture seemed to have changed even in the last few minutes, as if the darkest shades were balling up beneath the outer layers in response to something...

Winterfig marched over to the painting. "You expect me to believe that the thieves smuggled themselves into a statue, broke free of it when no one was looking, shed their cryostorage sleeves which splattered water into this painting, reawakening the alleged larvae inside, who then launched themselves off the canvas and through the skylight when they saw the brights of a passing ship, thinking it was their parents?!"

Jolene Fort nodded. "And in breaking the skylight, the explosive decompression would have caused the thieves—and any treasures not bolted down—to blow out into the sky. Case closed. Can I have some oysters, now?"

Officer Cipriano gasped. "It *does* match the evidence we've seen."

"Nonsense!" Winterfig roared. "Absolute nonsense woven by a clever space pirate! You think a painting is dangerous?"

Fort tensed, sensing the great man's next move. She grabbed Officer Cipriano's hand even as she entwined one leg around a bolted-down banister. "Um...Bradley? I really wouldn't do—"

"I spit on your theory, Jolene Fort!" Winterfig boomed. "I spit on it!"

Then he turned to the painting, and did exactly that.

> *The heist, not surprisingly, has been the talk of the entire planet and is fueling all sorts of odd reports. Case in point: a few minutes ago, our own newscopter drone in orbit around the vault experienced some kind of mechanical failure. Before crashing, it transmitted video of what really seems to be Bradley Winterfig himself flying straight into their windshield . . .*

Brian Trent's work regularly appears in *Analog, Fantasy & Science Fiction, The Year's Best Military and Adventure SF, Orson Scott Card's Intergalactic Medicine Show, Third Flatiron, Escape Pod, Galaxy's Edge,* and numerous year's best anthologies. The author of the recently published sci-fi novel *Ten Thousand Thunders,* Trent is also the 2019 recipient of the Readers' Choice Award from Baen Books. He lives in New England. Visit Trent's website at www.briantrent.com.

Teen Angel

R. Garcia y Robertson

*Deidre had been strikingly beautiful when still a child,
which was all that saved her life when space pirates on
a raid for slaves found her. Now eighteen, she recalls
how the slavers' leader told her he would never let her
go before preparing to do battle with the military fleet
closing in on the pirate base—and wonders if she will
finally be freed, or blown into glowing plasma along
with her captors.*

Deirdre of the Sorrows

"Here comes the Angel of Death." Deirdre heard
some thug say it in slaver slang as she stepped out
of the lock onto *Fafnir*'s E-deck. She fixed a smile
on her face. Nice greeting, shipmate, let us hope it
does not come true for you. The slaver's horrified
look turned instantly into a stare as blank as the
armored bulkhead.

Hardly the effect she hoped for. Having just shuttled up from Hades, she wore thigh-length leather boots beneath a shimmering cloth-of-silver kimono, cut short to show off her hips. With her came two SuperCat bodyguards, two-meter tall bioconstructs, Homo Smilodon—half human, half feline—with tawny fur, curved dagger-like canines, human hands and forebrains, and tiny bobbed tails. This particular pair wore battle armor, riot pistols, and stun grenades, but the *Fafnir*'s crew did not give the gene-spliced killers a second glance. She was what scared them.

Having hardened Eridani slavers blanch at the sight of her was something new to Deirdre. Since birth she had been outrageously beautiful, a gorgeous baby that only grew more lovely. So lovely, that for much of her short life, she had been treated more like a gaudy objet d'art than a real person—witness her current black-leather geisha outfit. Even as an infant, men oohed and cooed over Deirdre, telling her how cute and lovely she was, happily predicting she would become a "real heart breaker."

That had yet to happen. Until she was twelve, Deirdre took this adulation as just another adult extravagance. Attention was nice, but hardly turned her head. Who wanted to be "a heart breaker" anyway? Not her. Growing up on New Harmony, she had been far more concerned with sleepovers and sky sailing. Her home world lived the way the King would, with tolerance and mercy to all. Looks were not everything—or so her parents said.

At age twelve Deirdre found out looks could indeed be everything, literally life and death, teaching her just how unusually beautiful she was. Huddled in a public blast shelter during the tail end of a slaver raid on Goodwill City, she prayed for Priscilla's protection, listened in horror as a slaver went through the shelter eliminating witnesses.

Whatever weapon the slaver used was noiseless. Eyes shut tight, Deirdre heard terrified pleas and cries of terror, cut off one by one, sobs and begging replaced by silence. She recognized her friends' voices, fellow members of the Lisa-Marie middle school's Humanities Club, who had left school early for a field trip, to cheer up terminal patients at a local hospice. Now they were dying horribly.

Finally the killer's footsteps came to her. She looked up into the black muzzle of a silenced machine pistol.

Too terrified to cry, she watched the man's eyes widen, his finger frozen on the firing stud. For a long moment they stared at each other, killer and victim. Then she saw that familiar reassuring smile. He liked how she looked.

Holstering his pistol, the man helped Deirdre up and led her out of the shelter, stepping over the bodies of strangers and schoolmates, finding her a seat on a shuttle bound for orbit—bumping off a huge, heavily armed felon with hideous tattoos and a horrendous price on his head. Justice was closing in, and slavers were in a mad scramble to board, facing automatic death sentences if they failed. Slaving was the only capital offense left on New Harmony—since the King taught mercy and tolerance, not total suicide. Yet the fleeing raiders cheerfully made room for her, talking softly and trying not to scare her. All the way into orbit, a tattooed killer held Deirdre's hand, telling her not to be afraid as they left home far behind.

That was when she was twelve. Slavers saw that she grew even more beautiful, blossoming into a radiant young woman under strict diet and constant exercise, with biosculpt ridding her of any incipient blemish. At eighteen she was stunning, which made the hateful looks from the *Fafnir*'s crew all the more appalling.

Worse yet, Deirdre knew it was true. She was the Angel of Death, for them and for her. Konar would not have brought her aboard unless he meant to die. If Konar thought he could win the upcoming fight, he would have left her on Hades, which was honeycombed with blast shelters and secret bunkers dug by slavers over the centuries. Bringing her aboard was as good as saying there were no safe refuges, and this was the last fight. Konar would never leave his flagship alive, and had brought his sex toy aboard to die with him.

Her stomach heaved as she entered the starboard lift, and slavers hurriedly got out, leaving it to her and the SuperCats. Recycled air reeked of sweat, fear, and synthetic sealants. She ignored the hostile looks, knowing it was not her they hated, just what she represented—the ghastly fate hanging over them all. Nuclear annihilation was about the nicest future they could anticipate. Or explosive decompression.

Doors dilated for her. Tubes and ducts snaked overhead. *Fafnir* began life as the high-g survey ship *Endurance*, but slavers had taken her on her maiden voyage, turning her into a warship, with blast shields and armored bulkheads, stripping and reinforcing the hull, making *Fafnir* stronger, faster, more focused to a task, ruthlessly discarding whatever they did not want. Not unlike what they did to Deirdre.

Commander Hess of the *Hiryu* greeted her on

A-deck; dark-eyed, black-haired, and alert, he wore his dress uniform thrown open to show the flying dragon tattoo curled round his left nipple. Too professional to display fear, Hess bowed neatly, with a flick of his black curls, and a curt click of his heels. "If my lady will follow me." He showed the way with his palm.

"How goes the *Hiryu*?" This was a silly stab at making conversation, since all of Konar's ships were surely doomed.

"Could not be better," Hess lied casually. Things could hardly be worse, with Navy cruisers headed insystem, slowing from near light speed. *Hiryu* faced a losing battle along with the rest of Konar's little fleet, but the one nice thing about Hess was that he never deigned to show his feelings. Deirdre appreciated this reticence, since Commander Hess's inner workings sickened her. Physically. Being this close to Hess made her want to barf up her gourmet lunch.

Her quarters had a hemispherical pressure hatch, a sad indication that someone thought the main pressure would fail. The slaver on duty gulped at seeing her, asking Hess, "Is she wired?"

Hess nodded curtly. By now Deirdre was used to being discussed in third person. "Where's her remote?" the guard demanded. Hess gave him a "where-do-you-think" look, and the slaver shut up. Dismissing the SuperCats, Hess led her through the hatch, into the cabin.

Immense vistas opened up before her. Picture windows looked out over forest and sea, as if the cabin sat on a pine-clad pinnacle above a river valley filled with woods and farmland. In the foreground she saw a fishing village, and, farther down river, a port city stood at the mouth of a fjord. Storm clouds hung over the distant ocean, but an orange-red sun shone down on the cabin, framed by a small pair of moons. All extremely unreal, since the cabin was buried deep in a starship, behind layers of armored bulkheads. Living quarters on *Fafnir* were still those of a deep space survey ship, using 3V and sensurround to keep claustrophobia at bay.

Deirdre could smell the pines and hear birds singing above the drone of insects. Rock climbers waved to her from a nearby pinnacle, a fun group of healthy young people, close enough to call to from the "balcony" beyond the windows—if you wanted to talk to holos. She asked Hess, "Is this world real?"

"Elysium, Delta Eridani II, we raided it once!" Hess grinned at the virtual landscape. "Not a full out landing—Delta E is too far in for that—just a picked team with pre-set targets." Hess meant a kidnapping. Not all slaver crimes were on the horrific scale of the New Harmony Raid; sometimes they slipped into civilized systems, snatching up valuable individuals for ransom or resale. "But a rousing success nonetheless." Hess preened, as if she should congratulate him.

He already had her missing the SuperCats. "Can I change it?" Deirdre asked. Delta E meant nothing to her.

"Your bunkmates might object." Hess nodded at the balcony, where two children had come out to call to the climbers—a boy about eight or nine with impossibly purple hair, spiked on top, and a girl a couple of years older, whose squared-off blonde hair ended in a shoulder-level blue stripe.

"Bunkmates?" She thought they were holos. The

purple-haired boy scrambled up onto the balcony rail, leaning over the virtual gap, waving vigorously at the climbers, while the blonde girl with the blue fringe looked bored. Alike enough to be brother and sister, they wore expensive Home System outfits, cut down versions of adult fashions. Appalled to find there were real kids, Deirdre hissed, "Who are they?"

"Insurance," Hess replied airily.

"What does that mean?" It was bad enough that she was going to die—did she have to watch kids die as well?

"They are the grandchildren of Albrecht Van Ho, Director General of River Lines," Hess explained. "That pair of AMCs headed in system belong to River Lines. They might be a shade less eager to vaporize us with these two aboard."

Maybe. Personally, she hated staking her existence on corporate pity. River Lines had not operated for centuries in the worst stretches of the Eridani by pulling punches. Having no mercy themselves, slavers misjudged kindness in others—taking it for weakness, or stupidity. Did anyone really think the Navy would give up and go home rather than fry some CEO's grandkids? For Priscilla's sake, why not just load *Fafnir* up with baby puppies?

Deirdre had long ago stopped trying to explain compassion to Commander Hess. New Harmony had taught her to do good for others. "Love thy neighbor," is what the King said, and what he practiced, moving Priscilla in next door to Graceland. It worked for Elvis, and it worked for her. Compassion came easy, when a kind word or a simple favor from a girl so lovely as her brightened anyone's day. Deirdre liked people thinking her a darling angel—not knowing how little effort it took. Like giving away Cadillacs, when you owned a zillion of them.

When she first arrived on Hades, Deirdre tried diligently to live by the laws of New Harmony, treating everyone with kindness, sympathy, and understanding, hoping for fairness in return—vastly amusing her captors. Slavers raised the price of compassion, teaching Deirdre to keep such feelings to herself: They cared not a whit how others felt, which was their biggest failing, the one most likely to get them all killed. But try telling that to an Eridani slaver. Otherwise they were orderly and efficient and extremely good at what they did, which was kidnapping people for sale, ransom, or personal use. Deirdre complained, "Do I have to bunk with them?"

Her best chance of getting away was to convince some man that she was well worth saving. Hauling two kids about easily halved her slim chances.

Hess shrugged, "No room. Ship-of-war, and all that. Besides, this is not so bad," he looked happily about, running a keen reaver's gaze over the cabin's real ivory inlay, and pre-atomic cut crystal. Commander Hess was mysteriously immune to the pall her arrival cast over the flagship. Did Hess know something that she did not? Probably. His smile broadened, the first real smile she had seen since coming aboard. Hess asked, "We have come a long way, haven't we?"

Deirdre did not answer. Hess had saved her life, forming a weird bond between them, though it hardly made them close. She had been living with slavers since she was twelve, but Commander Hess was the one that gave her nightmares, scaring her more than any of them, more than Konar himself. Just being in the same room with him gave her the cold, screaming shivers.

Hess was the slaver who went through that Goodwill City blast shelter, killing everyone but her. Six years later, she could still hear her classmates' pleas and screams in her head, echoing off steel reinforced walls. And she always feared Hess would one day kill her, just to finish the job. Some nights Deirdre dreamed she was back in the blast shelter, staring into the pistol muzzle, only this time Hess pulled the trigger, and she felt the silent bullets strike.

Commander Hess of the *Hiryu* did another little heel-clicking bow, then left. Thank Gladys. Deirdre sank down into a glove leather chair, mulling options. The two well-dressed kids were still out on the balcony, waving stupidly at the holos—at least the boy was. Deirdre had friends and contacts on Hades that she ached to talk to, but *Fafnir* was under communications lock down—leaving her on her own.

Shutting her eyes, Deirdre tried desperately to think. She could not die, not with rescue only light-hours away. Somehow she would save herself. But how? Behind her blemishless, biosculpted features, lurked the hideous truth that beauty was only skin deep—it did not make her better, smarter, or more noble. It did not even make her nicer, though people liked to think so. So far it just made for incredibly weird relations with men.

"Cool boots."

She opened her eyes. Both kids had come in from the balcony, and the boy with spiked purple hair stood in front of her, staring at her black leather boots. He looked up at her, saying, "So, what are you doing in my Grand-dad's cabin?"

Her inquisitor wore a natty man's jacket, cut just for him, and neatly tailored pants. His own shoes were a pricy pair of snake-skin slippers over silk stockings. He asked again, "What are you doing in Grand-dad's cabin?"

"He still thinks we are on Elysium," the girl explained. She was older than her brother, but not by much. Up close they were clearly brother and sister, even though his hair was purple, and hers blue-blonde.

"Prove we are not," the boy insisted. His sister rolled her blue eyes like she really had to "prove" they were abducted by slavers, and light-years from anywhere.

Deirdre sighed. "Chuck him over the balcony rail, that will show him." Despite the yawning virtual cliff, there was no drop "outside." A swan dive off the balcony would end in a belly flop on the cabin deck, masked by holographic display. But it was not Deirdre's job to disillusion him. If the boy wanted to believe he was safe at home—instead of on a slaver starship about to be obliterated—what was the harm?

"Who are you?" the girl asked, wearing the junior miss version of her brother's outfit, right down to the snake-skin slippers, except she had on a pleated skirt in place of pants, and cuffs trimmed with lace. There was no need to ask their names—"Heather" and "Jason" were on their jacket collars.

"Deirdre." She made an effort to smile, sitting up in her seat. Just because they were all going to die was no reason not to be cheerful.

"Where are you from?" Jason demanded. "We're

from Elysium." He pointed to the panorama outside the picture windows.

Right. She glanced at the supposed scene outside. Skycycles circled over the village below, riding thermals off steep pine-clad cliffs, red-gold afternoon sun glinting on their control surfaces—too bad it was not true. "I'm from New Harmony," she admitted, sinking back in the chair, knowing what children raised in a place like this would think.

"New Hicksville," scoffed the boy. "Hippie planet."

Heather told him, "It's not nice to say that," though you could tell by her tone the blonde girl thought it was true.

Deirdre widened her smile to include Jason, thinking, "At least New Harmony is a real planet, you little preppy-suited marmoset. I'm not making do with a holo, and pretending it's home." But she did not say it, meeting rudeness with a smile. Her "hippie planet" had taught her not to taunt helpless doomed children, no matter how richly they deserved it.

"Where do you think we are?" Heather asked, stepping closer, ignoring her brother's pretense of being safe at home.

"You're off planet," Deidre told them, trying to break it to them slowly. Way off planet.

Heather nodded soberly, "I guessed that. We have been gone for so long without anyone finding us." She was smart, belying what folks said about dyed blondes. Smart enough to be far more scared than her brother.

"But if they could take us off planet, they could have taken us to Grandfather's lodge," the boy insisted. Kept alone like this, brother-sister bickering must be the main entertainment.

"Where off planet?" Heather asked, not bothering to contradict her brother.

"Tartarus system." She saw their blank stares. "Way the heck into the Outback. Triple system in the Far Eridani, a small red dwarf primary, Tartarus A, and a distant pair of white dwarf binaries—too far away to much affect Hades. That is the planet we are orbiting."

"Orbiting?" They both looked askance—the cabin seemed solidly rooted atop its mountain ridge.

"We are aboard a starship."

Jason scoffed, but Heather asked, "What starship?" Above hiding behind fantasy, Heather wanted to hear the whole truth.

Not that the girl would get that from Deirdre, who did not mean to tell these kids they would soon be blown to photons. "She's the *Fafnir*, used to be the survey ship *Endurance*. Slavers have her now." She must let the kids know that these were evil men, never to be trusted; though, needless to say, slavers had no sense of privacy, routinely recording everything important prisoners did and said, preventing escapes and providing amusement.

"Slavers?" Heather looked less horrified than she should have—but the girl could not possibly imagine how bad things were. So far they had treated the kids royally. "Is that who that man with the dragon tattoo was, the one you talked to?" Heather had been watching her and Hess.

"One of the worst." Deirdre nodded solemnly, knowing Hess would relish the compliment. "But their leader's name is Konar."

"Why have they brought us here?" Heather's hand took hold of the silver hem of Deirdre's kimono, silently twisting the fabric where it rested on the chair, the only sign of how much the question scared her.

"For ransom from your grandfather." Sort of. No harm in letting them hope to get home alive.

"What about you?" Jason asked, resenting her taking his sister's side. "Why are you here?" He stubbornly refused to admit that "here" was not his home.

Why indeed? "I was kidnapped too, from New Harmony."

"He means, why did they kidnap you?" Heather guessed that no hick from New Harmony had a trillionaire grandfather.

Deirdre heaved a sigh, not wanting to go into this too deeply. "Because I am pretty. And I am now Konar's girlfriend." Sort of. His property more precisely, but who needed to hear that? She had spent her teen years working her way up the slaver hierarchy, and at eighteen had hit the top. "He is the head slaver who commands this ship. The whole system, really."

"Why?" Jason looked disbelieving. "Isn't that gross?"

"Do you love him?" asked Heather.

Like she had a choice. Deirdre was saved from having to answer by a chime going off in her head—one only she could hear. She sat up in her chair, saying, "Have to go."

"Go where?" Heather was appalled to find her leaving.

Deirdre gently untwined Heather's fingers from the kimono, solemnly taking the girl's hand in hers. "I'll be back," she promised, hoping it was the truth. In less than an hour, she had gone from not wanting to see these kids, to not wanting to leave them. Even the condemned craved human contact.

Deirdre called out to the door, and it dilated. The slaver on duty stuck his head in, and she told him, "He wants to see me." By "he" she meant Konar. Konar had a garish title—Grand Dragon of the Free Brotherhood—but no one ever used it, least of all Deirdre. Konar was "he" or "him"—or in rare moments of affection, "the Old Man" or "Old Snake Nick." Otherwise, he was just Konar. Like Hitler, or Satan. Everyone knew who you meant.

Except for these two little rich kids. "Where are you going?" Heather asked plaintively. Jason looked truculent, but if he meant to throw a tantrum he was out of luck. *Fafnir* ran on raw testosterone, and when Konar called for her services, even a grandson of General Director Albrecht Van Ho had to wait.

"So let's not keep him," the slaver suggested. He casually aimed a remote at the kids, his finger on SLEEP.

Standing up, she bid the kids good-bye, following the slaver down to C-deck. Konar did not need holographic vistas to stay sane, and his command cabin seemed incredibly spare compared to the sumptuous quarters of his hostages—just four bulkheads and a float-a-bed. Slavers cared little for status, valuing people for their own sake. That was the sole way they resembled folks on New Harmony.

As she entered, Konar was meeting with his captains around a virtual conference table. Hess was there in the flesh, but the captains of the *Fukuryu* and the *Hydra*, and their first lieutenants, were holograms beamed from the ships.

Speed-of-light lag delayed their reactions to her entrance, but several looked shocked. None showed fear, though they knew best how thin the odds were.

These were old-time slavers, who had lived with their death sentences for so long they almost seemed born with them. All of them had survived botched raids, grueling life and death chases, hairbreadth escapes from hopeless situations, ghastly torture sessions, and gruesome prisoner eliminations. Incoming government cruisers did not frighten them much, and pretty teenagers did not scare them a whit. She was just one of the perks that made such horrendous risks worthwhile.

Her own remote lay on the float-a-bed, so she sat down beside it. Konar treated her like a piece of disappearing furniture—she came when he called, then left when he dismissed her. Other than that, she was an integral part of his life. On Hades she sat in on his conferences and private suppers, listened to his troubles, rubbed his temples while he thought, and told him stories about her childhood on New Harmony, attending to Konar's every need while they were together.

Watching him give orders, she tried to tell if Konar meant to die. He looked as vital as ever, his compact bull-like body stripped to the waist, with tattooed dragons crawling over his naked torso, his most fascinating feature by far. Sometimes Deirdre lost herself in those dragons, following them across his body for hours, forgetting everything else. Each dragon had a story, a successful raid, a ship he captured or commanded; occasionally he told her the stories, the closest he ever came to boasting. Otherwise he was nothing special to look at, with a blunt bald head, alert eyes, ferocious strength, and a genial smile. Except that this nondescript face was infamous, known and feared throughout the Eridani.

Floating above the table top was a 3V display, showing different parts of Tartarus system. Tartarus and Hades hung near the center of the display, along with Hades's two moons, Minos and Charon. Farther out came the gas giants Cerberus and Persephone. Still farther out, at the extreme edge of the display were Tartarus's twin companions, two white dwarfs spinning around each other. Seen as tiny sparks of light, the slavers' situation did not look so bad. Three government cruisers were headed insystem, accompanied by a pair of smaller corvettes. Four slaver ships stood ready to face them—*Fafnir*, *Hiryu*, *Fukuryu*, and *Hydra*.

Five to four did not seem overwhelming, but the numbers were horribly deceiving. *Hydra* was the converted colony ship *Liberia*, helpless in battle. And leading the incoming ships was the Navy light cruiser *Atalanta*, which outgunned the entire slaver fleet. For once the vastness of space worked against the slavers, giving them nowhere to hide. Abandon Tartarus system, and their ships would be run down in the emptiness of interstellar space. It was win or die. Typically Konar tackled the task head on, telling his captains that he and *Fafnir* would face *Atalanta*. "You gentlemen must make do with what is left."

They laughed. Konar wanted *Hiryu*, *Fukuryu*, and *Hydra* to face down two merchant cruisers and the corvettes—a stiff fight, but not half what Konar faced. Konar was using his fabled reputation to finesse the most alarming problem—the *Atalanta*. If anyone could defeat a Navy cruiser with a converted survey ship, it was Old Snake Nick.

On that light note Konar closed the conference.

Hologram captains winked out with their lieutenants, leaving Konar and Hess—the only ones physically aboard the *Fafnir*. Neither bothered to look at her. Leaning across the virtual table, Hess whispered conspiratorially, "You know there are other ways to do it than diving down their throats."

Konar settled back in his seat, eyeing Hess. Konar was the only person Hess was honest with. Deirdre did not think anyone could lie to Konar. Certainly not her, and probably not Hess. Konar did not bother with galvanic sensors or reading heart rates—having seen so many people saying anything to save themselves, he knew all the "tells" that gave liars away. Smiling grimly, he asked Hess, "How goes the escape pod?"

Hess nodded. "Totally operational. Waiting to be used."

"The pod only carries six," Konar pointed out.

Hess shrugged. "Whoever thought the hounds would get this far? There was no time to increase capacity. The others would just have to be convinced to carry on without us."

Konar laughed at that. Both of them acted like she was not there, casually discussing escapes and betrayals as if Deirdre were part of the float-a-bed. But neither did anything by accident. Hess had his own way of dealing with truth, and probably counted her as dead already. While Konar might want her to know all about the escape plan, to get her hopes up for some purpose known only to him.

And her hopes were up. Way up. Suddenly she might actually live through this nightmare. Six seats in this "escape pod" meant two for them, and four to be filled. Why bring her up from Hades, unless

Konar wanted her in one of those seats? He must have known she would scare the heck out of his crew.

"Escape to where?" Konar sounded doubtful. "Six of us in a tiny boat, alone in an awfully big cosmos." Right now Konar was king of his world, with a whole system-cum-slave-emporium at his command. Hades was not just his hide-out, but a hub for slaving throughout the Far Eridani, where ships and cargoes were fenced, where deals were struck and prisoners resold—all in a fleshy carnival mood catering to crews on leave. Why trade his personal pleasure planet for a tiny escape pod headed into the void?

"Where there is life, there is hope," Hess suggested. "The pod is on the hangar deck, in berth L, programmed to go—code word 'Medea.' Use it, or not." With that Hess got up, his chair vanishing into the deck along with the table, leaving the 3V display hanging in space. Hess grinned at her, doing a swift nodding bow, then left, tickled to see the girl he saved, all grown up and sitting on his boss's float-a-bed. Yet another coup for the *Hiryu*'s able commander.

Konar studied the hanging 3V display, not acknowledging her arrival. Deirdre waited. Without looking at her, Konar ordered, "Take off the kimono."

She got up and obeyed. Konar liked seeing her in just the leather boots, never letting her wear underwear. Other than that, his tastes were pretty plain. Sex was not that important to Konar. He did not need it all the time, or to twist it into anything kinky—not much at least. By now she was the galaxy's foremost authority on the Grand Dragon's sex preferences, and while Konar might be an insane mass murderer, he was thankfully not much of a sadist. So long as he had the most beautiful woman available at his complete command, Konar seemed fairly content with extreme mental cruelty.

He turned and grinned, liking what he saw. She smiled back, determined to win a seat in that escape pod, set to give Konar a reason to live, and to save her as well.

Picking up her remote, Konar stroked her cheek with his free hand. He was hardly taller than her. Konar always said size did not matter—"Napoleon was shorter than you." When she had to ask who Napoleon was, he laughed, telling her a story of Old Earth, from the days before Elvis. His fingers came to rest on her bare shoulder. "Are you nervous?"

Her smile had not fooled him. She nodded earnestly, knowing she could not lie her way into that escape pod, not to Konar.

"Don't be frightened," he told her, thumbing her remote. "Be sexy."

Immediately she was not frightened, not in the least. Sharp urgent desire shot through her, going from groin to nipples. She wanted the slaver's strong, merciless tattooed body inside her—right now. Konar had skipped the setting for foreplay, and internal wiring allowed him to bring her to orgasm at the press of a button. She opened her mouth to say how much she wanted him, to beg Konar to take her with him—just her and him, so they could be together forever and ever. Konar pushed MUTE.

Sex with Konar was never boring. Sometimes he liked to play with the remote, forcing her through every physical-emotional state from abject terror to repeated multiple orgasm, merely for his private amusement. Or to entertain a guest. Twice he did it for Hess. But no one needed that now, least of all Deirdre. She had already gone through every emotion she could imagine, from abject horror at leaving Hades to orgiastic hope that she might somehow survive this, if she just pleased Konar totally. She had been by turns scared, surprised, amused, maternal, wary, hopeful, and now sex-crazed. And it was still the morning watch.

When he was fully inside her, Konar whispered, "Do not worry about being left behind."

His words cut through the haze of desire. Deirdre very much wanted to be left on Hades, but she could not say it, even if she had dared. All her being was fixed on pleasing Konar, and earning a seat on that escape pod. Konar could tell, and when he was done, he patted her butt, saying, "I will never give you up."

Just what every girl wants to hear. Even Konar had a human side, somewhere. Back in her shared cabin, Deirdre collapsed in the sauna, telling warm water to cascade over her. Too wrung out to think, she listened to the drops pound down on her, glad to have a moment to herself with nothing to plan, or evaluate, or submit to—just pure, clean, clear, warm water, carrying her worries away.

Despite all the glowing predictions, Deirdre's luck with men had been ghastly. Fate had simply fallen on her out of orbit. Had she left school later, or ducked into a different shelter when the sirens sounded, her life would have been totally different. She might already be dead. Deirdre thanked Elvis for giving her life and hope, glad he had an undying love for teenage girls—who had first made him King.

Jason was there when she got out, saying his sister

was asleep, wanting to know, "Where did you go? Was that guy you talked with really a slaver?" He was warming to the idea that they were on a warship full of space pirates.

"Let's not talk about it," she told him, settling into the soft pneumatic leather chair. With just four free seats on the escape pod, there was plainly no room for an opinionated little brat. If Konar wanted a hostage, he would take Heather. Most likely they would leave both kids to die. Horrible, but hardly her fault.

"Well, tell me about this planet we are supposed to be orbiting." Another male needing to be entertained.

She stared at the purple-haired punk, wondering if she was doing him any favors, coddling and protecting him with her lying smiles. It only made her look like a pretty push-over with a space pirate boyfriend. "Do you want to see Hades?"

"Sure." He practically dared her to show him.

You asked for it. She told the cabin to reconfigure, projecting an image of Hades's surface outside the picture windows. Water, people, homes, greenery, blue skies, and sail planes vanished—replaced by a fiery vision of hell. Red searing landscape stretched away toward scarlet wind-carved cliffs, topped with orange-brown storm clouds, rent by violet lightning. Their cabin appeared to rest on a tall pink sand dune, surrounded by red rubble crushed beneath dense carbon dioxide atmosphere, flat as a sea floor and hot as hell's basement. Sulfuric rain fell on the highlands from the brown clouds, forming boiling acid rivers that vaporized before reaching the sizzling valley floor. Deirdre could taste the ozone on her tongue.

"Too cool." Jason looked awestruck, and not the least frightened.

Her smile returned. There was hope for the boy after all, who had the plain good sense to compliment her boots. Konar's favorites as well. "That's just the surface," she told him, "the good stuff is all underground."

Jason ran out onto the balcony to get a better look. She closed her eyes, hoping that Hades's seething cauldron would give her some time to rest. She needed sleep if Konar called again. Thank Elvis she was not trying to please Hess.

Konar did not call, and Hess left to command the *Hiryu*—both ominous signs, of which Konar not calling was the worst. She desperately needed to be with him, to know for sure she too would live. Not even her remote had ever made her want Konar so much.

Hess's leaving implied the escape plan was on hold, since she could hardly picture Hess giving up his seat to someone else. Deirdre doubted the slaver Hess bumped for her in New Harmony ever got out of Goodwill City. Desperate to save herself, she asked the ship's computer what was stored on H-deck, berth L, and the answer came back—"Berth L contains *Endurance*'s spare lifeboat, reconditioned for special use, coded access only." Originally, *Endurance* had two such lifeboats—each able to carry the entire survey crew. There was no record of what happened to the other one. Deirdre weighed using the code word "Medea" to get more information, but that might draw unwanted attention. She had to trust that Hess did his job right, and escape was waiting if Konar wanted to use it.

Time passed, terrifying her even more. Her hot sweaty visit with Konar began to look like one last boink for old times' sake, because they were soon headed up-sun on a high-g boost, going headfirst into battle—making it even harder to keep up a cheery front for Heather and Jason. Deirdre wanted to shriek and scream in protest, but that would have done nothing for the children's morale.

Her worst fears were confirmed when Konar came on AV to send a mocking challenge to the cruiser *Atalanta*, complete with holos of Heather and Jason, telling the Navy to vacate Tartarus system tout de suite. Or get set to die.

Atalanta's answer was a long-range salvo of Toryu— "Dragon Killer"—torpedoes. *Fafnir* replied with anti-missile fire and the fight was on.

Konar left the AV channel open so his crew could follow the action. Deirdre watched horrified, holding Heather's hand, as high-g torpedoes raced toward the *Fafnir*. "What's happening?" Jason asked, enthralled by the notion of being in a battle, but unable to make much out of the 3V display. Missiles and counter-missiles flashed between the fleets, but there were no explosions in space, since antimatter warheads released most of their energy as hard radiation, not visible light. Only ship movements showed clearly. As *Fafnir* engaged *Atalanta*, the rest of the slaver ships, led by *Fukuryu*, attacked the two merchant cruisers.

"Who's winning?" Jason demanded, as *Fukuryu*—the "Lucky Dragon"—took on the lead merchant cruiser, the converted River Lines packet *Niger*.

No one, you idiot, thought Deirdre. A lot of folks— good, bad, and in between—were going to die for nothing, and Deirdre did not want to be one of them. She squeezed Heather's hand. "How good an actress are you?"

Heather looked hopefully up at her. "I was Romeo in our class play. None of the boys wanted to do the balcony scene."

Sounds promising. "Can you pretend to be hurt?"

"How hurt?" Heather asked.

"Badly hurt. Can you do convulsive shock?"

Heather nodded; if she could play a boy she could play anything. "Show me," Deirdre demanded.

Throwing herself on the cabin deck, Heather started shaking and rolling her eyes, tossing herself about, and gagging horribly.

"Great," Deirdre whispered, "drool a little, too." Arching her back, limbs twitching, Heather dribbled spittle on the deck. Perfect. "Keep it up," Deirdre hissed, then she called for the slaver on duty.

Dilating the door, the slaver stuck his head in. Seeing Heather flopping about, he asked, "What is wrong with her?"

Grabbing the guard's arm, Deirdre dragged him over to where Heather lay writhing, saying, "She's having a fit and needs to go to the infirmary." The slaver looked convinced.

Jason cheered. Everyone but Heather looked at the display. Great plumes of gas shot out of the lead merchant cruiser, which immediately lost power and fell behind. *Fukuryu* had gotten a direct hit on the *Niger*, knocking out its fusion reactor and gravity drive. Only a fried warhead kept the missile from blowing the converted liner to pieces. The slaver cheered too, using the "Lucky Dragons" nickname—"Good

Old Fuck-a-You. Hit her again you bastards." He was shaking as hard as Heather.

"Look, if you won't take her to sickbay, I will." Deirdre seized the children's remote from the slaver's belt.

"Sure, sure," he did not even look at her, still fixated on the display, where his life or death was being decided. The second merchant cruiser, *Jordan River*, was taking on the *Fukuryu*.

Helping Heather up, she hustled the twitching girl toward the door, grabbing Jason with her free hand. He started to protest, saying there was nothing wrong with him, or his sister, but Deirdre stabbed MUTE on the remote. At the door, she heard a groan from the slaver. Looking back at the cabin display, she saw *Fukuryu* disintegrate under fire. The "Lucky Dragon"—Good Old Fuck-a-You—was gone, blasted to bits by the *Jordan River*.

The last words she heard from the slaver were, "Damn you Hess to hell." *Hiryu* had turned away, leaving the slower *Hydra* to face *Jordan River*, and the crippled *Niger*. *Hiryu* was a converted gravity yacht, the fastest ship Konar had, and Commander Hess was not the type to face death happily. Not when others could face it for him.

Telling Heather to stop shaking, she headed straight for the hangar deck with the two children in tow. Personal access codes got her past the hangar door, and "Medea" got her into berth L, where the *Endurance*'s reconditioned lifeboat sat waiting, covered in curved battle armor. Inside were six crash couches; all the rest of the crew space had been sacrificed to double the gravity drive. Too bad three of the couches were going to lift empty, but there was literally no one aboard she could trust to take with her, no one who would not happily rape her and sell the children to the highest bidder.

Deirdre baby-strapped the kids in the command couches, tilting them back to keep their hands away from the controls, then picked the crewchief's couch for herself—there she could run things while keeping watch on her charges. Hoping Hess knew what he was doing, she gave the command, and the escape pod flung itself away from *Fafnir*, headed outsystem at better than twenty gees.

And not a minute too soon. Fifty-three point two seconds after they separated, an antimatter warhead penetrated *Fafnir*'s defenses, burying itself in Konar's flagship. Matter and antimatter came together, and *Fafnir* disappeared in a flash of hard radiation that blanked the escape pod's screens. Built to withstand the particle storm at near light speed, the redesigned lifeboat easily bucked the blast that obliterated *Fafnir*.

Inferno

"Still think we're on Elysium?" snorted Heather. Jason glared at her but did not answer. Screens in front of him had flashed back on, showing Hades and the rest of the inner system receding at high speed.

Unfazed by the bickering, Deirdre was ecstatic, feeling gloriously alive and free. Not only would she live, but her every act was no longer monitored and recorded. She could shower or change without leaving a permanent record for slavers to enjoy, and she could do it whenever she wished. Her remote had been blown to atoms along with the *Fafnir*. She was still wired for control, but, without the coded remote, she was effectively free. No one could play with her emotions, or force her to do what she did not want.

Not even Konar. Her lord and master was gone too. How strange to think that Konar was dead, his tattooed body vaporized. He had been such a force of nature, controlling her life and the lives of everyone around her. Konar certainly deserved to die, no doubt about it. Slaving was the only capital offense left in most systems, a distinction that slavers had worked hard to earn, overcoming every human impulse for forgiveness. By the time Deirdre became Konar's property, she had given up hating every slaver she met, instead responding to how they treated her. And Konar had treated her well—up until the end. The worst thing he ever did was to call her up from Hades to die, and that resulted in setting her free.

"Where are we anyway?" Heather asked, staring at an enhanced view of local space. "This does not look at all like home."

Jason did not rise to the bait, still baby-strapped to the command couch, giving his sister an intensely dirty look.

Deirdre studied the screens to get her bearings. Hades was still the closest planet, though shrinking visibly. *Hydra* was the nearest ship, loudly broadcasting her surrender. *Hiryu* was hurrying away at high acceleration, pursued by *Atalanta*, while the two accompanying corvettes, *Calais* and *Zetes*, were headed Deirdre's way at flank speed. Any survivors from Konar's flagship rated immediate naval attention. She told Heather, "We are headed outsystem, tailed by two high-g naval corvettes."

Heather asked, "If we just turned around, would they take us home?"

"Probably," Deirdre admitted, "but that would mean reprogramming this lifeboat without proper codes." Not something she felt up to doing. "Medea" set the program in motion, but did not let Deirdre change direction.

"We could just shut off the gravity drive," Heather suggested, "and let them catch up."

"Maybe." Deirdre was not so sure. Hess had designed this program, and would surely assume that anyone tampering with his system was better off dead. "But this drive could easily be set to blow if we try to shut it down."

"We could at least call the Navy," Heather protested, "and tell them who we are."

"Even that might be suicide," Deirdre pointed out. "We have to trust in the escape program." And in Commander Hess.

"What?" Heather could not believe her. "That's crazy." Looking to her brother for support, Heather only got a disgusted glare, so she turned back to Deirdre, asking, "Why keep faith with these dead pirates?"

"Because if we do not, they will kill us, too." That was Hess's hallmark, the utter willingness to kill whoever became even the least threat, or merely a nuisance. Which made him way worse than Konar—who preferred control and manipulation to outright murder. Konar had been a charismatic megalomaniac, who Deirdre feared and respected. Hess gave her the galloping creeps.

Heather turned back to her brother, saying, "You tell her. This is so totally silly...."

Jason replied with a withering look, but did not deign to answer. Which was odd, since the boy normally could not bear an unexpressed thought.

His sister asked, "What's the matter, still mad we are not at home?"

"Damn, left him on mute." Deirdre remembered the remote, fished it out and turned the boy's speech center back on.

"You silly blue-headed imbecile," Jason yelled at his sister, "I swear we are not related. Hello? Cosmos to Heather. I was muted, remember? That's why I was not answering!"

"Sorry," his big sister replied sarcastically. "I thought you were just listening for once, maybe even thinking ahead. Sadly I was wrong."

"Hallelujah," her brother rejoiced. "Tits-for-brains is wrong about something...."

Heather turned back to Deirdre, pleading, "Please, please turn him off."

While they fought, Deirdre looked about the escape pod, seeing a standard survey ship lifeboat with increased shielding, expanded powerplant, and added antimatter tanks. No wonder it could hold only a fraction of the survey ship's original crew. *Endurance* originally had two such lifeboats, each intended to carry all twenty-four crew members—if necessary. Now it was none too roomy for the three of them, with no privacy except in the bath cubicle. Six would have been a stretch.

Turning back to the screens, she watched the corvettes slowly cut the gap between them. Despite that expanded powerplant, they still had a snail's chance of outrunning a real starship—much less two naval corvettes. *Calais* and *Zetes* would easily run down the escape pod before it reached a neighboring system. How could Hess or Konar have hoped to escape? Elvis knows, neither of them was stupid. All Deirdre could do was pray Hess had planned this to perfection, relying on his ruthless sense of self-preservation to work in her favor for once.

Heather wanted to at least signal their pursuers, accusing her of still being the pirates' prisoner. "You are so used to doing their bidding that you are obeying their orders, even though they are dead."

"With damned good reason," Deirdre retorted. "If you knew them half as well as I do, you would, too." Besides, Hess was not dead. Commander Hess and the *Hiryu* had a good head start and half a chance of getting away—now that the two corvettes that could have caught him were coming after her. And she did not dare call them off. How horribly unfair.

Which pretty much summed up her life, from the moment slavers entered that public blast-shelter on New Harmony and began killing people. Heather was right, life among slavers had taught Deirdre obedient detachment, and she felt curiously unconcerned by the corvettes closing in on them. Hess had planned for this, and he knew every hiding place and bolt hole in this part of space. Slavers had hideouts the Navy knew nothing about, accessed by secret gates in out of the way worlds. Deirdre had never heard of any such gates in Tartarus system—but Hess might have.

Hours into their flight, the drive fields suddenly reversed, and they were decelerating toward Cerberus, a three-ringed gas giant in the outer system, with a litter of frozen moons, the largest of which were Styx and Lethe. Heather wanted to know, "What's there?"

Deirdre shrugged. Knowing Hess, it could be anything: a secret slaver base, or a hidden missile battery set to blast the corvettes. To know for sure she had to think like Hess, which Deirdre hated to do.

Even Deirdre was disappointed when the capsule ducked behind Cerberus and set down on the frozen surface of Styx, the innermost major satellite. Screens showed a bleak cratered moonscape, half covered by heaps of frozen methane snow. Their pursuers were temporarily hidden by Cerberus, but the two corvettes were certainly decelerating to match orbits.

Suddenly a new craft burst onto the screens, lifting off the far side of Styx, headed outsystem at maximum acceleration, but keeping the bulk of Cerberus between it and the corvettes. Deirdre immediately recognized the vessel's profile; it was the *Endurance*'s other lifeboat, the exact twin of the craft they were in. This duplicate capsule had been stashed ahead of time on the backside of Styx, and it would now come streaking out from behind Cerberus, just as the corvettes were slowing to match orbits, mimicking the old slaver trick of using a star or gas giant to mask a tight maneuver. Only this time Hess had set up a fast shuffle, sending the corvettes tearing into interstellar space running down the wrong capsule. Yet another coup for the commander of the *Hiryu*.

Grasping what would happen, Heather announced, "We must tell the Navy they are after the wrong ship."

"How?" Deirdre was dead set against reprogramming the controls, or even flipping on the comlink.

"We could trigger an emergency beacon," Heather insisted, "then the corvettes could come get us."

"Maybe." Emergency beacons were self-contained,

with their own power and programming—so it should
be perfectly safe. And they could not just sit huddled
in the lifeboat while the Navy went rocketing away
into the unknown. But it was equally stupid to take
chances with a stone cold killer like Hess. "Only if
we suit up first and take a beacon outside."

"Suit up?" Jason looked surprised, but intrigued.

"And go outside?" Heather was horrified. "It is
ghastly cold out there."

"Then stay safe and snug in here," Deirdre suggested. "I am not going to break programming while
sitting in this capsule."

"Go outside! Super cool." Jason started pawing
through the suit locker, producing an emergency kit
and beacon. Deirdre helped him suit up, and Heather
had to do the same, or be left alone in the lifeboat.

Super cool indeed. Styx was stuck in perpetual
winter, with a bleak pitted surface where the only
atmosphere was the sort that you could pick up off
the ground, then watch as it vaporized in your glove.
Deirdre knelt in frozen methane, setting out a beacon with a twenty-minute delay, then led her charges
through the methane snow to put a low crater ring-wall
between them and whatever happened next. Heather
dragged her feet, plainly thinking the whole trek was
unnecessary, but since the suits had no comlinks, she
could not complain.

Before they even got to the ring-wall, Jason spied a
line of crisp bootprints heading off across the methane
field. Touching helmets with Deirdre, he demanded,
"Who the hell left those?"

Who indeed? They were on a frigid moon in an
uninhabited part of a slaver system deep in the Far

Eridani. People did not just stroll past. You had a better chance of seeing a Yeti, or some unknown xeno. Of course there was no telling when the tracks were made. With no atmosphere to speak of, tracks could last a long time before being covered up by methane geysers and outgassing.

Having no time to dally over new mysteries, Deirdre dragged the children behind the ring-wall, where they waited for the emergency beacon to trigger. She scanned the dark sky for some sign of the corvettes, which should look like small fast satellites. Precisely twenty minutes after setting the beacon, there was an intense flash, melting methane on the far side of the crater. Moments later Deirdre felt the bang in the insulated seat of her suit that was the escape pod blasting itself to bits. Clearly Hess planned for this possibility.

Without comlinks, Deirdre could not even say, "Told you so." Standing up, she saw frozen methane slowly falling on a huge melted patch where the lifeboat and beacon had been. Touching helmets with the children, she told them curtly, "Follow me."

Finding the line of prints, Deirdre followed them away from the falling methane, which is what Hess must have intended. Her sole attempt at deviating from the program had resulted in the complete obliteration of their only transport and shelter, leaving them stranded in vacuum suits on a lifeless world, without supplies or comlinks. If these boot prints did not lead somewhere, they could choose between freezing to death, or drowning in their own body wastes.

She followed the crisp prints across a field of frozen methane with the children trudging behind her, turning the line of prints into a trail. Above them, bright young stars burned amid the strange constellations of the Far Eridani. At the end of the methane field, the prints descended into a yawning ice cave at the base of a crater—something clearly artificial and encouraging. Suit-lights came on as they entered the cave, bathing gleaming crystalline walls in dazzling white light. But, after several klicks of shining tunnel, the trail ended in a smooth blank ice wall.

For once, Deirdre was grateful to have been owned by slavers, otherwise she might have despaired. This blank wall was typical of slaver gates, which opened into walls and floors, making them nearly invisible to the uninitiated. Touching helmets with the children, Deirdre told them to lean against the frozen wall, then she did the same. Gates were controlled by a simple knock code, so Deirdre tried Konar's personal knock, 3-1-1. Instantly the ice wall vanished, and they tumbled into a different world.

Dark woods surrounded Deirdre, tall scaly tree trunks that disappeared into hot inky night overhead. Without their suit lights, they would have been in total blackness. Picking herself up, Deirdre noted her suit heaters had cut out and cool air had begun to circulate. Her suit claimed outside temperature had risen hundreds of degrees, and that the air was breathable. She doffed her helmet to give it the sniff test. Hot but bearable.

Heather and Jason dutifully did the same, asking together, "Where are we?"

"Still on Styx," she hazarded, "but in a shielded and insulated underground cavity."

"It looks huge." Jason sounded dubious. "And what are woods doing klicks underground?"

"Just 3V," Deirdre explained. "This is an entrance maze, a safety check, or holding area to keep undesirables from using the gate. Trees give the illusion of space." They were surrounded by dark hologram woods that seemed to stretch into limitless night, filled with virtual twistings and turnings that would keep them going in circles. Twenty paces into the woods, and she would never find the entrance gate again, much less the exit.

"So which way should we go?" Heather somehow expected her to know.

Deirdre honestly did not know what to do next, wishing now she had not blown up the lifeboat trying to contact the Navy. She should have known Hess would not let go so easily.

"Hello, Deirdre, how truly delightful to see you." As if summoned up by her thoughts, a cheerful, dapper Commander Hess strolled out of the dark woods, saying, "I dearly hoped you escaped the *Fafnir*, but I could not be sure."

Deirdre stood frozen in shock, but Jason acted, reaching into the emergency kit and producing a recoilless pistol, pointing it at the slaver. Hess continued to grin, striding toward them, adding, "And you brought the kids too, bravo."

"Shoot!" shouted Heather, and Deirdre was jerked alert. Reaching out, she snatched the pistol from Jason.

"He has to be a holo," Deirdre told the protesting boy, who dearly wanted to bag his first slaver. Laws of physics did not allow Hess to be in two places at once. When they left the lifeboat, Hess and the *Hiryu* had been boosting outsystem at an incredible clip, so this had to be a holo.

To be sure, she aimed the pistol at Hess and pressed the firing stud, sending a volley of steel-jacketed rockets shooting through the slaver's virtual chest and vanishing into the hologram night, trailing points of fire. Hess grimaced. "That was uncalled for."

"Just proving a point." Deirdre shrugged. "I knew you must be a holo."

"Alas, it is true." Hess stopped in front of her and did a little bow, clicking virtual heels. "And what man would not rather be in the flesh with you?"

Gallant as always. This hologram was most likely a 3V guide, set up ahead of the time as part of the escape program. With a negligent wave, Hess indicated a dark path to the left, saying, "If m'lady will but follow me."

"He's a slaver," Heather protested.

"No, he is a holo." A real slaver would not be nearly so polite.

"Why trust him?" Jason sneered, still disappointed the pistol had not blown Hess apart.

So was Deirdre, but her only choice was to follow this hologram Hess. At worst he would lose her in the woods, but that might easily happen without him. Best to pretend cooperation, giving the program no reason to discard her.

"Give me the gun back," Jason demanded, trying to be the man of the group.

"No way." Deirdre was not giving in to attempts to run things from the bottom. Besides, the King believed that women ought to go armed, and had given Priscilla her first pistol.

"Great," Jason scoffed, "guess we can have Heather throw another fit if we have to."

"How about we throw you?" Heather suggested.

Deirdre pocketed the gun, threatening them with the remote instead. "Shut up, or I will put you both on mute."

"Children can be a trial." Hess smirked at her troubles, then led them down a dark crooked path that branched and twisted between low boles and thick protruding roots, while virtual bats twittered overhead, sounding like the souls of the damned. Eventually the hot hologram forest gave way to a grove of black poplars bordering a boiling stream. Which was no hologram effect. Deirdre could not even go near the searing stream without first sealing her suit.

Hess waded casually into the boiling water, and they were forced to follow, suit refrigerators whining in protest as the scalding stream came up to the kids' waists. So far Deirdre's survey vessel suit had taken her through frozen methane and superheated steam, showing slavers stole the best.

Beyond the billowing curtain of steam, they broke out into daylight, and the hot hellish woods vanished, replaced by a garden full of fruit trees. Pears, apples, oranges, plums, and tangerines hung from limbs twined with grape and berry vines, all miraculously bearing fruit together, filling the air with sweet scents. Music throbbed in the middle distance, and loud laughter came from the undergrowth.

Suddenly a naked woman burst from the brush, laughing and running, followed by a nude grinning slaver, covered with dragon tattoos, who was himself pursued by three more bare-naked women. Party time on Styx.

All five ran straight through the v-suited group, showing the slaver and his naked ladies were holos.

More nudists broke cover, and Deirdre realized there was a virtual orgy in progress, with hologram revelers playing sex games, and mating to ethereal music. Jason, for one, was disgusted, demanding to know, "What in hell is going on?"

"This is Elysium," Heather declared, giggling at the cross-country orgy.

Jason took that as a dig. "Dry up, blue bangs."

"No, it's true," his sister insisted. "Not our planet but the orchards of Elysium in the underworld. Did you sleep through planet studies? This is what our world is named after."

Jason looked unconvinced, but Heather was right; someone had created a virtual underworld beneath the frozen surface of Styx. Deirdre recognized slavers she knew wearing *Fafnir*'s blood-red dragon heart tattoo. Holos of dead men were dallying with virtual playmates in a 3V gardenscape. Grotesque even for slavers. She asked Hess, "What is all this?"

"Konar ordered it," the hologram answered airily, as if that justified anything, no matter how obscene and absurd. "He felt there should be some permanent record of the men who died under his command— beyond the usual list of aliases and DNA samples. What better way to preserve them than at play? Endlessly enjoying themselves."

"So are you dead too?" Deirdre asked hopefully.

"Heavens, I hope not." Hess looked aghast at the notion. "Last I heard, the *Hiryu* was headed outsystem at high-g, with yours truly in command, showing the Navy a clean pair of heels. I am merely here as a helpful subprogram."

Probably true. Deirdre saw no slavers with the

Hiryu's flying dragon tattoo. She asked, "So where are you taking us?"

"To your new home." Hess nodded at the holo-orgy. "None of this is real, and you would not like it much anyway."

His easy manner made her more suspicious. "Where is my new home?"

"Right where I am taking you," Hess replied cheerfully, setting out again on the garden path. Clearly a program loop would not let the holo tell her where they were going. Probably just as well.

Music faded behind them, along with the cries of pleasure. Finally, fruit trees parted to reveal a sunny beach ending in a long sandpit, with a white marble mortuary temple at the tip, surrounded on three sides by a china blue hologram sea, flat and placid in a perpetual noontide. Heat poured down from a hologram sun, and Deirdre's suit cooler kicked in again. Jason started to complain, but Heather told him to stuff it. "What heat? It is all in your head, remember? There is no sun, and we're not here."

But the big bronze temple doors were real, blended perfectly into virtual walls and columns. Deirdre had spent enough time in 3V to tell that the temple interior was carved from the living rock of Styx. Gold-skinned girls greeted them at the gilded door, small and slim, with wide grins and long blond hair; each wore nothing but a bit of kohl to show off wide amber eyes. They too were real, or as real as bioconstructs can be. Golden lips parted and the foremost girl told her, "How happy to have you here at last. Come, Deirdre, we have been waiting for you."

"For me?" Deirdre eyed the beautiful nude girls

who barely came up to her shoulder—more Heather's size than hers. They all laughed, as if her question were absurd. Small gold hands seized her v-suit, pulling Deirdre into the seaside tomb. She looked questioningly back at Hess.

"There, you see, right at home, just as I said." Hess happily turned his charges over to the gilded bioconstructs, giving Deirdre a little nodding bow, then vanishing. End of program.

Letting herself be hauled inside, Deirdre asked, "Have you really been waiting for me?"

"Yes indeed," the golden girls insisted. "You are Deirdre, are you not? We have been waiting years for you. Everything is ready."

"Years?" This made no sense. How could they have waited years, when she decided to come this way only hours ago? Her suit watch confirmed it—this time last week she was on Hades, hoping the Navy would soon rescue her. "What is ready?"

"Everything," they assured her. "We will show you."

Suddenly one of the golden girls shouted, "Look, this is a boy!"

Which produced shrill cries of amazement. "What? Are you sure? Which one?"

"With the purple hair," declared the girl, pointing at Jason.

Her companions crowded around, saying, "Are you really sure?"

"Of course," the first girl insisted, "just look at her."

"Him, you mean," her companion corrected her. "Just look at him."

Someone finally asked the fuming Jason, "Is it true, are you really a boy?"

"Yes, you gilded morons." Jason could barely believe such idiocy. "Are you blind as well as brainless?"

"He has a boy's temper." They giggled knowingly.

Proud of their discovery, the golden girls led them triumphantly down the great columned hall of the mortuary temple calling out, "Look, it is Deirdre, and a boy!"

Women and girls of various description emerged from side apartments. Human females. Greenies. Plus even weirder bioconstructs, like women with pointy goat horns or prehensile tails. The closest thing to men were a couple of hermaphrodites, fully erect, excited to get a look at her and the boy, saying, "Yes, and Deirdre is with him. Konar will be so pleased."

Konar was fried to photons, but Deirdre did not say it. Undoubtedly these girls did not get out much. This had be some secret slaver brothel-cum-biolab—one even Deirdre had never heard about. From the way they talked, the golden girls were raised here, as were the wilder constructs, while the humans and Greenies were either taken as children, or bred in captivity.

But her biggest surprise was to be herded into "her" room—an exact duplicate of her old apartments on Hades, complete with her favorite works of art, her personal refresher, and her extended wardrobe, right down to the school T-shirt she was wearing when she was snatched from that bunker on New Harmony. A lot of it was stuff she had thrown away years ago. Spooky and then some.

Feeling silly standing in her own entryway wearing a v-suit, Deirdre asked for a chance to change and use the refresher. For a moment she was alone, aside from whatever spying eyes were in the walls, so while using the refresher, she managed to stick the plastic recoilless pistol in the back of her harem pants—fairly sure no one could have seen her, unless there was a camera trained up her ass. She covered it with her favorite embroidered jacket, glad to feel the familiar silk against her skin.

Stepping out of the refresher, she found Heather and Jason staring at her, obviously waiting for her to reappear. Deirdre asked warily, "What's the matter?"

Heather rolled her eyes toward the suite door. Standing in the doorway was a beautiful little girl of five or so, who looked exactly like Deirdre in miniature. This little Deirdre announced blandly, "You are in my room, but you may use it. It is your room too."

Deirdre did not know what to say. It was an awful shock to see her own features on a small child, but there was no mistaking the lustrous eyes, the tilt of her nose and the shape of her chin, all done in miniature. Amazing. The girl seemed equally intrigued by her, asking, "You are truly Deirdre?"

"That's me. Who are you?" Things were now officially too weird.

Her child-double smiled broadly. "I am Deirdre II. When I grow up we will be twins."

Actually they already were. Deirdre guessed this girl had been cloned from her DNA when she first arrived. (Along with who knows how many others?) Slavers must have liked their catch and decided to make extra copies—just in case. Konar had been raising her replacement in an exact duplicate of her apartment on Hades. "When your grown-up clothes arrived, I knew you would be here soon." Clearly Deirdre II had eagerly anticipated her advent. "Now you can teach me to be exactly like you."

"Great," Jason groaned, "then there will be two of them."

Fat chance. She was not going to settle down and give Deirdre-lessons to a preschooler. With Konar dead, this place no longer had a purpose and was running on automatic, unaware that the slavers had been annihilated or driven from the system. Yet as isolated as this was, there still had to be some kind of control station where she could contact the Navy, or at least shut off the entry maze. Unless this was truly just a mausoleum, a monument to Konar's dead crews, and a repository for his most prized playthings. She asked the women waiting outside the suite, "Is there a command deck or control area?"

"Naturally," was the reply. "That is where we are taking you, now that you are refreshed and ready."

"And I can contact the outside from there?" Deirdre asked.

"Of course." They treated it like an incomprehensible request. Who could she possibly want to talk to? But whatever Deirdre wanted, Deirdre got.

At the C-deck door, Deirdre told everyone else to wait while she went in alone. They all obeyed, acting as if the place was now "hers"—in fact she found the door already keyed to her thumbprint, dilating at her touch. Deirdre stepped confidently onto the control deck, guessing that her arrival was the biggest thing that had ever happened hereabouts.

Make that the second biggest. Lounging relaxed and naked on the command couch, backed by the screens and control console, was her late unlamented master—Grand Dragon Konar. Unbelievable. Her first thought was this had to be 3V, like the holo Hess who guided her here, but then she saw her remote in his hand, the one that was blown up aboard *Fafnir*. Konar pressed a button, and Deirdre froze.

Shocked and appalled, unable to speak or move, she stood watching as Konar rose and walked over. His all-too-solid hand reached out, making her want to wince, but Deirdre could not even do that. All she could move were her eyes. Breath went in and out automatically. Konar stroked her cheek, saying, "Sorry, cute stuff; anything you could say would only spoil the moment. I told you I would never let you go."

Crushed at seeing Konar again, she damned herself for thinking she could just stroll in and take over. How was this even possible? Her mind groped for sane explanations. No one had gotten off the *Fafnir* alive, except for her, Heather, and Jason—Deirdre was sure of that.

Konar slid his fingers inside her silk jacket, running them down the front of her light blouse, enjoying the feel of her breasts through the thin fabric. Kissing her limp lips, he told her, "I am terribly proud of how you gave the Navy the slip. Hess and I had a bet on it. I feared they might catch you, but Hess was sure you would get through—so I have to pay up, when he comes for me."

With nothing to do but contemplate this latest disaster, Deirdre swiftly put the pieces together. Clearly Konar had not been aboard his flagship when *Fafnir* went on its death ride. He had been hiding out here on Styx, and his defiant "last battle" was an elaborate 3V ruse to make everyone think he was KIA. Bringing her aboard *Fafnir* for a "final" boink convinced both her and the crew that Konar was on the flagship—but once his captains had their orders, he secretly slipped away, leaving Hess and a holo-program in command. Project Medea and her own escape was an added diversion to decoy the corvettes, designed by Hess to get *Hiryu* safely away.

And it all worked as good as gravity. Even when outgunned and outnumbered, veteran slavers had centuries of experience at hoodwinking the Navy. Far from being finished with her, Konar was thrilled to have his property returned, running his hands over her hips while fingering the remote. Soon it would be just like old times.

Sick with fear, Deirdre could feel the recoilless pistol digging into the small of her back, its cold muzzle pressed in her butt crack, centimeters from her limp hand. If Konar released her without a strip search, she would get one chance to shoot. Would she take it? Lisa-Marie Middle School had not trained her for armed self-defense, much less premeditated homicide. She had shot Hess, knowing he was a holo. Could she shoot Konar for real? She prayed to Priscilla that she could—since that was what the King would do.

"And you brought the kids," Konar announced happily, "courageously saving River Lines from incinerating its innocent heirs. What a living doll you are, always doing just what you should. How could I ever give you up?"

And if he did, there was a little genetic understudy waiting just outside. Konar gave her fanny a pat, missing the gun muzzle by a millimeter or two, then he told the door to open, saying, "Send in the two children."

Heather walked into Deirdre's line of sight, looking terrified, followed by a defiant Jason. Konar greeted them with a cheery, "Happy to see you, too."

Ignoring the naked tattooed slaver, Heather looked hopefully at Deirdre. Seeing only one chance for them, Deirdre rolled her eyes significantly.

Heather rolled her eyes in response, then flipped over and fell to the deck, tossing and jerking violently, making ghastly gagging sounds.

"Oh, fuck! Another fit." Jason groaned. "Give it up."

Konar knelt next to the flopping and flailing Heather, asking, "Where is her remote?"

Jason shrugged, saying, "She'll get over it. Only does it to get attention."

Turning to Deirdre, Konar pushed UNMUTE and demanded, "Where is her remote?"

"Inside jacket pocket." Deirdre dared not lie.

"I'll get it." Jason jumped up and reached inside her jacket, ignoring the remote, feeling about frantically. Looking up at her, he complained, "I cannot find it."

He was looking for the gun. Deirdre stared down at Jason, realizing that the nine-year-old had already made the choice she was struggling with. For better or worse, Jason was determined to save himself—and he deserved the chance, even if it killed him. "Behind my back," she whispered, "but make it good."

"Got it!" Jason declared proudly, his hand going around behind her. It came out holding the recoilless pistol, and Jason spun swiftly about, pretending to give it to Konar. In the split second it took to see it was not the remote in his hand, Jason pointed and fired.

Distracted by the convulsing Heather, Konar caught Jason's movement out of the corner of his eye. Leaping up, he spun like a cat, throwing himself out of the line of fire.

And catching a cluster of rocket darts full in the

chest—since Jason had excitedly fired high and wide. Beginner's luck, but the results were impressive, spraying blood and bone all over the controls. And on Heather, who went into real hysterics.

Konar's body flipped backward, landing face up on the command couch. Deirdre stood impassively through it all, unable to move anything below her neck. When Jason looked questioningly over at her, she told him curtly, "Shoot him again."

Anything worth doing is worth doing right. Holding the gun steady with both hands, Jason shot Konar again in the chest, but the dead slaver did not even twitch. This time Konar was not coming back.

Then Deirdre told Jason to pick up the blood spattered remote and release her. Which he did, both elated and awed by having killed his first man.

She went to comfort Heather, calming the girl, then cleaning her up in the control deck refresher, which smelled heavily of Konar. Having soothed Heather's hysterics, Deirdre walked gingerly over to the bloody command console and opened an emergency channel, broadcasting their identity and position to the Navy. Armed merchant cruiser *Niger* returned the call, surprised to have a signal coming from a supposedly dead moon.

Informed that help was on the way, Deirdre opened the control room door. Women and girls stared in horror at the bloody mess. Greenies turned and fled. Only the golden girls knew what to do, bowing down to Jason, who was the new man in charge, and to Deirdre, the lovely angel who brought death into their secluded little world. With tears in her eyes, Deirdre II looked worshipfully up at her miraculous twin sister.

Atalanta was off hunting *Hiryu*, and *Calais* and *Zetes* were chasing down an empty lifeboat, but River Lines was elated to have unexpected custody of Konar's body and the two lost River Lines heirs, who were now child heroes as well—turning the Battle of Tartarus into a triumphant victory, at least for River Lines. Only Hess and *Hiryu* got away. In a burst of corporate gratitude, River Lines gave Deirdre free first-class tickets to New Harmony for her and Deirdre II, plus a thousand bonus light-years to use or sell.

Heather begged Deirdre to stay with them, promising to make her rich forever. Deirdre said she would think about it, "But I must see my folks again." New Harmony might be hicksville, but it was home. Then Jason got his first real kiss from a grateful young woman, to go along with his first slaver kill and his immense inheritance. At this rate the boy would be running River Lines by the time he turned twelve.

Even going first class on a high-g ticket, it took Deirdre nearly a year to get home, and by then she was nineteen. To her, seven years had passed—but, thanks to relativity effects, it was thirty-something years later on New Harmony. Her parents were two divorced old people, who were nevertheless overjoyed to get back the daughter they'd given up for lost. Friends and siblings were in their forties and fifties, many with kids of their own, and they all made a great fuss over their teen "angel"—brought miraculously back from the dead. Which made Deirdre feel even more out of place.

Despite this awkward transition, going from slaver's head mistress to teen mom to her own twin, Deirdre was thrilled to be home, glad to see her parents and friends again, no matter how strange and aged they had become. Everyone doted on Deirdre II, telling the girl she would grow up to be a real heartbreaker, "just like her big sister."

When the time was right, Deirdre took her little sister to put flowers in the public shelter she was kidnapped from. Long ago made into a shrine, the shelter was a grim, underground place, dedicated to people brought together by death, but there was bold new lettering above her memorial—RECOVERED ALIVE.

These two simple words radiated civic pride, celebrating Goodwill City's tiny triumph over a remorseless enemy. Deirdre helped her six-year-old twin lay daisies on the spots where Hess had shot her schoolmates, saying prayers to Saint Michael in Neverland, who watches over little children. Long dead members of the Lisa-Marie Middle School's Humanities Club looked up from their memorials, smiling in 3V. She told Deidre II each child's name, and what each one was like, what hopes they had, and what made them happy. They were the only people on New Harmony who were just as Deirdre remembered.

R. Garcia y Robertson (b. 1949) holds a PhD in history and lectured at UCLA and Villanova University. His first published SF story, "The Flying Mountain," appeared in the May 1987 *Amazing Stories*, and he soon left teaching to become a full time writer. He has written an impressive number of striking SF and fantasy stories, a selection of which appeared in his *The Moon Maid and Other Fantastic Adventures*, and eight novels. Perhaps appropriately for a historian, many of his tales involve time travel, while other stories are set in past times. Noted critic John Clute observed that "his range of protagonists is, in ethnic terms, extremely wide and his use of characters who occupy sidebar roles in conventional versions of Western History is markedly effective." His novels include the intriguingly titled *The Virgin and the Dinosaur*, first of a time travel series, and *Knight Errant*, beginning of a second series, as well as the fantasy *Firebird*, one of three standalone novels. He lives in Mount Vernon, Washington.

Blackout in Cygni

James Blish

On ships traveling between the stars, the lights had to be on all the time, or the human minds of passengers and crews dissolved into gibbering panic—and somehow the ruthless space pirate Jason was taking advantage of that. But Dirk, crewman on the luxury liner Telemachus was determined that his ship wasn't going to disappear en route like the others, and he was prepared to shed light on the mystery.

The main lights on D-Deck were out when Dirk Phillips came off watch, and only the dim glo-pups whiled away their half-lives behind the moldings above. Far down in the bowels of the *Telemachus* the geotrons purred, a deep, sonorous sound, somehow vaguely comforting.

Dirk was not comforted. Things were too quiet, and too much hell was waiting to pop somewhere along the Long Arc. Down the corridor the blank doors of the deluxe suites regarded him, and from behind one

319

of them came a muffled feminine giggle. Dirk scowled
and increased his pace. The empty-headed whinny
followed him as he rounded a corner.

You'll giggle out of the other side of your mouth if
you get in Jason's hands, you damned parasite!

Dirk hated the passengers on D-Deck on principle.
They were his charges, but no more so than the thousand Centaurian laborers and their families packed into
the cubicles down in Supercargo—pioneers bound for
a world that hadn't even been named yet: 61 Cygni
C-II. These gilded loungers topside were the spectators,
the pleasure-palace builders, the representatives of the
big power and mining cartels . . . people who could pay
two thousand credits for a D-Deck suite only because
of the sweating of people like the ones below.

It would be nice, Dirk reflected idly, if the *Telemachus* could be split horizontally up her middle, sending
the Centaurians on to their epochal job of establishing
Earth's second interstellar colony—and leaving the top
two decks behind, floundering in subspace, waiting
for the man who called himself Jason. Or perhaps to
let Jason himself pick over the moneyed cream for
ransom—no, that wouldn't work. Jason would simply
pitch the poorer people out the airlocks, for they had
no one back home who might pay ransom for them;
that was S.O.P. with Jason.

Voices murmured ahead of him. He stepped over
the low doorway into the Star Deck: the big bubble
forward of center, on the midline of the ship. It was
an odd hour for anyone to be looking at the scenery, but then, few passengers ever got oriented to
the twenty-hour Ship's Day. Third Watch might be
sleepy-time for Dirk, but for a passenger it might just

as easily be the equivalent of 9:30 a.m. Earth time, or 14:50 Centaurian.

He recognized one of the figures at once: Jerry Sanders, the *Telemachus*'s new Third Mate. There was a girl with him and a stocky, broad-shouldered man in civvies. The man saw Dirk at the same time and gestured.

"There's another officer—maybe he knows. I say, Commodore."

For a moment Dirk was tempted to go on without answering. Among the people on D-Deck whom he would cheerfully dunk in boiling wine, those who hailed him as if he were a bellhop were high on the list. However, he couldn't pretend that he hadn't heard the summons—it had rung like a tocsin through the big dome—and rank discourtesy to a passenger would be out of character. Grudgingly he swerved and walked over to the little group.

"What can I do for you?" he said mildly.

"Couple of questions," the heavy man said, with bluff heartiness. "Mr. Sanders here can't seem to make them quite clear. We're on overdrive now, aren't we?"

"Certainly. You can hear the geotrons."

"Aha, that's what I said. Now then: how does it happen that things don't look any different?" He gestured through the clear stellite, including the whole universe in his category of "things."

"Shouldn't there be warping or something?"

"There is," Dirk said, a little stiffly. "But it takes some knowledge of the stars to recognize it. Had you been up here when overdrive first went on, you'd have seen the starfield scramble itself thoroughly."

"But shouldn't there be some color changes, too?"

"Yes and no. You're not seeing by light, you know. You're looking at what might be called the backsides of the stars—not the components which exist in free space, but the considerable masses of their cores which are extruded into subspace."

"Rather disappointing," the big man said. "I expected something more, ah, unusual."

"Such as the 'nameless hues' the 'vision writers prate about? Well, those hues are probably there, but your eyes can't see them. That's why they're nameless; they don't need names."

The big man laughed. "That settles me," he said jovially. "Eh, Nadya? If some of the scripters back home could hear their boss told off like that—"

Dirk stiffened momentarily. Their boss! There was only one man on Earth or Centaurus who could call himself that. This burly bird must be James Henry Stapledon, kingpin of the visicast networks of two systems. Evidently he was on his way to extend his empire over a third. The girl was probably his secretary—

Dirk became aware suddenly that the girl was watching him with dark-eyed amusement.

He swung angrily on Jerry. "Mr. Sanders, aren't you aware that the next watch is yours? If we run into any trouble, you'll wish you'd had your sleep."

Sanders flushed. "My off-watch time's my own."

"Oh, come now, don't be hard on the lad," Stapledon protested. "He's here at my request. Anyhow, what trouble could we encounter out here?"

The questions seemed rhetorical; surely the 'vision magnate knew all there was to know about Jason. "Knock off, Jerry," Dirk said. "You've got four hours left to go, and I don't relish the idea of a shaky hand at the boards up front."

"Yessir," Sanders said sullenly. It was obvious that he hated to be ordered to bed in front of the girl, but he had no choice. Dirk watched him until his slender back was framed against the glo-pup shimmer in the levitator shaft, then he turned to the two passengers.

"Sorry," he said. "But we're a little on edge this trip. There's a lot at stake. If Jason's greed stops this third wave of colonization, there may never be another; we can't any of us afford a moment's inattention."

"Quite right, quite right," Stapledon said. "We appreciate the attention, Commodore. Goodnight."

"Goodnight," Dirk said through suddenly clenched teeth. He turned his back on them and strode off. Just as he was entering the shaft, the girl laughed. The silvery sound cascaded through the dome. He felt himself flushing and cut off the shaft at B-Deck.

It had been nearly a century since the first interstellar passenger liner had turned back toward Earth, only a quarter of the way along toward Centaurus III, with a cargo of madness and death.

It had happened, according to the few surviving crewmen, when the lights had been turned off for the second Watch. Dozens of learned tomes had been written about it since then, but no one had ever gotten much beyond the simple facts: the lights had gone off, and the passengers had rioted. There was something about being driven between the stars at nine times the speed of light that was different from ordinary interplanetary flight: in a lightless cabin the darkness closed in, you were horribly, uniquely alone, pitching headlong into a pit of absolute emptiness...

Perhaps—just perhaps—that was the way it was. Those who had come sane through the first blackout could not be sure; they had been lucky enough to be on duty, near a source of light. Those who had been in the cabins had gone mad within a few moments.

After that, the switchless, inextinguishable glo-pups had been installed by Act of Council, and the General Orders on Blackouts had become a part of the Spaceways Manual. There was even a glo-pup at the head of every bed, next to the visitape screen, casting its dim radiance up toward the ceiling. On the ledge next to the pillow there was also a mask for the glo-pup, but most of the masks gathered dust.

Dirk stripped off his jacket, took off his shoes and socks, and put the mask over the light. He was as afraid of the interstellar pit as any spaceman, but he had sense enough to know that half his fear was of something he knew to be harmless while he was alone: the fear of what other people might do while he could not see them. On this flight, there was no telling who or what might be watching wherever there was light...

In the stifling darkness he groped to his locker and spun the combination, working with fingers which had often conquered tougher puzzles than an ordinary baggage locker. Inside, behind his gaudy dress jacket, was a worn holster with a 76 heavy cyclast in it. It was a tough starman's boast that he slept in the dark, and the man who was telling the truth had little to fear from marauders—it took something more than guts to walk into a totally black room out here—but

Dirk slept with the cyclast all the same. There was no telling what was due to happen this trip—

His fingers found the holster. The heatstained, familiar weapon was gone.

The shock of surprise was doubled and redoubled in the boundless gloom. Fighting down his panic, he ran quick fingers through his jacket, along the floor of the locker. Gone, all right. Of course it was illegal for an officer to maintain arms outside the ship's arsenal, but nobody on the bridge had any reason to be pawing through Dirk's effects—

Sanders?

Ridiculous. Dirk had hardly spoken to Sanders until tonight. The fledgling resentment the third mate might have felt at being packed off to his crib couldn't have taken wing this quickly.

There was only one answer. There was someone on board the *Telemachus* who was an agent of Jason.

Dirk padded back to his bunk and sat down, rubbing the blond stubble on his chin. It fitted; almost it seemed as if it fitted too patly to be true. After the Centrale-Ganymede war, some units of the Ganymedian Navy had been sold as surplus to private firms, before the Centrale Council could get a complete inventory of what it had won. Among the sold ships had been several heavy sub-cruisers. The man who called himself Jason had somehow had the liquid cash to buy one; he'd turned it to piracy, and had made a good thing of intercepting the big, clumsy liners on the interstellar run—

Except that a ship on overdrive was supposed to be indetectable. Every physicist in the system swore that it was impossible to pirate a sub-ship, no matter how big it was. So the obvious conclusion was that

the piracies had been inside jobs; and the theft of
Dirk's cyclast, on this trip of all trips, seemed to
point the same way. Disgustedly, he reached for the
glo-pup mask.

A soft knock on the cabin door arrested his hand,
in mid-air. There was a kangaroo-shiv in the belt of
his dress jacket; but it was a duelling weapon, and
he decided against fighting over trifles.

"Yes?" he said.

The door opened hesitantly. It was the girl. Modeled
against the hazy glow, she was startlingly lovely. She
peered helplessly into the unexpected darkness, one
hand at her throat, one smooth knee bent.

"Mr. Phillips?"

Dirk's hand resumed its arrested arc, and the glo-
pup once more stared innocently at the ceiling. He
leaned on one elbow and studied his visitor. He'd
hardly gotten a glance at her before—and she was
something to look at.

Her hair was a waterfall of black silk with blue
highlights in it, and her eyes were violet and slightly
slanted—not enough to suggest the Oriental, yet giving her face a piquancy that was hard to resist. The
fashionable Centaurian toga, with its slit from waist
to toe and its heavy golden shiv-chain locking the
waist, wouldn't have been tolerated on taburidden
Earth—but then, there were few women left on Earth
who could wear such clothing successfully. The active,
lithe-bodied people who roamed the interstellar frontier
were almost a different race. Dirk noticed wryly that
the shiv-chain wasn't empty; the massive handle of
the weapon itself lay across one gently rounded hip.

"That's me," he said, somewhat belatedly. Then, "You're armed."

The girl bit her lip and reached for the clasp of the golden chain. Dirk raised his hand quickly.

"Please don't. Those damned togas look like nightgowns when they're unbound, and I'm not sure I could stand the shock. What do you want?"

"May I close the door?" she said stiffly.

"It's your reputation, not mine. Get on with it. Sanders may want to lose sleep off watch, but I don't."

"You're very gracious," she said. She shut the door and leaned against it, her hands behind her back. "I'm Nadya Storm."

Dirk's eyebrows shot up. "I wish I'd had a chance to look at the passenger list! First Stapledon—and now the daughter of Kurt Storm, top Centrale Council woodenhead! And to think I took you for a Centaurian. I should have known better."

"Oh?" Nadya said coldly. "Why?"

"Because the real Centaurians are down in Supercargo—not lolling around on D-Deck at two thousand per."

She shrugged. "I'm going to Cygni for the same reason they are—to work. I'm covering the colonization for ITN; the D-Deck rooms were Mr. Stapledon's idea...but that doesn't matter. You seem to be spoiling for a fight. If you can't stop fencing, I'll take my questions to Captain Muir."

"You'll get short shrift there, Stapledon notwithstanding, I promise you." But Dirk relaxed a little. It was hard not to be curious over what had brought her here at this hour, and harder still to resist the sheer beauty of her. "Well, maybe I have been a bit brusque. But the Long Arc is a dangerous one, and I haven't had much time for polishing up my manners. Go ahead."

She straightened with an impossibly graceful, flowing motion and walked over to the single chair, her slim legs kicking the toga into a swirl about her knees. "Why is it so dangerous?" she said. "This Jason, whoever he is, has worked out a way to pirate an overdrive ship. But surely it would be possible to give merchant vessels an escort—or even to arm them. We did both during the war."

"Sure, it's possible. The *Telemachus* is armed—you didn't know that? Well, she is; you can't see it from Star Deck, but there's a turret with two synchrons in it under the ship's belly, and murder-guns—pom-poms—all along her periphery. But during the war those guns were manned by Patrol crews who knew their business. Now the Patrol's being demobbed, and if we get into trouble we'll have to put ordinary merchant ratings into the turret. Our gunnery officer's a good man, but he can't be in the turret and on the bridge at the same time. As for a convoy—you should know more about that than I do."

"If I did, I wouldn't be asking."

"Your father and his egg-headed young crony Paul Haagen were the first Councilmen to call for eternal peace and prosperity—and the reduction of the Patrol to a fifth of its normal strength. The Patrol has its hands full now just enforcing the Spaceways Act in the System, let alone having monitors to spare this far out."

He saw her delicate eyebrows arch in puzzlement, and added, "This Jason has a demobbed Ganymedian cruiser. A screen of smaller vessels wouldn't do us a bit of good; he could immobilize them by threatening to blast us the minute the others fired on him. It takes a bigger vessel than a heavy to beat a heavy to the punch; a battleplane will do, but a monitor's better."

"But monitors are too big to use except outside the asteroids. Surely there must be some to spare out here."

Dirk laughed. "Sure. But there's a mass limit on overdrive. The liners are just under that limit. Monitors are way over it. With a monitor escort, it'd take us about 11.02 years to get to 61 Cygni from Centaurus, with everybody sick from acceleration pressure most of the time."

The girl frowned and was silent. Dirk said, "May I ask some questions?"

"Why not?"

"Why do you want to know all this?"

"I'm a 'vision announcer, as I said," Nadya replied abstractedly. "We're going to do a take on the first landing, and I wanted details about the dangers of the trip. I'm not sure I can use much of this, though—the political element is touchy."

"Why do you carry a shiv?" Dirk asked suddenly.

"It's fashionable," she said. Abruptly she came out of her study. She stood up, swung to the door, and stepped out into the corridor. At the last instant she looked back at him and smiled.

"Mine," she said, "has a propelling charge in it."

The next instant she was gone, leaving Dirk with his jaw hanging. The smile had been gorgeous, but that final speech certainly didn't go with it. He'd been pumped, out-thought, and shilled where it counted. He had half a mind to drag the girl back in again and demand an accounting—

A sudden, choking pall of darkness dropped over his head and shoulders, cutting the thought off. It took him nearly a second to accept what had happened. The glo-pup had gone out!

In the thick blackness, Dirk churned his way to the locker and into the dress blouse. The shiv, at least, was still in it. He zipped the heavy cloth closed with nervous fingers and jerked the blouse roughly into order. The shoes could sit where they were—whatever had happened, the silence of bare feet might be useful.

It was anything but silent in the corridor. The deck shuddered to the running of scores of feet, and doors banged in their slots. There were shouts and frantic scramblings and scattered screams. The glo-pups were out in the corridor, too; probably all over the ship. It was impossible, but they were out.

Blackout!

Someone thudded into Dirk's shoulder and grabbed at him. Hands locked around his throat, heavy shoes kicked at his shins. He balled one fist over the other and drove his arms up with all his strength—

The man hanging onto him howled and tumbled backward. Grimly Dirk ploughed through the struggling mob. Thirty meters ahead there was a companionway to the bow—if he could reach it. He wondered if Nadya had managed to reach her cabin before—

Btsiirrrrrrrr!

He threw himself flat against the cold metal of the deck. The shiv ricocheted and went racketing down the corridor, yowling blue murder.

Someone stepped on Dirk's right hand, hard. Someone was lying next to him. He dug his bare toes against the metal and tried to swim away from under the trampling feet. A small, wiry hand dug into his biceps.

"Lie still!" Nadya's voice hissed. "Or I'll put a shiv in your kidneys—"

Dirk didn't stop to bow from the waist; not exactly, anyhow. He doubled himself up suddenly, catching the girl a sickening blow in the solar plexus. Then he caught the suddenly-relaxed hand on his arm and dragged her after him. If he could get them both over against the wall—

Somehow, he made it. His captive was beginning to struggle again. He took her by the hair and dragged her ear over against his mouth.

"Stop it," he growled. The girl bucked once, but the cruel blow Dirk had dealt her had taken its toll. "It's me—Phillips. This is a blackout; there's worse to come. Don't attract any attention."

He locked his free arm about her. Under them, the deck shuddered spasmodically. A second later the wild howling of the General Alarm rang through the tubes. Dirk's lips skinned back from his teeth. Leave it to Muir! Nothing like a siren to pile madness on top of madness!

The mob surged toward the levitator shafts, every last man trying to claw up to Star Deck where there was at least an illusion of open spaces. After several eternities, B-Deck was quiet, except for a hopeless moaning somewhere astern. Dirk loosened his hold on the girl.

"All right," he said. "Let's go—and make it fast."

"I'm quite all right," she said angrily. "No thanks to you and your educated knees. If you'll let go of me I'll go to my cabin."

"You little fool, D-Deck is a madhouse now. Everyone's trying to jam up there. The only safe place in this whole ship is on the bridge. Travel!"

He drove her forward to the stairwell at the *Telemachus*'s nose. There was a light there, and Dirk felt a vague shame at the surge of relief that went through him when he saw it. Two of the crewmen were high up in the well, heat-rifles at the ready; the beam of a dismounted landing-light poured down the shaft. As Dirk propelled the girl into the column of light, both rifles snapped up.

"Ahoy, up there!" he called. "At ease. This is First Mate Phillips."

The flared muzzles did not waver.

"We know who you are," one of the spacemen said. "Point is, are you potty?"

"Nah, he ain't potty," the other one said. "He sleeps in the dark, ain't you heard? Come on up, sir."

Dirk went up the winding ladder, supporting the exhausted girl. At the port which let out onto Star Deck a red-headed little man in civvies crouched with his back to the well, a tape-ike jammed through the Judas. He was cursing exultantly. Dirk stopped and stared at him. "Hey, you—"

"It's Johnny Hask," Nadya said. "Cameraman. Johnny—"

The redhead waved them both away with his free hand. "Don't muss me up," he said. "Don't muss, see? What a picture! Two Thousand Passengers Riot in Interstellar Void! Terror On the Long Arc! What a picture! Go 'way, Nadya, you'll get your crack at it when we dub in the commentary."

Dirk grinned. However the little 'vision man had

gotten here, he was obviously having the time of his life. He took the girl's arm again.

On the bridge, Muir was jabbing at the power-boards and roaring anathemas at chicken livers who were afraid of a little darkness. The glow of a jury-rigged ethon-tube gleamed on his bald head. The navigator's desk was empty; Dirk let the girl slump into the empty seat and yanked the G. A. switch out of its blades. The siren wow-wowed away into silence like a damned soul dwindling into hell.

"What the—" Muir bellowed. Then, "Oh, it's you, Phillips! Get me an orbit check, fast, and cut that alarm in again!"

Dirk fed tape into the big integraph. "I'd advise against the alarm, sir. Everybody's at stations that can get to them in this ink. The siren just doubles the terror among the passengers."

"The passengers!" Muir looked stunned, as if the passengers were tilings he had forgotten until now. "They should have been gassed ten minutes ago."

Dirk automatically grabbed for his nose. The filters weren't there; he'd actually forgotten them—there'd been no gas! "That damned Sanders—"

"Here, sir," the Third Mate's voice said. He came through the D-Deck hatch with Stapledon, the 'vision boss, at his heels. Both of them looked considerably mussed up.

"What is this, a game?" Muir said. "A fine bunch of officers Interstellar gives me—too busy rescuing their favorite civilians to remember their General Orders. I suppose you wouldn't pull the gas 'til you had this man on the bridge, eh?"

"No, sir," Sanders said, swallowing. "I mean, yes, sir, I did. But nothing happened. I pulled toggles at every station from my cabin to here and didn't get any gas."

"Eh? No gas, no lights—I hope to Heaven we've got power! Phillips?"

"We're still on course, sir," Dirk said.

"All right. Sanders, get a party and run down the trouble in the main lighting lines." The Captain's blunt hands reached for the geotron cutout. At the same instant, Dirk hurled himself from the integraph in a flying tackle.

Muir came down with a heavy thud, but he struck fighting. He was a big man, and a hard one. It was like trying to wrestle a lion. Somehow he got one foot planted in Dirk's chest and heaved, his thigh muscles knotting under his tight uniform. Dirk felt himself flying. A second later he smashed into the far wall and Muir had a shiv pointed at his middle.

"Now then, Mr. Phillips," Muir said, breathing heavily. "Since you're the big, brave man who sleeps in the dark, we can't assume that you've got the madness. Explain yourself, and make it good."

Dirk fought for breath. Nadya was watching him with wide, terrified eyes. Sanders had snatched a heat-rifle from the rack and was hefting it uncertainly.

"The geotrons," Dirk gasped. "Don't cut them—"

"And why not, Mister? You know the General Orders on Blackouts—gas the passengers, cut the overdrive, send out visicarrier SOS—my God, we've had that stuff pounded into us ever since we were oilers."

"This is different. Jason's in the vicinity."

The shiv did not move. "Jason!" Muir said. "If he's

around, overdrive won't do us any good. I'd sooner be in free space where I could maneuver." He picked up the intercom mike. "Synchros!"

"Gunnery officer."

"Hello, Sims, I thought you'd been trampled. Battle stations. Report down the line on the murder guns."

"Begging your pardon, sir," the interphone said, "but I don't have any handlers or any power. If you could give me a rig from the accumulators I could manhandle the turret."

Muir swore. "All right," he said. "Good boy. Build a field, quick." His blunt fingers clacked plungers, banking the accumulators into the synchrotron circuits.

"You'll never make it," Dirk said flatly. "The pompoms are pea-shooters even if you do get them manned, and Sims can't beat a cruiser to the draw without handlers. You can't fight Jason with the Telemachus, Captain."

"I mean to try, Mister," Muir said. "I won't surrender my ship, fat pig as she is. And if Jason is out there, you can explain to a summary court-martial how you knew about it beforehand." He grasped the big jackknife handle. The twin plungers of the overdrive switch leapt out of their sockets.

The humming of the geotrons died. In the forward viewplate the stars swirled like dust motes in a sunbeam, changing colors with impossible rapidity, skyrocketing up into the violet, blinking out, reappearing at the red end of the spectrum and running the gamut again. It was as if a god's dream of stellar order had been broken and dispersed by some cosmic alarm clock.

Muir watched, his fists clenching and opening.

Dirk tensed for a new spring, but Sanders had the heat-rifle on him. The Third Mate was biting his lip, keeping his eyes off the plate by sheer funk. It was not pleasant to be a green officer in a space-bound madhouse . . .

Against the swirling stars, a ghostly ship formed.

There was a sobbing breath from Stapledon. He stumbled to the bulkhead, yanked the hatch open. It was dark beyond the hatch, but Stapledon suddenly did not appear to care. He went out, his ragged breathing merging with the surf of terrified moaning beating up from below.

The ghost ship solidified: a long, turret-knotted torpedo scarcely ten miles away. The stars scuttled affrightedly for their proper places and froze.

"Well?" Dirk said grimly.

Muir spun on him. "That's the *Argo II*, all right. And she's already got her turrets coming to bear on us." He glared at Dirk, like an infuriated bear. "Talk!"

Dirk shrugged. "Simple enough, Captain. It's impossible to pirate a ship on overdrive. We have to assume that; the main body of evidence—not all of it, but most of it—points that way, and to assume the opposite is to leave ourselves without any jumping-off place."

"I didn't ask for a lesson in logic, Mister!"

"Consequently," Dirk said evenly, "it followed that the liners Jason pirated were in free space—not on overdrive. Why? What reason could a liner have for cutting overdrive?"

"They had a Blackout?" Sanders whispered.

"Yes. They cut their geotrons as the General Orders require. Jason evidently knew in advance when the lights would go out and could manage to be nearby, on a matched course. Then, the moment the liner appeared in free space, his detectors spotted it and he got there in nothing flat on his own overdrive. If the liner sent out an SOS as the Orders require, why, so much the better. It led Jason to his victim practically by the nose."

"Very pretty." Muir frowned. Obviously Dirk's sudden assault upon his authority was hard to reconcile with his view of the situation. Yet if the *Telemachus* was actually under threat of piracy—

After a long moment, he jammed his shiv back into its scabbard. "I'll have to trust you, Phillips, though God knows you could have engineered the Blackout as well as anyone else on board. But I need you to fight the ship. Put up that rifle, Mr. Sanders, and muster me some pom-pom crews."

As if in answer, twin bolts of greenish light leapt from the *Argo II*'s dorsal turret. The *Telemachus* boomed like a cracked bass drum. The concussion knocked them all to the deck. The alarm siren cut in again. Muir surged to his knees and glowered at the blinkers.

"Aft cargo hold," he said. His nose was bleeding, but he didn't look a bit funny. "Where the hell—ah!"

A ragged comb of death swept along the port side of the *Telemachus*. The murder guns—some of them, anyhow. Dirk touched Nadya's shoulder reassuringly and squeezed himself into the gunnery officer's chair. There was a chance—Jason might not have expected the liner to be in any shape to fight back—

A bright, blue-white flower burst into bloom on the *Argo II*'s flank. One of the thermite-loaded pom-pom shells had found a home. With a grin of satisfaction Muir threw the *Telemachus*'s helm up and over. The big ship rose clumsily on her jets.

Dirk watched his crosshair and prayed that the lone man in the belly turret had had time to build a field. If it had been even barely possible, Sims was the man to get it done. But with no handlers—

The pirate's synchros fountained deutrons again, but this time there was no answering crash. In space, the target booms, not the guns; silence meant a clean miss. The crosshair slid toward the image of the gray cruiser. Dirk's hand tensed above the firing key—

James Henry Stapledon's voice said, "I wouldn't touch that, if I were you, Mr. Phillips."

Dirk froze. After a moment he turned his head, slowly.

Stapledon was standing in the darkness of the open hatch, smiling lazily. From behind him the dull horror of the passengers still rose and fell. Cradled in his arms was Dirk's cyclast.

The heavy sub-cruiser lay off, its guns centered watchfully on the *Telemachus*. From the boarding-launch at the liner's keel airlock, arrogant, greedy-eyed men with blasters filed along the corridors, and a few seconds later the main lights came on again. In the shambles on Star Deck, passengers looked at each other and at what they had done. Some of them wept. Some of them were beyond all tears. The rest were dead.

Jason had to bend low to get through the hatch to the bridge. He was a tall man, with the mild, weak face of a momma's darling. With him was an entity even taller than he was, a ten-foot figure with tattered ears like a mongrel dog's: a Martian.

"This," Jason said, waving his hand at the Outlander, "is my First Mate, Willie Peng. If he gives any orders in my absence, jump, or you'll bloat. Now then. Who's Captain Muir?"

"Me," Muir said disgustedly.

"Oho; the surly type. Take his shiv, Willie—and you might lighten these other heroes of their loads, too."

Stapledon shifted to keep the others in the line of fire while the Martian blocked Jason's blaster. The pirate's eyes encountered the girl, and his almost-invisible eyebrows kinked.

"My dear girl!" he said. "What a shame!"

Nadya said, "Hello, Paul."

Dirk stared at them both. Paul? The raider's face was familiar—

"I see," he said slowly. "Paul Haagen. No wonder you were in such a hurry to demobilize the Patrol." Another thought crept unbidden into his mind. There had been another Councilman who had been strong for "letting the boys go home"—Kurt Storm, Nadya's father.

"I'm really quite sorry," Jason was saying, rather too smoothly. He did not seem to notice that Dirk existed. "I'd supposed you'd be back there among the rabble; you could have been ransomed and no one would have been the wiser. Now—"

"Now," Nadya said, "you'll have to kill me along with the officers?"

Stapledon stirred. "I say," he protested. "Look, Paul, there's a limit. I can't continue to romanticize your exploits if you victimize my best stars—"

"Be quiet," Jason said sharply. "No, I don't think I'll do that, Nadya. Contrariwise, you can't go free. Hmm. A nice problem." The washed-out blue eyes scanned her speculatively.

"All got, chief," Willie Peng said. He threw the shivs in a corner. "Female got one, too. Rf?"

"It's ornamental; no propellant; Centaurian fashion," Jason said. Willie looked puzzled, but his Captain's indifference was clear enough. "Muir, where's the mail stored?"

"Six paces from the nearest firing squad," Muir said. "Take a look."

"I shall. Willie, the passenger list is probably in that locker over there. You know the names to look for."

"Rf."

Dirk felt his muscles cording. The locker, unlike the baggage-safes below, had a tough five-tumbler electrolock on it. If Willie, like most Outlanders, was short on patience—

He was. He fumbled tentatively and swore in his own hoarse language. Then he turned his blaster on the lock. A blaster in a confined space kicks up quite a fuss—

Dirk threw himself forward with every erg of power he could slam into his legs. Stapledon shouted incoherently. Dirk's head butted into Jason's middle.

The pirate's clubbed blaster glanced stunningly off Dirk's left temple. The deck hit him on the forehead. He ground his teeth and fought to his knees, spitting blood. The toe of a hard-driven spaceboot crashed into his side.

On the edge of the tangle Stapledon scuttled, trying to get in position to blast Dirk and still cover

Muir and Sanders. The Martian's weapon would take about eighty seconds to recharge; Willie threw it at Dirk and went around the other way. Sanders stuck a foot out and the ten-foot dog-man came down on the deck like a scarecrow. Jason kicked Dirk again and brought the muzzle of his own blaster into line—

Ptsiirr-tchk!

Jason dropped the blaster and grabbed at his throat. Blood cascaded down the front of his jacket. A half-inch of shiv-blade protruded from his Adam's apple; it had nearly taken his head off. Dirk retched and snatched at the weapon on the deck, but it wasn't needed. As Stapledon swung on Dirk, Muir lobbed a balled fist as big as a grapefruit into his ear. He dropped as if stoned.

That left Willie Peng. He had a clear field, but when Dirk dropped the blaster and snatched the cyclast from the fallen 'vision magnate, Willie laid back his ears, bared his teeth, and dived under the chart table. A man will face up to a blaster or a heat-rifle, but a cyclast is something else again; nobody likes to feel his flesh running fluidly off his bones...

"Nice going, Nadya," Dirk gasped.

The girl was crying convulsively. "I had to do it," she sobbed. "When I think what a fool he made of Dad—and the awful thing down below—"

"Cripes," Dirk said. "We're still full up with boarders. Quick, Sanders, pull the gas—they've got the lights back on, and money says the same short was what cut the gas-toggles."

The Third Mate jumped to the wall toggle and pulled it. It cut the alarm siren on again, but for once Dirk was glad to hear it. The gas was on. Under the wailing alarm he could hear it hissing beyond the open hatch. He slammed the hatch shut.

Muir was already at the interphone. "Sims!" he roared. "You still free?"

"Yissir," the intercom said. "What the hell's going on? I've been sitting on my key for twenty minutes. Isn't anybody going to fire these damned guns?"

Muir grinned savagely. "Keep sitting." He gestured Dirk to the firing table. The single vertical crosshair was a little to the left of the image of the *Argo II*; if Sims had his key down, it meant that his own horizontal crosshair was still on the pirate. Muir fired a short burst from the port jets and the sub-cruiser's image began to drift.

When the vertical crosshair split it fairly across the middle, Dirk put down the bridge key. Under the *Telemachus*'s belly the synchros screamed triumphantly—

A silent burst of white-hot gas jetted away from the *Argo II*'s middle. Dirk held the key down as her image continued to drift. The cancer of destruction ate its way forward. The big cruiser jerked spasmodically, but before she could get underway the blast of deutrons reached her bridge.

One side of the *Argo II*, just foreward of the overdrive assembly, fell away, and a lifeship clawed spaceward. Muir shook a fist at it. "Small fry," he snarled, "but I hate to see a one of 'em stay alive—"

At the nose of the *Telemachus*, a single pom-pom spouted. Some crewman had kept his head long enough to remember his nose-filters. The murder gun was coming into its own. The life-ship ran head on into a thermit shell. After that it drifted . . .

As an afterthought, Dirk dragged Willie Peng out

from under the chart table and chucked him out the hatch into the gas. "A sleeping prisoner," he said to no one in particular, "is a good prisoner."

Sanders said unsteadily, "One thing I don't get. How did Stapledon get into it?"

"Remember his editorials last year about peace and plenty?" Dirk said. "His chain supported Haagen and Storm in the demobilization campaign. And he financed Jason. He had every reason to want this colonization stopped; Earth's empire was getting too big for him. As things stood, he could sway public opinion, control Council decisions, get things played the way he wanted them. But every new star system conquered made his hold more tenuous. Jason, he hoped, would terrorize the colonists, ruin all chance of the Cygni system—or any other new system—being settled by people he couldn't manipulate."

"I can see why," Muir said. "What I want to know is how."

"That's easy. Stapledon was the only person who could have bollixed up the ship's circuits that way. There's a 'vision set in every room. His technies had plenty of opportunity to disconnect the gas-trips at the same time they installed the sets. And plenty of time to take out the real glo-pups—the radioactive ones that never go out—and install colored ethons instead. They were spliced onto the regular lighting circuit. When Jason wanted a Blackout, all his henchman had to do was cause a short somewhere, and *blooey!* What chance would we have of finding where the short was in the middle of a riot?"

He felt his kicked side tenderly. "But they had to have light to work by when they boarded us. They knew where the short was and fixed it. The 'vision technies had had no chance to disconnect the gas toggle on the bridge and depended on the pirates to incapacitate the bridge. When that failed, they were sunk—nobody but the Patrol knows how to make gasproof nosepieces, and Jason couldn't steal a tenth as many as he'd need to equip his crew.

"It's no wonder Jason owned a heavy sub-cruiser. He had Stapledon behind him to put up the two million or so it took to buy the ship from Ganymede. Two million's a lot of credits, but they probably got it back in the first attack—not that the money itself interested Stapledon any. He probably let Jason keep it all.

"We figured that might be the story, but 'til now we had no proof; and the demobbing left us without enough men to put Marines aboard every ship—"

"We?" Muir said suspiciously. "Who's we?"

Dirk grinned. "Intelligence, who else? Commander John H. Dalton, at your service."

"Not," Sanders said, on cue, "not Jack Dalton of the Centrale Patrol!"

"Sir, the very same." Dirk looked at the girl. "Aren't you going to say, 'My hero'?"

She didn't, but the substitute she offered was eminently satisfactory.

James Blish (1921–1975) may be best known for his *Star Trek* novel adaptations, but his enduring reputation in SF rests on his classic *Cities in Flight* series, comprising four novels: *They Shall Have Stars*, *A Life for the Stars*, *Earthman, Come Home*, and *The Triumph of Time* (also published as *A Clash of Cymbals*), in which the invention of the "spindizzy" and anti-gravity/faster-than-light drive/force field leads to whole cities leaving the Earth and wandering the stars. Another series of note is his "pantropy" series, which has humans colonizing the stars by being genetically altered to survive in vastly different conditions rather than living in domes or terraforming the colony worlds. A third series, less orthodoxly linked, is his "After Such Knowledge" series, comprising his Hugo-winning novel, *A Case of Conscience*, a historical novel, *Dr. Mirabilis*, based on the life of Roger Bacon, and the novel *Black Easter* and its sequel, *The Day After Judgment*, which share a theme, but are set in very different time periods and different universes. His novel, *A Case of Conscience*, was a continuation of a novella with the same title, which itself won a Retro-Hugo in 2001. Writing critical reviews of SF stories under the pseudonym "William Atheling, Jr.," he became known as one of the field's premiere critics. He was a noted authority on the works of James Branch Cabell, Ezra Pound, and James Joyce. He was the Guest of Honor at the 1960 World Science Fiction Convention and was one of the field's true polymaths.

Postmark Ganymede

Robert Silverberg

*What a comedown! Preston was trained in space combat
by the Patrol . . . and now he's a mere mail carrier. But
then he is menaced by space pirates and finds there
are even worse things waiting on Ganymede . . .*

"I'm washed up," Preston growled bitterly. "They made
a postman out of me. Me—a postman!"

He crumpled the assignment memo into a small,
hard ball and hurled it at the bristly image of himself
in the bar mirror. He hadn't shaved in three days—
which was how long it had been since he had been
notified of his removal from Space Patrol Service and
his transfer to Postal Delivery.

Suddenly, Preston felt a hand on his shoulder.
He looked up and saw a man in the trim gray of a
Patrolman's uniform.

"What do you want, Dawes?"

"Chief's been looking for you, Preston. It's time for you to get going on your run."

Preston scowled. "Time to go deliver the mail, eh?" He spat. "Don't they have anything better to do with good spacemen than make letter carriers out of them?"

The other man shook his head. "You won't get anywhere grousing about it, Preston. Your papers don't specify which branch you're assigned to, and if they want to make you carry the mail—that's it." His voice became suddenly gentle. "Come on, Pres. One last drink, and then let's go. You don't want to spoil a good record, do you?"

"No," Preston said reflectively. He gulped his drink and stood up. "Okay. I'm ready. Neither snow nor rain shall stay me from my appointed rounds, or however the damned thing goes."

"That's a smart attitude, Preston. Come on—I'll walk you over to Administration."

Savagely, Preston ripped away the hand that the other had put around his shoulders. "I can get there myself. At least give me credit for that!"

"Okay," Dawes said, shrugging. "Well—good luck, Preston."

"Yeah. Thanks. Thanks real lots."

He pushed his way past the man in Space Grays and shouldered past a couple of barflies as he left. He pushed open the door of the bar and stood outside for a moment.

It was near midnight, and the sky over Nome Spaceport was bright with stars. Preston's trained eye picked out Mars, Jupiter, Uranus. There they were—waiting. But he would spend the rest of his days ferrying letters on the Ganymede run.

He sucked in the cold night air of summertime Alaska and squared his shoulders.

Two hours later, Preston sat at the controls of a one-man patrol ship just as he had in the old days. Only the control panel was bare where the firing studs for the heavy guns were found in regular patrol ships. And in the cargo hold instead of crates of spare ammo there were three bulging sacks of mail destined for the colony on Ganymede.

Slight difference, Preston thought, as he set up his blasting pattern.

"Okay, Preston," came the voice from the tower. "You've got clearance."

"Cheers," Preston said, and yanked the blast-lever. The ship jolted upward, and for a second he felt a little of the old thrill—until he remembered.

He took the ship out in space, saw the blackness in the viewplate. The radio crackled.

"Come in, Postal Ship. Come in, Postal Ship."

"I'm in. What do you want?"

"We're your convoy," a hard voice said. "Patrol Ship 08756, Lieutenant Mellors, above you. Down at three o'clock, Patrol Ship 10732, Lieutenant Gunderson. We'll take you through the Pirate Belt."

Preston felt his face go hot with shame. Mellors! Gunderson! They would stick two of his old sidekicks on the job of guarding him.

"Please acknowledge," Mellors said.

Preston paused. Then: "Postal Ship 1872, Lieutenant Preston aboard. I acknowledge message."

There was a stunned silence. "*Preston?* Hal Preston?"

"The one and only," Preston said.

"What are you doing on a Postal ship?" Mellors asked.

"Why don't you ask the Chief that? He's the one who yanked me out of the Patrol and put me here."

"Can you beat that?" Gunderson asked incredulously. "Hal Preston, on a Postal ship."

"Yeah. Incredible, isn't it?" Preston asked bitterly. "You can't believe your ears. Well, you better believe it, because here I am."

"Must be some clerical error," Gunderson said.

"Let's change the subject," Preston snapped.

They were silent for a few moments as the three ships—two armed, one loaded with mail for Ganymede—streaked outward away from Earth. Manipulating his controls with the ease of long experience, Preston guided the ship smoothly toward the gleaming bulk of far-off Jupiter. Even at this distance, he could see five or six bright pips surrounding the huge planet. There was Callisto, and—ah—there was Ganymede.

He made computations, checked his controls, figured orbits. Anything to keep from having to talk to his two ex-Patrolmates or from having to think about the humiliating job he was on. Anything to—

"Pirates! Moving up at two o'clock!"

Preston came awake. He picked off the location of the pirate ships—there were two of them, coming up out of the asteroid belt. Small, deadly, compact, they orbited toward him.

He pounded the instrument panel in impotent rage, looking for the guns that weren't there.

"Don't worry, Pres," came Mellors's voice. "We'll take care of them for you."

"Thanks," Preston said bitterly. He watched as the

pirate ships approached, longing to trade places with the men in the Patrol ships above and below him.

Suddenly a bright spear of flame lashed out across space and the hull of Gunderson's ship glowed cherry red. "I'm okay," Gunderson reported immediately. "Screens took the charge."

Preston gripped his controls and threw the ship into a plunging dive that dropped it back behind the protection of both Patrol ships. He saw Gunderson and Mellors converge on one of the pirates. Two blue beams licked out, and the pirate ship exploded.

But then the second pirate swooped down in an unexpected dive. "Look out!" Preston yelled helplessly—but it was too late. Beams ripped into the hull of Mellors's ship, and a dark fissure line opened down the side of the ship. Preston smashed his hand against the control panel. Better to die in an honest dogfight than to live this way!

It was one against one, now—Gunderson against the pirate. Preston dropped back again to take advantage of the Patrol ship's protection.

"I'm going to try a diversionary tactic," Gunderson said on untappable tight-beam. "Get ready to cut under and streak for Ganymede with all you got."

"Check."

Preston watched as the tactic got under way. Gunderson's ship traveled in a long, looping spiral that drew the pirate into the upper quadrant of space. His path free, Preston guided his ship under the other two and toward unobstructed freedom. As he looked back, he saw Gunderson steaming for the pirate on a sure collision orbit. He turned away. The score was two Patrolmen dead, two ships wrecked—but the mail would get through. Shaking his head, Preston leaned forward over his control board and headed on toward Ganymede.

The blue-white, frozen moon hung beneath him. Preston snapped on the radio.

"Ganymede Colony? Come in, please. This is your Postal Ship." The words tasted sour in his mouth.

There was silence for a second. "Come in, Ganymede," Preston repeated impatiently, and then the sound of a distress signal cut across his audio pickup.

It was coming on wide beam from the satellite below—they had cut out all receiving facilities in an attempt to step up their transmitter. Preston reached for the wide-beam stud, pressed it.

"Okay, I pick up your signal, Ganymede. Come in, now!"

"This is Ganymede," a tense voice said. "We've got trouble down here. Who are you?"

"Mail Ship," Preston said. "From Earth. What's going on?"

There was the sound of voices whispering somewhere near the microphone. Finally: "Hello, Mail Ship?"

"Yeah?"

"You're going to have to turn back to Earth, fellow. You can't land here. It's rough on us, missing a mail trip, but—"

Preston said impatiently, "Why can't I land? What the devil's going on down there?"

"We've been invaded," the tired voice said. "The colony's been completely surrounded by iceworms."

"Iceworms?"

"The local native life," the colonist explained.

"They're about thirty feet long, a foot wide, and mostly mouth. There's a ring of them about a hundred yards wide surrounding the Dome. They can't get in and we can't get out—and we can't figure out any possible approach for you."

"Pretty," Preston said. "But why didn't the things bother you while you were building your Dome?"

"Apparently they have a very long hibernation-cycle. We've only been here two years, you know. The ice-worms must all have been asleep when we came. But they came swarming out of the ice by the hundreds last month."

"How come Earth doesn't know?"

"The antenna for our long-range transmitter was outside the Dome. One of the worms came by and chewed the antenna right off. All we've got left is this short-range thing we're using and it's no good more than ten thousand miles from here. You're the first one who's been this close since it happened."

"I get it." Preston closed his eyes for a second, trying to think things out.

The Colony was under blockade by hostile alien life, thereby making it impossible for him to deliver the mail. Okay. If he'd been a regular member of the Postal Service, he'd have given it up as a bad job and gone back to Earth to report the difficulty.

But I'm not going back. I'll be the best damned mailman they've got.

"Give me a landing orbit anyway, Ganymede."

"But you can't come down! How will you leave your ship?"

"Don't worry about that," Preston said calmly.

"We have to worry! We don't dare open the Dome,

with those creatures outside. You *can't* come down, Postal Ship."

"You want your mail or don't you?"

The colonist paused. "Well—"

"Okay, then," Preston said. "Shut up and give me landing coordinates!"

There was a pause, and then the figures started coming over. Preston jotted them down on a scratch-pad.

"Okay, I've got them. Now sit tight and wait." He glanced contemptuously at the three mail-pouches behind him, grinned, and started setting up the orbit.

Mailman, am I? I'll show them!

He brought the Postal Ship down with all the skill of his years in the Patrol, spiralling in around the big satellite of Jupiter as cautiously and as precisely as if he were zeroing in on a pirate lair in the asteroid belt. In its own way, this was as dangerous, perhaps even more so.

Preston guided the ship into an ever-narrowing orbit, which he stabilized about a hundred miles over the surface of Ganymede. As his ship swung around the moon's poles in its tight orbit, he began to figure some fuel computations.

His scratch-pad began to fill with notations.

Fuel storage—
Escape velocity—
Margin of error—
Safety factor—

Finally he looked up. He had computed exactly how much spare fuel he had, how much he could afford to waste. It was a small figure—too small, perhaps.

He turned to the radio. "Ganymede?"

"Where are you, Postal Ship?"

"I'm in a tight orbit about a hundred miles up,"

Preston said. "Give me the figures on the circumference of your Dome. Ganymede?"

"Seven miles," the colonist said. "What are you planning to do?"

Preston didn't answer. He broke contact and scribbled some more figures. Seven miles of iceworms, eh? That was too much to handle. He had planned on dropping flaming fuel on them and burning them out, but he couldn't do it that way.

He'd have to try a different tactic.

Down below, he could see the blue-white ammonia ice that was the frozen atmosphere of Ganymede. Shimmering gently amid the whiteness was the transparent yellow of the Dome beneath whose curved walls lived the Ganymede Colony. Even forewarned, Preston shuddered. Surrounding the Dome was a living, writhing belt of giant worms.

"Lovely," he said. "Just lovely."

Getting up, he clambered over the mail sacks and headed toward the rear of the ship, hunting for the auxiliary fuel tanks.

Working rapidly, he lugged one out and strapped it into an empty gun turret, making sure he could get it loose again when he'd need it.

He wiped away sweat and checked the angle at which the fuel tank would face the ground when he came down for a landing. Satisfied, he knocked a hole in the side of the fuel tank.

"Okay, Ganymede," he radioed. "I'm coming down."

He blasted loose from the tight orbit and rocked the ship down on manual. The forbidding surface of Ganymede grew closer and closer. Now he could see the iceworms plainly.

Hideous, thick creatures, lying coiled in masses around the Dome. Preston checked his spacesuit, making sure it was sealed. The instruments told him he was a bare ten miles above Ganymede now. One more swing around the poles would do it.

He peered out as the Dome came below and once again snapped on the radio.

"I'm going to come down and burn a path through those worms of yours. Watch me carefully, and jump to it when you see me land. I want that airlock open, or else."

"But—"

"No buts!"

He was right overhead now. Just one ordinary-type gun would solve the whole problem, he thought. But Postal Ships didn't get guns. They weren't supposed to need them.

He centered the ship as well as he could on the Dome below and threw it into automatic pilot. Jumping from the control panel, he ran back toward the gun turret and slammed shut the plexilite screen. Its outer wall opened and the fuel tank went tumbling outward and down. He returned to his control-panel seat and looked at the viewscreen. He smiled. The fuel tank was lying near the Dome—right in the middle of the nest of iceworms. The fuel was leaking from the puncture.

The iceworms writhed in from all sides.

"Now!" Preston said grimly.

The ship roared down, jets blasting. The fire licked out, heated the ground, melted snow—ignited the fuel tank! A gigantic flame blazed up, reflected harshly off the snows of Ganymede.

And the mindless iceworms came, marching toward

the fire, being consumed, as still others devoured the bodies of the dead and dying.

Preston looked away and concentrated on the business of finding a place to land the ship.

The holocaust still raged as he leaped down from the catwalk of the ship, clutching one of the heavy mail sacks, and struggled through the melting snows to the airlock.

He grinned. The airlock was open.

Arms grabbed him, pulled him through. Someone opened his helmet.

"Great job, Postman!"

"There are two more mail sacks," Preston said. "Get men out after them."

The man in charge gestured to two young colonists who donned spacesuits and dashed through the airlock. Preston watched as they raced to the ship, climbed in, and returned a few moments later with the mail sacks.

"You've got it all," Preston said. "I'm checking out. I'll get word to the Patrol to get here and clean up that mess for you."

"How can we thank you?" the official-looking man asked.

"No need to," Preston said casually. "I had to get that mail down here some way, didn't I?"

He turned away, smiling to himself. Maybe the Chief *had* known what he was doing when he took an experienced Patrol man and dumped him into Postal. Delivering the mail to Ganymede had been more hazardous than fighting off half a dozen space pirates. *I guess I was wrong,* Preston thought. *This is no snap job for old men.*

Preoccupied, he started out through the airlock. The man in charge caught his arm. "Say, we don't even know your name! Here you are a hero, and—"

"Hero?" Preston shrugged. "All I did was deliver the mail. It's all in a day's work, you know. The mail's got to get through!"

Robert Silverberg, prolific author not just of SF, but of authoritative nonfiction books, columnist for *Asimov's SF Magazine*, winner of a constellation of awards, and renowned bon vivant surely needs no introduction—but that's never stopped me before. Born in 1935, Robert Silverberg sold his first SF story, "Gorgon Planet," before he was out of his teens, to the British magazine *Nebula*. Two years later, his first SF novel, a juvenile, *Revolt on Alpha C* followed. Decades later, his total SF titles stands at 82 SF novels and 457 short stories. Early on, he won a Hugo Award for most promising new writer—rarely have the Hugo voters been so perceptive.

Toward the end of the 1960s and continuing into the 1970s, he wrote a string of novels much darker in tone and deeper in characterization than his work of the 1950s, such as the novels *Nightwings*, *Dying Inside*, and *The Book of Skulls*. He took occasional sabbaticals from writing to return with new works, such as the Majipoor series. His most recent novels include *The Alien Years*, *The Longest Way Home*, and a new trilogy of Majipoor novels. He was inducted into the Science Fiction and Fantasy Hall of Fame in 1999.

In 2004, the Science Fiction Writers of America presented him with the Damon Knight Memorial Grand Master Award. For more information, see his "quasi-official" website at www.majipoor.com. The site is heroically maintained by Jon Davis (no relation).

Mystery of the Space Pirates

Arlan Andrews, Sr.

When Mr. Andrews included this short-short punstory in his collection, Future Flash, he gave it this brief intro-duction: "No excuses. Not one." Fortunately, being an editor means never having to say you're sorry. You may be sorry, but you don't have to say so. My excuse is that I am one of those unfortunates hopelessly addicted to puns. Give generously to help find the cure, but in the meantime, if you are among the immune, You have been warned! Proceed at your own risk . . .

Dr. Panlener Spoon stood in front of the press confer-ence, his confidence emanating to the known galaxy through the tri-cams and the bright lights.

"I have solved the mystery of the missing Meiner Brothers," he declared, waving a curiously woven feathered headdress of primitive origin.

"While hunting these vile evil-doers through the J. P. Getty private planetary system, I received a hyperspace distress signal from Ms. Lynn King, archaeologist from Burke University who was doing research on Planet Four, the avian preserve.

"I immediately landed and found Ms. King being cared for by the native inhabitants, the humanoid 'Fours.' She had been studying the microglyphs that the Fours carve on the animal bones of their headgear, one glyph for each day of their life—their way of being remembered. She, too, had learned their craft.

"She also learned that these previously unresearched natives are telepathic. Not only do they communicate with a related race on Planet Seven of the system, they use their mental powers to shield themselves from the savage telepathic attacks of the carnivorous animals that still roam the outback. No human can withstand the animals alone without that protection. Fascinating, don't you think?

"Well, just a few days before I arrived, the Meiner Brothers, Hal and Barth, along with their one crewperson, Ann Deck, a human from Avis II, had landed on Planet Seven and absolutely ransacked the place for the precious spices, taking even seeds and sprouts— everything. Then they came to Four for the most valuable loot of all—the fabulous Golden Eagles of Four, worth any price on the black market zoo worlds of the Federation.

"This is where they made their mistake—Ann Deck was a born-again fanatic of the Audubon Church on her home planet. Not only did she refuse to help catch the birds, but she even defected to the natives to try to stop the pirates. The Meiners, for their part, didn't mind seeing her depart. They hated her religion and they hated her for the one psychic power that all Avis

II'ers inherit—paradentistry, the useful-but-painful talent that gave her race its nickname, 'Toothy.'

"Sensing trouble, Barth unloaded the boxes of stolen spice around their ship as a barrier against native attacks, while Hal took a land vehicle, his stun rifle, and some large crates, and went looking for the Golden Eagles.

"When the natives heard Ann Deck's news, they went berserk. They were already upset with the looting of their cousins on Seven, and Ms. Deck proposed a fitting retribution should either of the men touch their bird-gods: A Shun, the withdrawing of psychic protection from the pirates, meaning they'd be subject to attack by the telepathic predators of Four.

"The grateful natives adopted Ann Deck into their tribe and dressed her in the head-to-toe garment indicating she was a servant of their chief. Then they all went to attack the Meiners.

"The Fours waited outside the Meiners' spice-box barricade until the Holy Hour when their one moon reached the point of its daily orbit, where it would begin a visible wobble caused by tidal forces. Called 'nutation' by astronomers, the natives regarded the phenomenon as propitious for their cause.

"They charged.

"Barth Meiner fought off the first attack with superior weapons. But then Hal Meiner arrived with the caged eagles and the natives went wild. At Ms. King's urging, they captured Hal, then let the waiting telepathic animals storm Barth's fortress and dispose of him among his ill-gotten loot."

Dr. Spoon waved the headdress for all of the tri-cams to view. "Unfortunately, the natives' microglyph records end there, but Ms. King has recorded the whole story on her own headdress here. She tells how the pirates finally met their fates at the hand of the grim Fours."

He smiled. "You must remember, of course, that although these events transpired yesterday for me, it was years ago by your own time; quicker-than-light flight does have its disadvantages.

"To summarize: 'For scouring Seven, years ago Fours further fought Barth upon his condiments at nutation; concealed in livery, Ann Deck, hated Toothy, proposed a Shun—that Hal Meiner crated eagles!'

"This, of course, is from Lynn King's Getty-Burke headdress!"

Arlan Andrews, Sr., began selling articles in 1972, dealing with Forteana, UFOs, the paranormal, and other esoteric subjects. His first science fiction sale was to *Asimov's* SF Magazine in 1979, followed since by ten dozen more in *Analog*, anthologies, and other magazines. A retired engineer, he founded SIGMA, the science fiction think tank, while working at the White House Science Office in 1992. SIGMA's professional writers provide SFnal type futurism for free to the Federal Government, and have worked with many well-known agencies and military branches. Arlan's latest novels are available on Amazon and elsewhere: *Paradox Lost, Silicon Blood, Valley of the Shaman*, and story collections *Future Flash, Other Heads & Other Tales*, and *The Great Moon Hoax: How It Really Happened*.

Collision Orbit

Katherine MacLean

The escaped convicts from Earth stole a spaceship and headed out to the asteroid belt, where they burst in on a settler running a sort of spacefaring general store for settlers. They thought he'd be harmless and helpless, but hadn't considered that settlers in space had to be tough and resourceful. He had figured out his countermove before he even had his pants on...

I was drowsing when I heard the airlock clanking and banging. Anyone can come into my ship, glance through the magazines, play the films, and select food from the stock without me bothering to wake up until they're ready to buy something, but this sound was different. By the way they were clanging and cursing and trying to get the airlock to work, they were strangers. I came wide awake. Last month's load of news from Earth had some interesting stories. Four convicts were missing from New San Quentin. There had been a bank robbery three days later with a really terrific haul of money taken. After that the Earth-to-Moon lift ship had taken off with apparently a full load, but six of the passengers never reported in on the Moon after the ship landed and were considered to be missing, and one of them had been found dead on Earth a mile away from takeoff point. An hour and a half after the lift ship had landed at Luna, the space ship *Phobos*, of the Luna to Phobos-Mars run, took off suddenly without waiting for cargo and vanished into space with only her pilot and first engineer known to be on board. The news was a month old by the time it got to me, but it was easy to add those three items up. The convicts had the ship and were heading for the Asteroid Belt.

Well, here they were at the Asteroid Belt. First stop, Sam's Place. I grinned slightly and unscrewed two of the knobs on the radio, screwed one back in the wrong place and put the other under the counter. Then I switched the radio on to Send, in spite of the fact the knob said Receive. They were coming. Yawning, I swung around on my revolving chair.

"Careful with the airlock. Air's not free around here."

They crowded in, four figures muffled in heavy spacesuits with green globes concealing their heads.

"Don't move, Mister." Two guns were suddenly pointed at my middle.

"Good evening, gentlemen," I said amiably. "I was expecting you would drop in. What can I sell you?"

"You didn't expect us, Fatty," said one, taking off his helmet and showing a young haggard face that needed a shave. He snickered nervously, put out his hand, and was given a gun by one who reached up and began taking off his own helmet. The young one was nervous but not stupid, for with the gun pointing steadily at me he moved quickly to one side as far as he could get. He leaned against the front wall to cover me from the opposite direction of the other gun holder. Whatever ideas I'd had about maneuvering one in front of the other and grabbing a gun vanished right then.

"Shove that funny-talk, Mister," said the other, a husky with a stiff crewcut. "We're not buying anything; we're taking this place over."

The other two had their helmets off now. There was a big thoughtful-looking one who went over to look at the supplies, and a lean one who went off looking for the can. They all looked haggard, underfed and tired. Probably they were haggard from having trouble holding down their food. Spacesickness gets practically anyone the first months out.

The big one wandered into the stacks of supplies and began opening cartons and nibbling anything edible.

That made me mad, but I didn't say anything, just got up and looked to see what he was opening, and almost got shot as the young gunman's hand jerked nervously at my motion.

"Sit down and turn off those neon signs and radio beams. We've got to get moving."

"Yeah," said the husky, as if surprised that he'd thought of it. "Turn 'em off."

There was a big neon sign wrapped around my ship, saying, SAM'S. I flipped a couple of switches, and it went off for the first time in a long time. There was also a set of swinging radio beams like lighthouse beams which said "Sam's Merchandise" in my voice. It was a sound that spacemen could home in on when they ran out of food or something broke and they needed a spare part. I flipped another switch and that went off too for the first time since I'd set it up. A lot of men depended on that radio beam.

But I didn't expect it would stay off long.

The radio was humming quietly at "Rec." as if waiting for incoming calls, but what it was doing was broadcasting everything that was said inside the store. It wasn't beamed at anyone, so the signal was weak, but anyone who wanted to know why my homing beams had gone off could find out by turning to my frequency and listening.

Fergason's place was on my orbit, somewhere close ahead. If he noticed me going by, he'd wonder why I didn't stop to deliver the mail and the groceries.

All I had to do was to stay alive for awhile, or make sure they killed me in a certain way.

"Man the controls, Mister," said the husky one. "Take us out of here before someone comes to see why the lights went off."

"Any direction," added the big man who was chewing at the supplies. He had an easy deep drawl. "We'll tell you later where to go."

The fourth man came out of the can and laughed at that, bringing clear the idea that I wasn't going to be around long.

Abruptly I realized I had made a bad mistake. "Wait a minute," I said, letting myself sound startled. "I'm not wearing my coverall." I was wearing jockey shorts, nothing else, and I figured that they'd think I was modest. I spotted the coverall lying across a case of algin butter and reached for it. "Mind?"

The husky with the gun waved it at me, "Get those jets going," he snarled. "Stop stalling around."

"Let him put his pants on," smiled the big one, coming forward again with an open magazine in his hand. "No reason for anyone to be closer than a thousand miles; people spread thin in space. They won't all arrive here for a picnic before he gets dressed."

I didn't wait for the gunman's nod, just took a chance and grabbed the coverall to put it on. They did not object again, apparently taking the big one's say as the final word.

The coverall slipped silkily over bare feet and legs, pulled up and zipped tight to cover body, arms, and hands comfortably in thin, flexible, silky fabric, with a fancy looking collar, high behind the neck, low and open in front, and held in shape by the edge being a light metal ring, with another light metal ring and a little mirror-like limp plastic hanging down the back attached from the collar, like the space suitish touches that were the style in men and women's coats on Earth.

The material had a mixture of slow and fast elastic threads so that it fitted like a skin, but gave easily with every motion, and it was painted with a coating of aluminum, so that it shone like a flexible mirror.

It was an intensely practical outfit, used by almost everyone in the Belt. The rest of mankind didn't have anything like it. Give an amateur necessity and not much material to work with and he can out-invent any hired expert. But it looked useless, ornamental and gaudy, and I did not cut much of a figure in it. Lots of people get fat around the waistline in space. Something to do with not enough exercise for the legs. No place to walk to.

I looked like I'd just put on a coat of aluminum paint and a fancy collar, and knew it. There were stares and grins.

Let them laugh now. "Look at that, a silver-plated man."

"Isn't he purty."

"Look at those muscles bulge, Or are they muscles?"

I clenched my teeth together, climbed into the pilot's chair, and pushed the steering rod forward cautiously until I could feel the jets beginning to thrust.

The big one, the one who was probably the brains of the outfit, came forward and leaned over my shoulder watching what I was doing. He chewed crackers noisily beside my ear and turned the pages of a magazine. "We're well stocked back there. Enough food and entertainment for a year."

"It's all due to customers," I said. "Two months' worth, per person, to be delivered here and there." I was bearing down on an irregularly shaped lump of rock on the screen that was probably Fergason's camouflaged place. It turned red on the screen, meaning I was on a collision course. I couldn't tell that it was Fergason's without having the radio open to his signal, but if that was his place, probably all his alarm bells were ringing inside, and he was screeching into his mike, trying to warn me to change course.

I moved the control rod a notch sideways to avoid it, and the screen turned it white again, showing it was no longer a danger.

"How about putting on some more speed," drawled the thinker. He was used to having people take his advice; it showed in his voice.

"Don't want to shift the cargo, might break the

eggs," I pushed the rod forward a notch more, and with the extra fraction of a gee acceleration the inertial pull toward the rear grew noticeable, and everyone stood slanted as though the floor were tilting back.

"Eggs." They all laughed nervously. I could tell from the sound they still weren't used to space travel, and the tilting floor had them queasy again.

"Yeah, eggs," I said irritably. "It took me fifteen hundred dollars to have them ship a box of fertilized eggs and hatching chicks out here. That's investment enough to make sure there are eggs for the store."

"You kidding?" asked the young gunholder and laughed. "Where's the chickens?"

"Some of the boys took on the job of raising them. If you boys will tell me your specialties, safe cracking or what—I'll tell you what kind of job you'll fit."

For an instant there was an angry surprised silence, then the nervous gunboy with a smile that was half a snarl walked over behind me and clunked me on the side of the head with his gun, not hard, just enough to hurt a little as a warning.

"Look, Fatty, we aren't here to apply for a job."

"You'll be working anyhow," I said.

The blow that hit my head that time crossed my eyes for a minute. The young gunman's voice was pitched almost to a falsetto with irritation. "We don't need any work. We've got nine hundred thousand to hide out with until it cools, and we ain't going to spend it buying eggs!"

The husky made a reproving noise, and the gunboy turned on him defensively and barked, "Why not tell him? He won't tell anybody anything, after now."

I had not expected them to keep me around their

hideout for a pet after they took the store back to the stolen spaceship, but this sounded like I was closer to getting a bullet in the back of the head than I expected.

"We won't need him for a pilot much longer," the Brains of the gang said calmly, still looking over my shoulder. He had not made a sound of objection when the kid clunked me. "The way I see him working this rig, you just push that stick forward to go, sideways to turn, and harder to go faster. If you're going to hit anything the screen turns it red and you steer around. Simple. I can handle the piloting myself."

I hadn't expected him to catch on to the way the controls worked. Suddenly they didn't have any use for me, and no reason to keep me alive. I had to give them a reason, and fast.

I turned and grinned. "You'd better try another tack, boys, or you're likely to find yourselves kicking in space with your spacesuits off." I should have planted the idea sooner. This late, talking big might set off those already tightened triggers.

Nobody pulled any triggers; they were a cool bunch.

"Find out what he means," said the Brains. He slid calmly into the control seat as the others yanked me out and rested his hand lightly on the control rod. "Maybe he wasn't kidding when he said he expected us."

They dragged me upright, and Husky swung a blow to my wind. It didn't penetrate. I keep fit. He looked surprised when I didn't double up. "Blubber," he growled uncertainly, rubbing his fist. "You got a trap for us? Talk quick." He rubbed his knuckles and looked at my nose.

I value my nose. "No trap. There are better ways of approaching the Belt than you boys are using. The woods are full of fugitives. I'll give any of them a stake and start and a place to live where no one knows the orbit but the guy who delivers supplies, that's me. But if you try anything else...."

He grunted something and swung, and I barely moved my nose out of the way before getting a fist in the face. The second swing connected and made my nose a throbbing radiating ache in my face. The two men at my arms hung on while I tried to pull loose and get at the husky, and we thrashed around the room for a few moments until I cooled off and they brought me back standing facing him.

He was getting impatient, hefting a pistol by its barrel like a short club. He glanced from it to my face.

"Spit it out!"

Behind me at the controls came the Brains's smooth drawl. "He was probably running us into a trap. I've changed course."

"Brother," I said, breathing through my mouth. "If you do anything to me—" While I was talking they let me turn to the Brains, and he swung around to look at me. I kept talking.

"If you do anything to me, you are running yourself into a trap. I've got friends. Around here, when people get obnoxious they are likely to find themselves stuffed alive into a garbage chute and the lever pulled for them to go fight space, if they like making trouble! It's an interesting way to die, and it doesn't leave a mark."

During that speech the Brains and I were staring into each other's eyes. I jerked my head sideways to indicate the garbage chute when I mentioned it and his glance flicked over to see where it was, and then locked with mine again until I finished talking. Then he spoke coldly.

"You've named it, Buster."

He looked at the others. "Stuff this bag of wind down the garbage chute. And make sure he's conscious."

It took all three of them some fifteen minutes to do it. I was careful to keep the fight away from the supplies so as not to break anything, but otherwise I gave a good Br'er Rabbit imitation of a man fighting to stay away from death. Their faces were the only part that stuck out of their spacesuits, but I bent Gunboy's nose, almost closed both of Number Four's eyes, and made a good try at yanking off a part of Husky's left ear.

I don't like being called Fatty.

They got mad enough to have shot me, but they had already put their guns away to make sure I'd be alive to appreciate what was going to happen to me.

For one lucky moment in the scramble I had all three of them tripped and down, and had a knee on Gunboy's back, fishing in his spacesuit leg pocket for his gun. Then somebody kicked me in the groin. I lost track of what was happening and just tried to breathe. When I came back to noticing anything they were busy stuffing me into the garbage chute, putting muscle into straightening me out from my curled up crouch, and making laughing cracks about it being a tight fit.

I clawed to get out and tried to choke down a few more deep breaths, but I was still too weak for my arm-waving to bother them.

They pushed my head down with the lid, clanged the lid on and locked it into place. It cut off the sound of their laughing to a distant murmur.

Then someone must have found and pulled the disposal lever.

The bottom of the chute opened. Air pressure fired

me out into space like a human cannonball from a circus cannon.

For a moment, I flung end over end, the multicolored lights of the Milky Way and the intermittent harsh burning glare of the sun flashed into my naked eyes, then I shut my eyes tightly while the pressure of air bulged my chest out and whooshed out my mouth, pushing it open like a soft expanding pillow.

I clenched my eyes more tightly closed. I wasn't going to explode like the characters in visio stories; pressure drop was not enough for that, because I never kept more than three pounds pressure in the store atmosphere anyhow. A pressure drop like that can't kill, but it might rupture the blood vessels in my eyes.

Like a mousetrap the ring that hung down from the back of my collar swung up on a hinge, bringing a collapsed balloon of mirror-coated plastic over my head and swung down past my face, nearly taking off the tip of my battered nose. As it clanked into place over the collar ring, suddenly the air pushing out of my lungs filled the soft plastic bag and it expanded with a pop into a helmet globe, darkly transparent from the inside, mirrorcoated on the outside to reflect most of the sun's destructive glare.

I was protected by an emergency spacesuit. From the outside now I looked like a solid silver figure with a round silver sphere instead of a head. The mousetrap spring on the helmet globe was set to dangle down the back, and its catch was supposed to hold it back there until a sudden pressure drop expanded a tiny balloon under the catch and slipped the spring free.

I'd tested them in space before distributing them, but this was the first time my coverall had been tested with me in it, and I found myself considerably surprised and grateful that it really worked.

There wasn't much air in the emergency headglobe with me. I should have been breathing heavily up to the last minute to store oxygen in my blood, but the kick had stopped that. There was barely enough breath to pray with.

I had to be lucky twice. My second guess had to be right too.

It was.

Just about the time I could no longer tell the sun from the spinning bursts of white light in my head, Fergason's scooter showed up alongside with its jets trailing blue light and his anxious face peered out.

After that I was out of the fight.

For three hours the store went on, picking up more and more quiet little scooters as the settlers trailed after the interesting conversation being broadcast by my radio. They followed closely, but always a little to one side, so none of them ever went on "collision" course and rang an alarm in the store control board. They were quiet and inconspicuous, listening on their radios with great interest to the talk of nine hundred thousand dollars, and to the fugitives' talk of hiding out with the supplies in the store.

It was not until my stolen ship came to a meeting place where floated the huge shiny expensive *Phobos*, the ship they had taken from the commercial line, not until the convicts began coming out the airlock to go back to the *Phobos*—not until then did the scooters close in.

The settlers brought my store back to me, its thin walls plugged full of holes and patched, and brought back one survivor, Mister Brains. He must have needed brains to survive, since the settlers had probably been over-enthusiastic in the capture. I did not ask what became of the other five convicts or the kidnapped pilot and first engineer of the *Phobos*. I believe in being tactful.

I took the survivor's fingerprints and gave him a stake of supplies and a spinhouse to grow vegetables in until he decided what kind of work he could do.

We called a conference of all settlers over the radio to decide what to do with the loot and, on vote, divided up the nine hundred thousand among us as a penalty to the Brains for not using his brains for barging in and making a row when he could have found out on Earth how to be smuggled out here quietly on the regular run. He had a vote too, and voted against it, but it didn't do him much good. We're a democracy, and one vote doesn't go far. Nine hundred thousand divided fifty ways is pinmoney compared to the prices of things out here anyhow. Frontiers always get bad inflation.

I sent the new one's fingerprints down to my strongbox in a bank on Earth. Everyone's fingerprints are in there, and everyone knows that anytime I disappear suddenly the box will be opened and the prints handed to the police. But I don't blackmail them, and they trust me to keep that box closed, because my prints are in there too.

It just makes everyone very careful of my health, so that they are inclined to resent outsiders trying to kill me.

That's why I can leave the airlock open for anyone to walk in. I know when I'm safe.

The parts of the *Phobos* are coming in very handy for building. We'll have a city here yet.

Katherine MacLean (1925–2019) began writing science fiction with "Defense Mechanism," in a 1949 *Astounding Science-Fiction*, and went on to produce a distinguished body of work. *Astounding* also published her novella "Incommunicado," a strongly human story extrapolating the still-young field of computer science. Shortly afterward, she was trying to sneak into a conference of scientists and engineers to learn about new developments that she could turn into stories, but the man watching the entrance saw she had no badge and asked her name. On hearing that she was the same Katherine MacLean who had written "Incommunicado," he shouted her name to the other attendees, and she found herself not being ejected, but treated like visiting royalty. She also received a Nebula Award for her 1971 novella, "The Missing Man," (later combined with two other linked novelets into the novel of the same title), she was a Guest of Honor at the 1977 Wiscon (the Wisconsin SF convention), she was made an Author Emeritus of the Science Fiction Writers of America in 2007, and she received the Cordwainer Smith Rediscovery Award in 2011. Her work is very worthy of rediscovery, and fortunately her story collections *The Diploids* and *The Trouble with You Earth People* are available as e-books. I (Hank) was glad to reprint two of her stories in earlier anthologies for Baen, and deeply regret that her passing a few months ago means she will not see this story from her "Hills of Earth" series returned to print.

The Barbary Shore

James L. Cambias

While the classic image of space pirates involves matching orbits, blowing airlocks open, and blaster battles between the crew and the marauders, our present day world involves no shortage of crimes committed online, some of which are accurately described as piracy. In the interplanetary future, such crime by keyboard likely could be extended into space, with the buccaneer sitting in the comfort of his computer room, eye patch optional.

David Arnold sat in a king-sized hotel bed and watched for his next prize. As "Captain Black" the space pirate he had five fan sites on the Web and at least as many highly secure law-enforcement sites devoted to tracking him. He was twenty-six years old and the absolute gold-anodized titanium pinnacle of the techno-badass pyramid.

On his laptop screen he saw a tiny bright dot rising above Mare Smythii: a booster carrying four tons of helium-3. A treasure ship, worth two billion dollars on the spot market. It was a Westinghouse cargo from the American base at Babcock, on course for the Micronesia drop zone. "Ship ho, me hearties," David said.

He had six ships lurking at the L-1 libration point, balanced between Earth and Moon. They were listed as "lunar resource satellites," which was true in its own way, and the owners of record were perfectly legal companies incorporated in small Central Asian countries. David picked one and set up a burn that would put it right at the turnover point when the helium payload finished climbing up from the Moon and began falling toward the Earth.

Having done that, David went out for lunch. He was currently commanding his pirate fleet from the Shangri-La hotel in Bangkok. His business partners kept trying to lure him to control centers in the Dasht-i-Kvir or Inner Mongolia, but David had no desire to sit in some desert blockhouse surrounded by other people's gun-toting goons. Much better to run missions from a luxury hotel surrounded by adventurous college girls on vacation.

A hundred and two hours later his pirate satellite was within fifty kilometers of the helium treasure ship, and David was in full battle gear. He was propped up on pillows in his hotel room with a pair of VR goggles on, running a really cool interface that used images from his favorite pirate shooter game. The helium payload was represented by a galleon flying the Westinghouse flag, and he was on the deck of a pirate sloop with guns, loyal crew, and a big spoked ship's wheel all available at the touch of a gloved hand.

He used up two-thirds of the sat's remaining fuel to match velocities with the galleon. Then he phoned his attorneys in Singapore and told them to liquidate the company which owned the satellite. That was running up the Jolly Roger. Until that moment if the Americans or the Japanese tried to intercept his pirate orbiter, it would be a hostile act against a sovereign state. Now he was revealing himself as a Rogue Entity.

His patrons would be shocked, *shocked* to learn of this criminal activity. Investigating the newly defunct Rogue Entity company would reveal that it owned nothing but a post-office box and an empty bank account. If his piracy was successful and the victims really raised a stink, some poor dissident might be identified as the mastermind and locked up until David's next score. Or beaten to death while trying to escape.

David turned the ship's wheel a notch to close with the target, and one of the animated pirates filling his vision said, "Burn complete, Cap'n." Then they all froze for a moment. David's computer was set up to take him offline every minute or so if he wasn't doing anything important. He didn't want to create a big signal profile for himself.

His crew came alive again and he picked up a virtual spyglass to check the distance. Ten kilometers now. Had SPACECOM noticed yet?

Yes. His satellite picked up a tightbeam from Goldstone, and a yellowed parchment unrolled in front of him, warning him of "potentially unsafe proximity." A shot across his bow. But they didn't have any cannonballs. If he ignored the warning, the only thing they could do was send him a more strongly worded one. He laughed aloud.

A second scroll appeared with tracking data from his business partners in Macao. It matched what the pirate ship's own radar was telling him. One kilometer. When he looked through his spyglass he could see that the cheap little camera bolted onto the satellite was showing the target now. The treasure ship was maneuvering, trying to get away. But it just didn't have the fuel for major velocity changes after struggling up from the surface of the Moon. It was wallowing and heavy-laden while his pirate sloop was fast and deadly, with a half a kilometer per second still in the tank.

David checked the status of all his weapons and systems, each represented by a different pirate icon. When he finished, his satellite was closing with its target again. SPACECOM had given up on proximity warnings. Two hundred meters now. The helium carrier gave one last futile spurt of its motor, then the Westinghouse ground team decided to separate, maybe hoping to confuse him. The payload module began drifting away from the booster, just beginning the long fall to Earth.

Now it was time to fire his broadside. He already knew what channel the Westinghouse ground controllers were on. They were using minimal encryption—just enough to stop some casual hacker or stray signal. But David had some of the best software anywhere. He touched a cannon and it fired a blast of smoke and flame.

The pirate ship began drowning out the ground signal with its own instructions, telling the payload to, in effect, heave to and prepare to be boarded. It obeyed. Animated pirates on the deck swung grappling hooks, and David's satellite docked with the payload's attachment hardpoint. Its manipulator arm found the data bus where the boost stage had been connected, and plugged in. The galleon's deck was red with blood and her flag fluttered down.

David took command of his prize as quickly as he could, replacing parts of the onboard software with his own versions, locking out the real ground control and loading new instructions.

His orders left the payload on course until just before reentry. Then it would take a dive, falling short into the Celebes Sea. Real pirate waters, and real pirates with boats and guns would recover the cargo. The helium-3 would find its way to market through several layers of cut-outs and shell companies. The whole scheme rested on the simple fact that helium atoms don't have serial numbers.

David's work was done. His pirate sloop cut away from the prize, and once they were a safe distance apart, blew itself to bits. David pulled off his goggles and called room service for a pitcher of Bloody Marys and a masseuse.

Captain Elizabeth Santiago lived off-base in Fountain and bicycled to work every morning. A good tough ride up the mountain in the early morning sunlight made up for a lot of hours spent in the Pit living on commissary pizza and Coke.

But although it was an absolutely perfect fall day, Elizabeth barely noticed. She left her apartment an hour early, nearly beat her record time getting up the mountain, and waved her ID at the gate guard as she shot through the checkpoint. Today was the day. MARIO was going to war.

Down in the bowels of Cheyenne Mountain she

changed into her fatigues and got an extra large, double-strength latte before heading for the Pit.

The Space Control Center was a lot more crowded than usual. Elizabeth wasn't the only Gold team member to show up early, and none of the White team wanted to leave. Some of the Blue shift were hanging around as well.

She glanced up at the big board. There was MARIO, a bright blue circle moving along its orbit plot. Two hours until the stabilizing burn to park it at L-1. Then things would get interesting.

Elizabeth conferred with her White counterpart, Richard Lee. "Status?"

"Everything's go so far. Power's good and we did the yaw maneuver at 0300."

"Targets?"

"Just sitting there acting innocent. The Singaporean one just did a stationkeeping burn."

"Do you think they're all pirate sats?" Elizabeth looked over at the smaller display showing the dozen or so vehicles at L-1.

"We know the French one isn't, and the Brazilian one probably isn't. But all the ones owned by dodgy companies in offshore-banking countries are likely pirates. Another one launched today."

"Really?"

"Yep. Lunar Science Observer. A real model UN— sea launch off Venezuela, Chinese booster, payload's flagged Liberian—"

"Always a good sign."

"And the ownership's Laotian."

"Because Laos has so many big space investors. Jesus. Why don't they just say it's a helium pirate sat?"

"Then we'd have to quit calling MARIO a 'Resupply and Inspection Orbiter.'"

"Fine with me. I always preferred 'Space Superiority Fighter' myself."

A chime rang to announce the 0800 shift change. Whites gave way to Golds and Elizabeth slipped into the command chair. It was going to be a busy day.

For the rest of the morning the Gold Team busied themselves getting MARIO parked and stable at the L-1 point. Their bird was an aluminum box very much like a two-drawer filing cabinet, with long photovoltaic wings stretching out on either side. Its ion motor could take it almost anywhere within the Earth-Moon system.

MARIO's original purpose was entirely benign— inspection and resupply of other satellites. Elizabeth's bird, MARIO 5, was a bit more aggressive. In the bay where other MARIO orbiters carried new components or fuel supplies to their satellite customers, MARIO 5 carried a weapon.

It was a curious sort of weapon, though. The Electromagnetic Interrogation system literally couldn't harm a fly, unless you felt like using a multi-million dollar piece of electronics as a swatter. It was nothing but a very fast and sensitive wireless data handler, capable of reaching past most emission shielding to let a skilled operator read and manipulate a satellite's computer memory. A rather staggering sum had gone into developing it so that the Air Force could separate the law-abiding payloads from the pirates lurking among them.

By two o'clock MARIO was closing on its first target.

"Twenty meters and holding," said Lieutenant Cameron from the Flight console.

"Right. Keep it there. Arm, I want a visual inspection please."

The camera on MARIO's manipulator arm came live, giving them a look at the suspect satellite. It was a simple aluminum can, with a thruster nozzle at one end, a manipulator and some antennas at the other, and some surface photovoltaics. Elizabeth could barely make out some logos on an exposed patch of the vehicle's skin.

"Zoom in on those, please, and let's get a record."

Some flags—Kazakh, Venezuela, and a mysterious one which Captain Lee finally pegged as Mauritius. The logo of China Space Machinery, presumably the builders. Another for the owners of record, the remarkably generic Space Satellite Company. And a mission-patch logo of a square-rigged ship steered by a peg-legged cartoon character.

Elizabeth enlarged the image of the ship on her screen until it was like a mosaic, filtering over and over to squeeze more resolution from the camera. The hair was standing up on the backs of her arms. "What does that word look like to you?" she asked Lee.

He leaned over the back of her seat and peered at the screen. "Scabby Whore?"

Could it be a coincidence? She did a search for the name, to see if it was just some pop-culture reference she'd missed. Nothing that seemed likely.

Elizabeth walked down Massachusetts Avenue, feeling like a fool. There were so many reasons to feel like a fool that afternoon.

She was a fool for getting involved with a younger guy. A boy, really. The difference between nineteen and twenty-two was a lot more than what simple subtraction would indicate. Of course, that had been just as true three months ago, so she'd been a fool for three months at least.

She crossed Prospect and decided she was also a fool for going to his room to have it out in person. When someone you've been seeing stops answering your messages, there's really only one reason. You're being dumped. Only a fool would think otherwise. Only a fool would insist on hearing it from him personally.

The security guard at Random Hall waved her through. She'd been there enough times. She and David tended to have sex in the afternoons between the end of class and dinnertime. For a while it had been every day except Thursdays, when he had a lab that ran late. If she hadn't been a fool she might have noticed that they didn't do much together aside from sex.

His door was open. A bunch of his pals were gathered around on beds and the floor. David was sitting in his swivel chair with his back to the door. They were watching *Treasure Island* on TV, and talking in bad pirate accents.

"Arr, 'tis the dread pirate Captain Skullraper," David crowed. "And his first mate Mr. Sodomy, and Billy Barecheeks the cabin boy. The fearsome crew of the pirate sloop *Scabby Whore!*"

He stopped as he realized everyone was looking at the door, and turned around.

If he'd at least been embarrassed she might have spared him, but instead he smiled at her as if he hadn't just been making seventh-grade playground jokes. "Oh, hi, Liz. I've been meaning to call you."

That was when Elizabeth realized how much of a fool she had really been. She had enough self-control to keep it all together as she said, "Goodbye, David," then turned and walked away.

"Bird's coming alive, sir!" said Hirsch.

The satellite was turning its thruster bell toward MARIO. Elizabeth kept one eye on it while typing furiously. "Flight, if they do a burn are we in any danger?"

"Not at this distance."

"That's fine. Sergeant. Commo? Any traffic for us?"

Corporal Whitman shook his head. "All encrypted."

"Send a text message, please. 'Strike your colors, Captain Skullraper.'"

Lee bent to whisper in her ear. "A little too much comedy. This all gets logged."

"I know." She finished one message and sent it off, then started another. "I'm cc'ing this to you. See if you can get NSA or somebody to follow the traffic."

Lee looked at the note she was sending out and raised his eyebrows. "You sure about this?"

"No, but it's worth trying." She looked up at the board. "Flight, we need a close rendezvous with that vehicle. Ten meters. SIGINT, start warming up the EMI gear. Arm, be ready for a resisted capture." She beckoned Lee to bend close again. "Tell command that unless I receive orders to the contrary, I'm going to catch and inspect that bird."

David had been watching the USAF satellite for two days, and now it was nosing into his pirate anchorage. He was ready for battle. His skin was pink and rose-scented from a hot bath and he was sitting nude in lotus position on his bed, his virtual pirate ship surrounding him.

Arrogant bastards, cruising in and trying to hack

his satellite without even a court order! David kept up with the trade magazines; he knew what this supposedly harmless "inspection" probe could do.

He tried to back off casually, doing a little "station keeping" burn which would take him away from the Air Force bird. But then he got a message, plain text relayed from their satellite to his: "Strike your colors, Captain Skullraper."

David froze, fighting panic. Had someone *talked?* What did they know? His first impulse was to blow up the ship and start packing. He got as far as selecting the one-eyed pirate holding a sputtering bomb labeled "DESTRUCT," but his curiosity got the upper hand. Who sent him that message? It wasn't his public "Captain Black" persona, but a very inside joke only half a dozen old friends from MIT would understand, if they even remembered.

It had to be Liz. Ruining his fun again. Even with the Lunar helium mines there still weren't very many people in the space operations business, and fewer still who'd been at MIT with him. First she'd dumped him in front of everybody, and now she was interfering with his pirate operation. Bitch.

They knew who he was. That was bad, but not excessively bad. They'd have to prove it. He was in Bangkok on a different passport anyway. And if worst came to worst, his business partners could help him vanish. He could work in China. Shanghai and Hong Kong were pretty cool places. Definitely cooler than Colorado Springs or Lompoc or wherever she was sitting in a bunker under government-issue fluorescent lights.

And if he was going to spend the rest of his life under another name, at least he'd go out with a bang. Time to earn enough street cred to last the rest of his natural life. David called up a display of the battlespace and began giving orders to his crew.

The pirate sat was scooting away with erratic thruster burns. MARIO followed, its ion engine pumping out a steady thousandth of a gee.

Four o'clock came, and Blue controllers pulled up spare chairs next to Gold ones. A few switched seats, when the Blue operator was more experienced than the Gold. Alex Masters, the Blue director, took a folding chair next to Elizabeth, feeding her reports from Air Force Intel and NRO. Lee was still on duty, acting as her link to command and the legal people. The back of the room had filled up with a lot of oak leaves and eagles. Even a star or two.

"Commo? Send another text message." She typed it out. "You can't escape, Captain Skullraper. Heave to."

That brought a response, not in text but a compressed sound file. "Arr! Belay that fool talk, ye cowardly lubbers! I be Captain Black, the terror of the spaceways! If it's a fight you're after, come on, then!"

"Just got a note from SEC about the owners of that satellite," said Adamski.

"Liquidated."

"As of noon GMT."

"A criminal enterprise masquerading as a legitimate business. Who'd have guessed it?"

The pirate had opened the range to about a kilometer, but after half an hour, MARIO was closing again. It looked like the target was trying to rendezvous with another mystery satellite. Elizabeth wasn't sure what her enemy was up to.

"How much juice does our target have?" she asked Masters.

"Based on past missions, best guess is that model carries about a kilometer per second of delta-V."

"So, Captain Black, are you going to run and use up your fuel? You won't catch any helium payloads that way."

On MARIO's camera view the pirate probe suddenly brightened.

"Burning," said the Tracking controller. "Looks like a braking burn. Taking up station next to that other bird." The two pirate satellites were about forty meters apart. That would make it a little tricky for MARIO to close and inspect them, but Elizabeth wasn't worried about that. What was David up to?

Elizabeth turned twenty-two on a rainy Sunday in November. She spent that morning crouching with David on the roof of Building 54. They wore their winter coats because of the rain, and David had wrapped his computer in clear plastic so he could use it out in the open.

"Can't we do this some other time?"

"No," he said, staring at the screen and turning the salvaged satellite-TV antenna until it pointed south. "It's got to be today."

"You keep saying that but you don't tell me why. I could be in bed right now." She leaned closer and made her voice seductive. "I could be sprawled naked on my bed right now."

"Save it," he said. "Do you see anything in the air that way? My glasses are all wet."

Elizabeth squinted at the Boston skyline. "In the air? No—wait. There's a little blimp over by the Hancock Center."

"That's what I want." He adjusted the antenna again. "There it is. Come to Daddy." He typed some instructions, wiped raindrops off the plastic covering the screen, and typed some more.

"What are you doing?"

"It's an RPV—some low-wage drone in the traffic control office flies it around looking for jams. Cheaper than a helicopter, and quieter. And oh by the way it means the Boston cops have a camera in the sky all the time looking at people's rooftop gardens for pot plants, reading license plates, and probably photographing sunbathers."

"Welcome to the new millennium, David. There's cameras everywhere you look."

"Well, I just took control of that one."

"You did? How?"

"Hacked the control channel. I've been snooping it for a while. Now I'm changing the channel and installing encryption so the cops are locked out."

"Very nifty," she said. The little blimp was coming toward them across the Charles, and she waved as it passed overhead. The image appeared on David's screen. "Too bad it's such a wet day," she said. "There isn't much to look at."

"How about a football game?"

"What?"

"Harvard Stadium. The Harvard-Yale game's just starting and I haven't heard of any hacks planned for this year. So I'm doing my part for school tradition."

She peered off to the west, where the RPV was crossing the Charles again. "You're losing altitude," she said.

"I want to buzz the stands. Otherwise nobody will notice."

A police helicopter thundered past overhead. She could see a man with a sniper rifle through the open side door. She watched it circle the stadium. A second chopper approached from the north—National Guard from the look of it. She heard sirens. Lots of sirens.

"David, I think this just got too serious. They don't know this is a hack. You've got a blimp about to crash into a stadium full of people."

"Well, duh! Look at them!"

She crouched next to him and looked at the screen. The view from the RPV's camera showed pure chaos: people climbing over seats, over each other, packing the aisles.

"David, stop it! People are getting hurt!"

"They're all rich. They've got insurance."

Elizabeth didn't hesitate. She got to her feet and grabbed the antenna, yanked the cable free from David's laptop, and tossed it off the roof.

"Hey!" He finally looked up from the screen.

"That's enough."

He stood up, fists balled. "You ruined it!"

"Oh, for God's sake. David, people were panicking. Someone could get hurt. It's over."

She looked over toward the stadium. The blimp was climbing, back under police control. The helicopters still flanked it.

"Come on. We'd better get out of here. This won't be campus police taking the cow off the dome. City cops and FBI and half a dozen others will be all over Cambridge."

David stayed sulky until they were riding the elevator down. Then his mood turned triumphant. "But it was still a great hack! Black Sunday!"

In the end, nobody died. David grudgingly admitted it was reckless, and against her better judgment Elizabeth forgave him again. After all, it *had* been a great hack.

David watched the damned Air Force sat creeping up on his pirate sloop. Closing now to fifty meters. He switched between the two satellites, getting them ready to spring his trap.

Twenty meters, and Captain Santiago's bird began to probe the brain of his first satellite. David fought back, encrypting and overwriting to hide any useful data. He was a little disappointed that his interface couldn't represent this as a sword fight on the deck.

When he wasn't holding off the inspection, he was switching over to his second satellite, using the gyros to turn it as slowly as possible until it was aimed directly at the Air Force bird. It would be expensive, but they'd be talking about Captain Black's Revenge on the net until he died. His business partners were sending him worried emails every thirty seconds or so, but he ignored them.

"SIGINT, anything?"

"It's tough. He's changing encryption schemes every minute, and he keeps moving stuff around and overwriting with random junk."

"Keep at it."

"Second bird's awake!" said Tracking.

The second pirate sat did a short thruster burn. Elizabeth called up the radar display. "Is he trying to ram us?"

"No lateral vector."

"Okay, consider it hostile." On the screen the little green square turned into a red triangle. MARIO's solar panels were big and fragile; either pirate sat could ram and smash them, crippling the vehicle.

"Another sound file," said Commo.

"So, Captain Santiago, we meet again. But this time the advantage is mine! Arr!" A couple of people even laughed.

"I guess you were right," said Lee. "He knows you."

"Commo, relay this." She typed one-handed, using her left to control the tactical display. The message she wrote was "Hell hath no fury."

"Flight, get us out of there," she ordered. That second bird was closing too fast.

MARIO's ion thruster began feebly shoving it away from the pirates. Given enough time it could get Elizabeth's vehicle moving faster than almost anything in space, but there wasn't enough time.

"Roll!" she ordered. MARIO began to swing its huge solar panels like a windmill in a faint breeze. On the display the approaching red triangle merged with the blue circle, and Elizabeth tensed as if Cheyenne Mountain was about to hit something.

But a moment later the two shapes on the screen separated and Elizabeth exhaled. The pirate sat had passed between MARIO's swinging solar wings. Then Tracking said, "Hey, where—" and half the screens suddenly displayed gibberish as the pirate sat blew itself up.

The three controllers at Systems announced the damage. "Power's down to sixty watts, arm position sensors out. Rendezvous camera's gone. EMI passive mode only. Pitch gyro is unstable..."

MARIO was crippled, and might end up being steered into the southeastern Pacific. But Elizabeth was smiling and shaking hands with Lee and Masters.

"WOOHOO!" David bounced up and down on the bed, scattering pillows and knocking the room service tray to the floor. "Score! Gotcha! Captain Black is the supreme badass of space!"

There was a knock at the door.

"Come back later with some champagne!"

Louder knocking.

"Leave me the fuck alone!"

David shut down his remaining pirate sat. No reason to blow it up yet—maybe he could give the Air Force another black eye if they tried poking around L-1.

The door unlocked and opened three inches until the chain stopped it.

"I said leave me the fuck alone! Are you deaf or just fucking retarded?"

It was only when he heard the chain being cut that David took off his goggles and reached for his robe. By then four large white men in suits and sunglasses were in his room.

"Hello, David," said one of them. "Why don't you come down to the Embassy with us?"

"I want my lawyer."

"If you want a lawyer that means someone will have to *arrest* you."

"So what are you here for?"

"We're *inviting* you to come down to the Embassy until we can transport you Stateside. If you cooperate, I bet you can get a short sentence. Maybe even community service."

"And if I don't want to go?"

"Then we'll keep you here until the Thai police show up. And they'll put you in a Thai jail. And we'll announce that you're being a big help with our investigation."

"Bastards." Thai jails were full of Muslims and Chinese expats, perfectly willing to silence him for a carton of smokes if his partners thought he was talking.

"It's your call."

"Let me get dressed. How'd you find me, anyway?"

"I don't know all the details, but they tell me running satellites from your hotel room attracts attention if you do it long enough."

David winced at that. Poor signals management. He'd been undone by poor signals management.

About a month after the battle, Elizabeth was a little surprised to get a phone call from David Arnold. She'd been busy getting MARIO 5 repaired and refueled, and there was talk of equipping her squadron with armed sats. She'd barely had time to go biking.

"Hello, Liz," he said. "It's me, David. David Arnold."

"Um, hi," she said. "Where are you? Should you be talking to me?"

"Oh, it's cool. I made a deal. I'm—somewhere in the States."

"That's good. I'm glad you made the right choice."

"Yeah. So anyway, I was wondering—do you want to get back together?"

"What?"

"You know, you and me. Like we were back at MIT."

For a second she couldn't quite understand what he meant. Then she had to suppress the urge to laugh.

"Are you okay?" he asked. "Are you crying?"

"No, I'm fine. Really."

"So what do you think?"

"I don't think that's a good idea."

"But—but I've been cooperating. We're on the same side now. Isn't that what this was all about?"

"What? David, I didn't spend five years working to get where I am because of some great undying love for you."

"Aw, come on. Admit it."

"Goodbye, David."

"But if it wasn't about me then why'd you attack my sats?" He sounded genuinely puzzled.

"*Goodbye*, David." She hung up while he was still protesting, then unplugged the phone.

"Who was that?" asked her husband.

"Captain Black the Space Pirate," she said, rolling over to rest her head over his heart.

James L. Cambias writes science fiction and designs games. His new urban fantasy novel *The Initiate* was published in February 2020 by Baen Books. Originally from New Orleans, he was educated at the University of Chicago and lives in western Massachusetts. His first novel, *A Darkling Sea*, was published by Tor Books in 2014, followed by *Corsair* in 2015. Baen Books released his third novel, *Arkad's World*, in 2019. His short stories have appeared in *The Magazine of Fantasy & Science Fiction*, *Shimmer*, *Nature*, and several original anthologies—most recently in the collection *Retellings of the Inner Seas*. In March of 2020, his story "Treatment Option" was adapted for audio by DUST Studios, starring Danny Trejo. As a game designer, Mr. Cambias has written for Steve Jackson Games, Hero Games, and other roleplaying publishers, and he co-founded Zygote Games. Since 2015 he has been a member of the XPrize Foundation's Science Fiction Advisory Board. Check out his blog at www.jamescambias.com.

Captives of the Thieve-Star

James H. Schmitz

*Schmitz was a master of SF adventures set in unforget-
table universes, and while this yarn doesn't connect to
any of his other series, it has no shortage of Schmitz's
trademarks, including hints of a bigger universe than
appears on the pages, with the feeling that if you'd
come into the story a little earlier, or came in through
a different entrance, you would have had a completely
different story. It also has no shortage of action, a
mysterious alien structure that humans really should stay
away from, two typically plucky Schmitz heroines (though
we only meet one), and raises the question of which
of the opposed sides has the real space pirates on it.*

I

The celebration of the wedding of Peer and Channok
had to be cut a little short, because a flock of police-
boats from Irrek showed up at detector-range about

midway. But it was carried off with a flourish nevertheless.

The oxygen-bubble in the small mooncrater was filled with colorful solidographs, creating the impression of an outdoor banquet hall. The best bands playing in the Empire that night unwittingly contributed their efforts, and food and drink were beyond reproach.

Though somewhat dazed throughout, Channok was startled to discover at one point that the thick carpets on which he stood were a genuine priceless Gaifornaab weave—and no solidographs either! The eighty-four small ships of the space-rat tribe—or voyageurs, as they distinctly preferred to be called—lined up along the outer edges of the banquet hall looked eerily out of place to him; but Peer didn't seem to mind. Her people rarely did go far away from their ships, and the lawless, precarious life they led made that an advisable practice.

It would be up to him now, Channok reflected, beaming down on Peer, to educate her into customs and attitudes more fitting for the wife of a regular citizen of the Empire and probable future member of the Imperial Secret Service—

And then, suddenly, the whole ceremony seemed to be over! A bit puzzled by the abruptness with which everybody had begun to pack up and leave, Channok was standing beside the ramp of his own ship, the *Asteroid*—an honest, licensed trader—when Santis strolled over to talk to him. Santis was Peer's father and the pint-sized chieftain of the tribe.

"Didn't tell you before, son," he remarked, "because you were already nervous enough. But as soon as they finish collapsing the bubble, you'll have about six minutes to get your *Asteroid* aloft and off this moon before the cops from Irrek arrive."

"I heard you, Pop, and everything's packed!" Peer called down from the open lock of the *Asteroid*. "Come up and kiss me goodbye and we'll seal her up!"

Frowning suspiciously, Channok followed Santis up the ramp. "Why should I worry about cops?" he inquired, looking down at the two little people while they briefly embraced. Peer came about up to his shoulder, though perfectly formed, and Santis was an inch or two shorter. The tribe didn't run to bulk. "Nobody's hunting for me."

"Not yet, son," Santis conceded. He twirled his fierce brown mustache-tips thoughtfully and glanced at Peer.

"If you're passing anywhere near Old Nameless, you might cache that special cargo you're carrying for me there," he told her. "Around the foot of the Mound. Too bulky for the ships I've got here! I put a dowser plate in with it, and I'll come pick it up with a transport sometime in the next four months."

"Yes, Pop," said Peer.

"The Fourth Voyageur Fleet will rendezvous at New Gyrnovaan next Terra spring. If you can talk this big lug into it, try to make it there, daughter!"

"We'll be there," promised Peer.

Channok cleared his throat impatiently. Not if he could help it, they wouldn't!

"Those cops are looking for the missing Crown jewels of Irrek," Santis resumed, looking at him. "After they've opened you up from stem to stern to make sure you're not hiding them, they might apologize. And again they might not."

"Holy Satellites!" Channok said, stunned. "Did you actually—"

"Not I, son. I just mastermind these things. Some of the boys did the job. There goes the oxygen-bubble! Now will you get going?"

They got going, Channok speechless for once.

Some two months later, he stood in the *Asteroid*'s control room, watching a pale blur creep up along the starboard screen.

"That's not just one ship—that's at least a hundred," he announced presently, somewhat startled. "Looks like they've turned out the entire Dardrean war-fleet! Wonder what's up?"

Peer laid the cargo list she was checking down on the desk and came over to look at the screen.

"Hm," she said.

"It couldn't possibly have anything to do with us, could it?" he inquired, on a sudden alarming hunch. Being unfamiliar with the dialect used on Dardrea, he had left most of the bargaining there to her.

Peer shrugged. She showed the bland, innocent look of a ten-year-old child, but that was habitual with her. On one occasion she'd been mistaken for his daughter, and at times he even had to remind himself that she'd been eighteen and a student at the Imperial Institute of Technology when he first met her there—and then unwittingly became Santis's tool in the abstraction of a small but important section of the IIT's top-secret experimental files! He'd been trying to counteract that little brigand's influence on Peer ever since, but he wasn't too sure of his degree of success so far.

"We took the Merchants Guild for plenty on our auction," she admitted.

"Well," Channok frowned, "they'd hardly send a fleet after us for that."

"And, of course," added Peer, "we got the Duke of Dardrea's fabulous Coronet. Forgot to mention that. Perfectly legal, though! Some local-crook swiped it and we took it in trade."

Channok winced. As a matter of fact, fencing was a perfectly legitimate business on Dardrea. But a man who planned to enter the Imperial Secret Service, as soon as he could save up the money to pay his way through the Academy, couldn't afford any stains on his past. Throughout the Empire, the Service was renowned in song and story as the one body of men who stood above the suspicion of reproach.

"The Duke won't know it's gone for another week," Peer consoled him. "Anyway, it looks to me as if those ships are beginning to pull off our course."

There followed some seconds of tense observation.

"So they are," Channok acknowledged then. He mopped his forehead. "But I wish you wouldn't be quite so technical in your interpretation of local laws, Peer! Those babies are really traveling. Wonder who or what they're chasing?"

Three days later, as the *Asteroid* approached the area of the red giant sun of Old Nameless, where they were going to cache Santis's cargo for him—hot cargo, probably; and it would be a load off Channok's mind to get rid of it—they picked up the trail of the foundering spaceship *Ra-Twelve* and found part of the answer on board.

II

"It seemed to me," Channok remarked, watching the *Ra-Twelve* in the viewscreen before them, "as if her drives had cut off completely just then. But they're on again now. What do you think, crew-member Peer?"

"Let's just follow her a bit," Peer suggested. "I've seen ships act like that that were just running out of juice. But this one won't even answer signals."

"It could be," Channok said hopefully, "a case of fair salvage! You might keep working the communicators, though..."

However, the *Ra-Twelve* continued to ignore them while she plodded on toward the distant red glare of the Nameless System like a blind, thirsty beast following its nose to a water-hole. Presently, she began a series of quavering zigzag motions, wandered aimlessly off her course, returned to it again on a few final puffs of invisible energy, and at last went drifting off through space with her drives now obviously dead.

The *Asteroid* continued to follow at a discreet distance like a chunky vulture, watching. If there was anyone on board the *Ra-Twelve*, it almost had to be a ghost. Her rear lock was wide open, and the hull showed deep scars and marks of some recent space-action.

"But she wasn't really badly hurt," Channok pointed out. "What do you suppose could have happened to her crew?"

Peer gave him a nervous grin. "Maybe a space-ghost came on board!"

"You don't really believe those spooky voyageur stories, do you?" he said tolerantly.

"Sure I do—and so will you some day," Peer promised him. "I'll tell you a few true ones just before your next sleep-period."

"No, you won't," Channok said firmly. "Aside from space-ghosts, though, that crate has a downright creepy look to her. But I suppose I'd better go over and check, as soon as she slows down enough so we can latch on. And you're going to stay on the *Asteroid*, Peer."

"In a pig's eye, I am!" Peer said indignantly. And though Channok wished to know if she had forgotten that he was the *Asteroid*'s skipper, it turned out that this was one time he'd have to yield.

"Because, Channy dear," Peer said, her big dark eyes welling slow tears, "I'd just die if something happened to you over there and I was left all alone in space!"

"All you'd have to do," Channok said uncomfortably, "is to head the *Asteroid* for New Gyrnovaan, and you know it. Well—you've got to promise to stay right behind me, anyway."

"Of course," promised Peer, the tears vanishing miraculously. "Santis says a wife should always stick with her husband in space, because he might lead her into a jam, all right, but nothing like the !!°°°°!; !°°!! jams she's likely to run into if she strays around by herself."

"Whereas Ship's Regulation 66-B says," said Channok with grim satisfaction, "that crew-member Peer gets her mouth washed out with soap just before the next sleep-period because of another uncontrolled lapse into vituperous profanity—and what was that comment?"

"That one was under my breath," said Peer, crestfallen, "so it doesn't count."

❖   ❖   ❖

Without making any particular remarks about it, both of them had fastened a brace of guns to their jet-harnesses. At close range—held thirty feet away against the *Asteroid*'s ring-bumpers by a set of dock grapnels—the *Ra-Twelve*'s yawning lock looked more than ever like the black mouth of a cavern in which something was lurking for them.

Channok went over first, propelled by a single squirt of his jets, and landed a little heavier than he had intended to. Peer, following instructions to keep right behind him, came down an instant later in the middle of his back. They got untangled hurriedly, stood up and started swiveling their helmet beams about the *Ra-Twelve*'s storage lock.

It was practically empty. So was the big rack that had held the ship's single big lifeboat. There were some tools scattered around. They kicked at them thoughtfully, looked at each other and started forward through an open door up a dark passageway, switching their lights ahead and from side to side.

There was a locked door which probably led into the *Ra-Twelve*'s engine section, and then four cabins, each of which had been used by two men. The cabins were in considerable disorder, but from what one could tell in a brief look-around, each of the occupants had found time to pack up about what you would expect a man to take along when he was planning on a lifeboat trip. So whatever had happened probably hadn't been entirely unexpected.

The mess-room, all tidied up, was next; two locked doors were at the back of it, and also an open entrance to the kitchen and food storage. They glanced around at everything, briefly, and went on to the control-room.

It was considerably bigger than the one on the *Asteroid* and luxuriously equipped. The pilot's section was in a transparently walled little office by itself. The instruments showed both Dardrean and Empire markings and instructions. Channok switched the dead drives off first and then reached out, quite automatically, for the spot above the control desk where a light button ought to be—

Light instantly flooded the interior of the *Ra-Twelve*.

The intruders jumped a foot. It was as if the ship had suddenly come alive around them! Then they looked at each other and grinned.

"Automatic," Channok sighed.

"Might as well do it the easy way," Peer admitted. She slid the Ophto Needle she'd half-drawn back into its holster.

The *Ra-Twelve* had eighteen fully charged drive batteries still untouched. With some system of automatic power transfer working, she could have gone cruising along on her course for months to come. However, she hadn't been cruising, Channok discovered next; the speed controls were set to "Full Emergency." An empty ship, racing through space till the battery she was operating on went dead—

He shook his head. And then Peer was tapping his arm.

"Look what I found! I think it's her log!"

It was a flat steel box with an illuminated tape at its front end, on which a date was printed. A line of spidery Dardrean script was engraved on a plate on the top of the box.

"*Ra-Twelve*," Peer translated. "That's her name."

"So it's a Dardrean ship! But they're using the Empire calendar," Channok pointed out, "which would make it an Empire crew... How do you work this thing? If it is her log, it might give us an idea of what's happened."

"Afterwards, Channy! I just found another door leading off the other end of the control room—"

The door opened into a second passage, parallel to the one by which they had come forward, but only half as long and very dimly lit. Filled with uneasy speculations, Channok forgot his own instructions and let Peer take the lead.

"More cabins," her voice said, just as he became aware of the wrecked door-frame out of which the light was spilling ahead of her.

A woman had been using that cabin. A woman who had liked beautiful and expensive things, judging by what was strewn about. It looked, Channok thought, as if she hadn't had time to finish her packing.

"Her spacesuit's gone, though," Peer's voice announced from the interior of a disordered closet.

Channok was inspecting the door. This was the first indication that there had been any violence connected with whatever had happened on the *Ra-Twelve*. The door had been locked from without and literally ripped open from within by a stream of incandescence played on it by a gun held probably not much more than a foot away. That woman had wanted out in an awful hurry!

Peer came over to watch him. He couldn't quite read her expression, but he had a notion she wanted to bawl.

"Let's take a quick look at the rest of it and get back to the *Asteroid*," he suggested, somewhat disturbed himself. "We ought to talk this over."

The one remaining cabin lay just beyond the point

where the passage angled back into the ship. There was light in that one, too, and the door was half open. Channok got there first and pushed it open a little farther. Then he stood frozen in the door-frame for a moment.

"What's stopping you?" Peer inquired impatiently, poking his ribs from behind.

He stepped back into the passage, pulled the door shut all the way, scooped her up, and heaved her to his shoulder. His space-boots felt like iron anchors as he clunk-clunked hastily back through the passages to the derelict's lock. There was nothing definite to run from any more; but he knew now what had happened on the *Ra-Twelve*, and he felt nightmare pacing after him all the way.

He crossed to the *Asteroid's* control room lock in a jump, without bothering with his jets.

"Close the outer lock!" he told Peer hoarsely, reaching up for the switch marked "Decontaminant" above him.

A fourfold spray of yellowish Killall was misting the trapped air in the lock about them an instant later.

"What was it?" Peer's voice came out of the fog.

"Antibiotic," Channok said, his scalp still crawling. "What you—what voyageurs call a lich, I think. I don't know that kind. But it got the guy in that last cabin."

The occupant of the last cabin had looked as if somebody had used a particularly vicious sort of acid gun on him, which somehow had missed damaging his clothing. To the grisly class of life-forms that produced that effect, an ordinary spacesuit offered exactly no resistance.

"A lich can't last more than an hour or so in space, Channy," Peer's voice came shakily after a pause. "It's a pretty awful way to get it, but that stuff over there must have been dead for a long time now."

"I know," said Channok. He hesitated and then cut off the Killall spray and started the blowers to clear the lock. "I guess I just panicked for a moment. But I'm going to go over that ship with decontaminant before we do any more investigating. And meanwhile you'd better get in a few hours of sleep."

"Wouldn't hurt any," Peer agreed. "How do you suppose the lich got on board?"

He could tell her that. He'd seen a heavy, steel-framed glassite container in a corner of the cabin, opened. They must have been transporting some virulent form of antibiotic; there might have been an accident—

Five hours later, they had come to the conclusion that it had been no accident. Four hours of that time, Channok had been engaged in disinfecting the *Ra-Twelve*, even her engine sections. He'd given the one man left on board space-burial in one of the *Asteroid*'s steel cargo crates. The crate hadn't been launched very far and presently hung suspended some eighty yards above the two ships, visible as a black oblong that obscured the stars behind it.

It and its contents were one of the reasons Channok was anxious to get done with the job of salvaging the *Ra-Twelve*. She was a streamlined, beautiful ship; but after what had happened, he knew he would never be able to work up any liking for her. She seemed to be waiting sullenly and silently for a chance to deal with the two humans who had dared come on board her again.

He sealed her up presently, filled her with a fresh airmix and, having once more checked everything he could think of, let Peer come over again for a final briefing on their run to Old Nameless.

Peer wandered promptly into the cabin where the dead man had been and there discovered the wall-safe.

III

She called him. He couldn't imagine how he had overlooked it. Perhaps because it was so obviously *there*. It was an ordinary enough safe, from what they could see of the front of it, and there was a tiny key in its lock.

They looked at it thoughtfully.

"You didn't try to open it, did you?" Channok inquired.

"No," said Peer, "because—"

"That's what I was thinking," Channok admitted.

There had been, they had decided, at least two groups working against each other in the ship. The dead man had been in charge of the antibiotic. Perhaps the woman had been on his side, perhaps not. But the eight other men had acted together and had controlled the ship. What action or threat of theirs had caused the dead man to release his terrible weapon would be hard to discover now. But he had done it, and the eight men had abandoned the *Ra-Twelve* promptly, leaving the woman locked in her cabin.

It looked pretty much as if she had been the one who had switched the drives to full speed—before jumping out into space. A pretty tough, desperate lot all around, in Channok's opinion. The *Ra-Twelve*'s log offered the information that they had left Dard-rea three calendric days earlier, but had been of no further help in identifying crew or passengers. That most of them were professional criminals, however, seemed a pretty safe bet—as Peer had pointed out, in voyageur terms, amateurs didn't play around with taboo-weapons like a bottled lich.

Also, amateurs—Peer and Channok, for example— could have sense enough not to blunder into a booby-trap...

"He'd know, of course," Channok said reflectively, "that everybody would be wondering what's hidden in that safe. And it could be anything up to and including full instructions on how to set up an artificial culture of antibiotics. Plenty of governments would pay twenty times what the *Ra-Twelve* is worth as salvage for that kind of information. But it's nothing we need to know."

"Not that bad," Peer agreed.

"And the guy who opens that wall-safe had better be an armaments expert! Which we're not. But now, crew-member Peer, if we want to get Santis's cargo cached on Old Nameless before I fall asleep, we ought to get started. Idle curiosity is something we can satisfy some other time."

"Two hours past your sleep-period right now." said Peer, glancing at her wristwatch. "Tsk, tsk! That always makes you so grouchy."

Half an hour later, they were on their way—Channok in the *Ra-Twelve*, Peer in the *Asteroid,* keeping as close to each other as two ships in flight could safely get. With the red glare of the Old Nameless sun a trifle off-center before him, Channok settled down in the most comfortable pilot-seat he'd ever found on any ship and decided he could relax a trifle. Peer was obviously having a wonderful time doing her first solo-piloting job on a ship of the *Asteroid*'s size; since she'd run and landed the *Asteroid* any number of times under his supervision, he wasn't worried about her ability to handle it. However, he continued to check in on her over the communicators every five minutes or so and grinned at the brisk, spacemanlike replies he got in return. Crew-member Peer was on her best behavior right now!

By and by, then—he couldn't have said just when it started—Channok began to realize that some very odd things were happening around him—

It appeared that the Thing he had put out for burial in a space-crate hadn't liked the idea of being left alone. So it was following him.

Channok decided uneasily that it might be best to ignore it. But it kept coming closer and closer until, finally, the crate was floating just outside the *Ra-Twelve*'s control room port, spinning slowly like a running-down top.

The crate stayed shut, but he knew the Thing inside it was watching him.

"That's my ship," the Thing remarked presently.

Channok ignored it.

"And you're all alone," said the Thing.

"No, I'm not!" said Channok. "Peer's with me."

"Peer's gone back to Santis," said the Thing. "You're all alone. Except," it added, "for me."

"Well, good-bye!" Channok said firmly. There was no point in getting too chummy with it. He punched the *Ra-Twelve*'s drives down as far as they would go, and the crate vanished.

How that ship could travel! Nothing could hope to keep up with him now—except, Perhaps, that round, red glare of light just behind the *Ra-Twelve*.

That was actually overtaking him, and fast. It was coming up like a cosmic police-ship, with a huge, hollow noise rushing before it. Channok listened apprehensively. Suddenly, there were words:

"WHOO-WHOOO!" it howled. *"This is the Space Ghost!"*

He shot up out of his chair like a jabbed cat, knocking it over, and glared around.

The *Ra-Twelve*'s control room lay brightly lit and silent behind him.

"Ha-ha!" Peer's chuckle came from the communicator. "That woke you up, I bet! Was that you that fell over?"

"Aw-awk!" breathed Channok. Articulation came back to him. "All right, crew-member Peer! Just wait till we get to Old Nameless! I'll fix you good!"

"Shall I tell you the story now about the Horror Ship from Mizar?" Peer inquired intrepidly.

"Go right ahead," Channok challenged, righting his chair and settling back into it. "You can't scare me with that sort of stuff." He began checking their position.

He must have been asleep for quite a while! The Nameless System was less than two hours ahead now. He switched on the front screen; the sun swam up like a big, glowing coal before him. He began checking for the seventh planet.

"Well," he reminded the communicator grimly, "you were going to tell me a story."

The communicator remained silent a moment.

"I don't think I will, anyway," Peer said then, rather quietly.

"Why not?" Channok inquired, getting his screen-viewer disentangled from a meteor-belt in the Nameless System.

"I made that Space Ghost too good," whispered Peer. "I'm getting scared myself now."

"Aha!" said Channok. "See what behaving like that will get you?" He got Old Nameless VII into the viewer.

The communicator remained still. He looked over at it.

"Of course, there's really nothing to be scared of," he added reassuringly.

"How do you know?" quavered Peer. "I'm all alone."

"Nonsense!" Channok said heartily. "I can see the *Asteroid* right over there on the screen. You can see me, can't you?"

"Sure," said Peer. "That's a long way off, though. You couldn't do anything!"

"It's not safe for two ships to travel much closer together," Channok reminded her. "We're only two hours from Old Nameless right now—I'm already focussed on it."

"I've been focussed on it for an hour," said Peer. "While you were snoring," she added. "Two hours is an awful long time!"

"Tell you what," suggested Channok. "I'll race you to it. The *Ra-Twelve*'s a mighty fast boat—" He checked himself. He'd only dreamed that, after all.

"Let's go," Peer said briefly.

He let Peer stay just ahead of him all the way in, though the streamlined derelict probably could have flown rings around the *Asteroid*, at that. Just an hour later, they went around Old Nameless VII twice, braking down, and then coasted into its atmosphere on their secondary drives.

"That's the place," Peer's voice said suddenly. "I

can see the old Mound in the plain. In the evening strip, Channy—that straight-up cliff."

He set the *Ra-Twelve* down first, at the base of a mountain that reared up almost vertically for eighteen thousand feet or so out of a flat, dimly lit stretch of rocky desert land.

The *Asteroid* came down in a very neat landing, two hundred yards away. He got there on the run, just as the front lock opened. Peer came tumbling out of it into his arms and hung on fiercely, while her skipper hugged her.

"Let that scare be a lesson to you!" he remarked when he set her down.

"It certainly will," said Peer, still clutching his arm as they started over to the *Ra-Twelve*. "That old Space Ghost had me going!"

"Me, too," he confessed, "just for a moment, anyway. Well, let's get busy."

They went over the *Ra-Twelve* again from bow to stern to make sure there was nothing they would want to take along immediately, and found there wasn't. They gave the unopened wall-safe a last calculating regard, and decided once more that they'd better not. Then they shut off everything, closed the front lock behind them, and safetied it with the dock bolts.

The plain was darkening when they came out, but the top of the mountain still glowed with red light. They climbed into the *Asteroid*, and Channok closed the lock. He started for the control desk then; but Peer beat him to it and anchored herself into the seat of command with hands, knees and feet. It became apparent almost at once that he couldn't get her out of it without running the risk of pulling off her head.

"Now look here, crew-member Peer," he said persuasively, "you know good and well that if these top-heavy cargo crates have one weakness, it's the take-off."

"It could be the pilot, too," Peer said meaningly. "I've been studying the manual, and I've watched you do it. It's my turn now."

He considered her thoughtfully.

"Suppose you die of old age, all of a sudden?" argued Peer. "Wouldn't want me to sit here alone without knowing even how to take her off, would you?"

That did it.

"Go ahead," said Channok with dignity, taking a position back of the chair. "Go right ahead! This decrepit old man of twenty-eight is going to stand right here and laugh himself sick!"

"You'll be sick, all right," promised Peer. "But it won't be from laughing! I'll read that chapter out of the manual to you sometime."

She *had* studied it, too, he decided. She sat perched forward on the edge of the chair, alert and cocky, and went through the starting operations without hitch or hesitation. The *Asteroid* rumbled beneath them, briefly building up power...

Channok braced himself—

IV

For the next few seconds, the question seemed to be whether they'd pile into the plain or the mountain first; for another improbable moment, they were distinctly skidding along upside down. Then Peer got them straightened out, and they soared up rapidly into the night sky above Old Nameless.

Channok's hair settled slowly back into place.

Peer looked around at him, puzzled and rather pale.

"That's not the way it said in the manual!" she stated.

Channok whooped. Then he sat down on the floor, bent over and yelled.

When he got around to wiping the tears from his eyes, Peer was looking down at him disgustedly from the control chair.

"It wasn't the way it said in the manual!" she repeated firmly. "We're going to have this old crate overhauled before she'll be safe to fly—and if you weren't my husband, I'd really let you have it now!"

He stood up, muttering some sort of apology.

"I've done some just as bad," he assured her.

"Hum," said Peer coldly, studying Old Nameless in the screen below them. It seemed safe to pat her on the head then, but he kept his hand well out of biting range.

"We'd better get back to that mountain and bury the *Ra-Twelve* before it gets too dark to find the spot," he suggested.

"It's still just in sight," said Peer. "You get the guns ready, and I'll run us past it slowly."

Spaceships being what they were, there wasn't much ceremony about caching the *Ra-Twelve*. Channok got the bow-turret out; and as Peer ran the *Asteroid* slowly along the mountainside a few hundred feet above the *Ra-Twelve*, he cut a jagged line into the rock with the gun's twin beams. A few dozen tons of rock came thundering down on the *Ra-Twelve*.

They came back from the other side, a little higher up, and he loosened it some more. This time, it looked as if a sizable section of the mountain were descending;

when the dust had settled the *Ra-Twelve* was fifty feet under a sloping pile of very natural-looking debris. To get her out again, they'd only have to cut a path down to her lock and start her drives. She'd come out of the stuff then, like a trout breaking water.

Satisfied, they went off and got the *Asteroid* on an orbit around Old Nameless, not too far out. Peer had assured Channok that Santis's investigations had proved the planet safe for human beings, so it probably was. But he knew he'd feel more comfortable if they put in their sleep-periods outside its atmosphere. Bathed in the dismal light of its giant sun, Old Nameless looked like a desolate backyard of Hell. It was rocky, sandy, apparently waterless and lifeless and splotched with pale stretches of dry salt seas. Incongruously delicate auroras went crawling about its poles, like lopsided haloes circling a squat, brooding demon. It wasn't, Channok decided, the kind of planet be would have stopped at of his own accord, for any purpose.

The cliff against which they had buried the *Ra-Twelve* was the loftiest section of an almost unbroken chain of mountains, surrounding the roughly circular hundred-mile plain, which was littered with beds of boulders and sand-hills, like a moon crater. What Peer had referred to as the "Mound" lay approximately at the center of the plain. It turned out, next morning, to be a heavily weathered, dome-shaped structure half a mile high and five miles across, which gave the impression that all but the top tenth of a giant's skull had been buried in the sand, dented here and there with massive hammers, and sprinkled thickly with rock dust. It was obviously an artifact—constructed with hundred-foot bricks! As the *Asteroid* drifted down closer to it, Channok became interested.

"Who built it?" he asked.

Peer shrugged. She didn't know. "Santis spent a few hours jetting around the edges of it once," she said. "But he wouldn't tell us much; and, afterward, he wouldn't let us get nearer than a mile to it. He didn't go back himself, either—said it was dangerous to get too close."

It didn't look dangerous. But fifty thousand years ago, it might have been a fortress of some sort.

"You oughtn't to be flying so low over it, even!" Peer said warningly. "Right in the middle on top is where it's the most dangerous, Santis said!"

Channok didn't argue the matter—they had to get Santis's special cargo cached and off their hands first, anyway. He lifted the *Asteroid* a mile or so and then brought her down a couple of miles beyond the Mound, at the point Peer had designated.

They got out of the ship and gazed about the broken, rocky plain. The red light of the Nameless Sun was spilling across it in what passed for morning on this world. In it, the black mountain chains rearing about the horizon and the craggy waves of flat land had the general effect of a bomb-shattered and slowly burning city. Far off to their left, he could see the upper half of the towering precipice which marked the *Ra-Twelve*'s resting place.

"How long a time did you say you spent here?" he asked.

Peer reflected. "About two Terra-months, I guess. I'm not sure, though. That was a long time ago. My youngest brother Dobby wasn't born yet."

He shook his head. "What a spot for a nice family picnic!"

"It wasn't a picnic," Peer said. "But my kid brother Wilf and I had a lot of fun anyway, just running around and teasing the ghouls. I guess you don't notice so much what a place looks like when you're little."

"Teasing the what?"

"Ghouls," said Peer carelessly.

He looked at her suspiciously, but she seemed to be studying the nearby terrain for a good spot to start digging.

"And what were Santis and your mother doing?" he inquired.

"They were looking for some sort of mineral deposit on Old Nameless; I forget just what. How about that spot—just under that little overhang? It looks like good, solid top-rock."

Channok agreed it was just the place. He'd got a drilling attachment mounted to the *Asteroid*'s small all-purpose tractor; now he went back and ran the machine down the ramp from the storage lock. He ordered Peer, who wanted to help, up a rock about twenty feet overhead, where she perched looking like an indignant elf, out of reach of any stray puffs of the drill-blast. Then he started running a slanting, narrow tunnel down under the overhang.

Half an hour later, when he backed the tractor out of the tunnel, pushing a pile of cooking slag behind him, he saw her standing up on the rock with a small stungun in her hand. She beckoned to him.

Channok pulled off his breather-mask, shut off the tractor, and jumped from the saddle.

"What is it?" he called anxiously, trotting toward her, while the machine's clacking and roaring subsided.

"Some of those ghouls!" Peer called back. "Climb up here and I'll show you." She didn't seem worried.

"They've ducked behind those rocks now," she said as he clambered up beside her; "but they won't stay there long. They're curious, and I think some of them remember the time we were here before."

"Are they dangerous?" he inquired, patting his bolstered set of heavy-duty Reaper guns.

"No," said Peer. "They look sort of awful, but you mustn't shoot them! If they get inside of thirty feet I'll hit them in the stomach with a stunner. They grunt then and run. Santis said that was the right way to teach them not to get too nosey."

They waited a moment in silence, scanning the rocks.

Then Channok started violently.

"Holy !!°°?°° Satellites!" he swore, his hair bristling.

A big, dead-white shape had popped up springily on a rock about fifty feet away, stared at him for an instant out of eyes like gray glass-platters, and popped down out of sight again. Awful was right!

"Aha!" crew-member Peer gloated, grinning. "You shouldn't have said that! Tonight you've got to let me soap out your mouth!"

A light dawned gradually.

"You did it on purpose!" he accused her. "You knew I'd say something like that the first time I saw one!"

Peer didn't deny it.

"It's the soap for you, just the same," she shrugged. "People ought to have some self-control—that's what you said. Look, another one now—no, two!"

V

When he came up for lunch, he found about fifty ghouls collected around the area. By that time he had dug the cache, steel-lined it, disinfected it, and installed preservatives, a humidifier and a dowser plate. Loading it up would take most of the rest of the day.

He avoided looking at the local population as much as he could while he ate. However, the occasional glimpses he got suggested that the Nameless System had made a half-hearted and badly botched attempt at developing its own type of humanoid inhabitant. They had extremely capable looking jaws, at any rate, and their wide, lipless mouths were wreathed in perpetual idiot grins. The most completely disagreeable parts of them, Channok decided, were the enormous, red-nailed hands and feet. Like fat, white gargoyles, they sat perched around the tops of the rocks in a wide circle and just stared.

"Sloppy-looking things," he remarked, noticing Peer's observant eyes on him. "But at least they're not trying to strike up a conversation."

"They never say anything until you hit them in the stomach with a stunner," she informed him. "Then they just grunt and run."

"Sure they mightn't get mean about that? The smallest of this lot looks plenty big enough to take us both apart."

Peer laughed. "All of them together wouldn't try it! They're real yellow. Wilf got mad at a couple of 'em once and ran 'em halfway over to the Mound before mother caught up with him and stopped him. Wilf had his blood up, that time!"

"Maybe the ghouls built the Mound," Channok suggested. "Their great-great-ancestors, anyway."

"They won't go near it now," Peer said, following his gaze. "They're scared of that, too."

They studied the rugged, ungainly slopes of the huge artifact for a moment. There was something fascinating about it, Channok thought. Perhaps just its size.

"Santis said the plain was the bottom of a sea a while ago," Peer offered. "So it could have been some sort of sea-things that built it."

"Any entrances into it?" he asked casually.

"Just one, right at the top."

"You know," he said, "I think I'd like to go over and have a look at that thing before we leave."

"No!" said Peer, alarmed. "You'd better not. Santis said it was dangerous—and there *is* something there! We saw a light one night."

"What kind of a light?"

"Like someone walking around the top of it, near that entrance, with a big lamp in his hand," Peer remembered. "Like he might have been looking for something."

"Sounds a bit like your old friend, the Space Ghost," Channok murmured suspiciously.

"No," Peer grinned. "This was a *real* light—and we took off the next evening. Santis said it might be as well if we moved somewhere else for a while."

Channok considered a moment. "Look," he said finally, "we can do it like this. I'll jet myself over there and stroll around it a bit in daylight; if you're worried, you could hang overhead in the *Asteroid* with a couple of turrets out. Just in case someone gets tough."

"I could, maybe," said Peer, in a tight voice, "but I'm not going to. If you're going to go walking around there, after all Santis said, I'm going to be walking right behind you."

"Oh, no, you're not," Channok said.

"Oh, yes, I am!" said Peer. "You can't make me stay here!"

He looked at her in surprise. Her eyes were angry, but her lower lip quivered.

"Hey," he said, startled. "Maybe I'm being a pig!"

"You sure are!" Peer said, relieved. The lip stopped quivering. "You're not going over there, then?"

"Not if you feel that way about it," Channok said. He paused. "I guess," he admitted awkwardly, "I just didn't like the idea of Santis flitting around space, Holy Aynstyn knows where, and still putting in his two millicredits worth every so often, through crew-member Peer."

Peer blew her nose and considered in turn. "Just the same," she concluded, "when Santis says something like that, it's a lot better if people do it. Is 'Holy Aynstyn knows where' a swear-word?"

"No," said Channok. "Not exactly."

He'd finished his lunch and was just going to suggest they run the tractor out of the cache and back the few hundred yards to the *Asteroid* for the first load of Santis's cargo, when he noticed that all the ghouls had vanished.

He called Peer's attention to the fact.

"Uh-huh," she said in an absentminded tone. "They do that sometimes..."

Channok looked at her. She was staring at a high

boulder a short distance away, with a queer, intent expression, as if she were deep in thought about something. He hoped she wasn't still brooding about their little argument—

Then she glanced at him, gave him a sudden grin, swung herself around, and slid nimbly off the rock.

"Come on down quick!" she said. "I want to show you something before you get back to work. A ghoul-burrow!"

"A ghoul-burrow?" Channok repeated unenthusiastically.

"Yes, sure!" said Peer impatiently. "They're cute! They're all lined with glass or something." She spread her arms wide. "Jump, and I'll catch you!"

Channok laughed, flopped over on his stomach with his legs over the edge of the rock, and slid down in a fair imitation of Peer's nonchalant style of descent, spraining his ankle only a little. Well, he hadn't grown up skipping from craggy moon to asteroid to heavy-planet to whatnot like she had.

They threaded their way about the rocks to the spot she had been studying. She explained that he'd have to climb into the burrow to get a good idea of what it was like.

"Well, look now, Peer!" Channok protested, staring into the big, round hole that slanted downward under a big boulder—it did seem to be lined with black glass or some similar stuff. "That cave's got 'No Trespassing' written all over it. Supposing I slide down a half a mile and land in a mess of ghouls?"

"No, you won't," Peer said hurriedly. "It goes level right away, and they're never more than thirty feet long. And the ghoul's out—there's never more than one to a burrow; and I saw this one pop out and run off just before we started here. You're not scared, are you? Wilf and I crawled in and out of hundreds of them!"

"Well, just for a moment then," said Channok resignedly.

He got down on hands and knees and crept into the tunnel. After about six feet, he stopped and found he could turn around without too much trouble. "Peer?" be called back.

"Yes?" said Peer.

"How can I see anything here," Channok demanded peevishly, "when it's all dark?"

"Well, you're in far enough now," said Peer, who had sat down before the entrance of the tunnel and was looking in after him. "And now—I've got to ask you to do something. You know how I always promptly carry out any orders you give me, like getting in my full sleep-period and all?" she added anxiously.

"No, you do not!" Channok stated flatly, resting on his elbows. "Half the time I practically have to drag you to the cabin. Anyway, what's that got to do with—"

"It's like this," Peer said desperately. She glanced up for a moment, as if she had caught sight of something in the dim red sky overhead. "You've got to stay in there a while, Channy."

"Eh?" said Channok.

"When those ghouls pop out of sight in daytime like that, it's because there's a ship or something coming."

"Peer, are you crazy? A ship! Who— I'm coming right out!"

"Stay there, Channy! It's hanging over the *Asteroid* right now. A big lifeboat with its guns out—it must

be those men from the *Ra-Twelve*. They must have
had a tracer of some sort on her."

"Then get in here quick, Peer!" Channok choked,
hauling out one of the Reapers. "You know good and
well that bunch would kill a woman as soon as a man!"

"They've already seen me—I wanted them to," Peer
informed him. She was talking out of the side of her
mouth, looking straight ahead of her, away from the
cave. "I'm not going to be a woman. I'm going to be
a dumb little girl, ordinary size. I can pull that one
off any time."

"But—"

"They'll want to ask questions. I think I can get
them to send that lifeboat away. We can't fight that,
Channy; it's a regular armed launch. Santis says you
can always get the other side to split its forces, if
you're smart about it."

"But how—"

"And then, when I yell 'Here we go!' then you
pop out. That'll be the right moment—" She stood
up suddenly. "We can't talk anymore. They're getting
close—" She vanished with that from before the mouth
of the burrow.

"Hold on there!" a voice yelled in the distance a
few seconds later, as Channok came crawling clumsily
up the glassy floor of the tunnel, hampered by the
Reaper he still clutched in one hand. It seemed to
come from up in the air, and it was using the Empire's
universal dialect.

Peer's footsteps stopped abruptly.

"Who you people?" her voice screeched in shrill
alarm. "You cops? I ain't done nothing!"

VI

"And just look at those guns she's carrying!" the deeper of the two strange voices commented. "The real stuff, too—a stunner and an Ophto Needle! Better get them from her. If it isn't a baby Flauval!"

"I didn't shoot nobody lately!" Peer said, tremblyvoiced.

"No, and you ain't going to shoot nobody either!" the other strange voice mimicked her. That one was highpitched and thin, with a pronounced nasal twang to it. "Chief, if there're kids with them, it's just a bunch of space-rats that happened along. It couldn't be Flauval!"

"I'd say 'it couldn't be Flauval,' if we'd found her dead in her cabin," the deep voice said irritably. "But that door was burned out from inside—and *somebody* ditched the *Ra-Twelve* on this clod." It sounded as if the discovery of Peer had interrupted an argument between them.

"I still can't see how she got out," Nasal-voice Ezeff said sullenly. "She must have been sleeping in her spacesuit. We were out of the ship thirty seconds after I slap-welded that lock across her door. She must have felt the boat leaving and started burning her way out the same instant—"

"It doesn't matter how she did it," said the deep voice. Apparently, it belonged to someone with authority. "If Flauval could think and move fast enough to switch the drives to Full Emergency and still get alive out of a ship full of the Yomm, she could cheat space, too! She always did have the luck of the devil. If we'd had just that minute to spare before leaving, to make sure—"

It paused a moment and resumed gloomily, "That stubborn old maniac of a Koyle—'I'm the Duke's man, sir!' Committing suicide like *that*—so no one else would get control of the Yomm! If we hadn't managed to start the launch's locators in time . . . Well, I hope I'll never have to sweat out another four days like the last. And now we still have to find whoever got Koyle's records."

"Flauval ain't here," Peer offered at that point, brightly.

There was a pause. It seemed that the two newcomers must have almost forgotten their prisoner for a moment.

"What was that you said, kid?" Nasal-voice inquired carefully.

"Those space-rats are all half crazy," the deep voice said contemptuously. "She doesn't know what we're talking about."

"Sure I know!" Peer said indignantly. "You was talking about Flauval. It's Wilf that's the crazy one—I ain't! And she ain't here. Flauval."

"She ain't, eh?" Nasal-voice said, with speculative alertness.

"No, sir," Peer said, timid again. "She's went with the rest of'm."

Both voices swore together in startled shock.

"Where are they?" the deep voice demanded. "Hiding on the ship?"

"No, sir," quavered Peer. "It's just me on the ship, till they come back."

"You mean," the deep voice said, with strained patience, "you're supposed to be on the ship?"

"Yes, sir," said Peer. She added in a guilty mutter, "Sleepin'..."

"Where did the others go?" Nasal-voice inquired sharply.

"But I ain't tired," said Peer. "Well, with the boxes and stuff! What Flauval wants buried."

There was another duet of exclamations which Channok, at almost any other time, would have considered highly unsuitable for Peer's ears. Right now, it escaped his attention.

"She's got Koyle's records," stated the deep voice then.

"What's in those boxes?" Nasal-voice snapped.

"D-d-don't shake me!" wept Peer. "Papers and stuff—I don't know. They don't never tell me nothing," she wailed, "because I'm just a little girl!"

"Yes, you're just a little girl," said Nasal-voice, exasperated. "You're not going to get much bigger either."

"Cut that," said the deep voice. "No sense scaring the kid."

"Well, you're not figuring on taking them back, are you?" Nasal-voice inquired.

"No. Just Flauval. The colonel will be glad to chat with Flauval a bit, now that she's turned up alive again. Koyle may have told her plenty before we soured him on her. But there's no point in making the rest of them desperate. It's easier when they surrender."

There was a short pause. Then the deep voice addressed Peer with a sort of amiable gruffness:

"So they all went off to bury the boxes, but you don't know where they went—is that it, little girl?"

"Oh, sure!" Peer said, anxious to please. "Yes, sir! I know that!"

"WHERE?" said both voices together, chorusing for the third time.

"It's that big Mound over there," Peer said, and Channok started nervously. "It's got a big door on top. No," she added, "I guess you can't see from down here—and you can't see from the ship. That's why I came out. To watch for'm. But you can see it plain from the top of the rocks."

"That would be the old reservoir or whatever it was we passed back there," said the deep voice.

"That's right," said Peer. "That's just what Flauval called it at lunch! The word you said. There was water there once, she said. They flew the boxes over with jets, but they'll be back before it's dark, they said."

There was a brief silence.

"Scares me when it's dark, it does," grumbled the idiot-child.

"Well, that ties it up," the deep voice said, satisfied. "It's the exact kind of stunt Flauval would try. But she's outsmarted herself, this time."

"How do you figure on handling it?" Nasal-voice inquired.

"Get up on one of those rocks with the kid where you can watch both that 'mound' and the lock of their ship. Yes, I know it's more trouble that way—but don't, ah, do anything conclusive about the—uh—aforementioned, before we've corralled the rest. Much more useful while capable of inhaling. Hostage possibilities. Inducement to surrender."

"Uh-huh," Nasal-voice said, comprehendingly.

"Yes, sir!" added Peer.

There was another short pause.

"Might as well skip the circumlocutions," the deep voice continued. "Barely human! I'll send a couple of men through the ship and, if it's empty, I'll leave one of them in the forward lock where you can see him. That's just in case anyone slips past us and comes back. The rest of us will go over to the reservoir in the launch. If the entrance is where she says it is, we've got them bottled. If it looks right, we'll go in."

"That'll be only four of you," said Nasal-voice. "No, three—you're keeping one at the launch-guns, aren't you?"

"Yes, of course. Hey, little girl—how many are with Flauval?"

"Of us, you mean?" Peer asked.

"Of what else?" snarled Nasal-voice.

"Now don't get her so scared she can't talk," the deep voice reproved. "That's right, little girl—how many of you?"

"Well, there's me," sniffled Peer, "and my old man, and my big brother Dobby. And then there's Wilf— that's all. But I don't like Wilf!"

"I don't like Wilf either," agreed Nasal-voice. "Four against three, chief. It might be safer to bring over the two from the *Ra-Twelve* first—no point in searching her anyway, now that we know where the records are."

"No," said the deep voice. "Flauval could just happen to decide to come out in the few minutes we're gone. It's sewed up too neatly right now. We'll have the heavy guns from the launch and we'll give them a chance to surrender. Flauval's too intelligent to pass that up—she never stops hoping. The chances are there won't be any shooting, till afterward."

"Any friends of hers are likely to be tough," Nasal-voice warned.

"Very tough," said his chief. "Like the kid there! You worry at the wrong times, my boy. A parcel of space-rats that happened along." He swore again. "That woman's unbelievable luck! Well, take care of yourself, Ezeff. I'm off. Keep your eyes open both ways. Just in case."

VII

There was silence for a moment. Then footsteps came crunching over the rocks toward the ghoul-burrow, and Channok got set. But the footsteps halted a few yards away.

"That's the one I was sitting on," Peer volunteered. "Nice, easy one to climb."

"Yeah, I never saw a nicer looking rock," Nasal-voice said sourly. "We've got to climb it, too. I'm not trying any point-landings with jets. Get on up there then, before I boot you up!"

There were sounds of scrambling.

"Don't you move now!" Peer said suddenly.

"What are you talking about?" demanded Nasal-voice.

"Durn rock come loose," muttered Peer. "Near flung me off!"

But Channok, meanwhile, had got the idea and settled back. It was not yet the Right Moment...

There were more scrambling sounds and some breathless swearing from Ezeff, who obviously had not spent his formative years in asteroid-hopping either. But at last all became quiet.

"And here we are!" Peer's voice floated down clearly.

A small chunk of rock dropped right in front of the burrow's entrance, like a punctuation mark.

"Sit still, blast you!" said Nasal-voice, badly out of breath.

A large, dim shadow swept silently over the ground before the ghoul's burrow just then. That would be the launch, going toward the Mound. A prolonged silence overhead confirmed the impression.

"They want to give Flauval a surprise?" Peer inquired meekly at last.

Rather startlingly, Nasal-voice laughed.

"They sure do," he agreed. "That's a good one! Yes, sir, they sure do."

"Flauval's nice, don't you think?" continued Peer conversationally, picking up courage.

"Depends a lot on how you look at it," Nasal-voice said dreamily. "She's a real pretty thing anyhow, that Flauval. Luck of the devil she's had, too. But it's got to run out sometime."

There was another silence. Then Peer remarked, "Boy, he set that launch down nice! Right quick spang on top of the—what the big guy said it was. On the Mound."

"We've got a good pilot," Nasal-voice agreed. "Flauval's going to get her surprise in just a minute now."

"And there they come out of the launch," continued Peer. "One, two, three, four. All four of them. Marching right down into the Mound."

"You've got sharp eyes," Nasal-voice acknowledged. "But that's funny!" he continued worriedly. "One of them was to stay with the guns."

"And now look at the launch!" cried Peer in a high, bright voice. "Getting *pulled* right into the Mound!"

Nasal-voice was making loud, choking sounds.

"What was that?" he screamed then. "What's happened? What's that over there?"

"Let go my arm!" cried Peer. "Don't pull it—you're pushing me off! *Here we go!*"

A small avalanche of weathered rock came down before the burrow's mouth as Channok shot out through it into the open. He looked up. In what looked like an inextricable tangle of arms and legs, Peer and Nasal-voice were sliding and scuffling down the steep side of the rock together. Nasal-voice was trying to hang on to the rock, but Peer was hanging on to him and jerking like a hooked fish whenever he got a momentary hold.

She looked down and saw Channok, put her boots into the small of Nasal-voice's back, pushed off, and landed two yards from Channok on hands and feet. He flattened himself back against the boulder while Nasal-voice skidded down the rest of the way unaided, wisely refraining from triggering his jets. In the position he was in, they simply would have accelerated his descent to a fatal degree.

He arrived more or less on his feet. Peer bounced up and down before him, her finger pointed, like a small lunatic.

"Surprise!" she screamed. "Surprise! Like Flauval got! When you locked her in her cabin and ran off with the launch, so she'd have to jump out into space!"

"That's right, kid," Nasal-voice panted softly, fumbling for his gun without taking his eyes off her. He looked somewhat like a white-faced lunatic himself just then. "Don't get scared, kid! Don't run off! I won't shoot."

He pulled the gun out suddenly.

But Channok had taken two soft steps forward by then, and he had only to swing. The Reaper was clubbed in his right hand, and he brought the butt end down on the top of Nasal-voice Ezeff's skull-tight flying cap as if he were trying to ram a stake through the surface rock of Old Nameless.

"What happened over there on the Mound?" he inquired, in a voice that kept wanting to quaver. He was hurriedly pulling on Nasal-voice's flight suit.

"Here's his goggles," said Peer, also shakily. "Tell you tonight about the Mound. But Santis was right!"

"That's what it sounded like," Channok admitted. He slipped on the goggles. "Do I look like this Ezeff now?"

"Not very much," Peer said doubtfully. "You still got that nose and that jaw. Better hold me close up to your face! I'll put on a good act."

"All right. As soon as I set you down in the lock, jump past the guard and yell, or something. If he looks after you, we mightn't have to kill this one." He held out his arms. "Hop up! We'd better get started before those last two on the *Ra-Twelve* decide to come over."

Peer hopped up. Channok wrapped his right arm carefully around her. They looked at each other thoughtfully for a moment.

"All set?" he asked.

"Sure," said crew-member Peer. She smiled faintly.

He triggered the jets with his left hand, and they shot upward. Peer drew a deep breath.

"Quit bossing me around all the time, you big lug!" she yelled suddenly. She reached up for that nose and gave it a good yank.

"All right," Channok muttered, startled. "You don't have to be so realistic! He can't even see us yet."

"Just because you're bigger'n me!" shrieked Peer, as they soared over the top of the rocks into view of the *Asteroid*'s lock. She hooked a smart right to Channok's left ear.

"Cut that out now, Peer," he ordered futilely.

He was lightly battered all around by the time they reached the *Asteroid*'s lock, though the act did get them in safely. But then—whether it was the nose or the jaw—the instant he dropped Peer to her feet, the guard stopped laughing and brought a gun out and up, faster than Channok ever had seen a man produce one before. However, the Reaper had been ready in his hand all the time; so, with a safe fraction of a second to spare, it talked first—

The glare of the discharge seemed about fifty times brighter than normal.

"Hit the floor, Channy!" he heard Peer's shout.

He hit it without thought, dropping over the dead guard's legs.

Sound rammed at him enormously, roared on and began banging itself about and away among distant mountains. The *Asteroid*'s floor had surged up ponderously, settled back, quivered a bit, and become stable again.

"An earthquake," Channok muttered, sitting up dazedly, "was exactly all we needed right now!"

"That wasn't any earthquake!" said Peer, standing pale-faced above him. "Get up and look!"

Long veils of stuff, presumably solid chunks of mountain, were drifting down the distant, towering face of the cliff at the foot of which they had buried the *Ra-Twelve*. Rising to meet them, its source concealed beyond the horizon of the plain, was the slow, gray cloud of some super-explosion.

"I guess," he said slowly, "one of those two must have got curious about Koyle's wall-safe!"

"We were pretty smart about that," nodded Peer.

"We were, for once!" Channok agreed. He was looking around for something to sit down on quietly when he caught sight of the dead guard again. He started violently.

"Almost forgot about him! I guess now I'll have to bury him, and that Ezeff, the first thing. Maybe this one is carrying something that will show who they were."

He found something almost instantly and he was glad then that Peer was still watching the oily writhings of the cloud across the plain. It was in a flat steel case he took out of one of the dead man's pockets: the identification disk of a member of the Imperial Secret Service—

The Service!

And they would have murdered us, he thought, shocked. They were going to do it!

He turned the guard over on his back. A big muscular young man with a look of sudden purpose and confidence still fixed on his face. It was the same face as the one on the disk.

Channok put the disk back in its case and shoved the case into the dead man's pocket. He stood up, feeling rather sick. Peer turned around from the lock and regarded him reflectively for a moment.

"You know, Channy," she stated carefully, "if you can't help it, it doesn't count."

He looked back at her. "I guess not," he said—
and suddenly, for a moment, he could see four men
marching one after the other down into the Mound.
"Of course, it doesn't count!" he told her firmly.

VIII

They worked hard at shifting the cargo into the cache,
but the Nameless Sun was beginning to slide down
behind the mountains before they were finished. And
by the time Channok had rammed the tunnel full of
rocks with the tractor and cemented them into a glassy
plug with the drill-blast, and scattered a camouflaging
mess of boulders over everything, only a foggy red
glow over the mountain crests, half obscured by the
lingering upper drifts of the explosion of the *Ra-Twelve*,
remained of the day.

There was no moon, but the sky had come full of
stars big and little over the opposite section of the
plain; and so there was light enough to make out the
dark bump of the Mound in the distance. Every time
Channok looked in that direction, the low, sinister pile
seemed to have edged a little closer; and he looked as
often as his work gave him a chance to do it. Santis
might have been right in stating that the Mound
wasn't dangerous if you didn't get too close to it—but
the instant he suspected there might be something
going on over there, Channok was going to hop off
the tractor, grab up Peer and get off Old Nameless
at the best speed he and the *Asteroid* could produce.

However, the Mound remained quiet. With everything done, he gave Peer a last ride back to the
Asteroid on the tractor, ran it up the ramp into the

storage section, and closed the rear lock. Then they discovered they'd left their lunch containers lying among the rocks.

If he'd been alone, Channok would have left them there. But Peer looked so matter-of-fact about it that he detached the tractor's headlight and started back with her on foot. It was only a couple of hundred yards, and they found the containers without any difficulty. The Mound seemed to have moved a little closer again, but not too much. He gave it only a casual glance this time.

"Where are your friends, the ghouls?" he inquired, shining the light around the rocks as they started back. The grisly creatures had put in a few cautious appearances during the afternoon, but their nerves seemed to have suffered even more than his own from all that had happened.

"The ghouls always hit their burrows at sundown," Peer explained. "They're not like the story ones."

"What do they find to eat around here?" Channok inquired.

"Some sorts of rocks. They've got no real teeth but their mouth is like a grinder inside. Most of the rest of their insides, too, Santis said. I had a tame one I used to pitch stones at and he'd snap 'em up. But all that weren't blue he'd spit out. The blue ones went right down—you could hear them crunching for about a foot."

"What a diet!" Channok commented. Then he stopped short. "Say, Peer! If they bite like that, they could chew right into our cache!"

"They won't," said Peer. "Come on."

"How do you know?" Channok asked, following her.

"They can't bite through a good grade of steel-alloy. And they don't like its taste anyhow. Santis said so."

Well, it had been Santis this and Santis that for quite a while now! Peer's father seemed to be on record with a definite opinion on just about everything. And what made him think he knew what a ghoul liked to chew on?

Perhaps Channok couldn't be blamed too much. He was dog-tired and dirty and hungry. He'd killed his first two men that day, and not in fair fight either but with an assassin's sneak thrusts, from behind and by trickery; he'd buried them, too. He'd seen the shining ISS disclose itself in action as something very tarnished and ugly, and a salvaged ship worth a fortune go up in a cloud of writhing gray smoke...

There had been a number of other things—close shaves that had felt too close, mostly.

At any rate, Channok stated, in flat unequivocal terms, that he didn't wish to hear anything else that Santis had said. Not ever!

"You're taking the wrong attitude," Peer informed him, frowning. "Santis is a very smart man. He could teach you a lot!"

"What makes you think I want to learn anything from a space-rat?" Channok inquired, exasperated.

Peer stopped short. "That was a dirty thing to say!" she said in a low, furious voice. "I'm not talking to you any more."

She drew away till there was a space of about six feet between them and marched on briskly toward the *Asteroid*, looking straight ahead.

Channok had to hurry to keep abreast of her. He

watched her in the starlight for a few moments from the corners of his eyes. He probably shouldn't have used that term—the half-pint did look good and mad!

"Tsk! Tsk!" he said, disturbed.

Peer said nothing. She walked a bit faster. Channok lengthened his stride again.

"Who's my nice little girlfriend?" he inquired wheedlingly.

"Shuddup," growled Peer.

She climbed into the *Asteroid* ahead of him and disappeared while he sealed the locks. The control room was dark, but he felt she was around somewhere. He switched on the power and the instruments. Familiar dim pools of green and pink gleamings sprang up in quick sequence like witchfire quivering over the control desk. Perhaps it wasn't an exceptionally beautiful sight, but it looked homelike to Channok. Like fires lighting up on a hearth.

"Well, let's see you handle this take-off," he invited the shadows around him briskly. This time there weren't any mountains nearby to worry about.

"You handle it," Peer said from behind his shoulder. "It's my turn to laugh."

She did, too, a few minutes later—loud and long. After he'd got over the first shock of narrowly missing the Mound, Channok gave a convincing imitation of a chagrined pilot and indignantly blamed the *Asteroid*.

He'd guided them halfway out of the Nameless System when she came behind the control chair in the dark, wrapped her arms in a stranglehold around his neck, and fondly bit his ear.

"Cut it out," Channok choked.

"Just the same," stated Peer, loosening her grip a trifle, "you're *not* so smart, like Santis is."

"I'm not, eh?"

"No," said Peer. "But Santis said you would be some time. 'That Channok's going to make a real spacer,' he said. 'Just give him a chance to catch on.'"

"Well," Channok muttered, secretly flattered, "we'll hope he was right."

"And, anyway," said Peer, "I *LOVE* you just as much!"

"Well, that's something, too," Channok admitted. He was beginning to feel very much better.

"And guess what I've got here," Peer said tenderly.

"What?"

"A nice, soapy cloth. For what you said when you saw the first ghoul. So just open that big trap right up now, Channy!"

He couldn't tell in the dark, but it tasted like she'd taken the trouble to mix something extra foul into the soap lather, too.

"And after you've stopped spitting bubbles," said crew-member Peer, who was switching on all lights to observe that part of the business, "I'll tell you what I saw on the Mound."

Channok shuddered.

"If you don't mind, Peer," he suggested soapily, "let's wait with that till we're a light-year or two farther out!"

James H. Schmitz was born in Hamburg, Germany, in 1911 to American parents. Aside from several trips to the USA, he lived in Germany until 1938, when the outbreak of WWII prompted his family to move to America. He sold his first story, "Greenface," to the now-legendary magazine *Unknown Worlds* shortly before Pearl Harbor. By the time it was published, he was flying with the Army Air Corps in the South Pacific. In 1949, he began publishing his "Agents of Vega" series in *Astounding* (later *Analog*), and was one of that magazine's most popular contributors over the next three decades, introducing Telzey Amberdon and Trigger Argee, the heroines of his "Federation of the Hub" series. He died in 1981.